# PRATT, PRATT, WALLY & PRATT INVESTIGATE

David A. Wardle

# A WORD FROM THE AUTHOR

This story has previously been published under the title 'Trouble Cross'. One of the reviews on that book suggested that the back story and the text of 'Doctor, Oh No!' could be taken out and that would make the story move along faster. That is what I have done here but the back story and 'Doctor, Oh No!' are now separate books in themselves.

'Trouble Cross' in its original form is still available for those who wish to read the lot in one go as originally intended.

Alternatively, 'T is for ...' can be used as a taster to see if you like the character as this is the previous 'Trouble Cross' back story and acts as an introduction to the main novel now.

Or if you just want a chuckle at a James Bond spoof 80's style then 'Doctor, Oh No! may be just what the doctor ordered.

# TABLE OF CONTENTS

# CHAPTER 1

It had begun like any other day, the sky gradually lightening in the east about cock crow. However, that day in February 1996 proved to be no ordinary day. This was the day that my big adventure began. This was the day that I obtained my first client. This was the day that I wore my red socks for the first time. This was the day that my red socks became my lucky red socks. It was a red-letter day as well as a red sock day.

I arrived at the office early. It was raining and I was, as Blackadder might have said of Baldrick, as wet as a wet fish that has just been awarded the Wettest Fish of the Year Award during a monsoon. This was very wet indeed and there was no heating, but at least the concrete was drip-dry. The offices of Pratt, Pratt, Wally and Pratt could not have been termed plush, not unless you were comparing them to an outside public convenience and even then only if there was no attendant. It was a plasterboard partitioned area on the second floor of a Victorian building where a slight push on any wall would have created an open-plan effect out of the thirty-four office units via the domino principle. It was cheap office accommodation for small service trades such as employment agencies, secretarial agencies or newly established insurance investigators. The rabbit hutch of an area occupied by PPWP was dissected by a further partition thereby creating an inner and outer office, the latter doubling as reception. The furnishings were sparse in the inner office; desk, chair (non-swivel, non-leather), filing cabinet and a loose square of carpet. Reception was even sparser; desk, chair (hardback, uncomfortable) and no carpet. All in all reception was hardly receptive. Still there had been no complaints. There had been no visitors either. The way things were panning out the prospect of visitors seemed remote. The prospect of any paying customers was non-existent. There wasn't even any sign of a non-paying customer. This being the case the state of the reception area hardly mattered.

I sat at my desk, feet up, drying millimetre by microscopic millimetre via a portable heater I had borrowed from an early bird neighbour, promising to return it prior to the arrival of his full complement of staff at nine o'clock. Slowly drying I may have been but there was certainly no compensatory warming effect, I was freezing and shivering uncontrollably. This was the pits. It was not just my current cold and wet condition that made me feel this way. My enthusiasm for insurance investigating had taken a severe dampening before my sojourn in a downpour. Exactly one week into my new job and I was totally fed up. I was an insurance investigator with nothing to investigate. I was beginning to feel like Mike Hammer and had the grotty office to prove it. However, unlike Stacey Keach's alter-ego, I doubted very much that I would be rescued from boredom and financial destitution by a beautiful woman dropping a case in my lap. This was not TV, this was the real world, and in the real world convenient fortuitousness is inconveniently lacking. It just goes to show how wrong one can be, well partially wrong anyway.

It was about 8.45am when I was startled from my melancholy musings by an unfamiliar sound, the opening of the outer office door, heralding an intrepid visitor to the unexplored reaches of reception. Figuring it would be a disgruntled employee of my neighbour who had discovered the missing heater and was no doubt madder than the proverbial wet hen and wetter too; I stayed put. I wanted to snatch every last second that I could from the tiny finger of heat. No sooner had three of these precious seconds elapsed than a female form darkened my doorway. "Excuse me," said the form, promptly tripping over the edge of the carpet. My visitor fell full length and bashed her head on the bottom drawer of the cabinet. The U to Z drawer; highly appropriate given the circumstances. U for unconscious which she undoubtedly was. This sort of thing never happened to Mike Hammer.

There was no couch so my natural reaction was to sweep all the contents from my desk to the floor. A wasted reaction as it happened for my desk was already completely empty. I lay her prone form across the desk top, pulling down her skirt which had ridden up her thighs. Then I retrieved her glasses which had fallen off as she hit the floor. It was the first time I'd had a woman in a horizontal position in a very long time and as usual she was comatose. For a moment I was tempted, but only a moment. I told myself I wasn't that desperate. In reality I was but I was just too much of a gentleman. Call me old-fashioned but I liked to have a lady's permission before jumping in, so to speak. Instead I decided to take my first-aid responsibilities seriously. Not that I knew the first thing about it, I didn't even qualify as a second-aider. Fortunately, the drawer had been shut so there was no cut just a nasty developing lump. I hurried off to locate something cold and wet. The good old days of paper towels were long gone which was a pity in those circumstances. To my mind a roller towel or hot air blower could just not provide the same function. My nearly clean hankie was the only solution.

In such business centres as that in which the office was based, the nearest toilets were conveniently located two corridors and three floors away. I ran both ways. On my return it was obvious that Sleeping Beauty had not yet been kissed by a prince as she was still dead to the world. As I was only a lowly frog, which was a different story altogether, I just applied the sodden cloth to her temple and waited.

During the interlude I tried to exercise my Sherlockian powers of observation and deduction. Female, medium height, medium build, aged between 16 and 65, brown hair in a severe bun, large owlish glasses and dressed in a smart business suit; so much for observation. My deductive powers were even less admirable. Unlike Holmes I was unable to discern what she had had for breakfast, how many brothers and sisters she had or what her mother's maiden name had been. In the best tradition of a private investigator therefore I decided to search her briefcase or I would have done if she hadn't chosen that moment to regain consciousness. She sat up moaning and holding her head. I helped her into the chair and she moaned some more.

"Are you alright?" I asked her, showing the right amount of concern from a person not worrying about being sued for personal injury.

"I think so," was the reply. "What happened?"

She was American I was sure of that now. I had had my suspicions before but it had been a little difficult to tell from just the two words she had previously uttered. Her accent was not that of a Southern belle, nor did it contain the brashness of a New Yorker. Other than that I had no idea from which part of the States she hailed from.

"You had rather a nasty fall. Hit your head on the filing cabinet. I wouldn't be surprised if you had rather a headache."

"I do actually. Yours I believe." She handed me the balled wet cloth. "Nice socks."

I was slightly taken aback. At least she could have thanked me before criticising my fashion sense, or lack of it.

"First thing I noticed," she continued. "I like a man not dictated to by fashion."

"The first thing you should have noticed was the carpet," I countered defensively. "Or did my socks distract you?"

"Well they are quite dazzling," she pointed out. "However, the reason I fell was your negligently placed piece of Fire Sale floor covering. You are properly insured I take it?"

Typical American. Sue first, sue last.

I declined to reply. An insurance investigator involved himself in fraudulent claims and sometimes the recovery of stolen property. He does not expect to be taken to court over defective carpeting. I decided to side-step the issue. "Can I offer you a coffee or anything?"

"No, thank you. Enough time has been wasted already. I think we'd better get down to business. Perhaps you'd like to find yourself a chair."

There was only the chair in reception so I had to use that.

There was not much in it but she definitely had the more comfortable one. I made a mental note that if I ever had the occasion to hire a secretary I had better purchase a new chair first. At the same time I also came to the conclusion that I was not warming to this lady. I had preferred her the way she had been five minutes previously. Then I had thought that with her hair down and wearing different clothes she could have been very attractive but now that I looked at her properly she had that predatory look of the Inland Revenue about her. The interviewing of my first client, if indeed she proved to be so, was not going according to how I had envisaged it on many an occasion.

"Have I the pleasure of addressing Mr Wally or one of the Pratts?" She made Pratt sound like a common noun.

"Neither!" I had to resist a Scrooge like "It is no pleasure to be addressed by you". If she was a client the last thing I needed to do was antagonise her. Well no more than tripping her up on the carpet had already done. "My name's Robel. Thomas Robel."

"Oh! That is unfortunate." She was clearly exasperated. "I was hoping to speak with one of the partners."

"This is a new office," I informed her. "I'm in charge here." It did not seem the time to let her know that nary a Wally nor Pratt existed. Well, of course, they do exist; you only have to open the phone book to find a Pratt, but not in relation to the firm. I was founder member and sole employee to date. I hadn't exactly lied, just stated the plain facts. It was a new office and as I was the only one there, I was in charge.

"Well, that's different then." She pushed her chair away from the desk and crossed her legs. "Mr Robel, I, or rather my company, have a little job for you to do."

"I'm all ears," I said, which I was in more ways than one. I could have given flying lessons to Dumbo. For that matter, for an honest guy my nose bore a striking resemblance to that of another Disney favourite. Unfortunately, I had no chance of any remission.

"I am the Director of Claims, East Division, for the Fidelity Insurance Corporation," my visitor informed me. "In the past year there have been a number of disturbing and sizeable claims involving one of our major clients, the Fairfax Corporation. There is the possibility that there is some gigantic fraud in progress. It is, however, only a possibility. There is no actual evidence, only too many coincidences." She stopped and threw a faint smile in my direction. "I believe I would like that coffee after all."

There was only one mug so I went without, stoic was my middle name, and I'd been without my chair for ten minutes. I mentally added another mug under the new chair. After the kettle had boiled and she was furnished with her black, no sugar, I resumed my seat and she continued.

"The Fairfax Corporation has a diverse base of operation; manufacturing, distribution, catering, hotels, television and film production, haulage, research laboratories and even a museum. That's just in the States; there are various foreign interests in addition. In the UK there is a property management company, a research laboratory, a leisure company and a bottling plant." She took a sip of her coffee. "The Corporation started with a small haulage company started by James Fairfax II in 1940. By the time his son took the reins in 1977 the business had mushroomed into a multi-million dollar operation. Last year the reins passed again, this time to the two grandsons, James III and Simon, who are president and vice president respectively. It is since the new management took over that the whole account has deteriorated to an alarming degree. It could be an unfortunate coincidence but certain suspicions have arisen recently. Fidelity Insurance holds a substantial portfolio of the Corporation's insurances and some concern is inevitable at such recent losses as have occurred. Particularly as in previous years this has been a very profitable account. My job at the moment is to determine whether this is just a blip or something more sinister." Another sip. "Any questions so far?"

"Only one burning one comes to mind at present," I responded. "What's your name?"

"Oh! Sorry!" She reddened slightly. "Jane Fulwood. Here's

my card. Must be the jet lag."

"Or the bump on the head," I suggested. "Please carry on Miss Fulwood."

"Mrs," she corrected quickly.

"I'm sorry. It's just that you have no ring."

"It's at the jewellers being repaired." Just for a moment she seemed nervous as though she'd made a mistake and was not sure on how to proceed.

"Engagement ring as well?" I asked innocently.

"I never had one," she replied, testily. "O.K.?"

"No offence." I held my hands up. "I was only trying to prove I can be observant."

"Very impressive. Now where was I?"

"Investigating a blip," I reminded her.

"Right," she agreed, back on track. "I guess you want to know where you fit in." She reached into her briefcase.

"I knew you'd get there in the end. Take your time; you're my only appointment this morning."

"And all the rest of the week I imagine," she smiled sweetly. "And all last week too for that matter."

"Sounds to me that you know more about this firm than you should do if you've just walked in off the street." I was getting annoyed now. Someone had obviously been spying on me, otherwise how would she know that on that Monday, my eighth day in business, I still had not one client to speak of. I wanted to know. "How do you know that? Have you been spying on me? You'd better level with me lady. How much of what you've told me is really the truth? I've the distinct feeling that there's more to this than meets the eye."

"I don't know what you mean." She was on the defensive now. "It was just a throwaway remark. This is not exactly a working office is it? Even the waste paper basket is empty." She started rummaging in her briefcase, a delaying tactic I was sure until she collected herself. Having apparently found what she was looking for she again directed her attention to me. "Look, it was just a quip on the state of the business. OK!"

"We've only been open a week," I said and left it at that, knowing full well that she knew that already.

"That's good! With no other clients you can concentrate all your efforts on our behalf. I was going to request that from one of the partners anyway. At least one man dedicated to Fidelity Insurance for the duration of the investigation."

"I don't know what the investigation is yet," I pointed out.

"I was just coming to that. Here!" She passed me a photograph. "That's Peter Hobson. UK Operations Manager for the Fairfax Corporation. Prior to the new management in the States the UK operation had had complete autonomy, only responsible to the main board of directors for quarterly results. All decision making regarding the UK operation was carried out by the man in the field, Hobson's predecessor. Recently, we know that Hobson has had various meetings with Simon Fairfax both here and in the States; some even of a clandestine nature. Even though we have not got to the bottom of what's going on at our end, it is feared that the UK operation may soon become involved. We want your firm to investigate at this end."

"You suspect Fairfax? The man at the top?"

"One of the men at the top," she corrected. "He is the managing director and his brother is the chairman. And no we don't really suspect him. It's just that we're checking out every angle. Anything out of the ordinary and this new and serious concern about the UK side is exactly that. It could just be that Fairfax is worried about the recent spate of fires and thefts and just wishes to ensure that the UK takes the appropriate precautions."

"You don't have much to go on," I observed. "It seems a bit flimsy. Like clutching at straws. Have you nothing more tangible?"

"Not as yet but with both investigations on the go there will no doubt be a rapid interchange of information."

"Why did you choose this firm?" I asked curiously. "I'm assuming this is a surveillance job. Why not a detective agency?

"Various reasons," the reply came. "Number one, we wanted an unknown outfit and what better than a newly established one. Two, you're in the right area. The Head Office for the UK operation is not twenty miles from here. Three, we needed someone with insurance experience, able to identify the relevant facts that a P.I. might not notice or realise the implication of."

"Most detective agencies do insurance work," I informed her. I knew because I had let my fingers do the walking through the relevant sections of a certain coloured phone-book before I opened my doors.

"True," she admitted, "but only as a side-line. It's not their main sphere of operation. You advertise as an insurance investigator full stop."

"Point taken," I agreed. They must have seen my advert in the insurance press. I was certainly not in the Yellow Pages yet. You had more chance of locating a copy of 'Fly Fishing' by J.R. Hartley than finding a section for Insurance Investigators in the yellow peril.

"It will be surveillance initially," confirming my guess. "Just keep an eye on Hobson and see if anything develops."

And now for the important question, I thought to myself. "What does the job pay?"

Much to my surprise she handed me a cheque that had been made out beforehand. "That's a retainer," she explained, "for your services as long as they are required. Of course, if it transpires that there is a conspiracy to defraud my company and your firm is instrumental in eliminating or reducing the financial effects then a reward would be in order. About 10% of any monies saved."

The only insurance investigator I had seen had been on TV and that was Banacek, George Peppard starring. He usually received 10% but he never had a retainer prior to the commencement of a case. Especially a retainer of £20,000.

"OK! I accept. What are the ground rules?"

"Play it your own way. In here," she continued, passing me a large envelope, "are details of the Fairfax UK operation and what little we know on Hobson. I will be at our London office for a while and will act as liaison. Any information you require, contact me."

"Fine," I agreed. "First of all I will need details of all the insurances in place for the UK companies."

"That will be no problem. I'll have it here by tomorrow."

"I'll also need a full list of the American losses over the past year together with any information that has come to light following the various investigations." I hoped I sounded professional for in reality I was winging it.

"OK. I'll have that sent too," she promised. "There is one thing I'll need from you however."

"What would that be?"

"A weekly progress report."

"That shouldn't be a problem," I lied. At the speed I typed it would take a week to actually prepare the report.

"Good! Now is there anything else you need?"

"Not that I can think of," I shrugged. "How do I contact you?"

"I'm staying at the London Hilton whilst I'm over here. You should be able to get a message to me there or at the London office."

"You'd better write that down then. I've only got your card which only gives your number in Chicago."

"Silly me! Here!" She passed me another card. No name but the London address and phone-number. Pity. I had wanted her to show me she knew it from memory. "After a week or two I'll be back in the States for which, as you've just said, you've got my number."

"I don't suppose you can be reached there all the time. It could be the middle of the night over there when I need to reach you, say for instance, something urgent crops up on which I need instruction or clarification."

She seemed very reluctant but eventually, grudgingly, she wrote down her home number on the back of the American card. Why, I thought to myself, do all phone numbers in the States seem to have the area code 555. Every TV show I had seen had those three numbers in any number given. 'The Streets of San Francisco', 'L.A. Law', 'Friends' – whatever the decade, telephone number 555. If 666 was the number of the beast, 555 was certainly not the number of the least.

"Well," she declared, slamming shut her briefcase, "I think that's about everything, unless there is anything else you particularly wanted to discuss."

"Not really. But I'm sure I'll have some questions when I've looked through the information you're going to send me."

"Right then, I'll take my leave." She vacated my chair and held out her hand. "I'd like to say it's been a pleasure, Mr Robel, but I can't" She was feeling her head as she said this. "I don't think I'll forget this meeting in a hurry."

Just how I liked to do it, leave a lasting impression. Not looking suitably in awe, she wished me "Good luck" and departed.

I just stood and looked at the cheque. £20,000. Twenty thousand pounds. Say it any way you like, it sounded good. Sweet music to my bank manager's ears. A myriad of emotions overwhelmed me, each vying for supremacy. Excitement, gratitude, relief, fear and not least of all, suspicion.

Her story had sounded plausible enough from a certain standpoint but there were things that just didn't add up. First, there was the query on her marital status. She had made it plain that she was married, or at least wanted me to think that but her story of the ring didn't ring true. She hadn't been excessively tanned but enough for me to see that she had not had a ring on for some time. And believe me I was an expert at looking at the third finger of the left hand on the female of the species. I would have sworn on a stack of bibles there and then, if I hadn't been a lifelong atheist, that she wasn't married. As to why the deception I had no idea. Maybe it was just a ploy to protect her from unwanted advances. Maybe it was for another more sinister reason.

Next came the comment about the business. She gave the appearance of just having picked me at random but she let it slip that she knew I had not had any potential clients since opening the firm. How had she known I would be there at that time in a morning? Insurance people, in the main, were habitual nine to fivers. She had said that I had not been under surveillance but I was not so sure. I wandered over to the window and looked out onto the street from which the building was entered. There were kerb to kerb parked cars, meter controlled. It was impossible for me to see from my vantage point on the second floor whether the vehicles had any occupants, far less tell whether any of them displayed a more than healthy interest in the building. One thing was for certain, I would be on the lookout in future. As if I wasn't paranoid enough. I'd be watching them, watching me. Unless there was more than one, then it would be them watching me watching them watching me. Talk about 'Game for a Laugh'.

This Mrs Fulwood, to give her desired title, had had the firm checked out, of that I was almost sure. If she had she would know that there were no such persons as Pratt, Pratt, Wally and Pratt. Yet if she had checked me out without wanting to appear that she had, then she had acted as I would have expected, except, of course, for the gaffe about no visitors. Was it a gaffe? Perhaps she wanted me to know that she knew everything. It was fruitless to speculate at this stage.

Third on my list of suspicions was the fact that she had obviously gone to some lengths to make herself seem plain, even unattractive. The hair in a bun, the severe cut of her suit and now I realised no make-up. Again she had wanted me to think she was the person she appeared to be, unless that act was for some other party.

The clincher though was the glasses. More effort to detract from her original appearance, but this time this wasn't a guess, this time I was as sure as an angel betting on Red Rum in the Pearly Gates Grand National. When I had picked up the glasses from off the floor I had checked them to see they were not broken. She was neither long nor short sighted for the lens were glass, clear glass.

All in all I was going to treat Mrs F with the utmost caution. I mean the whole thing was too convenient. There I was; a bankrupt before I'd even really started, then 'POW!' up pops my fairy god-client. Wish number one was easy, a cheque for £20,000. Wish number two - who needed any more? I couldn't afford to even snatch a glimpse at a gift horse, let alone look in his mouth. I couldn't take the money and run. It was a case of pass Go, collect £20,000 and hope one didn't have to take a Chance card, go directly to jail or worse. I had never been very good at Monopoly.

For the time being I would have to give Mrs F the benefit of the doubt, with certain reservations. At least I could check her credentials.

I had wanted her to have to write down the London office number to see if she knew it but by producing another card she had avoided that little safety check. Undaunted I did not ring the number on the card but obtained the number from Direct Enquiries. It was the same number as on the card. I hadn't expected anything else. She had been telling the truth or I was dealing with extreme professionals. I rang the number and was told that Jane Fulwood was based there but she was away from the office until tomorrow. Would I like to leave a message? Not now, I said, I would ring again. So she did indeed work for Fidelity Insurance, and I had been paid their cheque so I was now working for them. Or was I just working for Jane? Plain Jane she would have me believe but I was not convinced.

Just then my neighbour came storming into the office. He was all fired up, or he would have been if I had returned his heater. My profuse apologies went unheard, presumably because his freezing staff had chewed his ears off. I somehow got the impression that I would be unable to borrow from him again. I added a heater under the chair and mug on my hypothetical shopping list. With just a small portion of the retainer I could make the office a trifle more respectable. I was free to spend the money. If the investigation proved nothing one way or the other the retainer would still be mine. I would still have to be prudently thrifty as that £20,000 might have to last me a long time.

# CHAPTER 2

With all that had happened that morning I wondered what I had done to deserve such luck and I came to the unmistakable conclusion that as today was the first day in my entire life I had worn red socks, other than on the football pitch; they had to be the answer. Hence they had to become my lucky red socks. The real question though was, was it the colour that was lucky or those particular socks? If the former I would have to buy some more, I was going to need all the luck I could get. If the latter it was a case of luck versus personal hygiene. It would give a whole new meaning to the phrase 'your luck stinks'.

I started to peruse the details in the envelope given to me by the dubious Mrs F. It was purely factual information from which no conclusions could be drawn regarding the pending investigation. I would at least require the other information I had asked her for before I could even possibly picture a likely chain of events and take preventive measures. However, I was getting way ahead of myself. All I had been employed to do so far was watch.

According to the papers Fairfax (UK) Ltd consisted of Fairfax Property Management Ltd, The Fairfax Entertainment Group, Fairfax Bottling Ltd and the J.F. Research Establishment. There was a fairly widespread field of operation. FPM owned properties all over the UK it seemed and FEG ran cinemas, bingo halls, bowling alleys and nightclubs in all major cities. The bottling plant was in Scotland, where else? The research laboratory was down South, some small village I had never even heard of. The centre of the spider's web was the Head Office and Administration Centre which was located some fifteen miles south of Manchester. This was where Hobson was based. From the photograph of him, he seemed to have an honest face - distinguished even, with black hair greying at the sides. He had a squat nose and a genuine smile on his lips which also radiated from his eyes. He did not seem the sort to get involved with the ungodly but the camera does in fact lie, and quite often at that. Anyway, my experience of the ungodly was extremely limited, and in all but one case, restricted to the TV screen.

There were a few notes on Hobson but they didn't amount to much. He lived with his wife and two daughters not far from the Head Office location. He was a family man and tried to spend as much time with them as he could, without, the notes said, detracting from his job.

This was the man I had to shadow, and without him realising it. Easy as pie! Anyone could do it. It could be seen on the silver screen all the time, amateurs and beginners both as successful as the professionals and at times even more so. A car could tail another one for miles on an empty road and only yards behind while the driver of the car in front remains blissfully unaware. In a traffic laden street, however, a tail can be spotted almost immediately and a high speed chase usually ensues. Sometimes these diametrically opposed outcomes could occur in the same show. Whether on foot or by car did not seem to matter.

My own personal opinion was that to keep a person under constant surveillance without being spotted was as difficult as getting an alcoholic to attend a temperance meeting. It was not an assignment for an amateur. To my mind if you were seen by the subject once you might get away with it but more than that and one might as well pack up and go home. I would have to give the forthcoming operation some considerable thought. I was no professional in the shadowing stakes; I didn't even qualify as a professional amateur. Investigation was still very much a learning process for me, by basic trial and error. I sincerely hoped that there were not going to be too many of the latter.

I now turned my attention to the possible ways to defraud insurance companies, as a way of taking my mind off the fact of my total unsuitability for the job I had been paid to do. It was no secret that to the majority of punters insurance companies were unscrupulous money grabbing organisations out to line their own pockets, and with a nice line of microscopic opt-outs. Most people would probably regard them as fair game and treat someone stealing from one as some sort of Robin Hood, little realising that this is one of the reasons for continually increasing premiums. Not that increasing premiums was a problem at present and hadn't been for some time. It was a soft market, meaning rates were kept low because of fierce competition, and everyone in the industry was working twice as hard just to stand still.

The myth that insurers just want to collect premiums but will always wriggle out of a claim was just that. It is true that in certain circumstances claims are repudiated. In reality it would be bad business to repudiate claims unless there was a valid reason to do so because it would just result in bad press and public distrust. In a lot of cases if the policyholder had read his policy and understood his own obligations in respect of the insurance contract, and also which events were not covered, there would be fewer claims turned down because then the non-valid claims would not be submitted.

A fraudulent claim benefits no one but the fraudulent party, unless caught of course. It has been a great concern to insurance companies that the number of incidences has increased dramatically over recent years. Fraudulent claims were rife in the 80s when the recession resulted in so many failed businesses and the debt ridden owners needed to find a way out. It had become so bad that all major insurance companies discussed the exchange of information between themselves to combat this ever growing threat. Even though this was some years ago fraudulent claims still cost the industry £585 million in 1995.

There are numerous ways that have been tried to profit from insurance policies. There was the 'Double Indemnity Ploy', where a loss is claimed for under more than one policy. This is against the general principle of insurance which is simply to place the policyholder in the same position he was before the loss, or in other words, he is not supposed to make a profit from it. This type of fraud can be combated by the free exchange of information between companies. It can then be seen if two policies indemnify the same interest.

A favourite with failed businesses is the 'Arson About Ploy'. Find a friendly pyromaniac, point him in the right direction and for a small fee your worries are over.

Also in the top ten is the 'Wot! No Theft! Ploy', where property is hidden away for later but reported stolen. This results in the enviable position of having your cake, eating it and being able to buy another one too.

Then there is the 'Price Is Right Ploy'. Here items are insured for a figure over their true value so that a profit is made at the time of a loss. This is not to be tried when the insurance company has seen the property because they would know the rough value. Nor can it be used for valuable items where the insurance company requires a written valuation, unless one happens to know a crooked valuer.

One of the favourites with film and TV producers is the 'Cat of Nine Lives Ploy'. One spouse has a large life policy or various policies on the life of their other half who, unfortunately, unlike the proverbial cat, only has one life which is forfeit for capital gain. Do it yourself or pay someone else to do it, just have an alibi so you won't be caught. From Perry Mason to Columbo, the Saint to Morse, it was a variation on a theme used many times. No doubt in real life it was as prevalent.

I supposed that with enough ingenuity it was possible to cheat on most insurance policies. The question to be answered was who was cheating on the Fairfax policies, if there was any cheating at all. Any claims cheques issued would be in the name of the company so on the face of it no individual would be able to benefit. Who stood to gain? That was the key. What I had to do was find that key. Then I had to find the door that it unlocked.

On that point I decided to shelve my thinking on the subject. It was fairly pointless speculating at this stage. I had to wait until I had something more to work with. It was time to do something much more practical. For once my bank manager would be happy to see me.

I pulled an empty buff file from my desk drawer and nearly choked on the dust cloud this produced. Having inserted the papers I then had a little trouble in deciding how to head the file. Fidelity Insurance or Fairfax Corporation. In the end I compromised with just an F. I was my own filing clerk but was at a loss because the office manager, also me, had not yet decided on the filing system. Alphabetical, numerical or chronological. It was a difficult choice and one on which the whole future of the business could depend. If I chose an alphabetical system the file would go under F, Fa or Fi was not yet decided. It was my first case so under a numerical system it would be Case Number One. Of course, even under an alphabetical system it was still the first file, F for First. Then in chronological terms it was also the first file. Decisions, decisions. In the end I just flung the file in the top drawer. I didn't think the file minded how it was filed, it was just glad to exist.

I left the office and was proceeding at a leisurely pace down the corridor when I was hit by a ballistic missile and was knocked off my feet, arms and legs all over the place. Fortunately, this misguided missile was not of the exploding variety, more the frantic female variety. "Sorry!" she yelled over her shoulder as she ran on.

"Hold on!" I called after her. "What's the big hurry?"

She stopped and walked back a few steps. "I'm late for an interview at the job agency," she informed me in breathless tones.

"What do you do?" I asked, a weird idea forming in my head, assuming she gave the right answer.

"Secretary." Bingo! "At least that was my last job."

"Believe it or not I'm currently looking for a secretary," I told her. It was news to me. The idea seemed to have jumped straight from the subconscious to my mouth. Still it was not such a bad idea. I could be out on the case most of the time and I would need someone to man or, to be politically correct, person the office. I thought I read distrust on her face and I was right.

"Oh! Are you?" she asked suspiciously, as if every man she bumped into offered her a job. "What are you?"

Straight to the point this one. "I'm an investigator. My office is just around the corner. Why not pop in for a chat? I don't bite. Honest! And you can tell the agency where you are." I suddenly stopped, pound signs showing in my eyes. "Of course, if you did, I would have to pay them a fee to employ you," I smiled.

"You're on your way out," she observed.

"That can wait five minutes," I assured her. "Come to the office."

She came and her face fell five feet when she stepped into what would be her domain. First impressions count they say but I hoped they were wrong in this case. Now that the idea of having a secretary had taken a firm root in my brain I wanted to act fast. I knew I would have no time to recruit one as from the next day because I would be fully occupied on the case in hand, subject to a courier bearing gifts. There was one other tiny reason I was suddenly so keen, hardly worth mentioning really. Money. Why pay an agency's fees or advertising costs when you can bump into someone suitable in the corridor.

"Don't let the appearance fool you," I said on seeing her face. "Improvements are in the offing."

"It doesn't look like a thriving business." She looked around with obvious distaste.

"I've only just opened," I explained in my most soothing tones. I showed her the cheque. "Got my first client today. This cheque means the office can be furnished better for a start. That can be your first assignment, if you take the job." She would without doubt do a better job of making the office more personable than I would.

The inevitable question came next. "How much are you paying?"

I tried to sum her up which was difficult on an acquaintanceship of a few minutes. She was young, pretty, in her early twenties and not too keen. "I'll pay you £1,000 for the first two months; then if we're still in business, we'll review it."

"I'd like to think about it," she said, sensibly. "I'll go to the agency, see what they've got and let you know. OK?"

"Fair enough," I acknowledged. "You know where I am."

She was gone in a flash. It was then that I realised that I had done the exact same thing that I had accused my earlier visitor of. It seemed to be the day for not giving names. Still a name wasn't necessary if she wasn't going to work for me. I doubted she would be back, which said a lot for my detective instincts.

I set about the relatively easy task of depositing the cheque into my bank account. Note the use of the word 'relatively'. I referred to it as the 'Stand in a queue for an hour before we listen to your request bank' as well as 'the bank that likes to say no, but not straight away'. I was in luck that day, the queue was only an half an hour long and I couldn't see them saying no to a sizeable deposit. Surprise, surprise, I was right. I wasn't an investigator for nothing.

Back at the office there was another surprise waiting for me. A piece of paper had been pushed under the door. 'I will start tomorrow' it read. So now I had a secretary. It was turning into a momentous day - my first client, a fat retainer and an employee. I needed to hurry to M & S to buy some more red socks. However, I soon discovered that the trouble with buying red socks is that they only seem to be available in a multicolour pack of five. One pair of red socks for each day of the week left me with twenty-four non-red pairs. I had to put it down to the price of success.

I had a long, lavish and leisurely lunch in celebration, which came as a welcome respite from home-made sandwiches. As a result I was not back at the office until gone two o'clock. I spent what was left of the afternoon making a list of furnishings so my secretary would believe she was working in an office and not some theatrical agent's waiting room. After a couple of hours I called it a day. Early closing I decided, for tomorrow promised to be the start of a busy period for me. I figured to spend the morning studying the case history, provided the courier arrived early. In the afternoon I could perhaps make my first reconnoitre. The best laid plans of mice, men and red sock wearers.

There was obviously a limit on the amount of luck that can be generated by one pair of red socks in a day. My car had been stolen from where I had parked it a few streets away from the office. I still had an hour left on the meter too.

It is one of life's great mysteries how a fully locked and secure vehicle can be unlawfully taken from a main street in broad daylight without interference. You never see that on the small screen. The hero stops his car, gets out, slams the door, never locks it, usually doesn't even have the keys in his hand, sometimes leaves a window open, comes back a week and a half later and it is still there. Opportune car thieves would just ruin the storyline. Imagine! The baddie rushes out of a building, jumps into a car and speeds away. The pursuing goodie runs out to his car, but it's gone. A passing octogenarian spotted the keys in the ignition, found the door unlocked and drove away. Wot! No car chase!

By the time I had finished with the police it was later than if I had finished work at the normal time. The cost of a taxi was an unwarranted drain on my newly achieved resources. Perhaps red socks were not so lucky after all. If for every piece of good luck there had to be an equal amount of bad luck I thought I preferred no luck at all.

As it turned out my luck was about to run out in the very near future, red socks or no red socks.

I was still in a bad mood the next morning. It wasn't the best day for displaying a sunny disposition to my new colleague. I had to take another taxi to the office to be there in time for her arrival, which I assumed would be nine o'clock although she had not said in her note. After a cheery welcome I would have to arrange for a hire car, more unwarranted expense.

Stoically, in spite of everything, I wore what I hoped was my most welcoming smile when my new recruit arrived at 8.55. She was not out of breath this time so I assumed she had not been bombing along, head down, bowling over prospective employers.

"Morning boss," she greeted me.

She was immaculately turned out in ladies business suit and blouse and would have been entirely suitable for a top class hotel. She made me feel drab and the surroundings seem drabber than ever. And I still did not know her name.

"Morning Mildred," I responded. Not having offered me her name I had used the name of someone else's secretary, although I was sure Remington Steele would have agreed that with her long dark hair she was a younger version of Laura Holt.

Whilst not understanding the reference, obviously not a telly addict like me, she did realise that I was ignorant of her name for she stood stiffly to attention, saluted and barked, "Jenny Fox reporting for duty. Sir!"

What a coincidence. Before Mildred, Remington Steele's secretary had been a Miss Wolf who he had persistently insisted on calling Miss Fox. Or was it vice versa? There seemed no point in mentioning this so instead a mere introduction was in order. "Welcome to the firm, Jenny. My name is Thomas Robel but most people call me Tommy."

"Tommy Trouble?" she asked, mischievously.

"Exactly," I had to confirm. She was quick this one. Identified my nickname in seconds, not that it took much thought. "I'm afraid this is your chair for now but it won't be for long. The first thing you can do is make a list of everything you think the office needs. I have to go out for a while. We'll have a chat when I return. OK?"

"OK," she agreed. "What do I do if the phone rings?"

"This is only my opinion of course but I've always felt that the best thing to do in such circumstances is pick up the receiver, otherwise you'll never know who was calling." I was smiling to rob my words of any offence. I was just setting the scene for what I hoped would be the usual every day quick fire office banter. She had already shown she could hold her own in that way. "You'll have to use the phone in my office until I have another extension put in. However, I doubt whether there will be cause to use it. There is as much chance of the phone ringing as Britain leading the medal table at the Olympics."

"That good, eh! Business must be booming." She took off her coat and put it over the back of her chair. Another item for the list, a coat rack.

"Well, I'll see you later then," I said, turning towards the door. "Oh, one thing," I remembered something important. "I'm expecting a courier today, hopefully this morning. If he arrives whilst I'm out, please do the necessary."

"That's what secretaries do isn't it?" she pointed out. "By the way, a secretary should know where her boss is at all times, during working hours that is."

"Point taken," I acknowledged. "I have to hire a car. Mine was stolen yesterday. I should be back within an hour."

"Fine," she said and let me go.

I hadn't heard anything from the police since I had reported my car missing. They just said they would be in touch if they learnt anything. If this had happened at any other time I would have just relied on public transport, I would have had to as I would not have had sufficient funds to hire a replacement vehicle. Things were different now. I would need a car to carry out my investigation and fortunately I had the money to hire one, once the cheque cleared that is. Before I could pick up my rental I had to square it with the bank to loan me the necessary amount pending the clearance of the cheque paid in the day before.

I chose the cheapest model available so I ended up with a hire Ka. With my new found propensity for red I was disappointed that it was blue in colour but this was an advantage in the unobtrusive stakes. A blue car is less distinctive and therefore more suitable for surveillance. However, with my finely honed skills in that area I would be just as unobtrusive in a pink car with yellow spots. What I really needed was a car in invisible colours.

Back at the office I found that Jenny had completed her list of office necessities which on comparison with mine proved twice as long. It takes a female mind to remember such items as blinds for the windows, pictures to adorn the walls, to ease the waiting eye, and coffee cups for those waiting. With only one case on the go I couldn't foresee a lot of waiting people, but she was probably planning ahead. I called her into my office to compare notes. She brought her chair with her.

"OK Jenny," I began, "let's have a chat. First, I've been over your list, which I have to admit is far more comprehensive than mine and shows a lot of thought went into it. After lunch you can start ringing round and pricing things up. The smaller items you can go out and buy, but you'll have to wait until the cheque clears."

She nodded her head in understanding. "One item I didn't put on the list was a typewriter. Most offices use word-processors these days. I don't know how much typing there will be to do but if you bought a PC package I could do your accounts on it too."

"Cost it up with the other items and let me see the damage," I told her, not wishing to dismiss her idea out of hand but feeling that a computer would probably be too much expense on an item which would not see much use. "Now, as regards yourself, I'll need your P45. I've never had an employee before so I need to find out what to do. Contact the Inland Revenue for one thing." And take out insurance for another, said a voice in my head. Now I had an employee I had a legal obligation to do so. Further, my office contents were about to increase in value, dramatically if my new secretary had her way. At least I could afford the premium now.

"Tell me about yourself," I invited her. We had time to kill; the courier had not been.

"Well, I'm twenty-two, live with my parents and have been doing mostly secretarial work since I left school at sixteen." She paused, biting her lip in thought for a moment. "I resigned from my last job because my boss expected more than a secretary, if you know what I mean." That was a warning if ever I heard one, followed by another one. "I have a boyfriend, he's a security guard."

"Duly noted and warned off," I assured her. "You've no need to worry. I've never forced myself on a woman in my life. I'm too scared of being beaten up by the boyfriend or husband, or even the woman herself. Please continue."

"There's nothing more to tell really. I work hard and will not be walked on."

"Fair enough," I agreed. "Like I said, I've never employed anybody before so this will be a learning experience for me. Let me know at once if there is something you're not happy about."

"I will," she said, emphatically, and I believed her. "Tell me something about my new boss," she carried on. "How did you become an investigator?"

It was a long story but there was nothing more important to do, so in the interests of good employer/employee relations I started to recount the events that had brought me to that particular place in time and space. It was about an insurance broker who suspects a new client of arson and tries to carry out his own investigation rather than report his suspicions to the police.

There was a lesson in it too. How poking one's nose into something that didn't concern you can land you in very hot water.

# CHAPTER 3

A shrill and unusual sound interrupted my narration. It took me a few seconds to realise what it was. Well, the phone had never rung before. It was a very important call. The first since the start of business and with any luck it could be for me. On the other hand, it could have been a wrong number. The latter was more likely, yet I was wearing my red socks for the second day running and the call was for me. It was the carpet tripper. She had rung to let me know that Hobson was currently in the States with James Fairfax. I should begin my surveillance on his return. She said she would give me advanced notice of this so I could be waiting at the airport. I thought I ought to let her know that the courier had not arrived but my comment that she would have been better using a courier pigeon did not go down too well. Americans just don't understand the British sense of humour.

Mrs F wasn't concerned, promising that the information would arrive soon. As a premonition it was spot on because Jenny had taken receipt of a package whilst I was on the phone. Like a dutiful receptionist/secretary she had signed for it rather than interrupt me.

"I'll have to concentrate on these now, Jenny," I told her, taking a sheaf of paper from the large envelope. "The rest of my exploits will have to wait for another time."

"OK," she acknowledged. "What do you want me to do?"

"Well, you can start by costing up your list of improvements. I think most of the items are necessary. Shop around for the best price and then place an order. Not the computer though. I'd like to know the cost beforehand on that." She was just about to enter her own domain but I stopped her. "We'll have to swap offices for now. I've got the only phone remember. Which reminds me, the first item on your list should be to arrange for B.T. to install an extension in reception. Then we'll really be in business."

"You're the boss, Boss," she said, and for the second time in twenty-four hours I gave my seat and desk over to a member of the fair sex.

In reception, I checked the papers I had been sent. It appeared to be everything I had requested. There were copies of all the insurance schedules of the policies relating to the Fairfax UK companies and more importantly, from my own point of view, details of the incidents that had caused concern in the States. That was where I had to start from. The alleged deterioration in the claims experience was the crux of the matter, I felt sure of that. Anything that happened in the UK would only be a derivative.

The details proved interesting to say the least. With a multi-million corporation involving various companies in a variety of industries, I would have expected a lengthy list of claims but I was greatly surprised. Over the years since its birth, excepting the last year, the experience was exceptional. No more than two or three claims each year. The majority of these were liability claims for personal injury or property damage. This was not surprising for a fan of LA Law. Over there one can be sued for mispronouncing someone's name during a conversation. However, the low number of overall claims, excluding that last year, told me a lot about the Fairfax management. Sound management is one of the most vital ingredients in a good insurance risk. A management that acts as though uninsured, taking all the necessary precautions to minimise any potential risk and receptive to any suggested improvements, is the best type of risk. The underwriter can be confident that everything possible has been done and will continue to be done to prevent a potential loss.

Despite the low number of claims I guessed that there were even more liability claims that never reached court or the insurance company files. The Corporation probably had an army of top drawer lawyers on its payroll to prevent many of the claims getting through. Most of them were probably settled at a cost less than the policy excess, hence the lack of notification to the insurers.

To say the contrast in the past year's figures was startling would have been a gross understatement. It had to be the most unbelievable transformation since the ugly duckling became a protected species. The number of claims in that year would not have been unusual for an organisation of such size except for the stark contrast with the previous phenomenally good record.

There were thirteen claims, unlucky for someone. Unlucky for the Fidelity Insurance Company. Those thirteen claims, all of which had occurred since the change of management, totalled, in respect of monies paid and estimated payments currently outstanding, $192,514,000. Admittedly $175,000,000 related to just three of those claims but even the balance of $17,000,000 was well in excess of the previous largest total in any previous one year. This being 1977 when $6,000,000 had been paid out, the majority in respect of a fatality due to a design fault in a car.

When the probably not married Mrs Fulwood had expressed her company's concern over the alarming downturn she had not been overstating the case. Considering the size of the losses I wondered whether F.I.C. would be trading at all in the future. Without doubt, some of the risks would be syndicated; but even so, that one year's results were going to prove crippling for my new employers. No wonder they suspected fraud. If I was in their shoes I would be down on my knees praying for it. Even I.M. Gullible, model citizen of Trustville in Veracity County and winner of the Most Trusting Person of the Year Award three years in a row, would have been suspicious.

All this I had gleaned from the top three pages of the wad of papers which consisted of a chronological list of the claims, merely listing the date, incident and amount involved. On the next sheet there were some explanatory notes, typewritten but presumably from my liaison, the doubtable Mrs F, to the effect that each claim had been thoroughly investigated at the time of occurrence according to normal standard practice. The question of a possible co-ordinated fraud attempt had not been raised until after the fire in August. At that time, there had been a growing feeling that someone had a personnel vendetta against the Fairfax Corporation, or that someone inside the organisation was trying to benefit from insurance monies paid.

I felt that the former was more likely because it was hard to visualise how one person could profit. Whilst the Fairfax brothers presumably had overall control of the Corporation they would not have day to day control over each tentacle of such a vast octopus-like empire. According to the notes at least seven different divisions had been involved in the recent catastrophes and I was assuming that meant seven different financial controllers. Unless they were all in it together the insider theory was not even supposition at this stage. All the claims cheques would have been issued in the relevant individual company's name and would have to be cleared through separate bank accounts. Financial checks were currently being undertaken, read the notes, to determine the stability of each division and the Corporation overall. The latest claims had not been paid nor any interim payments made pending investigations. The situation had prompted F.I.C. to reopen the previously settled 1995 claims which were to be scrutinised for any details that had been overlooked, especially anything which tied in with any other incident that had occurred.

On the following pages, the details of each individual incident were set out. There were seven pages of this which was the nitty-gritty of the information I had requested. On those seven pages I had to concentrate fully so my mind could take in all factors, for present surmises and future reference.

I felt that some stimulation was needed to assist the little grey cells. Whatever else I couldn't do there was one thing I had excelled at and that was to choose a secretary that made a damn fine cup of coffee. Suitably armed I went into battle.

The insurance year for the Fairfax Corporation ran 1st January to 31st December. The notes on the losses for 1995 read as follows:

## 12.1.95 - Fire at Fairfax (Coast to Coast) Haulage

Fire Department notified 3.53am by a local resident of fire at San Francisco warehouse. Fire had already taken a firm hold by the time of their arrival and before blaze could be extinguished both buildings and contents totally destroyed. Nothing could be salvaged.

Forensics concluded discarded cigarette or match had set oil impregnated rags alight which spread to the fuel tanks of vehicles garaged overnight. There were a number of explosions as tanks caught fire.

Premises secured at 7.30pm by duty manager but each driver had keys in order to garage vehicle if returning after lock-up time. Last driver this night, Sam Peters at 3.15am. Fire started not long after this time. Peters is non-smoker but against company regulations had given hitch-hiker a ride. Hitch-hiker left unattended whilst Peters deposited keys in office. Hitch-hiker was smoker but Peters not aware if he did in vehicle depot. However, most logical explanation. Peters only had first name of hitch-hiker so impossible to trace.

Possible fire started deliberately or negligently. However, hitch-hiker picked up miles from depot and showed no discrimination in selection of vehicles. Seems unlikely therefore fire started intentionally with knowledge of policyholder. If fire deliberate act must have been unpremeditated.

Company just managing to pay its way prior to fire. Least profitable area of Fairfax Corporation. Management decided not to re-establish company. Settlement agreed on market value of assets.

Peters certainly partly responsible but due to lack of positive proof of cause of fire and Peters' lack of funds no benefit in pursuing recovery.

Total Payment $750,000

## 17.1.95 - Theft at Fairfax Film and TV Studio

Several original paintings stolen from director's office and boardroom of Hollywood studio. Discovery by director, Lionel Witherspoon, at 8.45am, by which time police present.

Film crew were shooting in one of small studios during night so alarm not operative. No one saw anything suspicious. Fast and efficient raid.

Guard on gate to studio lot overpowered and immobilised at around 2.00am. Gang drove van through gates and guard, who was conscious, says about ten minutes elapsed before he heard it depart. Assumed items lowered on rope through window to reduce chance of being spotted by film crew members. Probably at least three persons involved, one to select items, one to lower, one to load van. Thieves exited building without being seen. No one legally in building aware of events.

Film crew left at 4.30am. None stopped to check why gates open and unmanned. On being questioned each crew member assumed gates open because guard knew number of persons leaving one after another within a few minutes. Such practice usual but guard normally present to oversee departures. Weather inhospitable, with driving rain, and guard's absence assumed due to this.

Guard found tied up by relief at 8.30am. Police and Witherspoon notified immediately.

Inside assistance suspected as thieves knew what to take, when and where from. None of film crew out of sight of others and therefore alibi each other. All other studio personnel also had unshakeable alibis. Investigations concentrated on those who knew film crew working that night. A make-up girl had mentioned it to a friend, ex secretary of Witherspoon. Police discovered she had left country previous day and this taken as proof of involvement but never located. Boyfriend also disappeared and assumed he was part of gang.

Paintings never recovered or seen by local fences. Probably abroad in private collection. Consisted of 2 Rembrandts, a Van Gogh, a Renoir and 2 Picassos.

Total Payment $1,000,000.

### 3.2.95 - Third Party Injury at Fairfax Grand, New York

Third party, Gladys Wainwright, tripped over broom handle and fell down flight of stairs breaking left leg in two places. Incident occurred on third floor of hotel when elevator being repaired. Maid left cleaning trolley outside room nearest to top of stairs with broom leant against wall. Broom slipped, protruding across stairwell. Mrs Wainwright, making her way from her room on fourth floor to lobby, fell over broom. Maid left trolley whilst opening door with passkey for guest who had mislaid his. She witnessed accident. Definite negligence claim. Out of court settlement agreed.

Total Payment $77,000

### 25.3.95 - Theft at Fairfax Distribution, Chicago

Substantial quantity of electrical equipment stolen from warehouse. Security guard surprised and overpowered by three masked men in early hours. Guard supposed to radio check with base every twenty minutes and had just done so prior to attack. Therefore, thieves had less than twenty minutes before alarm raised. Guard unable to see what happened but heard two trucks arrive. By time police arrived thieves had made clean getaway and despite swift cordon of area trucks not located.

Guard could give no details of thieves. Not even sure how many in gang, but probably more than the three who attacked him.

No attempt made to remove any other type of goods, but as

boxes clearly marked and as easily accessible as other goods in warehouse, not known whether electrical items were predetermined target, indicating inside information, or just opportune prize.

All employees and directors had alibis. No items recovered.

Total Payment $50,000

## 1.4.95 - Third Party Injury at Fairfax Hilton, New York

Bellboy, Pete Simpson, was travelling in lift to ground floor after showing guest to room. Lift fell from first floor. Simpson only occupant, found alive but unconscious in damaged car at bottom of shaft. Simpson left paralysed from waist down. Prognosis from three independent specialists: injury permanent.

Out of court settlement not possible. Simpson wanted day in court.

Damages Awarded $5,000,000

## 2.6.95 - Fire at Fairfax Research Establishment, New Jersey

Fire Department called to small fire in one of the labs. Lab animal upset burner which ignited chemicals. Lab assistants attempted to extinguish blaze and whilst not achieved fire kept under control until Fire Department arrived. Damage less than could have been as a result but some very expensive laboratory equipment damaged beyond repair.

Total Payment $12,000

## 22.6.95 - Theft at Fairfax Corporation HQ, New York

At 10.30pm whilst cleaning contractors still working in office building, gang of masked men burst in and locked cleaners in storeroom then proceeded to smash up offices. All portable equipment taken and other equipment damaged beyond repair.

Gang had vehicle in basement car park so other than cleaners no witnesses.

Police later notified by alarm company who noticed alarm had not been set by midnight when contractors supposed to have departed. No clues to intruders' identity but severe grudge against Corporation indicated.

Fortunately, no paper records destroyed and computer disc backups kept off site so interference to business only slight. Only replacement of equipment necessary.

Enquiries undertaken to determine who could have grudge. As far as can be ascertained there are no disgruntled employees or ex-employees or third parties and no other reason for act established. Police have no leads.

Total Payment $125,000.

### 19.8.95 - Fire at Fairfax Film and TV Studio, Hollywood

Large blaze destroyed three of larger studios on lot including sets, scenery and props connected to two major motion pictures in production. Fire occurred on one of few nights when lot was unoccupied except for guard on gate. Buildings concerned were on far side of lot so guard did not notice flames until roofs caught fire. By time Fire Department arrived no chance of saving property.

Forensics established fires deliberately started by remote controlled incendiary devices, remains of which were found in ruins of each building. Seems deliberate plot to prevent or severely delay production of both films. Could indicate involvement of rival studio. Devices must have been in position some time during the day but despite intensive questioning of cast and crew no further information found.

F.I.C. only insured assets whilst cover for production risk of specialist carrier, such cover including costs of re-shooting, loss of revenue due to delay in film release and extra fees for cast etc., estimate expected to run well over $100 Million dollars.

Estimated Costs on Assets $15,000,000

## 8.9.95 - Fire at Fairfax Research Establishment, New Jersey

Main lab fire bombed at approx. 4.00am. Only person on site at time was resident scientist Peter Cummings. No security guards as complex surrounded by electric fencing with two sets of gates, one each on the outer and inner perimeters, being remote controlled from inside the buildings. Bombers launched their projectiles from outside the outer fence and through the lab windows. Fire took hold very quickly due to numerous chemical compounds present. However, Cummings able to give immediate alarm and Fire Department arrived to contain fire within that one lab, which was totally destroyed together with some expensive pieces of equipment and vital experimental work for Fairfax Motors.

No witnesses so tracing of bombers impossible. Cast of tyre mark was taken but proved to be of common manufacture.

Work of research establishment seriously hampered by destruction of main lab and has resulted in reduction in number of projects handled at any one time. Fortunately, research for Fairfax Motors was at early stage and can be re-established in a smaller lab. This is most important current project and others have had to be shelved.

Total Estimated Damages & Loss of Revenue $500,000

## 11.9.95 - Employee Injury at Fairfax Distribution, Detroit

Fork lift truck knocked over a pile of crates causing one to fall onto an employee, Dave Gibbons. Accident resulted in paralysis from waist down, subsequently diagnosed as permanent. In view of court awarded damages of $5,000,000 for earlier incident involving Pete Simpson every effort made to keep this out of court.

Agreed Settlement $3,000,000

## 18.10.95 - Theft from Fairfax Research Establishment, New Jersey

Blueprint for new car stolen by force. Thieves lifted over fence by crane and able to reach buildings undetected. Entry made on far side of complex away from residential quarters of Peter Cummings so sound of crane not heard. Thieves made their way to Cummings' quarters and forced him at gun point to open the safe in the main building from which they took blueprints. They exited same way as they arrived, leaving Cummings bound and gagged. Getaway by car. Crane and carrier left at scene but clean.

Crane was reported stolen next morning by foreman of construction crew working five miles from complex. Enquiries made along route. Discovered that crane seen in early hours being transported on its carrier but no details of driver obtained. No accompanying vehicle noticed.

Only approximate age, height, weight etc. given by Cummings. There had been two, both wearing black Balaclavas. At least one operating the crane means at least three involved. Gloves were worn so no prints.

Highly probable that theft connected to previous fire as blueprints stolen related to same project disrupted by fire. Blueprint related to prototype vehicle to be pioneered by Fairfax Motors. Research Establishment working on fuel system aiming to vastly reduce carbon monoxide emissions. Appears someone does not want car built so could indicate competitors. However, prototype closely guarded secret with only handful of people in the know. Leak suggested but six persons involved had no motive as all would cash in on project and no evidence pointing to any of them. Later discovered that offices of Fairfax Motors bugged, by whom not known. Further, original plans missing from their safe. No signs of break-in and could have been missing for some time as currently not being worked upon pending results from Research Establishment tests.

Potential loss astronomical and discussions ongoing re settlement. Market research undertaken by Fairfax Motors shows carbon monoxide free car would be top seller. Loss of blueprints will lead to extremely lengthy delay in launch.
Possible project may even be scrapped.

Conservative Estimated Costs $50,000,000

## 11.11.95 - Theft from Fairfax Museum, New York

At 7.00pm museum about to close. Last party of foreign tourists just finished guided tour and all other visitors had left. Suddenly members of tour party produced firearms and held up security staff. Party consisted of six men and four women. Once in control another group arrived, these being masked as well as armed. Latter group took over allowing first group to leave via main entrance as normal visitors. Masked raiders then secured all doors and locked security and other staff in storeroom. Numerous valuable exhibits removed and presumably loaded into vehicle at rear of building. How long taken and when thieves left is unknown. Prisoners not discovered until four hours later when detectives from local precinct realised they were receiving missing persons reports on various people who worked at museum and went to investigate.

Hoped description of group posing as tourists would be detailed as unmasked, yet tour guide only able to give details on a couple and these not identifiable from police files. Guide adamant that they were foreigners due to numerous languages spoken when discussing exhibits. Spanish and French identified plus others not so. Questions to guide had been in stilted English. Police assume art thieves hired foreign petty criminals to pose as tourist group who had fled country immediately after.

All city hotels checked and whilst descriptions did not tally nine foreign guests had been found to have left false names and addresses.

None of items stolen appeared on black market or recovered.

Estimated Cost $7,000,000

## 27.12.95 - Theft from Fairfax Metropolitan Hotel, Los Angeles

Gang entered hotel at around 2.00am and held night porter hostage. All valuables removed from safes and pass keys used to enter guests' rooms. Knock-out gas from aerosols used to render guests unconscious or deepen sleep. Gang had four hours until porter relieved. Porter unconscious when gang left. Size of gang not known but supposition of at least dozen necessary to tackle hotel of such size in time available.

Loss of items, many of which still to be finalised, insignificant compared to flood of liability claims from guests gassed in their rooms. One elderly couple never recovered consciousness.

Reserve $100,000,000

What an amazing read. Each individual incident had enough action to have resulted a best-selling novel, blockbuster film with huge star names, the usual three far inferior sequels and a chart topping soundtrack. No doubt about it, I thought to myself, once this was all over I had to write the novel. I could call it 'The American Jobs'.

For now I had to try and link the incidents together. Admittedly, it was not my job to do so as I had been employed to prevent similar disasters in the UK but I felt that if I could identify the common denominator it would greatly assist me in my own endeavours. So far everything made as much sense to me as a Terry Pratchet novel. I hoped Death would be taking a holiday whilst I was on the case.

The three personal injury claims could be disregarded. They were surely just unfortunate accidents, although two cases of paralysis were a bit of a coincidence. That left ten claims, four fires and six thefts. If one discounted the first two fires that left eight incidents to review. Eight deliberate acts against the Fairfax Corporation.

The first thing I noticed, which was as obvious as Baldrick's lack of IQ points, was that the six thefts appeared to be linked. All involved a gang of masked raiders. No surprise there but there were other similarities. The time of the raids had all been so perfect. In the early morning when guards were less vigilant, just after a regular radio check to leave as much time as possible before the alarm was raised, when security is off guard just before closing or when the only opposition is a team of cleaners. They knew what to hit and they knew when to hit. Their intelligence network was second to none. They obviously made use of inside information when necessary and imported further recruits when required.

None of the items stolen ever surfaced either. Not via a fence or otherwise on the black market. Unusual because this seemed to indicate the perpetrators were not profiting from their plunder. In six separate cases I suspected that this would be unheard of.

Same MO, same result, same gang.

So I knew that there was definitely a group of people, say a gang of at least twelve, who had it in for the Fairfax Corporation. This A.F.G. as I nicknamed them, standing for Anti Fairfax Group, were highly professional and extremely mobile, able it seemed to operate all over the States. They were also totally cool. Entering hotel rooms armed with knock-out spray took some nerve. They could have encountered a light sleeper with a gun under the pillow. At least the aerosols meant I could rule out Greenpeace.

The raids had been well planned in advance. To corrupt insiders took time and the gang must have been working on preparation for a considerable time prior to the first raid. Unless there was someone else doing the planning. Some elaborate puppet-master pulling numerous strings.

Another common link appeared to be the Fairfax Research Establishment. Arson and theft. Someone did not want the new prototype car to be built. Was it a competitor of Fairfax Motors? Their offices had been bugged. Or was it someone on the inside making it look like someone from the outside?

The tactics of the A.F.G. appeared to be the three D's, destroy, disrupt and deprive, the latter seemingly the top priority due to the greater number of thefts. Either we were dealing with a massive grudge, one that must have involved great personal loss and merited the total destruction of the Fairfax empire, a great desire for personal wealth at the expense of the Corporation, or a madman. Possibly it was a combination of all three. If there was a grudge it seemed likely this had something to do with the Research Establishment. This appeared to be the best bet and I was sure that the authorities in the States would be following up this angle. I still thought it unlikely that someone was trying to profit out of all this because in that case surely the stolen items would have been off loaded. After all that was the main reason for theft, to profit from that owned by others.

I spent an hour on this conjecture then realised I had wasted my time. On the next sheet of paper were certain points which had come to light from the local investigations. Points such as it was almost a certainty that all the thefts had been carried out by the same gang and more than likely the arsons were their work too. I had taken that as read anyway.

It was also felt that the gang had access to a personal plane to enable them to easily and quickly travel to each target area of operation. If this was so it was not using the major airports according to protracted enquiries. It was also mentioned that the research contracts undertaken by the F.R.E. over the past ten years were being thoroughly investigated. Nothing had been discovered so far which could provide motive for the attacks although the competitors of Fairfax Motors were certainly not being overlooked.

Nothing awe-inspiring really, merely the conclusions I had come to myself. All that is except the last two points mentioned which I had not visualised because I had discounted the incidents.

They concerned the two cases of paralysis. It appeared that Simpson, the first victim, had been found murdered three days after being given his cheque for $5,000,000. The cheque had not been deposited in his bank account but had been cleared. It was later discovered that another account existed, a joint account with a Miss Veronica Lamb who did not exist according to enquiries made. In addition the autopsy on Simpson's body failed to locate any reason for the paralysis. In fact the coroner's report stated that in his opinion there had been none.

Even more intriguing were the notes on the second victim, Dave Gibbons. He had disappeared according to his wife, who knew nothing about the $3,000,000 damages he had received. It had not been paid into their account. Again the cheque had been cleared through another joint account with a Miss Tanya Stevens. Surprise, surprise, she was found not to exist either. It looked like he had run off with another woman, or that was how it was supposed to look, but Mrs Gibbons had had no suspicions of another woman. She would have known if there had been she had stated.

There was only one thing to say about the coincidence of two employees being paralysed from the waist down in two separate incidents that occurred five months apart and in two different states, where the substantial awards for damages go missing. It was no coincidence.

I had been wrong to exempt these two incidents. The first may have occurred on the first of April but nobody was that much of a fool. This had to have been planned and because one cannot predict what a falling lift or crate will damage, the paralysis had to have been induced. The F.B.I. was on to this, the notes said. I doubted if anything could be proved. As sure as Shergar was in that stable in the sky, Dave Gibbons was there feeding it sugar lumps. I assumed that there must have been some drug that could induce temporary paralysis and both Simpson and Gibbons had been persuaded to have an injection, of cash as well as the drug. Whoever had hit upon the scheme to extract $8,000,000 from F.I.C. had eliminated the witnesses. Was the A.F.G. involved or just the puppet-master? Or was it just a coincidence that the non-coincidental accidents coincided with the actions of the A.F.G.?

I gave up on this line of thought for it was taking me around in circles. Let the Americans sort their own end out; I would have my hands full in the UK. All I had to prevent was probably only half a dozen thefts, the odd case of arson and maybe cure a couple cases of paralysis. Nothing to it. The problem would be to fill in the rest of the day.

Of course it was all conjecture. The meetings between Fairfax and Hobson were probably due to a fear that the attacks in the States might spread to the UK. No doubt Hobson was taking instructions on how to improve security. And if this was the case I was in for a very tedious time. On the other hand James Fairfax could be the big fat spider in the middle of an intricate web of dirty dealing. He could be the puppet-master pulling everybody's strings. If he was the big cheese it was certainly very smelly cheese.

Enough was enough. My brain wasn't powered by Duracell batteries and I needed some sustenance. It was well past lunch time and the sandwich shop only had a choice of cheese or egg. As a migraine sufferer I had no option but to choose the cheese, I hate egg. Just one of my many aversions and nothing to do with Sam N Ella's Curried eggscapade that had shell shocked so many people. Jenny was more sensible for she had brought a packed lunch from home.

For the rest of the day Jenny and I finalised the furnishing of the office. She had ordered everything to be delivered on Friday, except the computer which I had put on hold. Weighing the cost against the tenuous hold PPWP had on the investigative market I had decided that an ordinary typewriter would have to do for the time being. I did concede to an electric one though.

Before retiring for the day I also made enquiries on how to pay wages, employer's tax and National Insurance contributions. I also learnt the other secrets of employees' welfare and made certain arrangements in connection therewith, including taking out the necessary insurance. It had been the busiest day in the history of the company and I hoped it was a sign of things to come.

I locked up bang on five o'clock as Jenny was leaving at the same time. "How did you enjoy your first day?" I asked her.

"Fine," she said. "It was nice to be eased in slowly."

"I've got news for you," I told her. "Today was extremely busy."

"Oh! Well, I'm sure things will change. Tomorrow is another day."

"And today has gone with the wind," I countered.

She laughed and left. Maybe my jokes were getting better.

# CHAPTER 4

'Home Sweet Home'. 'Home is where the heart is'. 'Home is where you hang your hat'. Of the three statements the latter was probably more appropriate in my case although I didn't own a hat. My flat was not a home, merely a place to stay. Only a one bedroom flat, it would have been cosy for two but was empty with one. The furnishings were sparse and functional, lending a certain Spartan look. There were definitely no female touches about the place. Still it did me. It was not a place for entertaining but then I never had to entertain. There was no need for a Welcome mat outside the door and the phone rang less than the one in the office. My answering machine message was "You must have the wrong number, please redial." and was so seldom used it kept forgetting its line.

I unlocked the door of my castle at 6.30pm. As my date with a striking redhead was not until nine o'clock I had given Jenny a lift home after spotting her at the bus stop. I didn't think Scully would mind too much. The traffic had been heavy and the journey had taken twice as long as it should have done. I hoped Jenny wasn't going to take the act as a precedent.

The first thing I did was change into something more comfortable. I hate wearing a suit and only did so to impress prospective clients. As an office worker I had been obliged to wear one, as an investigator I could have worn what I liked. For preference that would be jeans and T-shirt which is what I had changed into. Not having an extensive wardrobe, I only had three pairs of jeans. My blue pair were awaiting ironing. My black pair were on the clothes horse drying after having been washed the night before following an accident with a mug of coffee. It had been hot and went in my lap dead centre. Unless I got out the iron that only left my white jeans so I wore them, a choice I would sorely regret at a later date.

It was the calm before the storm. My last night of freedom before committing myself to the case full time. The question was how to spend my last evening of leisure? I could take it easy and watch TV or do something a bit different like putting a video on. Not that I was a couch potato always stuck in front of the goggle box with a TV dinner to hand. Not on your life. You wouldn't see me dead eating a TV dinner, not even as an appetiser, because a microwave meal for one was not enough to keep the proverbial sparrow alive. No, I preferred more wholesome and nourishing food. Domino's was the only number programmed into my phone. I was thinking of listing it as one of my B.T. Family and Friends numbers. Trouble was I needed nine more. I had only got the doctor, dentist, optician and the Samaritans so far.

The food on its way, it was time to plan the evening's entertainment. Easier said than done. Things had been much simpler when there had only been four options. Those were the days when it only took half an hour to decide which of the offered repeats you hadn't seen for the longest period of time so you wouldn't remember the entire plot. Of course in those days a repeat was a repeat and was called such. These days the word 'repeat' is avoided in favour of a little psychology. I often wondered who had coined the phrase 'another chance to see' which is supposed to hoodwink the viewer into believing they are being granted a great honour to watch a programme for the second time in less than a year. It was a clever ploy, only seen through by regular viewers over the age of five.

Mind you, when it comes to clever ploys the B.B.C., I.TV, Channel 4 and Channel 5 are left way behind by satellite TV where the sky is the limit. They say there is one born every minute and if so the majority of them must reside in the UK. There is nothing we like better than succumbing to someone's money making scheme. Want a licence to print money? Just follow these basic steps:-

1. Buy a load of old programmes, say from the 60s, 70s and

   80s, from British and American TV.

2. Add just a smidgen of new items.

3. Don't forget to mix in a good dollop of movies, the best of which most people have already seen at the cinema or on video. (Important - it is essential to have at least three dedicated channels to spread the movies over so each one can be shown at least three times a month).

4. Ensure only the privileged few can view by making sure only special equipment can access the programmes.

5. Even though these privileged viewers have bought the equipment it is still essential to charge them a monthly fee to view the programmes.

This was the basic premise but satellite television did not initially take off as predicted and a further incentive was necessary. Perhaps stealing one of the more popular U.S. shows to be shown over here would help, so only satellite viewers saw the last two series of L.A. Law. Still even this produced no great results. What next? Of course! The great British game. Soccer. Like many people I was outraged when satellite TV bought the monopoly for live football and like many this was the only reason I subscribed.

Having been manipulated into becoming a satellite viewer at least, I consoled myself, I would have a greater choice of other programmes to watch. At first it's great. Wallowing in nostalgia, watching long forgotten programmes which it is a joy to view again. However, this does not last long. There are only so many watchable programmes to go round and too many channels to fill. Fear not; for the satellite guys know what they are doing.

First. Never show a programme just once a day, two or three times is better, morning, afternoon and evening.

Second. Introduce the concept of perpetual motion where a series is shown in a never ending circle. I first noticed this when trying to recapture my childhood by watching the Cartoon Network. At the same time as asking myself questions like 'Why does Dick Dastardly, when he has forced himself to the front of the Wacky Race, stop to lay a trap instead of just racing away to win?' and 'Why did Fred, Daphne, Wilma and Shaggy never change their clothes?' I noticed that after three weeks I was watching the same episodes. I thought it was just that particular channel, after all small children would not notice. Then I realised that Star Trek: The Next Generation was in continuous orbit. It should now really be referred to as Star Trek: The Ancestors of the Previous Generation. Talk about a never ending story. After this it only took me a short time to realise that this was generally a satellite TV thing. When they start repeating quiz shows you realise how desperate they are to fill air time.

There is sometimes a special treat for some fans though because some of the programmes in perpetual motion are still being made and at the end of each circuit it is possible 'an all new episode' could be tagged onto the end.

To be fair though, if you subscribe to satellite TV you are not just paying to watch what you have watched for nothing years before. One channel did introduce the innovative Prime Time slot. An exquisite whole two hours between 8.00pm and 10.00pm when only brand new programmes were seen. That was 8% of the day when nary a repeat would be seen. Of course this was only just one of the numerous channels and as a concept it didn't last very long.

Finally, when you have been a subscriber for six months and have come to terms with all this the frequencies of the channels are changed so you need a new piece of equipment called a channel expander. This new box can receive the frequencies your decoder cannot (unless you buy a more up to date one) so basically the decoder you scrimp and save to buy to unscramble the encrypted programmes cannot even receive the programmes because they are out of its range.

Only the British would pay over £300 a year to watch programmes that our own TV companies would be too embarrassed to screen again as they have been seen so often. Yet, we subscribers, when taunted over this just point out the one big advantage. For our £29.99 a month we get a free programme guide. The fact that we still need to buy a TV Times or Radio Times is beside the point.

Eventually I decided that there was nothing worth watching until 'The X Files' at nine. Temporarily I was at a loss but then I recalled there was something I had promised to do for an ex colleague which I had not yet started. She had asked me to write a send up of James Bond who her boyfriend was addicted to, this after I had proven myself to have a talent for sending up the people and procedures of the office. This had been during my last week of employment and I found that my writing could actually make people laugh. I might as well give it a shot, I thought. It would be a challenge.

The first thing I needed was a title. Ian Fleming's first Bond story had been Casino Royale but this had been already been made into a spoof movie starring David Niven. The first real Bond movie was 'Doctor No' and I decided to use a derivative of this. My version was 'Doctor! Oh No!' My mind seemed to be in a creative mood. The ideas started to flow like blood from a severed jugular so I sat at my typewriter and began to write.

I had been writing for nearly two hours, ninety minutes if one took into account the pizza break. What possessed me to finish Chapter 1 then, when my creative juices were in full flow, I wasn't sure. Perhaps it was because the Spooky and Scully Show was about to start, or maybe it was because I'd run out of paper. Whatever the reason I was quite pleased with the result; however, the proof would lay in the reaction of the commissioner of the piece. If it got a good reaction I had half a mind to send it to Mel Brooks. Mind you, some people would say I only had half a mind anyway.

What with studying the case notes that morning and my recent creative exertions I was mentally exhausted. All I wanted to do now was unwind in front of the telly. Easier said than done. I was halfway there watching "The X Files" with my mug of Ovaltine Light but I hadn't taken into account the counter-effect of watching the football on "Sportsnight". Tension and irritation teamed up to assault my easing body and mind, and United hadn't even been playing.

In the old days agitation and nervousness were states that were only achieved when watching one's own team live. At times when your team was just managing to cling to a 1-0 defeat or were completely dominating a 0-0 draw. Edge of the seat stuff, except in those days seats were the vantage point of the elite. How many in the terraces lived in terraces?

Suddenly live televised matches were born, edge of the sofa stuff, and because one wasn't just watching one's own team live any match having a bearing on one's own team's achievement could have one biting the fingernails. If top of the league, one became an anxious supporter of the opponents of the team in second. Through to the cup final, cheer the weakest of the other semi-finalists. Only your team mattered. Simple halcyon days. The days before Fantasy Football.

Every paper under and over the Sun had a Fantasy Football competition. With prizes ranging from a season ticket for your own team to a £50,000 cash sum. To someone like me who never read newspapers there was no real interest. I only had seventeen teams. I must have been the first F.F. junkie. I'd entered every competition going. I had spent the obligatory three hours per team deciding how to spend my thirty, thirty-two or thirty-five million. I had tried various tactics; the most expensive strike-force with the rest of the team makeshift, the strongest defence and keeper with a mediocre midfield and so-so forwards and the most creative midfielders with a middling defence and the cheapest strikers, not forgetting the eleven best foreigners, the best eleven British players (a difficult selection, I had money left over), the teams with all the players names starting with the same letter and the team aiming for the booby prize i.e. the cheapest I could find. Feeling like I could do with a two week cruise to get over the strain I had realised the job was only half over.

It was compulsory to furnish your team with a witty name. Football Foreign Legion was about the easiest to come up with. In the end I came up with only four really original names. The best I gave to the team with the most expensive attack, 'Goals R US', and it was a good job I hadn't used Points R Us as for each goal my attack scored the sieve like defence let in three.

Another of my teams, Cole's Goalgetters, were nothing of the kind. That season had been one for the strikeless stricken striker. In less than a year Cole the Goal had dug himself into a Cole hole, Villa had a chap called Missalotovich, and then there was every Fantasy Football Leaguers favourite, and that means followers of the Baddiel and Skinner appreciation society show, Jason 'He's Got A Pineapple On His Head' Lee. As bad luck would have it the team I had chosen to win the booby prize, called The Team With No Name, was my highest points scorer.

With so many teams on the go things had become very complicated, especially with the points system differing among papers. Some allowed points for goals and clean sheets only, some allowed assists; one paper used its own match ratings. Some deducted points for bookings, players sent off and penalties, others didn't. Most papers only used Premiership players but some allowed Endsleigh First Division and Scottish Premier players. Some competitions only applied in respect of league matches, some included the F.A. Cup but not replays; some included the replays too. It was all very confusing and as good a way of developing a migraine as any. But as someone once paraphrased "Fantasy Football is a funny old game."

Being such a widespread manager every result in the Premiership affected my teams in one way or the other, usually the other. I didn't know the results prior to "Sportsnight" so every match was agony and ecstasy, agony being the dominant force. It was less a question of "Yes! Yes! Yes!" and more a question of "Do I not like that". I couldn't work out why whenever one of my strikers scored it was against one of my defenders or goalkeeper or both. When my strikers were playing Manchester City, Sheffield Wednesday, Wimbledon and Bolton, teams from which I would never select a defender or goalkeeper, they never scored. No doubt for the same reason that my defenders and goalkeeper conceded goals against the same teams, from which I had also not selected my midfielders or forwards.

It was another unprofitable round of matches for me. What with all the stamps and the 0891 calls to register my team selections I must have been £100 adrift and from all those entries I hadn't even managed one measly Manager of the Week award. I decided there and then not to enter the next season. When your own team are awarded a penalty for a blatant professional foul yet instead of screaming at the ref "Send him off" you're thinking "Don't send him off I'll lose 2 points" it gets beyond a joke.

Thoroughly demoralised the TV went off and it was time to retire. That was the plan.

I went into the bathroom to clean my teeth. Whilst I stood there brushing, I was reflecting and seeing a reflection. I was reflecting on the case. The reflection was me. Some people cannot survive without a mirror, seeking one out at every single opportunity, preening and always assuring themselves of their perfect appearance. Me? I went out of my way to avoid them. I couldn't avoid the one in my bathroom; it was a fixture, secured to the wall and two feet square, situated right over the sink.

I could never reconcile my face with the person inside. The unruly, short brown hair that thwarted all attempts at styling, the Concorde nose, the elephant ears and the crooked teeth. The face that cracked a thousand mirrors.

I was thirty-five and my chin was beginning to sag. My stomach was more than just beginning. In my younger days I could eat anything without putting on weight, indeed in the matter of football it had been a problem in my early twenties, I was too easily nudged off the ball. Now I had a chocolate belly. I wasn't fat but compared to the years gone by it seemed that way and seeing my body in that mirror, unshielded by clothes, depressed me. Even my height had deserted me. At twenty-one I had been six feet exactly but now I was five feet ten and a half inches. I often wondered where those one and a half inches went. I had hoped it had moved to another part of my anatomy but it hadn't.

For the second time that day I was startled by the call of the lesser rung telephone. It was the redoubtable Mrs Fulwood.

"Hobson will be in Manchester within the hour," she told me.

"Right. I'll start first thing tomorrow."

"You'll start right now. We want him watched constantly."

"OK!" I agreed with resignation. "I'll leave now." How she expected me alone to maintain a constant watch I didn't know. But then perhaps she didn't really know there was only one of me at the firm.

I was still dressed so could leave immediately. However, the patron saint of insurance investigators had abandoned me, I had a flat. I don't know what it was but I was just unlucky with cars.

# CHAPTER 5

Question. What is worse than trying to change a wheel in the dark? Answer. Trying to change a wheel on an unfamiliar car in the dark when the handbook is missing. I would have thought it essential that all rental cars had a handbook in the glove compartment, after all that is what they were invented for; no one actually kept gloves in there. I suppose I only had myself to blame. That's what you get for renting cheap. Mind you, the car had a sticker proclaiming full A.A. membership, although I didn't have the nerve to ring them to come out to fix a flat tyre. I doubted very much whether that fell within their jurisdiction. No, it was down to me. Just me and the dark. It shouldn't have been quite so dark but the street lamp under which I was parked was not working. I had had to park on the street because the car park attached to the block of flats was full. There were no designated spaces so if there was no space you were on the street. Unfortunately, all the people living in the neighbouring houses were also parked in the street. Murphy's Law meant all the other lamps on the street were in full working order. Sod's law meant there were no spaces under any of them. I'd been extremely lucky to find the spot I'd got.

Loosening the wheel nuts I could do by touch, my fingers marrying the wheel brace and nut together. Either the wheel had not been changed from new or the last person to change the wheel had been someone with a nasty malicious streak. You can't get better than a stick fit fitter. Each nut took more than one concentrated effort to turn them even a fraction. Eventually though they were all loose. That had been the easy bit. Locating the jacking point proved impossible; so in the end, I just guessed and put my trust in the god of red socks, being particularly careful not to let any appendages stray under the chassis.

It must have taken me at least twenty minutes to do

what any normal competent person could have done in three flat. Even Mr Bean could have done it in seventeen and a half minutes. It was the sort of time one prayed for a passing lady driver to stop and yell out of the window "Need a hand darling?" In these days of sexual equality anything was possible. Unfortunately I just didn't have the legs for it.

One thing now was certain; I wasn't going to make the airport in time. Besides, it had only just occurred to me that although I had a picture of Hobson so could probably recognise him, I did not know which flight he was on. Presumably he had flown in from the States, but which one? Even at that time of night there would be too many flights for one person to cover. Hobson's choice. I did the only thing I could do and drove to the Hobson residence, which was in fact further for me to drive than Hobson was from the airport. Hopefully his plane would not touch down for another half an hour. Once on the ground I estimated it would take him thirty minutes maximum to collect his luggage, pass through Customs and get a taxi home. Therefore, if he was not home by 1.00am either his flight had been delayed or he had called off somewhere. If he did the latter I was sunk because at that time of night there was likely to be some nefarious purpose involved.

Hobson lived in a large, detached house off a quiet country lane. It had a lengthy private driveway, creeping ivy and certainly smacked of affluence if not downright wealth. I could only see the front of the house but as surely as soaps will soon dominate 90% of channel viewing time, there would be a full sized covered swimming pool at the rear. There was a double garage and a B.M.W. parked outside the front door. A three car family no doubt. How nice it must be to have money I couldn't help thinking, not that I was jealous, just poor.

On the left hand side of the driveway, as I looked at it, lay a wood which stretched from the lane to well past the house. Perfect cover to get nearer if necessary. I drove past the driveway and with a view to parking the car on the verge as near to the trees as possible I attempted a three point turn. Fail. The narrow width made it into a 9.5 turn. I parked some way from the drive but still near enough to see if any vehicle turned into it. All I could do now was wait.

It was while I was waiting that the full enormity of the task in front of me hit home. Who was I kidding? Twenty-four hour surveillance on Hobson. Pretty straightforward might think the uninitiated but it was far from it, even I could figure that out and I was one of the uninitiated. Firstly, such surveillance would normally be taken in shifts. How one person was supposed to keep up a constant vigil was beyond me, even if sometimes I was a fully paid up member of the International Fellowship of Sleep Deprivation. There is a big difference between being awake because one cannot sleep to staying awake; such being that in the latter case sleep is exactly what your body and mind decide is of utmost importance unlike the former when they are out of sync. I assumed that this would be even more so in a passive capacity such as keeping watch. Action and its resultant flow of adrenaline would have kept sleep at bay more effectively. I was having difficulty keeping my eyes open even then. My mind was fuzzy and my thinking woolly, but on the other hand when wasn't it.

Secondly, I wasn't used to surveillance work. I hadn't been trained for it and I doubted whether I could last twenty minutes without being spotted, a doubt fully justified as it turned out.

Thirdly, surveillance usually meant more than just shadowing someone. It meant the collation of as much information as possible. I had no bugs, unless one counted the beetle that had flown onto the bonnet of the car and was attempting to climb the windscreen, and I would not have known how to install one anyway, so listening to conversations was out. Also, I did not have a degree in breaking and entering so I wasn't going to be in a position to carry out a search for incriminating evidence. All in all I failed to see what I could actually achieve. What exactly would I be contributing to the investigation? I was to investigation and surveillance what Clouseau was to French law enforcement. In fact he was probably more successful because he got results. More by luck than judgement admittedly but by then my red socks were wearing thin.

Hobson arrived home at 12.53. At least I assumed he was in the vehicle that turned into the driveway at that particular time. I ran along the edge of the wood to the bottom of the driveway. A man got out of the vehicle and entered the house. I couldn't tell if it was Hobson at that the distance but I felt that in this case two and two certainly made a number between three and five. Hobson was expected around that time, a man had arrived at that time and he had a key to the door. An open and shut assumption.

The vehicle had to be a taxi for it returned down the driveway. I dived into the woods for cover. I stood for a moment wondering what to do next. Some people had beginner's luck. Me? I had beginner's gross stupidity. Who else would commence such an operation without notebook, pen, camera or binoculars? I had to bite the bullet and get closer. If I was going to learn anything I would have to take a risk or two. I crept over the lawn towards the house, the drive being noisy gravel. Lights were on downstairs but curtains were drawn at the windows so I was able to approach unobserved, or so I thought. Fortunately, despite it being February, it was not a cold night and some small windows were open. At one of those open onto a lighted room I was rewarded with the sound of voices.

"You needn't have waited up dear," said a male voice which had to be Hobson.

"You know I can't sleep when you are away," a female voice replied. That would be his wife. "Are you alright? You look on your last legs."

"Fine. Just a bit tired that's all. It's these trips to the States."

"Well, why do you do it then?"

"Because I have to. It won't be for much longer according to Mr Fairfax. Come on let's go to bed."

Let's not, I thought, but they did. Only a few sentences but they told me something. The wife was definitely not involved in anything that was going on. That was the first thing. Also,

Hobson was looking the worse for wear according to his wife. This could be the result of him being put under pressure, to do something he was not happy about perhaps. The tone of his voice had said as much. To me it had seemed weary and resigned to its fate. And the final thing I had learnt was that things were going to happen soon, or so Fairfax had told Hobson.

The lights were out now and there was obviously going to be nothing else worth hearing so I made my way back to the car, inwardly smiling. Maybe I would be better at this than I had thought. Cockiness is usually short lived. My new found complacency lasted all of five minutes or more precisely until I was unlocking the car. Even at night and on a quiet deserted road it is still prudent to lock one's vehicle, TV portrayal to the contrary. My misplaced confidence melted away at the feel of cold steel against my temple. Not again, I thought to myself. For one horrible moment I thought the Tweedles were back for revenge. I didn't dare turn my head to see my tormentor as the gun pressed hard into the side of my head.

"Hands on the roof!" ordered a female voice.

Definitely not a Tweedle. I complied with alacrity. She frisked me. Whether this was done in a professional manner I couldn't say but under different circumstances I could have enjoyed it. Search complete she spun me around by the shoulder until I was facing her and her gun. I only had eyes for the latter. I didn't know much about guns but I could see it was an automatic. Fed by a clip it probably contained at least eight shots. She only needed one at that distance.

Concentrating as I was on the armament I only had a vague impression of the person behind it. She was tall for a woman, blonde and had a rock steady hand. Even when she spoke I couldn't lift me eyes from what it was holding.

"Who are you?" she demanded to know. "And no bullshit. I know how to use this and there are too few male sopranos in the world."

"Take it easy lady," I said in my most shakily soothing voice. I didn't want her tensing up, particularly her curling forefinger which needless to say was on the trigger.

"Name?"

"Robel ... Thomas Robel."

"What are you up to?"

"That's rather a long story."

"I'm not going anywhere," she announced. "And neither are you. Get in the car! Move over to the passenger side!" She was a natural for barking out orders. She should have been on a parade ground, for preference at precisely that moment.

She covered me the whole time with her unwavering firearm. I scuttled over from the driver's seat, not even yelling out when I got the gear stick up the rear in the process. She slid into the driver's seat, shut the door and turned to face me. "Now talk!"

I couldn't think up a plausible lie. I had already used up my creative juices for the night. As nothing else came springing to mind I told her the truth. After all I wasn't doing anything illegal. At least I hoped I wasn't. Was keeping watch on someone illegal? I knew that an unauthorised wire-tap was. On the other hand, I realised too late as usual, she could be the one on the illegal exercise. She could have been casing the joint with a view to a redistribution of wealth. If so she would want me out of the way, sort of permanently.

She had been watching my face all the time I had been speaking, trying to read it no doubt. Unfortunately I could read nothing in hers. It was as inscrutable as that of a Chinese poker player. Only her eyes said anything and they spoke in the most glaring terms. I soon knew the reason why.

"I think I ought to tell you my name before we go any further," she suddenly proclaimed when I had rather lamely finished my explanation. "I am Victoria Hobson. Peter Hobson is my father."

Great! A really outstanding start to the case. I might as well have walked up to Hobson's front door and announced my intentions. The result would have been the same. If there was something afoot he would now be on his guard and so would his fellow conspirator in the States. In just under two hours I had completely scuppered the investigations in two countries. Whoever was responsible would now go to ground. The case would be over because nothing would now be tried in the U.K. and I would have to return the £20,000. Even worse, depending on the stakes involved, the ungodly might just decide to take me out of the picture as I was the only person who knew, that they knew they were being investigated.

While all these thoughts had been going through my head Miss Hobson had not moved or spoken. She was still glaring and the gun was still pointing in my direction. Her finger was still on the trigger but now her hands were beginning to tremble, probably with anger at the accusations. I hoped the gun didn't have a hair trigger.

"Can you please put the gun down," I pleaded with her. "I'm not worth shooting."

She lowered the gun but still remained silent. She was studying my face again and thinking. I could almost hear the cogs whirling. Should she shoot me in the woods and so protect her father or hand me over to the police as a prowler. I put on my best prowler's look.

Finally she spoke. "Let me get this straight. Two days ago you had a visit from a woman purporting to be from Fidelity Insurance and she told you of this elaborate conspiracy to defraud her company? Or possibly a grudge against the Fairfax Corporation. And on the strength of that and a few meetings between James Fairfax and my father you think he is involved? In short you think my father is a criminal?"

"Not really," I appeased. "As I understand it anything unusual is being investigated. America's new avid interest in the UK is regarded as unusual. Your father isn't suspected of anything yet. It is Fairfax who is suspected, and even that is based on nothing concrete as far as I can gather." She didn't reply to this so I carried on in my defence. "Look! If you'd just started up in business and someone offered you a job with a fat retainer, your first job at that, then you'd take it wouldn't you? Especially as there are no other prospective clients banging at the door for attention. I cannot afford to think about the ethics, unless it is an illegal proposition which I would never contemplate. All I have is a watching brief. In all honesty I expected that I would have nothing to report."

"Maybe, maybe not," she said mysteriously.

"What do you mean?" I queried, more sure of myself now that the gun was out of sight.

"It's just something I've noticed. It might be connected or just a total coincidence." She looked directly into my eyes. "And I'm not sure if I should trust you."

"You can," I assured her. "I'm not your enemy. If your father is in trouble I'd like to help. By your own admission you've noticed something out of the ordinary. Surely you want to discover the truth? We can pool resources and help each other."

"I'm not going to tell you anything yet," she stated flatly. "I want to think about it. I'll contact you tomorrow at your office. You do have an office I take it?"

"Of course I have," I replied indignantly. What did she think I was running, a tin pot operation?

"Got a card?"

"Er ... No." It wasn't far off a tin pot operation. "I haven't got around to having any printed yet," I lied. "I'll give you my number though. Have you got a pen and paper handy?"

"You mean you haven't," she queried in disbelief. "You came out on a surveillance job without even a notebook and pen?"

"Well, I was in a rush," I explained.

"Just tell me the number, I'll remember it."

So I told her the number and also the address. I was eager to comply. I had the vaguest feeling that she was on my side and even if we were not comrades in arms we were both shooting at the same goal. She had her doubts about something. Something which made my presence, if not logical, certainly plausible.

"Right! I'll contact you tomorrow," she declared, reaching for the door handle.

"You're not going to tell your father about me are you?" It was a crucial question on which my future depended.

"I haven't decided yet," was her response. "You'll have to pray that I decide not to."

"I'll certainly do that alright," I confirmed. "If you let the cat out of the bag neither of us will be any the wiser."

"True," she agreed as she got out of the car. "By the way," she added, her head bobbing back in, "you do know you've been set up don't you?"

"How come?"

"A new business, one operative, no experience and a case involving millions of pounds, or dollars. No one would secure the services of a firm with no track record for a job of such size or importance. Besides, for this type of work, a private detective would have been hired; someone used to surveillance, who had access to listening equipment and someone who wouldn't dream of creeping around at night in white jeans." With that she was gone, walking back to the house, her black clothes soon melting into the night.

I sat and watched her disappear, this girl who had completely turned the tables on me. Strike one. Two more strikes and I would be out of there. It may not even have required that. If she elected to tell her father what had happened and what she had learnt then it was all over as far as I was concerned. There would be no more case. There would be no more business. And, if the ungodly had their way, there would be no more me. Still, I thought to myself, clutching at straws, it's not over until the fat lady sings, hoping at the same time for a severe case of laryngitis.

I was in a bit of a dilemma now. Had I been dismissed by Miss Hobson? Officially, for the time being anyway, I was still on the case. Did she expect me to leave my post? Abandon ship at the first sign of trouble? It was a tough call. Whether to sit there all night forcing myself to stay awake to keep watch on a house where everyone was asleep, for which I would end up stiff and cramped for no purpose. Or turn tail and run at the sight of one girl and her gun. No contest.

I had a bad night. An insomniac being fed coffee intraven-ously would have had more sleep than I did that night. But then I wasn't supposed to be getting any sleep. I should have been wide awake and alert at my post outside the Hobson residence. Was it my fault that I hadn't expected to meet Miss Rambo? My male ego was calling me a coward at being frightened off but my brain was endeavouring to fight this yellow fever with logic. One. Sit-ting outside the Hobson house all night would have achieved nothing other than annoying Miss Hobson, who spotting me still there may have disclosed to her father that which she might have kept to herself. My life, my business and my £20,000 lay in her hands. Two. The purpose of staying at my post would have been to follow Hobson when he left the house that morn-ing but I couldn't have done that anyway because I had to be at the office when his daughter called. Had she suggested that on purpose to keep me off his tail? It mattered not; I had to be pre-sent for her decision. There was no three. In fact one and two boiled down to the same thing, not to get on the wrong side of Miss Hobson. I had not stayed because I couldn't afford to upset her. Perfect logic. A strategic withdrawal. No cowardice there.

All night I had been thinking on her last words. Had I been set up? Was I so stupid? The points she had made about me having no experience and a surveillance job being more suited to a private detective, I had made myself to Mrs F. I had had my suspicions at the time but these had been swayed by the cheque. Anyway, her arguments for choosing PPWP had seemed fairly logical at the time. She had wanted an unknown firm, in that particular area of the country. Or perhaps, in hindsight, she had wanted a new and untried firm because it was less likely to achieve any results. If so why? Was a F.I.C. employee involved? Was it Mrs F? I had had my doubts about her too. Or was I just a diversion for them? A smokescreen? Was it my job to distract the ungodly whilst others did the proper surveillance? There were too many questions. I was as confused as an Arab sheikh at a wife swapping party.

It was possible that Miss Hobson had been correct in her statement. Still, I hadn't helped matters by behaving like a complete prat. No, make that three prats and a wally. Who would commence a surveillance operation with no equipment? No camera or binoculars, not even pen and paper to make notes of any observations. Me; that was who. But only because I'd had no time to prepare. I had been caught on the hop by the call from Mrs F. Maybe that had been part of the plan. Give me as little time as possible to prepare in the hope I would louse it up. If that had been the plan it had worked to perfection. I was beginning to feel like a puppet, reacting to every little pull on my string. Who the puppet master was I had no idea. I did know that I'd had enough of being manipulated. It was time to fight back, always assuming I wasn't fired first.

I went to the office early. Not that I expected Miss Hobson to call early, if at all, I was just on edge. What happened in the next few hours had a direct bearing on the future life span of PPWP. I was all set to make a new record, one that I did not care to hold. Hiring a secretary one day and making her redundant the next. What would I do with the new chair?

I didn't get any work done. Not because there was nothing to do, which in fact there wasn't, but because I wasn't in a working frame of mind. Jenny noticed something was wrong when she arrived. She seemed to sense I wasn't in the mood for witty repartee so she just made the coffee and left me alone.

Come on! Ring! I tried to use my mental telepathy on the phone. It was 9.04. At 9.05 it rang. At 9.05 and five seconds it was slammed back in its cradle. Not the time for a wrong number.

I was slightly surprised on how much I was relying on that call from Miss Hobson. I needed to know one way or the other. I was on tenterhooks waiting, yet when contact was made I was unprepared for she came in person.

# CHAPTER 6

"Good morning, Mr Gumshoe," she greeted me brightly. "I half expected you to be still parked in the lane outside our house."

"What, and have you push your gun into my face again?" I countered. "Not likely. I've been paid to watch not tackle pistol packing mammas."

"Oh! I didn't scare you did I?"

"No! I can't get enough of a lethal weapon jammed in my face," I responded. "Anyway, there was no point waiting through the night. There was nothing to go on and I couldn't follow your father this morning as I had to be here for your call. Phone call that is, I wasn't expecting you to put in a personal appearance." I picked up my chair and placed it on the other side of the desk. "As you are here you'd better take the seat, I'll use the desk." I sat on the edge facing her.

"I thought I would come in person so I could have a look through your file," she explained.

"I don't know whether I can let you do that," I pointed out. "Confidentiality to the client and all that."

"Look, I haven't told my father about you yet. I still could."

"OK. A two way deal," I acceded. "What can you give me?"

"I'll tell you what I know," she promised. "Agreed?"

"Agreed." I took her proffered hand and cemented our alliance. "Ladies first."

"I'd rather look at your file first," she said.

"I'm sure you would," I replied, "but that wouldn't be entirely fair would it. I have something you want to see but I only have your word that you know something which will be useful to me. I suggest you tell me what you know first and then I'll decide if it's worth a look at the file."

"You know," she said, with mock admiration in her voice,

"you're not as stupid as I first took you for."

"I'll take that as a compliment."

"Not too much of one I hope. Last night I couldn't have thought of anyone as more stupid."

Talk about a backhanded compliment.

"You caught me on a bad day," I conceded. "I was caught on the hop by a telephone call telling me your father was back. I had little enough notice. That's why I was unprepared. Mind you, I don't think any amount of preparation could have equipped me for our encounter."

"Well, much as I'd like to give you the benefit of the doubt, I think I'll reserve judgement for now on whether you'll be an ally or a nuisance."

"I'm flattered. In what?"

"That's what I'm here to find out. Whether we're on the same side."

"Why don't you enlighten me with your own thoughts on the matter? Tell me what you know and then you can see the file." I had nothing to lose and everything to gain. The file said nothing, at least in our short acquaintance it had never spoken to me, and the day that inanimate objects began to I would be booked down for a yellow van journey.

"Well, it's more what I think I know really," she admitted.

It was the first time since our dangerous liaison that I had noticed a tinge of uncertainty in her voice. Not much as tinges go but it was there.

"Go ahead anyway," I said. "It may help."

"OK." She sat forward in my seat, intent, wondering where to start. "It's Father. He's different."

"How do you mean?" I asked, intrigued. After all Hobson was the man I was supposed to be collecting information on.

"He's just changed," she replied. "He looks terrible. His face is all drawn and haggard. He looks older and I think he's lost weight." She stopped, momentarily lost for words. I thought I detected a tear in her eye. "He's so short tempered now," she continued. "Also he's started drinking. Heavily. He's scared."

"What makes you think that? These symptoms you describe are signs of stress. The pressure of business."

"I don't know. I just know," she stated firmly. A statement of logic if I ever heard one. I didn't know what to say but she hadn't finished. "He's definitely scared of something. His hands shake. He's really nervous about something. We can all see it but he won't talk about it. He persists in saying everything is alright. I think it's something he's trying to protect us from."

"When did all this start?" Something was forming in the back of my mind, not yet comprehensible, a bit like a Jim Carey film. "If I was to hazard a guess I would say just as he took over as head of UK operations."

"Exactly," she confirmed. "He was over the moon at first, we all were. It was a huge promotion. Unexpected though. I remember Father was surprised. His predecessor took early retirement so suddenly. Anyway, things changed quickly. It was just about a week after the promotion that we started to notice a change in him. He'd had an important meeting that day and when he came back it was like he was a completely different person. I haven't seen even the hint of a smile cross his face since."

This tied in with the few words I'd overheard at the house the night before. Hobson was definitely mixed up in something queer. Something that he was unhappy about. Something that went against the grain and was connected to his visits to the States. That funny smell in Denmark was getting stronger or the bacon was burning.

Usually when someone does something they don't want to it is because they are forced into it. In most cases some form of blackmail was used. But what would it be in Hobson's case. The fact that he was being coerced seemed to indicate whatever was going to happen would occur soon. The ungodly wouldn't want to show their hand too early. Either he was to make it happen or turn a blind eye to it.

"Interesting." I rose from the desk and sauntered over to the window. As I was looking out over the street I threw her a question, a complete change of tack, what the American's would call a curved ball, whilst she was vulnerable after letting her defences down over her feelings for her father. "Exactly how did you get onto me last night?"

"I saw you creeping up to the lounge window." Her answer was automatic, her mind still on her father, then she realised what I'd asked and elucidated. "I happened to be looking out of my bedroom window but even if I'd been sound asleep with the curtains drawn and wearing a blindfold the brightness of your attire would have woken me up."

"OK! No need to slide into sarcasm mode again."

I was never going to live those white jeans down. What is it with my clothes? I thought to myself. My first visitor had been against my socks and my second visitor against my pants. The fact that both my visitors had been of the female variety probably had something to do with it. Clothes maketh the man it is said, but to me clothes were just to keep warm, with the slight secondary advantage of disguising a body that was careering down the slippery road to middle age. I had about as much knowledge of fashion and what was in or out as I had about llama breeding in the Tibetan mountains.

"I just wanted to know if you'd seen me at the house or whether you'd spotted me before then," I continued by way of explanation. This wasn't quite the truth though. I wanted to know if she knew I had been earwigging at the window. In all probability she did and so it was best to come clean.

"I told you I spotted you approaching the house."

And no doubt she'd kept me under constant observation since then. She would know I'd been trying to listen at the window but would she know I'd heard anything? Better to be safe than sorry. I didn't want to antagonise her.

"What you've told me ties in with the little I overheard last night."

"And what exactly did you overhear?"

"Just that your father hates having to keep travelling to the States and your mother is worried and thinks he's overdoing it."

"So you already knew what I've just told you."

She sounded disappointed, although whether it was because she had given me nothing new, so might not now see my file, or the fact that I was not the absolute failure she'd pegged me for, I wasn't sure.

"Not really," I assured her. "I was assuming a lot. You've been the corroboration I needed."

"OK then, can I see the file now?"

"Sure. A deal's a deal."

I took my one and only file from its allocated space in the filing system and handed it across to her. She wouldn't learn much from it, except that what I'd told her had been the truth. It was hardly a fair trade. I'd come out of the deal better. I now had something to work with. Or rather I felt as if I should now have had something to work with, all I had to do was discover exactly what that was.

Now that I was not quaking in front of her gun barrel I had time to notice her properly. Gone was the black attire of the night before which would have sold like wildfire in Commandos R Us. She was now clad in white top and flowing, flowery skirt. Her blonde hair fell to her shoulders whereas the night before I had the vague impression it had been held in a ponytail, not that I had been too much into admiration of her coiffure at the time. I had visions of incredibly long legs but much of these were hidden beneath the skirt which was below knee length. Her face was meant for smiling though I had seen precious little of that from her. Her eyes were deep and blue, reminiscent of a young Lysette Anthony. She had a pert nose and firm lips. Her skin was as pale as the moon. All in all she was the loveliest person I had met in a long time. Physically at least, I wasn't too sure about her personality. Sarcasm seemed to be always to the fore, but she was going through trying times and it could just have been some sort of defence mechanism. I had used it myself on occasion. Only on occasion though. To be in the Premier League of Sarcasm one had to have a lightning quick mind that was always ready with a quick riposte to any given situation. The lowest form of wit it may be but then wit wasn't all it was cracked up to be. After all what is wit? About 75% of a twit, that's what.

She didn't take long to read the file. She perused the details of the Fairfax UK operation, scrutinised the details of her father, glanced at his photo for a few seconds, no doubt seeing the man he used to be, passed over the policy details and gave a little whistle over the American losses.

"There's not much here," she observed on closing the file. "Relating to my father I mean. There's only a very loose connection, hardly that even. It's sheer speculation."

"True," I readily agreed. "However, with what you've now told me together with what I heard last night I think the connection is a little tighter. The F.I.C. may have been grasping at straws when they employed me but I'm sure now that they were on the right track."

"How? What do they think is going on? Surely they don't believe my father is going to start setting fires and arranging for things to be stolen?"

She was indignant and I supposed she had a right to be. Mind you she was as mercurial as it was possible to be. She changed moods as quickly as a chameleon vying for the Quick Change World Record. I wanted her to be an ally. She had the inside track. It called for extreme subtlety and in such circumstances I wasn't known as Sir Subtle for nothing.

"Your father hasn't been accused of anything yet."

"Yet!"

Yes all the diplomacy of an elephant with a penchant for Doc Martens.

"What I mean is that there's nothing to worry about. There is no evidence against him at this time." Better. More like a bull in a china shop, but a graceful ballet dancing bull.

"So you expect to find some? You're waiting to catch him in the act?"

"On my past record, of about nine hours, I wouldn't bank on catching a cold in Siberia."

"That's not funny!" She was not amused but other than that

she bore no resemblance to Queen Vicky. "Your complete in-competence is immaterial. The insinuation is still there." She was stood up now prodding me in the chest. I was thankful that she didn't have long nails.

"Look! Sit down!" I didn't have time for these melodramat-ics. "We'll never get anywhere like this."

"Sorry," she apologised sheepishly, resuming her seat. "I'm angry at what is happening to Father and you happen to be a ra-ther convenient scapegoat."

"Well, this scapegoat is about to fight back," I announced in a positive fashion. "With your help if you'll give it."

"How? I'll do anything to help my father."

"That's the gist of it." Unfortunately I only had the gist. It was time to think and fast. I thrust my mind into forward gear.

"Let's look at this logically," I began. "I don't care about the mess in the States, that's their mess and they can deal with it any way they like. All we have to do is to prevent anything hap-pening here. Now, in spite of your protestations you do have misgivings about your father and what he may be involved in. Something is making him ill and so it is something that is put-ting a terrific strain on him. It is also connected to his visit to the States and in particular the meetings with James Fairfax. Now let's see ... " I paused for a moment trying to marshal my thoughts which was about as easy as rounding up sheep whilst on a space hopper.

"What we have to do," I continued, "is ease your father's plight. As far as I can see these meetings have one of two mean-ings. First there is the above board one. Fairfax is concerned about a vendetta against the Corporation and is worried that this might spread to the UK so has made your father responsible for the safeguard of the UK operation. That could be a strain, knowing that any little incident could be misconstrued. How-ever, I doubt that this would cause the downright despair you have described.

"The other meaning is the underhand one where Fairfax wants your father to arrange certain incidents. I'm afraid this is more likely. This would be against your father's code of ethics. Make him worry. Make him ill."

"It doesn't look good," she conceded. "I can't believe Father would resort to that though."

"In normal circumstances he would probably tell Fairfax to get lost. Even if he got fired for it." She nodded in agreement. "So what we have to find out is the hold that he has over your father. If we can remove the lever your father will get his freedom of choice back."

"Right," she enthused. "But what can he have? What could someone blackmail him with? Not an affair. Mother and Father have been happily married for over thirty years. Criminal record? No. Drugs? Certainly not. Embezzlement? No!" She was getting worked up again. She was a passionate person I noted for future reference. "It's no good," she stated. "You blackmail someone with a transgression and my father has not made any."

"None that you are aware of," I pointed out. "There could be something in his past. Whatever it is it will be something you know nothing about, otherwise it would be common knowledge and useless for blackmail purposes. However, it may not be blackmail we are dealing with. There are other forms of coercion."

"What else can it be?"

Last night she had got the better of me and ridiculed my attempts at the job in hand. She had been cool and threatening. Now, she was agitated and distraught. It was no doubt only a temporary condition. I didn't feel like playing the part she had assumed the night before now she was the one not thinking straight. Instead I just posed the question to set her thinking again.

"What is the most precious thing in the world to your father?" I asked her.

"His family," she responded immediately. "Mother, Sammy and me."

"Who's Sammy?"

"My sister."

I automatically wondered if her sister was anything like her. Two of them would be impossible to cope with.

"OK. Well, it may not be blackmail your father is reacting to but a threat to the dearest thing in his life. A threat to his family. You, your sister, your mother or all three."

"It has to be," she agreed. "That's the only thing I can think of that would make him concede to demands."

"Well, it's certainly plausible anyway. Still, it's only a supposition. We need proof." I sat on the edge of the desk again. "I think we might get a clue from your father's predecessor. You said earlier that the promotion came as a bit of a surprise. I think if we check it out, we'll find that the previous guy was forced out. That being the case, they, whoever they turn out to be, believe your father will be easier to manipulate. Why? Find the difference and we might be a bit closer to the truth."

This was better. Things were moving along. Instead of wading through treacle it was more like blancmange.

"I can check into that," she offered. "My father knows him, or knew him. Not very well, they were not great mates or anything, but probably enough to learn what we need to know."

"Don't just come out and ask him," I warned her. "We don't want to arouse any suspicion. It's better that we know what we think we know without him knowing that we know, otherwise he'll want to know how we know what he thinks nobody knows."

"Don't worry. He won't realise that I know more than he knows he wants me to know while I find out what I want to know about what I don't know." She looked at me slyly from under her eyelids; she suddenly jerked up straight in her chair and thumped the desk. "A brilliant idea!" she shouted.

"What?"

"That's what we need, a brilliant idea."

It was an old joke but I had walked right into it. I didn't dignify it with a reply. I had come to the recent conclusion that whatever I said or did I was never going to win with Miss Victoria Hobson.

"Well, don't you want to hear it?"

Was the joke now a two-parter? Had it a newly constructed extension?

"You mean you really have a brilliant idea?"

"Certainly," she affirmed. "It will help you out enormously and you won't even have to pay me."

"Shoot," I said, which considering the previous night's events was probably not the most appropriate thing to utter.

"OK, if you're sure." On which she extracted a gun from under her jumper where it had been stuck in the waistband of her skirt, pointed it in my direction and pulled the trigger. I heard an empty click from my new position under the desk. I had lightning reactions when it came to self-preservation.

"Nice quick reactions," she observed. "A pity they were negative and not positive."

She obviously had a playful spirit. I dreaded to think what she could get up to once the worry about her father had been dissipated.

"Is that an extension of your personality or just the latest fashion accessory?" I asked her whilst brushing myself off after literally biting the dust. I didn't even clean my flat that often let alone the office.

"Protection. One can't be too careful these days."

True enough, but who would protect the bad guys from her.

"This isn't America. How did you get hold of it and is it licensed?"

"Of course it is," came the indignant response. "What do you think I am? Some sort of criminal?" Little did either of us know that in just over a year from then it would be a criminal offence to own one except in very exceptional circumstances.

"Some years ago," she continued, "there were some threats against my father. Somehow he got permission to buy a gun for protection and we've had it ever since. And before you ask, yes I can use it. Two years T.A. and three Army. Best female shot and better than most males during that period."

I believed her. The self-assured way she handled herself the night before had displayed her training.

"Do you carry it around all the time?" I asked, fearing I might be teaming up with Annie Oakley but also reassured to have a pro on my side.

"No. I picked it up last night to nail you," she grinned. "But in the circumstances I think I'll keep it handy from now on."

"It's no good unloaded."

"I don't know about that," she purred. "You dropped to your knees pretty fast."

Again there was no arguing with that. She had the last word for everything. Little did I know that I was going to be relying heavily on that gun in the future, both loaded and unloaded. Lethal Unloaded Weapon. Sounded like a good name for a film to me.

"Tell me your idea," I said, getting back on track.

"My father asked me to work as his secretary. I could be your inside person."

"When was this?"

"Last week. His usual one was off sick. Something pretty serious I gather, or at least requires an operation anyway."

"Great! It couldn't have come at a better time."

"It could!" she disagreed accusingly. "It could have happened at a time when things were going swimmingly well for Father and I didn't need to spy on him."

"Granted," I admitted, "but in the present circumstances it could prove a godsend."

"Maybe, maybe not," she said doubtfully. "He made the offer at Mother's suggestion. It was a little half hearted, and no wonder with what we now know. He probably didn't want me involved in any way with this business."

"The offer was made though? And still stands?"

"I suppose so. I never really gave an answer. As far as I know he hasn't started a replacement yet."

"You don't sound too enthusiastic," I observed. "It was your idea."

"I know," she countered defensively. "The idea is good but the implementation is a problem. I've no way of forcing Father into letting me be his secretary, especially after being offered the job once and not accepting it."

"You didn't reject it either," I reminded her. "It will help us all out. I won't literally have to shadow your father everywhere, nor keep a constant watch outside his office. You could keep me in touch with what's going on and tip me off when he goes out so I can be on hand to tail him. That's what's in it for me. For you, you will be helping to set your father free from whatever is tormenting him. For your father, he will benefit from our sleuthing on his behalf, or at least I hope he will." On the off chance that we were successful. "And not forgetting your mother and sister who will have the husband and father back the way he used to be. Once we crack the case that is, which I have little chance of doing alone."

"OK! Stop preaching to the converted," she protested, holding up her hands to halt my barrage. "I'll get the job. I'll have to, if I left it to you he'd know he was under surveillance in two minutes flat and we wouldn't learn anything."

"Thanks a lot partner."

"Partner in your business?" she asked mockingly.

"No, just this venture. I couldn't handle a permanently bruised ego."

I couldn't help smiling. Things seemed to be falling into place. It had been a stroke of luck teaming up with Hobson's daughter. A pure fluke that I would not have dreamed of. But on the other hand neither would my employer, which I felt was to my advantage, especially if I was being offered up as the sacrificial lamb. Now I would have the inside track. It was little enough to be sure. Victoria Hobson knew as little as I did but she had the potential opportunity to learn a great deal more.

When I'd first taken the case I'd had as much chance of success as Morse entering a pub and ordering a Britvic orange. Now my chances had greatly improved. About as good as a British player winning Wimbledon, snooker player that is. All we had to do was prevent any staged insurance claims, protect Hobson from the ungodly and try to make sure we all came out alive on the other side. Easy peasy. I usually preferred something more challenging, like swimming in a piranha infested river.

"Right! So that's settled then," I said. "You try to find out about your father's predecessor first and let me know so I can start working on that angle. At the same time ask about the job. Let me know when you'll be in place. If you can get him to let you start tomorrow that would be ideal. He's already had this morning free to meet incriminating people and make enforced plans. In fact you could ring him now from here. Find out if he's going to be in his office all day. If he is I won't need to be outside the gates until clocking off time."

"Why? Have you something more important to do?" she asked accusingly, as if anything not connected to clearing her father was totally unimportant, which to her I suppose it was.

"Preparing lines of communication," I told her and left it at that.

She did not press me further but picked up the phone. While she was talking to daddy I went out to talk to Jenny. She was going to be a very crucial part of the operation, the centre of communication. I needed her to man, even person, the office, take any messages and relay them to the final recipient. Me to her, me to Miss Hobson, me to Mrs F and vice versa. I intended to keep Jenny well informed of my whereabouts and where necessary Miss Hobson, but no one else. That way I had to hope I could keep one step ahead of the opposition. The fewer who knew of my plan of action the less chance of the wrong people hearing about it. Only one thing remained: an actual plan. There was little point in going to extreme lengths to keep something secret if that something did not exist. What I needed was a cunning plan, but not of the Baldrick variety.

"All fixed." Miss Hobson came out of my office positively beaming. Her moods changed quicker than Manchester United's away strips. "I start this afternoon. He wasn't keen at first but because he'd already offered me the job there wasn't a lot he could do. He'll be in the office when I get there and has no plans to leave before six."

"Great! I quite like it when a plan comes together," I declared, not particularly feeling like the leader of even a C Team. Still I had a team and it was time to introduce the members to each other. "Miss Hobson, this is my secretary Jenny. Jenny, Miss Hobson."

"Call me Vicky."

Charming. She hadn't asked me to call her Vicky. Not even Victoria. I was still at the Miss Hobson stage.

They hit it off straight away and I left them to chat. Jenny knew what I wanted, and would pass it on. I went into my office to try and come up with the logical next step.

No thoughts presented themselves. Instead I started musing about the three women who had entered my life in the past few days. Old JB would have bedded them all by now. Mind you, at least one of them would have tried to kill him. I should be grateful for small mercies. At least I had one advantage over the great 007. If a beautiful woman came onto me I would know it was a set up. I held as much attraction to the opposite sex as Worzel to Aunt Sally. Even a blow up doll would feign a headache in my presence.

Five minutes chat was enough. My musings were just depressing me.

"Let's get this show on the road," I announced, interrupting their female flow.

Nary a defiant glance did I see.

"OK," agreed Miss Hobson. "I'll check in later."

With that she was gone.

"I've given her the office number, your home number and mine," Jenny told me.

"Fine," I acknowledged. "I've got to leave now too. I may be away from the office for some time. You have the key. I'll let you have a contact number as soon as I can."

I still had not decided on a plan of action but one thing had been clear from the start, I needed a base of operation. One that was within easy reach of Hobson's home and workplace. My office was too far away to respond at a moment's notice and my flat was further north still. A nearby hotel or some such establishment seemed the best option.

On leaving Jenny I went home to pack. The unwinking red light on my answerphone told the usual story, no messages. Even that was better than someone ringing up, listening to the message and replacing the receiver after the beep because this registered as a call. There is nothing more infuriating to see the winking red light and hear just the disengaged tone. I hate unknown callers. My exchange did not offer the 1471 service.

Perhaps it was the actual message that was putting people off. Answering machines were the bane of nervous callers everywhere. There is nothing worse than the ominous click when the ringing stops. Do you ring again later or do you leave some garbled mumblings which when played back sound like anything but a concise message. I found out, after eventually reaching the stage when I could afford such a status symbol as an answering machine, that actually recording the message was even worse than leaving one. First you have to decide what to say. Of course the thing that nearly everyone uses is the one thing you are advised not to. "Sorry I'm not in right now". This is an open invitation to perpetrators of felonious acts who have a team of telesales operatives, phone-books to hand, who advise the field operatives of all the addresses where an answering machine is on. One is supposed to say something like "I am not able to take your call right now but ... " which makes all the difference and results in the criminal element giving your residence a wide berth.

The really cool person has a witty message on his machine. This is sometimes so good you have to ring up a second time because you were laughing so much the first time to leave a message. You can buy these ready prepared or record your own. Me? "You must have the wrong number, please redial." It had been a joke but the trouble was that 99.9% of people took me at my word and never left a message, but then I didn't have many callers anyway, judging by the fact that those that didn't leave messages didn't ring back either.

In the early days when they were novel it was considered cool to have an answering machine. I always thought they were a product of the Yuppie era along with the ubiquitous mobile phone but that was in the 80s and Jim Rockford had one in the 70s or was it the 60s? Nowadays they were as common as warts on a toad. You were the odd one out if you didn't have one. In fact these days you had to have both an answering machine and a mobile phone. Anyone who is anyone has a mobile. Businessmen, doctors, housewives. Even the local delinquent gang leader would stop his assault on you to answer a call from his local dope suppliers about the next drop.

To make things easier for callers it was now etiquette to leave your mobile number in your answer message. The intrepid caller can then, after already having made a fruitless call, spend five times as much ringing the mobile number to achieve contact. Do they usually succeed in this extra expense you ask yourself? Not likely. One gets an answering service, in other words a mobile answering machine, possibly orange in colour but not necessarily. So it's another message taker. Or something even worse. In certain cases the words "This call is being transferred" herald your call being switched back to the original number so that you can leave a message on the machine that told you to ring the mobile in the first place. It's good to talk if you can get someone to answer. Mind you, how much good did it do Bob Hoskins? I think B.T. dispensed with his services when he started talking to the animals. After a whole film talking to a rabbit his best pals were suddenly a pig and a duck. What they had to do with phones was beyond me. Now a dog and bone I could have understood.

Despite my concerns over the vagaries of telecommunications I had to leave my machine on in case Jenny or Miss Hobson needed to convey some information and were unable to contact me directly. That had been my instruction to Jenny, to be used as a last resort. I had gone to the expense of buying one of those

PRATT, PRATT, WALLY & PRATT INVESTIGATE

instruments that instructs one's own machine to play its messages down the phone line. Not that I had ever had need to use it so far.

Having packed all I needed, including all my red socks, I thought it time to check in with my so called boss. She was not in so I left a message that I was making headway with the matter in hand but would not be contactable for some time so to leave any message with my secretary for onward transmission. I wondered what she would make of that. If she had expected me to make no progress she would be surprised, maybe annoyed and perhaps even worried. If she had set me up it would serve her right.

Little did I know that things were moving faster than I realised. Dead fast in fact. With the operative word being DEAD!

# CHAPTER 7

Within two hours I had managed to set up my base of operation. A room without a view in a local pub. Ideal was the word for the location but not the whole situation. The pub was located approximately halfway between Hobson's house and office. This was the ideal part. I could be at either place within a few minutes. The trouble was there was no phone in the room. Incoming calls came through the phone at the bar and outgoing calls made from a payphone in the same bar. It gave a whole new meaning to the phrase 'local call'. Anyway, it was the best I could do and I'd phoned Jenny to let her know the number. She already knew not to pass this on to anyone, other than Miss Hobson, and not even to let on she knew where I was.

The quickest way to the car park was through the bar but this would not be my route because during non-opening hours access through the bar was locked and during other times the landlord would not have been keen on having someone careering through his business and upsetting his customers. There were better reasons for getting thrown out of a pub but I wasn't intending fighting, drug dealing or getting legless either.

I had a pub lunch and cogitated, or was that vegetated, over events so far. I was at a bit of a loose end until my new partner reported back. It was a pity I couldn't have a partner like Marty Hopkirk but then I didn't stand a ghost of a chance of that happening. Not that I was complaining too much. Victoria Hobson was better looking and it was possible to touch her flesh, or so my subconscious was hoping.

It was going to get mighty boring in that room but I had to stay put so I was contactable. It was going to be a long vigil. There was no telling how Hobson would act, if he needed to act at all. He might need do nothing but act like the three wise monkeys. Hear no, see no, speak no. However once bitten twice extremely reserved. I had come prepared this time. Camera, binoculars, two pens, a writing pad and a book for long spells in the car. Essential items for an investigator on the move.

I figured I could use some of the time I undoubtedly had on my hands by starting my report on events thus far; the one required by she who would have been obeyed if I didn't have my doubts about her. A nice, concise, one page report including all she would have expected me to learn by myself i.e. nothing, but excluding what I had learned and achieved that she would not have expected. If she was on the level then later on it would come as a pleasant surprise. If she was very uneven then she would only know what she had expected to find out. However, I now regretted leaving the message that I was making headway. I hoped she took that as a line used to make her think I'd been worth hiring.

I was sat on the bed, pad and pen in hand, when it occurred to me I could use the time on something more productive instead. Better not, I thought to myself. Stay professional. With that in the forefront of my mind I began to write Chapter 2 of my JB spoof.

By the time I finished it was just about four o'clock and still no word from my erstwhile partner. Unfortunately this left me with time to do my report. As I trusted Mrs Fulwood about as much as an audience at the N.E.C. in Birmingham would trust Wolf to behave for an entire Gladiator's show, I was economical with the truth. I didn't mention the flat tyre, nor the fact that I didn't pick Hobson up at the airport, nor what I'd overheard at the window. I particularly didn't mention meeting Miss Hobson. She was the trump card in my hand against the ungodly. In fact, she was my only card and if her presence proved to be more of a hindrance than a help she may prove to be my joker.

All in all there wasn't much to report, still it was more than I expected it to be, a lengthy six lines, mind you one was for th heading and another for the date. I felt it was enough to fulfil m obligation to report without giving anything away that I h gleaned so far. If Mrs F wasn't on the level I'd not tipped my ha

That was, of course, unless I was a diversionary tactic and the real surveillance team had been watching me, watching Hobson and watching me watching Hobson. If so she would probably know everything anyway. Little enough to be sure but enough to know I wasn't playing it straight with her. It would tell her I was suspicious and if she knew that the next move would be hers.

Having sealed the largely blank piece of paper into an envelope and addressed it to F.I.C.'s London office I lay on the bed for a rest. I heard no word from Miss Hobson until she breezed into my room at about 6.30. No polite knock on the door, she just waltzed straight in.

"Charming," I snorted. "I could have been stark naked."

"That's alright," she responded, "I'm not that easily shocked."

"Were you not taught to knock before entering a room?"

"Not when I'm in a hurry," she retorted. "Do you want to know what I've found out or not?"

"Of course! I've been kicking my heels in here for nearly six hours waiting for you to call."

"Had no time. Besides I figured the phone in the office may have been tapped."

"Fair enough," I agreed, not having thought of that possibility. "But what is your father doing now whilst you're here?"

"Seeing a show with Mother. I can't see him undertaking anything nefarious tonight."

"Why all the rush then?" I asked her.

"I want to search the house while they are out just in case I can find anything of interest." She sat at the opposite end of the bed to where I was sitting.

"OK. I can see you are on the ball." Which was more than I

"What news have you?"

"Well, it seems that my father's predecessor was a bit of a ... wife or children and no living relatives according to ... nel file. A workaholic by all accounts. It was a big sur- ... he announced his retirement. An early retirement, he is only 55. Due to ill health it was stated but there was no forewarning of this. In fact his attendance record was second to none over the years."

"So," I said thoughtfully, "they replace one man who was eminently suitable for the position, totally dedicated to the job, with someone else less suited." That brought a frown to her forehead. "One who because of family commitments couldn't put in so many hours," I added hastily. "In normal circumstances that would make no sense at all."

"It doesn't make much sense anyway," Miss Hobson observed, but that was before she had given it any thought. Even then I saw it dawning on her by the expression in her eyes.

It had all fallen into place, like the fragmented pieces of a jigsaw suddenly jumping together to form the picture on the box lid that at the outset you thought you could never recreate. I knew now what the lever was. She knew too. We had spoken of it briefly back in the office. Then it was only a possible theory plucked from obscurity but now it was a black ominous probability. I didn't know how to proceed. I didn't want to alarm her but she was a bright girl and could figure out all the alarming points for herself.

"It is us," she mumbled, quietly. "The other guy had no one to threaten. That has to be the answer. We're all in danger."

"Not if your father plays along." I wanted to sit beside her and put my arm around her but restrained my instincts to comfort her. She was not the type of girl who would burst into hysterics and need a shoulder to cry on.

"But I don't want him to play along. I want him like he used to be. With no worries. That's what we all want."

"I know Miss Hobson," I assured her. "Yet we have to act carefully."

"I know that!" she snapped. "And stop calling me Miss Hobson. It's Vicky!"

It had taken long enough, I thought, but then she wasn't thinking straight. Normally she would have been delighted to keep me at Miss Hobson length.

"OK," I said soothingly. "Let's look at this thing logically. Emotion will only cloud your judgement and your whole family need us thinking clearly right now."

She looked me directly in the eye and she was defiant again. "I'm not going to let them win," she declared flatly.

"Vicky, I never had any intention of letting them win." Whoever they turn out to be, I thought.

"Then what do we do? Call the police in?"

"We can't do that yet. We have no proof, just speculation."

"You mean we carry on as planned, just the two of us?" Her expression told me she thought I was mad. "We won't be able to cover all the bases."

She had a point and it was one I had already been thinking about. We were spread thin. Thinner than Rowan Atkinson's 'Thin Blue Line' and as a crime fighting force that was thin. In fact, we were not even a line but a mere dot. It was the time to call in reinforcements. Unfortunately, I knew, as no doubt Custer had done as he stood surveying the carnage that had once been his troops, there were none to call.

"We'll have to do the best we can," I pointed out. "Unless you've got a private army you've not told me about."

"What about the people that employed you? Surely they can call in the cavalry?"

"There are two reason I can't get them involved," I explained. "Firstly, they employed me to find proof and I have about as much as when I started. Secondly, I don't entirely trust my contact. As you said yourself, who would choose someone with no experience for a job like this? I think they've got their own agenda and for the time being I'd like to keep mine from them."

"But what is your agenda?" She stood up in exasperation, throwing her arms out wide then turning in my direction.

"That's what we're now going to work on," I replied, in as positive tone of voice as a pessimist can sound positive.

"What have you got in mind?"

"Well, we know, or think we know, that your father has

been installed because the ungodly have a lever against him that they did not have against his predecessor. And we believe that lever is his family. No doubt your father would do anything to protect his wife and daughters."

"Of course he would," Vicky agreed. "But if he knew we were in danger surely he would have sent us off somewhere safe, on some made up pretext?"

"Not with the people we're dealing with here. They are very well organised and widespread. Your father probably hasn't got the connections to pull off a disappearing act in total secrecy."

"OK then. There's a threat against us. What do we do about it?"

"At first sight not a lot," I admitted. "We cannot ease the threat if we don't know who is posing it. All we can do is take extreme care which will involve you keeping a close eye on your mother and sister, without having to alarm them."

"There's only Mother to worry about at the moment," Vicky informed me. "Sammy's on holiday. Has been for nearly two weeks."

"Where's she gone?"

"Touring Europe. She had no set itinerary."

"When did you last hear from her?"

"Not since she set off?"

"No postcard?"

"It's not unusual. Sammy's always so busy running around she never gets around to writing. Why are you so concerned about it?"

"It's only a thought," I said, "but suppose she's not in Europe. Suppose she's already in the hands of the ungodly. She may be the lever. If she was already being held then your father would do anything he was asked."

"Oh no! Do you really think so?" She sat heavily on the bed as her legs collapsed beneath her.

"It would make sense. A threat only carries so much weight. The real thing brings better results. You said your father had been different since his promotion. Has there been any change recently?"

"Not that I can remember. We've been worried about him for a while. Much longer than two weeks."

"Well, we'll have to treat it as a possibility. As things stand at present nothing has happened. If there is a threat hanging over your family then maybe we could do something about it. If they already have your sister then your father is totally in their power and then there's not much we can do."

"Surely we have to know how things stand so we know which way to play it?" She was on her feet again, pacing in agitation now. "If they have got Sammy our hands are tied."

"Exactly," I agreed. "But you can't really come out and ask you father, can you? And that's the only way you'll find out for sure. Even then he would probably try and hide the truth from you. I think for the time being we just have to go with the flow. You work with your father and keep me informed of his movements so I can be on hand if he leaves the office. Until a move is made there's nothing we can do."

"What about Mother?" protested Vicky. "If they haven't got Sammy then she could well be in danger. Who will look after her?"

"Back to square one. No more resources."

Or maybe just one, it occurred to me moments later. The only other person I could trust in this venture. Jenny. The office would have to be closed for a while but that would only inconvenience Mrs F and that bothered me not one jot.

"Leave it to me, Vicky. I might have an idea on that. You go back and carry out your search. I doubt if you'll find anything but it's worth a try. Tomorrow, go to work as normal and I'll see if I can get someone to keep a protective eye on your mother."

The meeting was over. Vicky left as abruptly as she had arrived. Not much had been decided on. I needed something to happen. One should not wish for things. One really shouldn't.

It was my second night without sleep. Not that I was on stakeout this time, just in a strange bed. Like a lot of people I had trouble sleeping in new surroundings the first night. I tried counting sheep but they wouldn't even jump over the gate, it was open so they all rushed through on mass. I tried singing myself to sleep but real sleepers kept banging on the wall in appreciation. I even tried to exercise but gave up after the third press up. I eventually drifted off just as dawn was breaking. Consequently I wasn't up when the call came. The landlord aroused me from my hard won sleep and with eyes that had seemed to have grown an opaque skin overnight I stumbled downstairs.

"What kept you?" Guess who? "11.30".

We had agreed that if a call from the office was necessary we would dispense with pleasantries in favour of the plain facts. 11.30 meant that Hobson was leaving his office at that time so I would need to be in position.

I was parked a little way up the road at the appointed half hour. In fact it was nearer noon when Hobson's car turned out of the private road to the Fairfax offices into the main road. Sod's law told me I would be facing the wrong way and I was. There wasn't much on the road but by the time I'd turned the car around there were three vehicles between us.

The road was a winding country lane really. Sometimes I could glimpse Hobson's car ahead. Other times he was well out of sight. I couldn't overtake to get nearer as each bend approached so fast. Pity it wasn't a TV chase. I would have had no problems then. I could have moved out onto the other side of the road knowing that all the oncoming traffic would be very accommodating and swerve out of the way, even crashing into a tree if necessary, anything so as not to heed my progress. Unfortunately, I was driving in the real world so could not take this easy way out. I was fortunate in another way though. The road had no junctions so he couldn't turn off. Even so I nearly missed him. He'd stopped not two miles from the office.

I'd passed him before I realised. No problem. Just slide into the next convenient space which was just ahead of me and the only one available on either side of the road for three miles. Trouble was I wasn't Simon Templar who can find a parking space on any street he's driving down at short notice, especially in London.

Not that this extreme skill of always finding a parking place only applied to the Saint. It was a universal silver screen fallacy. Whether it be the baddie following the goodie, the goodie following the baddie or just the necessity for a character to enter a certain building, there was always a convenient empty space to pull into, and in the case of the latter it was usually in front of the correct building. The reason, of course, is clear. If a bit of real life was included in the plot and someone had to drive round and round the block for three hours until someone else moved their car and there was a space free, only to get beaten into the spot by a taxi, then the show would be over. Dramatic licence had to be taken to keep the plot flowing. No such licence for me, just a mere driving licence which was vulnerable to suspension for acts of dangerous driving such as a vicious U-turn in a busy high street. I had the sense not to try it and broke some other rules instead by stopping in the railway station car-park. I wasn't a rail passenger and I didn't 'Pay N Display'.

I hurried back up the street, trying to look as unhurried as one can when one is in fact hurrying as one has never hurried before. I could see Hobson on the other side of the street, meandering along and gazing in shop windows. Funny time to go window shopping, I thought to myself, with the forces of the ungodly closing in on his family.

I was walking towards him on the opposite side of the street. Suddenly he turned and made as if to cross to my side so I took an instinctive interest in the contents of the nearest shop window. What reason I could have given for being so engrossed in ladies underwear I'd no idea.

Just like the football fan that endures 90 minutes of boring midfield play and misses the only goal when putting the kettle on in injury time, I missed the action. I heard it though. A screech of rubber, a dull thud and a woman's scream. When I looked Hobson was lying motionless in the street. My first instinct was to rush over to see if he was alive but there were a crowd of people around him already. Traffic was at a standstill in both directions. Someone ran to a phone box to call an ambulance and people peered out of shop windows and doorways.

I wandered slowly across and saw through the crowd that he was conscious. He lay there looking dazed but definitely alive. There was nothing more I could do but act as a bystander and wait for the ambulance to arrive. No one tried to move him which was no doubt the right thing to do in such circumstances.

The driver of the car which had hit him was proclaiming his innocence to anyone who would listen. Middle aged, nondescript with a sad face. Some of those who had seen the incident agreed with him that Hobson had just walked out in front of his car. They reassured him that it wasn't his fault and that there was nothing he could have done to prevent the accident. By this time the police siren could be heard and I drifted away into the background. The last thing I needed was to be noted as a witness, particularly as I had witnessed nothing, about par for the course on my record for the case. I made my way back to the car and met the ambulance come speeding the other way.

Before driving from the scene down a back street I rang Vicky from the phone outside the station, wasting precious time obtaining the number from direct enquiries and when finally getting through enduring a torrent of emotions down my ear. Concern, fear and not least of all anger because I neglected to find out which hospital Hobson had been taken to.

That was not the worst of it. After I'd collected my things from the pub and arrived back at the office the bombshell dropped. Vicky rang from the hospital. Physically Hobson was fine apart from some bruises. Mentally he wasn't. He had total amnesia.

It struck me that this was totally convenient for Hobson and totally inconvenient for the ungodly. How had he not seen that car? It had been conspicuous enough. Funny though it wasn't, like that of my literary creation the car had been bright pink. Not a Morris Minor though but a Mini.

What a stroke of luck. With his memory went the ungodly's hold on Hobson. He was of no use to them like that and neither were his family. Vicky would probably not agree but this was the best thing that could have happened to him. Conversely it was the worst thing that could have happened as far as I was concerned. No Hobson, no case. Call it my suspicious nature but if it was a choice between Fate's twisted sense of humour or something more staged managed I favoured the latter, although the how or why did not really matter. The case seemed closed.

As I sat there in the office late that afternoon after Jenny had left, I could not help thinking that as one door closes the roof can cave in.

There was no improvement on the following day. I was back at the office busy doing nothing, except employing a secretary who was also busy doing nothing. Jenny's nothing was slightly more useful than mine as it consisted of making endless coffee.

Hobson was still in hospital, busy trying to remember everything he had forgotten or alternatively he was equally busy trying to make everyone think he had forgotten everything. Either way it all boiled down to the same thing as far as the case was concerned, no place to go. Vicky was keeping a bedside vigil but as a concerned daughter and not as the reluctant partner of an inept investigator. After all there was nothing to report on now.

At least the office was less depressing. It looked less like the office of a less than successful theatrical agent and more like a doctor's waiting room. A NHS one of course. There were blinds at the windows, pictures on the walls, comfy seats for the non-existent clients and even a coat rack. Jenny had done a good job but so she should have. She'd had the time. I'd been less than boss-like in generating other work for her to do.

I was just thinking to myself that things were looking that bad that I might have to start wearing two pairs of red socks when the telephone broke its vow of silence. It was Vicky ringing from the hospital.

"Any news?"

"Not about Father. He still doesn't know me. Mother's here now so I'm taking a rest. But I thought you'd like to know about the other visitor."

"What other visitor?" I was suddenly alert, the possibility of a reopening case awakening my interest.

"An American. He wouldn't talk to me but I heard him question the doctor."

"Did you hear exactly what was said?"

"Practically. He was extremely rude I thought. Demanded to know if the amnesia was total and whether it was likely to be permanent. If not, how long would it last, he wanted to know. How long is a piece of string, was the doctor's reply. The American wasn't best pleased and stormed off. No one knew his name or anything. He didn't disclose any information about himself at all, just asked questions."

"Curiouser and curiouser said the cat."

"What are you talking about?"

I didn't know myself. Sometimes phrases just popped into my head from out of the blue. I had the vague feeling it was from 'Alice in Wonderland' but I could have been wrong. Anyway, I knew what I meant even if I didn't know what I was saying.

"I meant that things are a bit strange."

"How do you mean?" queried Vicky. "It is to be expected that someone would check up on Father. Even if everything was on the level within the company someone would show concern for an employee."

"True," I conceded. "But I wouldn't have expected anyone to fly over from the States. In fact, I doubt if anyone could have made it in so short a time. The visitor, whoever he was, must have been in the UK already. A sort of overseer I suppose, on behalf of Fairfax. Chances are that he'll now have to run the operation. How he's introduced into the equation will be interesting. Pity you're not working there anymore."

"Actually, I was just going back to the office to clear out my desk," declared Vicky.

"I wouldn't have thought you'd been there long enough to have anything to clear out."

"I have some personal items there. I did rush out in a hurry yesterday!" She was getting touchy again.

"OK. See what you can find out. But be careful. Your father isn't there to protect you now."

"I can take care of myself," she snorted, defiant as ever. "I'll ring later if there's anything to report."

"OK. Bye."

There was no response. She had already broken the connection.

I sat back in my new leather swivel chair to ponder on recent events. I'd been getting myself accustomed to the fact that the case was over, steeling myself for the inaction of my previous existence and heaving a huge sigh of relief that the £20,000 was not refundable. However, suddenly there was a chance that the game was still afoot. It was a slim chance to be sure. As faint as the brightness of a glow-worm in a pea-souper when he has been on a low calorie diet, but even that pinprick was worth pursuing.

Hobson had been my only lead. With him out of the picture the ungodly had to replace him. If I could get a line on his replacement it would be business as usual. Or rather business as unusual, business as usual was no business at all. It was up to Vicky now. Only she had grounds to be in the Fairfax offices and even then she was on ice as thin as one ply toilet paper.

Jenny popped in with my sixth cup of coffee that morning. She was getting expert at it now with a new kettle and cups enough for six visitors. Not that there was any prospect of needing them. I could always return the five unused ones if we went under.

"Any news?" she asked.

"Won't know until later."

"I was hoping, as there is nothing on at present, if you could continue with the account of your previous case."

"Why not," I agreed. At least I was useful for something. I carried on with my tale of derring-do. We had left off last time where I had been kidnapped and then forced to retrieve, for the bad guys, the fictitious report of their activities from my office desk. I related how I had been shot, ended up in hospital and then when returning home had accidentally killed two of the bad guys in self-defence. Then suddenly there was an explosion.

"Aaaa ... aaaa ... aaaatishoooooooo."

"Bless you," said Jenny, handing me a tissue she had produced from nowhere. It being one of life's little coincidences that a sneeze sounds exactly like what one needs when sneezing, a tissue.

"Thaaa ... aaa ... nk yoooooooou."

It was a sneezing fit. I may not sneeze for months but once started a chain reaction sets in, sounding like a continuous staccato of a sub-machine gun. I reached for my own hankie as my second sneeze ripped through the tissue. It was the one with which I had wiped Mrs Fulwood's brow. Fortunately it was now dry. Not so the water Jenny thoughtfully provided. It could be she had my welfare at heart. Or maybe she just wanted to ensure that the storyteller could carry on. I didn't know which.

"What happened next?" she asked when the fit seemed to have abated. So much for my welfare.

"Weeee ... ellll."

I was at it again. The office must have been particularly dusty that day or the pollen count high. Probably the former as the office hadn't seen a cleaner since opening for business.

In the middle of the mini explosions the phone rang and I picked it up automatically. I didn't say anything as I was just about to sneeze again but the person on the other end did. I dropped the phone and the sneeze never happened.

# CHAPTER 8

"Hello darling," the voice had said in greeting, hence my bout of dropsy. I was dumbstruck. I had never been anyone's darling before, and the voice had been female too. I retrieved the receiver to see if the caller had realised that they had dialled a wrong number. Apparently not, for when I had my ear in place I heard "Really!", as if in response to a comment from my end. Either it was an obscene phone call from a schizophrenic or I was only required to be a silent observer, if one can be said to be an observer of a conversation.

"Listen sweetheart," the voice continued whilst I managed to retain my grip this time. "You know with Father being in hospital with amnesia he has been temporarily replaced at the office. I have a meeting with his replacement after work so I'll be late."

There was a pause now so I assumed that some response from my end was maybe necessary. As a line of improvisation I had to say it fitted to a T.

"How late?"

"About an hour I'd say," came the reply.

"No problem. I'll wait up." I was getting into the spirit of it now.

"Well, I had trouble with the car this morning. I was hoping you could come here to give me a lift just in case it doesn't start. Or to follow me even if it does in case I break down on the way home."

"OK"

"Great! See you later handsome."

To say I was in a state of shock was the understatement of the year. If Isaac Newton had found that the apple had bounced off his head and hung suspended in mid-air he could not have been more surprised. 'Darling'. 'Sweetheart'. 'Handsome'. All terms of endearment that were unused to heading in my direction. They were as familiar to my ears as the mating call of the lesser spotted Ooslem bird. 'Pratt'. 'Wally'. 'Loser'. These were the terms I associated with. Of course the shock did not last long. However, it was not replaced with the euphoria of having attracted an admirer but with the concern that my new partner was in trouble. Vicky would no doubt have had her fingernails extracted with pliers rather than have to make such overtures to me, so one had to assume that they had been used to avert something even worse.

It wasn't hard to figure; in fact the message was clear. She had been discovered by the new man and he wanted a chat, either to try to learn information on her father which he had been unable to obtain at the hospital or to see how much Vicky knew. Or both. Personally I hoped it was the former. If it was the latter then he must be suspicious about something. He must have been within earshot of her call to me but she had been clever. By inventing a problem with her car she had created a good reason for me to arrive. Also she had put a time limit on her possible ordeal. About an hour after clocking off time was six o'clock but I'd aim to be there earlier than that. It was getting on for eleven then. Seven hours to kill but there was something I wanted to check anyway.

I still wasn't totally convinced about the accident. It had been too convenient. I needed to know the truth. If Hobson was play-acting he wasn't about to disclose it to me or any of his family for that matter. He could not know how they would react and above all he needed the correct reaction to allay the fears of the ungodly, who had two choices as far as I could see. Keep him under surveillance to see if he recovered or avoid the necessity of this by taking him out of the equation. I favoured the former, the latter being too drastic. Killing Hobson would attract attention and precipitate a police investigation which would no doubt complicate operations. Better just to watch. With no memory he was no threat.

There was little point in us keeping a watch on Hobson

at this time I decided. With our small resources we would do better concentrating on Hobson's replacement, particularly if some action had been planned for the immediate future. Hobson had, in fact, probably been replaced by the American Vicky saw at the hospital. If so this was the man she was staying behind to see. He had tried being forceful then, Vicky had said, but had not got very far. Had he now changed tack or was Vicky in danger? She was obviously taking no chances by getting me involved.

It was all guesswork. What I needed were some hard facts. I needed to know if Hobson was bluffing, then I could plan further. If he had really lost his memory he would need close watching by friends as well as foe. As soon as he showed signs of recovery he became a liability to the ungodly and would be in grave danger. It would have to be a case of me watching them watching me watching him. Still game for a laugh. That analogy kept cropping up in connection with this case.

Leaving Jenny in charge as usual I drove to the scene of the accident. One couldn't miss it. A large 'Accident Here. Can You Help' notice was displayed on a lamppost. With all the attendant witnesses at the time I wondered why it was needed. I supposed just in case someone who was thus prompted to come forward had some information that could throw a new light on the incident.

What to do to learn the truth? One couldn't just stop people in the street, no matter that it works in the land of the scriptwriter. "Excuse me, did you happen to witness an accident that happened here yesterday?" "Well, yes. I just happened to be in this exact spot and saw the whole thing. And you know I thought it was strange but … " And suddenly the investigation at a dead end gets a vital clue out of the blue. The chances of approaching someone who had been there at the time were better than winning the lottery but only just. There were a lot less than fourteen million people living in and visiting the town and more than one person had been a witness to the accident but the odds were still too great to make an attempt worthwhile. What

I needed to do was to speak to the people who I knew for certain were in the same places as the previous day, the shopkeepers.

The idea was good, the execution satisfactory, and the results appalling. It seemed that half the shop assistants had not been on duty the day before and those that had been were too busy serving at the time in question until the screech of rubber brought them to their doors to see what was going on.

There was nothing for it. I would have to speak to the local police. Not that I expected them to be very forthcoming. One, I was not even a member of the family. Two, P.I.s and police don't mix and this was probably true of I.I.s too.

With these thoughts in mind I dispiritedly made my way back to the car. That was when my red socks kicked in and I encountered a piece of good luck.

The early edition of the evening paper was out, you know, the one that arrives in the shop at 10am. 'Prominent Townsman Mowed Down' was the headline. A bit over the top to my mind but I bought a copy anyway. Any information that I could lay my hands on would be useful. My own enquiries had turned up a great big nul points. I sympathised with Norway, or was it Turkey that were the perennial magpie songsters. However, the Liechtenstein judge came up with a cloud nine at the last moment. It wasn't the paper that helped me but the gnarled old man who stood behind the counter. This shop had not been subject to my enquiries because it was at the far end of the street and on the opposite side of the road to where the accident happened. One should never take things for granted.

If one buys a paper for the headline one tends to look at it immediately and I did.

"Nasty accident that," said the newsagent. "I saw the whole thing you know."

"I thought it happened down the street. You couldn't possibly have seen it from here." A glory seeker I thought to myself. Anything newsworthy and there were people who had to be known to be there at the time.

"True enough, if I'd been here, but I wasn't was I?" He was

triumphant. "I was there. As near to him as you are now to me."

I hadn't been as near to Hobson as I was to the old vendor and I hadn't seen him around. If he had been that close surely I would have noticed him. Mind you, there had been quite a crowd and there had been other focal points of attention. Hobson and the driver who hit him. Even then I took little notice of the latter. I doubted whether I could describe him properly. Maybe this old man was a witness.

"Did you notice anything unusual?"

"How d'you mean?"

"Oh, I don't know. Something not quite right. Something out of the ordinary."

"Seeing a guy knocked down isn't out of the ordinary then where you come from?"

"Of course, but there are conflicting stories," I lied.

"Well, I didn't actually see the incident," he admitted.

I was right. He was a glory hound wanting to feel part of something important. I was about ready to leave but he persisted.

"I was there though. I passed him on my way here."

"You actually saw him before the accident then?"

"Yeah. He was looking in shop windows."

"But you never saw him get hit by the car?"

"Nope." He was crestfallen about this. To be there but to have missed the event must have really been galling to him. "But there was something though."

"What?" I asked suspiciously. I felt this old guy was wasting my time.

"Well, I'm not positive you understand. I didn't take much notice at the time. I never realised until afterwards."

"Go on!"

"Well, just as I got near to him a car beeped its horn. He heard it too I think. I thought I saw him jerk then he looked at his watch. Then he turned away walking towards the road and I passed him as he came in front of me. I turned round as I heard the screech of the tyres but he was already down."

"Did you tell all this to the police?"

"Nope. There were enough witnesses. I figured they didn't need me as well."

Typical 'don't get involved' attitude. He was fine talking about it as though he were part of it but at the time only content to watch not participate. Perhaps the police made him nervous I thought charitably. Whatever, he had given me something to go on. I thanked him and left.

I was still intent on visiting the police station to see what they could tell me, if they would tell me anything. In the end I didn't have to because the reporter for the paper had done the job for me. The article was quite damning of the police handling of the matter. Apparently the driver of the vehicle, who had given his name to the police verified by his driving licence, was now untraceable. He had after the accident gone back to the police station, given a statement and taken a negative alcohol test, then as there were numerous witnesses who testified to Hobson walking out into the street without looking he was allowed to leave. That was the last anyone saw of him. It was later discovered that his name and address were false, both belonging to a Joseph Maguire who had been killed in a factory accident six months earlier. The number plates on the car were also false. The reporter's view was that Hobson had been unlucky enough to be hit by a car intended for some criminal caper. Me? I was working on a different scenario entirely. Hobson being hit by a car and losing his memory was convenient. Hobson being hit by a car and losing his memory when the car had false plates and was driven by an unknown person stretched the bounds of convenience too far. The cause and resulting effect of this incident were about as coincidental as Clark Kent's absences when Superman is around. Nothing questionable in that at all.

There was no doubt in my mind now that there had been a put up job. There was about as much chance of this not being the case as 'The Italian Job' and a particular episode of 'MacGyver' not having the same Mini chase scene. What was fairly clear now, which I hadn't even contemplated before, was that not only had Hobson deliberately walked into the path of the car but also that the driver was part of the plan also. It made sense. Walking out in front of any old car was too dangerous. One couldn't legislate for the driver's reactions. OK it was on a busy high street where no car could be travelling at excessive speeds but it was still incredibly risky. More risky to my mind than the situation Hobson had found himself in. However, a driver expecting it could have braked slightly early to lessen the impact. Even with a driver on your side it was still risky but then Hobson was obviously desperate.

It was a pity that I couldn't speak to him about it, to discover what the rest of his plan was. He wasn't going to talk though. He was playing his cards close to his chest and so would I have in his position. It was the last hand and he was banking on the bluff of all bluffs. No help there. Finding the driver would be useful though. He must have known Hobson. I couldn't see him trusting a complete stranger in such a venture. He must have been a close friend, someone he had complete faith in. Maybe Vicky could put a name to the face I wouldn't be able to describe to her. Even if she couldn't I owed it to Hobson not to spoil his plan. He would be feigning amnesia until all the danger was past. Provided the ungodly didn't decide to silence him I could concentrate on other points like his replacement in the scheme of things. Or rather Vicky could. Perhaps she had done so already. I would soon know.

Four hours later I was sat outside Fairfax UK HQ. I was early as had been my plan. It was only 5.30 but Vicky and her new boss knew I was waiting, the guard on the gate had seen to that for he'd had to ring through to check me out. I told him I would wait in the car park which I did. None of this TV super sleuthing for me. The outcome of snooping around the outside of buildings at night usually ends up with a gun in the ear and imprisonment within. Not that I was particularly worried about that. Apart from a few non-Caucasians in the woodpile this was a clean, legal and above board operation. I wasn't going to learn anything on the outside. Neither would I do much better on the inside, not that I could have got in undetected anyway. The place to learn anything, if there was anything to learn, was in Hobson's office and Vicky was in the best position to search that if the opportunity arose. In any event I had my doubts as to whether I could search a room under the threat of discovery. One had to be able to do a complete exhaustive scrutiny of the entire area in the time it takes the person under suspicion to make a cup of tea and be able to return everything to its correct place from a completely overturned room position in the time between the turning of the doorknob heralding the return of the suspect to the first sight of the tea-tray. No, I didn't possess such skills and I didn't want to tip my hand or Vicky's for that matter. As far as the ungodly were concerned Vicky was just a dutiful daughter who had been doing some secretarial work for her father. And me? I was her boyfriend just there to assist if her car wouldn't start.

At ten minutes to six I decided to make myself more visible and entered the automatic glass doors into the reception area. There was another security guard behind the desk.

"I'm here for Miss Vicky Hobson," I told him.

"Sit there!" he growled, indicating the three sided sofa with centre coffee table waiting area. "She'll be down shortly."

Having been put in my place, I took my place in the middle of the sofa facing the desk so I could see all before me. Behind lay just the glass frontage of the building. There were coffee mats on the table but no one offered me coffee. Hospitality Inc. The guard recommenced the book I had interrupted.

Presently I heard the ping of an arriving elevator, followed by the sound of footsteps and accompanying voices. Suddenly they came into view. Vicky, a bouncing, bubbly and chatty Vicky I'd not seen before, and a large, dark haired and bearded man who kept nodding in agreement. When Vicky saw me she rushed over.

"Hi Tommy!" she cried gleefully, jumping into my arms and planting a smacker right on the kisser. Pity this was just an act, I thought to myself, I could get used to such greetings. "It's OK. I'm not going to lose my job. Mr Montford is taking over Father's role for a while and is going to keep me on. Isn't that wonderful?"

"Great!" I agreed. I thought I should get into the act and nearly added something like "We'd better be off. We have to pick up the kids from your Mother's" but I didn't know the background story she had concocted. I would have assumed the correct one, except about me being her beau, because Hobson's family would have been checked out at the time of his new appointment. Instead I just followed with "Let's go and look at this car of yours then."

"OK. Goodbye Mr Montford," she gushed. "See you Monday."

"Goodbye Miss Hobson," said Montford the American. "Goodbye to you too ... er, Tommy."

Good, Vicky had not given him my surname. That might help. I didn't know quite how but it might.

"Goodbye Mr Montford."

For good measure Vicky kept up her meaningless chatter all the way to her car. To no one's surprise, although she feigned it very well, her car started first time.

"Don't you think we ought to kiss again before I go to my car?" I enquired hopefully. "They may still be watching."

"Don't push your luck, darling," she said sweetly, closing the door and driving away.

Well, it had been worth a try. The first one had caught me off guard and I'd had no time to savour it. I had to admit it, in the acting stakes she had me beat. All I had was one eyebrow position.

I ran to my car and followed in her wake. She was already through the security barrier before I arrived there but she had pulled over to the verge around the next bend. Thinking she wanted to talk I pulled in behind her but she put her arm out of the window and beckoned me to follow. We ended up at the Hobson residence which looked dark and unlived in. Hobson in hospital, his wife watching over him and their other daughter away. I wondered if houses got lonely.

"You'd better come in," she invited as I arrived whilst she

was locking her car. Obviously not an avid TV watcher. Who locks up their car outside their own house?

"Yes m'lady," said I tugging my non-existent forelock.

Inside the house she marched into the sitting room and sank into a deep and comfortable looking armchair with a huge sigh of relief. I sat on the sofa, in the middle again although this was of a far more opulent style. Vicky looked drained.

"I take it I'm not your love, darling or sweetheart any-more?" I tried to lighten the atmosphere.

"You didn't believe all that twaddle did you?" she snapped disgustedly.

"One lives in hope."

"You would have more luck with faith and charity. God I'm glad that's over."

"Hard day dear?"

"You could say that. I only went there to clear my desk. I never intended staying there all day."

She must have had a lot of things to clear from her desk. What could one accumulate in two days? Make-up, spare pair of tights, hand lotion, nail file, eyebrow plucker, nail varnish, sunglasses and maybe the ubiquitous potted plant. Good job she hadn't been working there two years or she would have needed a transit van. Yet that hadn't been her only reason for going, not even the overriding one, for she had stated her intention to find out what she could on the man who was now her boss.

"What happened?"

"Whatever you might think about me going back there to just snoop around I had to go back anyway. I'd left the gun there."

I'd done her a gross injustice. She had been carrying around that gun with her ever since I met her and I should know having been the only person thus far to have looked down the busi-ness end of it. When I had called her with the news of the ac-cident she would have rushed out, protection the last thing on her mind. If the ungodly had found it, the balloon would have more than just gone up, it would have had a hole blown in it and have crashed limp and lifeless. They would have realised then that certainly one family member of the man they were relying on had misgivings of some sort. Would they have believed that it was just a girl protecting herself? Maybe in the States that would have worked but not in the UK. There would have to have been a special reason for her to possess it. That would have been too much of a coincidence to overlook.

"Did you get it?"

"Yes. There was no problem there," she assured me. "But there was a note on my desk asking me to wait around to meet this Montford character. I couldn't have just left, it would have looked too suspicious."

"It might have done," I agreed, "but then again you could just have said that you were only working there because your father asked you to, and now that he didn't need you there you were no longer an employee subject to orders."

"Well, we needed to find out anything we could about the opposition so I decided to stay. He arrived not long afterwards. I'd had time to have a quick look around Father's office but found nothing useful. He didn't catch me. Montford's the guy who was at the hospital." She shuddered involuntarily. "He gives me the creeps. At the hospital he was belligerent and rude to the doctor. He didn't speak to me there. Suddenly he was all smiles and urbane civility. I don't think he knew that I'd seen his out-burst at the hospital. This happened in the corridor and I was in Father's room. He's a real Jekyll and Hyde but mostly Hyde I would guess."

"How did he explain the note?"

"He said he knew I was working there from the personnel records. He'd figured that I would think that I was now redundant but had wanted to speak to me about staying on as his secretary, show him the ropes so to speak. That was the bit that didn't make any sense. He must have known that I'd only been there a couple of days and knew less about the operation than he probably did."

"I suppose he intended to learn from you what he couldn't at the hospital," I ventured. "Probably felt you would be too upset to be defensive or evasive."

"He did ask. How was he? Did the doctors think the amnesia was permanent? I told him they didn't know. Truth is he could get his memory back at any time. There is no recognised time period involved. It could come back in bits and pieces or all at once. No one knows. Familiar people and surroundings are the best bet. But if things are as bad as we think they are I hope he never gets it back or at least until all this trouble has blown over."

Did she know something that I shouldn't but did? If not her mind and that of her father ran along the same gauge track.

"So he kept you back after office hours just to ask after your father's welfare? A bit inconsiderate. Anyone else would have figured on you rushing back to the hospital as soon as you could."

"That wasn't it. That had been earlier when he first arrived. The reason for the meeting was to persuade me to work for him. I fell into a trap I'm afraid. When he asked me why I'd started working for Father I told him that I'd lost my previous job and needed the money. He said I could continue to work there, in fact he hoped I would. He said he had been rushed over from the States and did not have the time to interview for a secretary. I think he was trying to paint over his "show me the ropes" gaffe."

"I take it that you agreed?"

"Of course. I mean he gives me the creeps and I wouldn't trust him as far as I could throw Jo Brand but we need a foothold in the enemy camp and this is as good as we are going to get."

"True enough. But you can be sure any work he gives you to do will be above board, nothing to raise any suspicions."

"That's only logical knowing what we know. In fact I've been typing ordinary letters all afternoon. Although even that was strange."

"How so?"

"When my father left the office the day of the accident, he gave me his dictation to type and told me that once that had been done everything would be up to date. He obviously hasn't dictated anything since then but this afternoon I have been typing dictation from my father. Tapes given to me by Montford that he said he'd found in the office. It was definitely Father's voice too."

That was indeed strange but maybe not as strange as me telling her that her father had deliberately walked out into the path of the car that had hit him, that the driver was probably in on it and the amnesia was all a ruse. Perhaps it would be better if I forgot to mention it. On the other hand she was my right hand at present and I needed all the hands I could get.

"I suppose it's just possible that the ungodly may have realised that they would have to make your father disappear at some time or another so had already prepared dictation to allay suspicion," I suggested. "Or they may have been prepared to keep the secretary busy whilst your father was away doing whatever he is being forced to do."

"My thoughts exactly. It was definitely premeditated." More like pre-dictated. "It made me glad I'd called you and that they knew you were coming to meet me."

"Yes. I meant to ask you what made you do that. You appear to have handled everything OK."

"I was a bit worried when he first arrived and said that we'd have to have a meeting later. I wanted to let you know the score."

"And it's the nicest phone call I've ever had." Pity it was contrived.

"I had to act on the spur of the moment. He came out to my desk as you answered."

"It was a piece of smart thinking anyway. It ensured that you got out. What exactly was said at this meeting?"

"He began by telling me how he was going to operate. He said as he was new and had rushed over with little knowledge of the operation in the UK, he would be out of the office a lot visiting various sites. He would, he said, dictate at night and leave them for me to do the next day along with any other instructions."

"In other words," I interceded, "he would be out arranging fires, explosions, thefts and the like."

"I suppose so," Vicky agreed. "But there's a difference now. Father was being forced to do something, probably turn a blind eye or get passes or something like that. Something menial. He could not have played a more active role than that. The incidents, whatever they happen to be, would have to be carried out by the initiating rather than the reluctantly initiated. Now it's too late to get another innocent third party involved. Montford must have an active role, otherwise he would remain visible at all times to give himself an alibi."

"Follow Montford and we may get to the bottom of things," I observed.

"Precisely." She rose and started to leave the room. "You know," turning back, "this accident definitely could be a blessing in disguise. Father's out of it now and because of this we could be that much closer to the truth."

"Er ... Funny you should mention that," I said.

"What do you mean?" She was suddenly startled. "Is Father alright? Has his memory returned?"

"Not as such," I responded. "I don't think it will for now. Not until this is all over."

"Why? How do you know? You're not a doctor."

"No," I admitted, "but I know something you don't."

She didn't say anything but just stood there in the doorway looking at me. I didn't know what she expected. Maybe she thought I was going to say that her father was still in danger, that the accident was all part of the great plan of the ungodly. Perhaps his part was complete and it had been a botched attempt to silence him.

"You'd better sit down," I advised her. "I need to tell you something."

She took her seat tentatively as if expecting the worst. I set out to put her out of her misery. Tact was the order of the day and in such circumstances people called me Mr Tact.

"The accident was deliberate."

Her face went ashen and her hands started to tremble, whether in anger or fear it was impossible to say. Perhaps I hadn't eased into the subject quite as skilfully as I'd hoped to.

"No one was trying to kill him," I quickly reassured her.

"What do you mean?" she demanded. "You just said it was done deliberately." Then she clapped her hands to her face. "Oh, no!" Her mind was working overtime. She had jumped from one extreme to the other. A deliberate act could only be carried out by one of the two parties. One who wanted to kill or one who wanted to be killed. "NO! He wouldn't! No matter how bad it got he wouldn't do that." She was close to tears now. She didn't want to believe it and was trying hard not to.

"You know, ten years ago that car wouldn't have even touched him. Father used to be a stunt man."

Eureka! That was it. That was the clincher.

"Look, if you'll let me finish." I tried to stop her torrent of words whilst my mind was assimilating this latest bit of information. If the other guy was privy to the plan, which everything seemed to indicate, chances are he was or used to be a stunt man too.

Vicky was looking at me expectantly.

"Just a minute I'm trying to sort something out in my head."

If he was a stunt man then maybe Vicky could point me in the right direction. She might even know who it was. First, I had to get her back on an even keel. The cool, confident, gun toting Vicky I could depend on.

"Let's have some coffee," I suggested. "Then I'll tell you what I know."

She rose and left the room without a word. Her stance was stiff now when seconds earlier it had been sagging. She was never vulnerable for long. There should have been a better word for her than mercurial. Even thermometers needed time to change but with her it was instantaneous. Like touching a switch. Still she was regaining control again which helped me; I had enough trouble just keeping control of myself. Half the time at least, I just wanted to run away and leave the whole mess behind.

# CHAPTER 9

I tried to get things straight in my own mind before she returned. This accomplice must have been a good friend of Hobson's for him to be involved in this, probably going back to his stunt man days. I couldn't help smiling to myself. I couldn't see Hobson, even a much younger version, as a dashing, heroic substitute for the stars. Still it made sense of the facts. However, I still needed corroboration for my own peace of mind. I couldn't confront Hobson with my theories. There was always someone around him and whilst he would undoubtedly act stupid to my suggestions, there was always the distinct possibility that this action could alert the ungodly pushing them into silencing safety tactics. If I could find the other guy maybe I could learn the truth. Well, not so much learn the truth because I was sure of that already but learn of Hobson's plan. It was a long shot. If he were that good a friend he would not yield anything either. However, I had Hobson's daughter on my side. He would know that she would have Hobson's best interests at heart. If he saw that we knew part of it he might divulge the rest.

One part of me was saying why bother. I was positive Hobson was acting. Why then the need to go to all this trouble to prove it? To be sure I told myself. If I knew what Hobson intended I could concentrate on the job I'd been hired to do. Since meeting Vicky I had digressed somewhat from my original task. Not that I gave a fig about Mrs Fulwood. She hardly entered into my thinking at all.

Vicky came back into the room with two steaming mugs of coffee which she placed on an expensive looking coffee table. It said much for her state of mind that she hadn't put coasters down first. The room was impeccably furnished and clean, except for two days dust and two recent coffee stains, very recent in fact, only seconds old. Vicky's touchdown had been slightly bumpy hence instant coffee stains, or fresh ground coffee stains if she had not used a jar.

"Now," I began as she resumed her seat, "are you sitting comfortably? Then let's begin."

"I beg your pardon?" She was baffled.

"Sorry. Just trying to lighten the mood."

"Well don't!" She was angry again. "It's not a laughing matter. You just accused my father of trying to commit suicide. What proof have you got?"

Just in case she decided to get up and hit me, or worse still treat me to another uninterrupted view of her gun barrel, I decided to come clean.

"First, we know your father is in trouble." She nodded in agreement. A vast improvement. When we had first met she was all denials. "We believe he is being pressured into something by a threat to his family. They want him to do something, or not to do something, as the case may be. He knows what that something is or he wouldn't be so tormented. He knows that if he doesn't do what they want his family is in danger. He needs a way out but what can he do?" No comment from his daughter so I continued. "He has to change the situation. Deal himself a new hand if you like."

"But his hands are tied," protested Vicky.

"Were tied," I corrected. "I think he found his way out. Think about it. In the same situation what would you do?"

She thought about it for a few seconds, her brow creased in concentration, before she answered. "I would have to find a way so as not to be of any use to them but also no threat to them either so they wouldn't need to punish anyone."

"Such as?" I led her.

"Loss of memory?" A question, not a statement. She was still unsure. She was thinking along the lines I had been leading her but the idea had not yet taken root.

"Exactly," I agreed. "With no memory he couldn't do what they ask, in fact he wouldn't even know who they are, or anyone else for that matter. Which means the family are safe also. A: Because as he doesn't know them any threat to them would carry no weight. B: What would they threaten him about? Get your memory back or else we'll kill this woman, who is your wife by the way. I don't think so."

"You could be right," she conceded. "But rather than taking advantage of a fortuitous incident you think it was all planned?"

"Precisely. Don't you see?"

"Not fully," she replied. "But then I haven't had as much time to get used to this idea as you have."

If I hadn't known better I would have said she was looking at me through different eyes now. Not that there was any noticeable change, they were still bright, blue and deep. Unfortunately, they were not come to bed eyes, not for me anyway. It wasn't admiration or even respect but I felt she was seeing me for the first time as an equal. Up until then she had obviously had me down as a bit of a mental lightweight but now she was reviewing her thinking. I must be light middleweight by now. I'd have to change her mind back again. Later, when she had forgotten I'd worked something out she hadn't considered. The last thing I needed was Vicky thinking me an astute, quick thinking guy. Better to be just a dufus.

"There was no genius involved," I hastened to point out to her. "I just had access to a couple of facts you were ignorant of. At first I thought it was just a sheer coincidence, outrageously fortuitous and extremely advantageous to your father, but a coincidence all the same. One that may have been short lived also as there is no telling when temporary amnesia will correct itself. Of course, I did think to myself that it was a pity he hadn't thought of it himself. That was probably when my subconscious started working on it. Then I read the paper and discovered that the driver of the car was untraceable, with a false address and number plates. That was when I really began to wonder. Then just now, when you told me that your father used to be a stunt man, I was sure."

"You said there were a couple of things that I didn't know," said Vicky. "One was that I hadn't seen the newspaper. What was the other?"

"Something I found out when I went back to the scene this morning," I replied. "When I saw the paper I went back to see if I could learn anymore." A little white lie but better than letting her know I had been suspicious all along.

"What did you find out?"

"Well, I found a guy, an old newspaper seller, who was there at the time. He told me that he heard a car beep its horn, and on hearing this, your father turned from his window shopping and walked into the road."

"You think it was some sort of signal?" She asked dubiously, not entirely convinced.

"Taken with all the other facts it seems likely. He would have had to make it look real. He couldn't just stand at the kerb waiting for the correct car to come by."

"That's if it was deliberate."

"I thought we'd already established that. It's as plain as that lovely nose on your face. One, he's in trouble and needs a way out. Two, loss of memory, as you've already admitted, solves all his problems. Three, the driver involved in this little accident just happens to have been dead for six months and the car has false plates. Four, your father used to be a stunt man and would have the necessary knowledge to carry it off. What more evidence do you need to believe?"

"OK," she conceded. "The facts all fit the theory. What now?"

"We need to find out the rest of your father's plan. He's not going to talk to me or you or anyone else. He has to keep up the pretence and can't take the risk of letting anybody in on the secret. If the ungodly find out he will be a dead man and maybe the rest of you with him."

"That's why he's not even let on to Mother?"

"Right. Even though it must be hurting him to see you all so worried, it's the only course of action open to him."

"But someone knows," Vicky pointed out. "The guy driving the car."

"I know. He will have been sworn to secrecy and must be someone your father trusts implicitly. We have to find him. We need to know what your father intends to do next and then we'll be one up on the enemy. If he keeps the ruse up, and personally I can see no other option, they will have to keep a constant watch on him in case he recovers at which time he becomes a liability. If the amnesia had been real we'd have had to be in constant attendance too for the same reason but the opposite purpose. Now that we know he will not be recovering, we can concentrate on other matters: always subject to the rest of his plan being equally as well thought out. He really has planned this brilliantly so far."

"Right. So how do we find this driver if the police can't"

"Because they don't have your family knowledge. The guy driving the car must be a stunt man or ex stunt man and a good friend of your father's. I was hoping you would know who it might be."

"I'd have to think about it. I said ten years ago but that was when he finished. In reality we need to go back twenty or more years. It might be someone I've never even met."

"Well put your thinking cap on," I instructed her. "What about photographs? There must be some from that period. Mementoes of various films he worked on for instance."

"I'll check the albums." She dashed out of the room, now in adrenaline mode. She didn't stay down for long.

I had my fingers crossed, mentally and physically, and my red socked toes also. It had already occurred to me that the guy we were trying to locate probably forged a close relationship with Hobson over many years. Maybe they had started in the business together before Vicky was born. It was quite possible she had not met him.

Vicky returned with a large and dusty album. She had to sit next to me on the sofa so we could both look at it. Fortunately for her it was a large sofa so she could still keep me at arm's length. The pictures were old and faded, most of them with a much younger looking Hobson standing by a burnt out car smash or some other such remnant of a successful stunt. It seemed that many of the stunts he'd been involved in concerned cars and driving. Tied up nicely with the matter in hand I thought.

Before the first dust had settled or even affected my sinuses we struck gold. We had been looking for a needle in a haystack, one needle in a host of haystacks. Luckily it turned out to be a knitting needle and I sat on it. Some stunts obviously require more than one stunt man so in certain photographs Hobson was not alone. One face cropped up a fair amount and it jogged Vicky's memory.

"That's Chalky," she announced.

He looked a younger version of the driver that had hit Hobson although I wouldn't have liked to swear on it.

"How do you know?"

"It's years since I last looked through this," she replied, "but Father used to show it to me when I was little and explain the photos. I remember him telling me about Chalky."

"I think it's the guy," I told her, although with some doubt, which completely disappeared with the next snap. "That's the car!" Hobson and Chalky stood one each side of a pink Mini.

This was too weird for words. To discover Hobson's ally had been odds against. To find the actual vehicle was beyond belief but there it was in full colour. The driver, the car and the victim all in one shot. Either this old stunt colleague of Hobson had an incredible grudge against him or we had found the proof we needed. All we had to do now was find Chalky.

"I don't suppose you have any idea where we can find this guy?"

Vicky broke into a smile. "At the circus," she proclaimed in triumph.

"Did you suddenly remember that too?"

"No. This fell out of the album when I picked it up." She handed me a folded piece of paper which turned out to be a circus poster. It was advertising Biggle's Circus and it was fairly new, certainly nowhere near as old as the photos in the album. It had to be there for a reason.

"Roll up, roll up, for the Greatest Show on Earth," cried Vicky.

"Have you a paper?" I asked her. "It'll tell us if it's in town."

"Don't need to." She was surprised. "It's on the poster."

"Oh, so it is." I agreed looking more closely at it.

So it was and so I had noticed. However, now I wasn't as perceptive as she was beginning to think I was.

"Let's go then," I stated. "I haven't been to a circus in years."

In fact I couldn't remember the last time, or indeed the first time. I must have been to one at some time. Sometime in my distant childhood. Every kid goes to the circus at least once. It had obviously left a lasting impression.

Mind you, I knew what circuses were supposed to look like. I'd seen the films; 'The Greatest Show On Earth', 'The Big Top' etc. A big top, loads of animals in wheeled cages, caravans or smaller tents for the performers preparations, not forgetting all the vehicles for transportation, unless the show was so great that a personal train was required. I couldn't remember which film it was but no doubt it starred Tony Curtis or Burt Lancaster or both, as they had had the training for it. Whatever the film or its stars Biggle's Circus, when we saw it next morning, in comparison was a big let-down. The big top would only have seemed so to the tiniest tot, I had been camping in bigger. Of animals caged or otherwise I could see nary a sign, except for a solitary horse-box. Most of the vehicles appeared clapped out, mainly Land Rovers but a few camper vans, too. The phrase flea bitten came to mind and it was an apt fit. I didn't think Billy Smart or the Chipperfields had anything to worry about, if indeed they were still the circus standard.

"The Greatest Show on Earth," observed Vicky with great irony, looking around her in amazement.

"It probably looks a lot better at night." I was feeling charitable. The only bits that would look better at night would be those obscured by the darkness. "Let's go and find the boss or ringmaster or whoever."

On the trip over we had formulated our plan of action. We had decided to wait until morning for a couple of reasons. By the time we had discovered the circus connection it had gone 7.00pm and there would have been a performance on by the time we had travelled the twenty miles to its location. Also the next day being Saturday there was no need for Vicky to go into the office. Armed with an old photo and a nickname we didn't have a lot to go on. No real name. We were not even certain that the man we were looking for had any connection with this circus, although the poster stored with the snapshots must have some significance. Rather than wander around uninvited trying to spot Chalky based on the photo and my brief glimpse of him we had mutually agreed, all bar one, to seek out the circus owner for permission and direction. It also meant that if we came upon Chalky he would be less suspicious with his boss on hand.

Biggles, the literary creation of Captain W E Johns, was a pilot around World War One. He had numerous adventures with his chums Bertie, Algy and Ginger. Biggles is what they called him, his real name being Bigglesworth. The owner of the circus could certainly have come from that era. He had the clipped English accent and a huge handlebar moustache, no doubt adding to his role as ringmaster. However, it was something of a disappointment to learn that this tall elderly showman was not called Biggles or even Bigglesworth. I supposed Smith's circus didn't have the same ring to it.

It was certainly the place for pseudonyms and as good a place to hide from the world as any. We showed Smith the photo, hoping he could see through the years as I'd been able to do and recognise that he knew and employed the older version. It was still a long shot.

"So you would like to speak to Chalky would you?"

Surprise was the order of the day. We hadn't given a name as it was just a nickname used in another age and might just have confused the issue.

"He and my father used to work together," said Vicky. "We

need his help on something."

"Important?"

"It's a matter of life and death."

"Well, come on then. I will show you the way. The clowns are rehearsing."

Clowns. Well, with a name like Chalky what else could he have been? A good cover. Half the time he would be unrecognisable. Why did I have the feeling that he had been hiding even before recent events.

Call me old fashioned but the sight of middle aged men running around throwing buckets of water over each other seemed absurd. Mind you their outfits of jeans and T-shirts didn't help and the only thing on their faces was sweat. This was obviously not a dress rehearsal.

I noticed Chalky immediately. He was the one doing most of the running around. It looked unreal but I guessed all dressed up and with painted faces what now looked stupid would then seem normal, as clowns go that is. Chalky saw us too and stopped dead. He didn't recognise me and there was no reason he should have done. I had just been a face in the crowd and not a memorable one at that. No, he was just curious, like his counterparts who had also stopped their shenanigans. Mind you, he should have been somewhat worried. I would have been. He had been involved in a hit and run, given false identification and had been driving a car sporting stolen plates. He would know the police were looking for him and the appearance of any strangers should have been disturbing. It wouldn't have surprised me if he'd taken to his heels on sight of us but he didn't, which vindicated us having gone through his boss, we had felt he was less likely to head for the hills if we proceeded that way.

"Chalky!" called Smith. "Some people to see you."

Chalky came over to the edge of the arena. "What's up boss?" he asked wiping his hands on his jeans.

"We would like to talk to you please," Vicky answered him.

"What about?" He was certainly a cool customer but as an ex stunt man I would have expected him to have a lot of nerve.

"In private please," she requested.

Some minutes later we were seated in Chalky's camper and got right down to business.

"I'm Victoria Hobson, Mr er ... "

"Chalky will do Miss Hobson. What's this all about? I have work to do you know." Just a hint of anxiety maybe. Not a crack but a definite scratch in the surface.

"You used to work with my father. In his stunt man days."

"Oh! You're Pete's daughter," he exclaimed in surprise. "Nice to meet you." He pumped her hand in welcome.

"We need your help Chalky," Vicky informed him when she had retrieved her arm and found that the hand was still attached.

"How? Is Pete OK? Haven't seen him in years."

"That's funny," I observed. "I've the distinct impression you saw him not so long ago."

"Who's he?" he asked Vicky, whilst casting a hostile glance in my direction. I don't know what it is but most people just warm to me straight away.

"Just a friend," she replied. "Father was hit by a car a couple of days ago."

"Oh, I'm sorry to hear that Miss Hobson. Is he alright?"

"That's a matter of opinion." This from me.

"Physically he's fine," said Vicky. "He has amnesia though."

"Why come to me? Like I said I haven't laid eyes on him in years. The sight of me isn't going to jog his memory."

"That's not why we're here Chalky. We know that my father's accident was nothing of the kind."

"What do you mean? Who would want to kill him?"

"I never said anyone did," Vicky pointed out. "It was deliberate, but a deliberate ploy. To help my father out of a jam."

There was no response to this but it seemed to me that for the first time there was a trace of panic in his eyes.

"Look Chalky, we know," continued Vicky. She showed him the photo. "This is you and my father. And behind you is the car that hit him."

That got him right between the eyes, but he wasn't about to collapse on us.

"Prove it."

His tone had changed. Pretence was over. The clown had gone and the steely nerved stunt man was before us.

"We don't need to. We don't want to." Vicky was placating. "What was done was to help Father. We know that. We want to help too. To do that we need to know the rest of the plan."

"You can't help." The first admission of his participation. "This was the only way he could think of. The only way he can survive is if everyone believes. What you know now places him in danger. I can tell you no more."

"We only want to know his intentions," protested Vicky. "I am his daughter."

"And if he had wanted you involved he would have told you." Chalky was steadfast. "I promised not to tell a soul and I won't"

"We could tell the police," I warned him. "They would be very interested in talking to you."

Vicky and I had decided to do our own version of good cop bad cop. It was called nice civilian and threatening not very civilian.

"You wouldn't do that, would you Miss Hobson?" He sounded confident. "Not to the one person who has helped your father out of a hole?"

"No," she admitted. "But please tell me the rest. I need to know."

"I'm sorry. I'm a man of my word." He stood up and opened the door. "I think you'd better go now."

I had to follow Vicky's lead and she made to leave. "I hope you know what you're doing," was her parting shot.

"I think so," said Chalky. "See you." He closed the door behind us.

It was a silly parting greeting. He clearly was not going to be forthcoming. There would be no reason to see him again unless he changed his mind and that did not seem likely. He would hope not to see us again. So why say "See you". In all probability we would never set eyes on him again.

Of course, one could be wrong about these things.

# CHAPTER 10

Yes, there was no doubt about it, in full costume and facial paint, clowns were a lot funnier, especially if they caught you off guard. I mean, if you were stood in front of some lift doors waiting for it to arrive and after the ping the doors opened to reveal a jovial, colourful clown, you couldn't help but smile. In the majority of cases that is. There may be a few reasons why this wouldn't amuse one. One could have forgotten to renew that multi-week lottery ticket on the week one's six numbers came up. One may have recently learnt of the infidelity of one's partner. Possibly it could just be that time of the month. Or maybe clowns just don't amuse one, especially when slumped in the corner with a large knife protruding from the chest. Certainly I wasn't smiling and neither was the screaming woman behind me.

I didn't make the classic mistake of rushing over to the body and instinctively grabbing hold of the knife. Not particular clever actions in the circumstances but always those taken in the stabbings I had been witness to. On the box, of course. For instance, Richard Hannay in 'The Thirty Nine Steps'. If he hadn't grabbed the knife in Scudder's back he would not have had to go on the run. Not that I was in any danger of anyone thinking that I'd done it. I hadn't moved since the lift doors had opened and it hadn't taken long for the screams to bring people running, including the resident manager whose office was just down the hall. The screaming woman had moved though. She was now in a horizontal position and quite out of it. The manager stepped over her body, took one look at the other body and relieved me of having to keep my finger on the lift call button by locking the lift in position.

"I'll go and call the police," he said.

"No, I'll do it," I offered. "You make sure no one touches the body." I had reasons for making the call myself.

I could have made the call from the manager's office but there was something I needed from the flat. I took the stairs two at a time and made the trip to my door in record time. The something I needed was a telephone number. I had to ring Cox. If I was going to be involved with the police over this it was better to deal with the devil I knew. In Italy all roads lead to Rome but in this affair all roads led to me.

Although I hadn't checked the body closely I knew it had to be Chalky. It was beyond belief that when I'd just met a clown that morning another one had got himself killed in my building. That wasn't the clincher though. There was the murder weapon. A long handled kitchen knife. One that could have come from one of a thousand homes. Only one thing made it stand out and that was where part of the plastic handle was missing. A small hole in the plastic which revealed the metal underneath, such as may have been made if the knife had fallen onto a hard surface. I remembered the incident well. It hadn't been so long ago.

I knew the victim. The knife had come from my kitchen. It was not difficult to guess where the finger of suspicion would fall, despite the fact that I had a witness to me discovering the body. How reliable Miss Swoon 1996 would be I had no idea and it was something I wouldn't like to rely on. Cox was my best hope. He might be my only hope of not being hung in the frame.

Cox wasn't available. He was out, investigating no doubt. I pleaded with a colleague to get a message through that he was to contact me ASAP or even sooner. I should have dialled 999 for I had no way of knowing how long he would be, but I didn't. Not that it mattered for when I returned to the scene I found out that someone else had. I couldn't really object and I didn't have any time to. The sound of sirens was approaching and the police arrival was very imminent. I had the overwhelming urge to run very far away. In this particular instance not to show resistance would have been futile.

The police were officious and efficient. The lift was taped off in short order and the foyer cleared of anyone who wasn't directly involved, namely the fainting woman, the manager and me. The former was hysterical and the sergeant trying to take down her particulars was getting nowhere. In the end she was allowed to go to her flat to calm down, accompanied by a WPC. That left the manager, Bob Foundling, and yours truly. Foundling was questioned in his office and I was sat on the sofa in the foyer with the sergeant. He seemed to be happy just getting some coherent response to his questions.

I told the bare facts which involved me waiting for the lift and discovering the body as the lift doors opened, not forgetting to emphasise the fact that I was not alone at the time. I didn't hazard a guess as to the identity of the body. I was asked of course but side-stepped the question nicely. Answer a question with a question. It was something I'd been accused of many times before. How could anyone identify anything under all that face paint? Neither did I admit to being the owner of the knife. It was only a matter of time before both these points were discovered but by then, hopefully, Cox would have arrived. DI Cox CID. Not exactly my man on the inside but the best I could hope for. It was his province anyway. CID would be called in, uniform didn't investigate murder. In fact, it was extremely lucky that we only had a small local police station with no resident CID officers or they would have been there already. Even then they would be speeding to the scene and so would the coroner or pathologist or whatever title he went by. It wasn't the time to wonder on how certain English and American words became intermingled within the two dimensions of the same language. I was hoping that whoever the Quincy type was he wouldn't remove the greasepaint on the spot. I wanted to feign ignorance of the deceased for as long as possible.

No sooner had I finished my skeletal statement than the plain clothes brigade arrived and I had to go through the whole routine again. Cox didn't put in an appearance. I was questioned by a DI Perkins and Foundling by a DI Pink. I kid you not, it was a real live Pinky and Perkins show.

This was a more serious affair. The sergeant had just taken

details with the odd clarification needed whereas Perkins asked probing questions whilst perusing my statement scribbled in the sergeant's notebook.

"At what time did you discover the body?"

"3.17."

"That's a very precise answer."

"I'd just looked at my watch."

"Do you remember what floor the lift was on when you called it?"

"The top floor. Tenth."

"Did it stop at any other floor on the way down?"

"Third."

My own floor. A coincidence? I thought not.

And so it went on. Did I know the victim? No. Had I seen him around? He would have been hard to miss. Why, did I suppose, the woman behind me fainted? Shock perhaps. Did I think she might have known the victim? Pass. Did I touch the body or the knife? No. Had I seen anyone leaving the building when I had been coming in? No. Had I seen anything or anyone acting suspicious recently? No. And so on.

"You'd better turn me over, I'm done this side," I joked after twenty minutes of grilling.

"We have to be thorough Mr Robel, as I'm sure you will no doubt appreciate." He was speaking with authority. "Can you come down to the station tomorrow and sign a full statement?"

"If it's really necessary."

"It is. Besides the body will have been cleaned up by then. You might be able to identify the deceased." He closed his own notebook. "That will be all for now Mr Robel. You can go home."

As I was practically home already I just made my way to the flat via the stairs, the lift understandably out of action. Past the PC who was preventing anyone from leaving the building via the rear door. His colleague was on the main front door.

Inside what should have been my own domain I no longer felt like king. The security had been breached. I went around checking for signs of intruders careful not to leave any more of my prints than were already all over the place. It was odds on that whoever had been there had been wearing gloves. There didn't seem to be anything out of place, except the missing knife. Either a search of extremely professional proportions had been carried out or none at all. Doing housework only once a week, if that, tended to leave the place fairly dusty but as far as I could see none had been displaced. It seemed that the intruder had only been interested in obtaining the knife.

As usual I later discovered I was wrong about this. There had been another purpose but one that never would have occurred to me in a million years.

How an entry had been effected was a mystery. The door to the flat had two locks, a latch lock and a deadlock. They must have been picked. I had a close look and thought I could detect faint scratches although these may have been there before for all I knew. Still the intruder had to have used the door. I was three floors up and there was no outside fire escape. Not that it mattered how an entry had been gained, it had and the damage was done. I had also been done. Done up like a kipper, whatever that phrase was meant to mean. I had a lot of thinking to do but first two calls to make. Another attempt to reach Cox was called for but first I had to check on my erstwhile partner. I was hoping she wasn't going to end up my late partner.

Dialling Vicky's number, I had my doubts as to whether she would be there. We had parted company that morning at 11 o'clock and she had been anxious to get to the hospital. The phone was answered on the first ring.

"Hello!"

I thought I could detect a slight concern in her voice even in that one word. Maybe she was dreading any phone call on the assumption that it could be bad news about her father.

"It's me." A classic opening gambit in phone conversations. Perhaps it was a little egotistical of me to assume that she would recognise my voice after so short an association but I was the guy who was trying to save her father after all.

"Who's me?

"Tommy!" I was pained.

"Oh hi. What's up?"

"It's more a case of what's down and out," I corrected her. "Mind you I think you could say the balloon's gone up."

"What are you yabbering on about?"

"Our friendly but uncooperative circus performer."

"Chalky? What about him? I thought we both decided he wasn't about to change his mind? It's a dead end."

"He won't be changing his mind now," I confirmed. "He is a dead end, with the emphasis on DEAD."

"You are kidding? How do you know this?" She was sceptical.

"He turned up here."

"What at the office?"

"No, my flat."

"What for? How did he find you? I don't even know where you live."

Did she want to I wondered.

"I didn't get the chance to ask him," I informed her. "He'd already thrown off his mortal coil."

"What did he die of?"

"A foreign body," I replied. "A knife to be precise. In the chest."

"Oh God! Why would anyone want to kill him?"

"That's the $64,000 question," I said, not having the time to wonder whether in the States under such circumstances they had the £64,000 question. "As the knife came from my kitchen it may have been to set me up. If it was I can only think of one party that would need to. It would appear that the forces of the ungodly are onto me and if they are then they are on to you too."

She was already one street ahead. "But if they knew about Chalky, then ... "

"Precisely. They could be on to your father's scheme as well."

"No! I've got to go." And before I could utter another word she was gone.

Great, I thought, talk about wasted energy. Instead of putting her on alert and advocating prudence, caution and extreme care I had just set her into impulse mode. I hoped she realised that turning up to the office on Monday morning was not going to be a good career move.

My second call was even less productive. Cox was now off duty and not expected in until the next day. Oh golly gosh, I said sotto voce, or words to that effect. Tomorrow I had to be at the police station signing a false statement. Was it perjury to warrant with a signature an inaccurate account of factual matters? I thought it was only perjury if done under oath, or at least I hoped it was. Where was Perry Mason when you needed him?

I had some serious thinking to do. To tell the truth, the whole truth or nothing like the truth. It was a case of heads they won, tails I lost. If I told the truth I would have to own up about knowing Chalky and that I had only met him the same day as he'd been killed. The whole truth also meant admitting that a piece of my kitchen had been found in the victim. Even if I kept quiet about the knife it wouldn't take them long to find out it was mine. They would take my prints, for elimination purposes only, except instead of eliminating me they would totally incriminate me. The knife was either going to be wiped clean or just contain my own prints. My bet was the latter. Why go to such lengths to implicate me and then wipe my prints off the murder weapon? On the other hand, I hadn't been the last person to use the knife so there must be a set of smudges over my prints, the killer having without doubt used gloves.

There was also the fact that I had been on the ground floor waiting for the lift when Chalky's body had been dumped in on the third floor. We all knew that it had been done on the third floor and not the tenth otherwise the person who had called the lift to the third floor on its way down would have raised the alarm. Surely Perkins would see this. There was no way I could have done the deed and been on the ground floor awaiting the lift at the same time. The only way I could possibly have done it would have been to load the body into the lift on the tenth floor, push the third floor button so the lift stopped there and sprinted down the stairs to be waiting for the lift when it arrived. I don't think it could have been physically done, certainly not by myself, not even when I was young and fit.

The one point in my favour was that the lady that had fainted, who I had learnt was called Mrs Tilehurst, had only been a few paces behind me when I had parked my car, having fortuitously found a space in the car park, and walked into the building through the rear door. I had even held the door open for her. She could corroborate that I couldn't possibly have placed the body in the lift. If she ever got herself together that is. Surely the shock would subside and she would be able to give a clear account of events.

There would still be the knife to explain. Chalky had been in my flat or at least his killer had. How? Why? Had Chalky paid me a visit voluntarily? How had he found out where I lived? If he had changed his mind and decided to divulge the great plan he would have chosen Vicky. He would have known where she lived. It made no sense. Unless he had been forcibly escorted there with the express intention of framing me for his murder. Either way someone was on to me and that had to be Fairfax's UK cronies and/or his American representatives on location. They knew who I was and where I could be found. They had decided to take me out of the frame by putting me in one.

This meant that they had to be on to Vicky too. Would she be safe at the hospital? Would she even get there? That was out of my hands. I would ring up the hospital though, just to check, once enough time had elapsed for her to have reached there.

How had they got onto me? The same way as Vicky no doubt, gross inexperience and incompetence. The difference was she had actually spotted me spying on her father. Since then I had tailed Hobson just once, for five minutes, and he wasn't telling anyone anything. So either they had been watching Hobson because they didn't trust him and had noticed my interest in him or they were naturally suspicious and had followed Vicky and me when we left the office on Friday.

If someone had followed us the next morning, that was just that morning, then we would have led them to Chalky but they would not have been able to tie him in with Hobson's accident. Not unless they had Hobson's house bugged and picked up our conversation the night before. If so they knew everything and no one was safe.

The current situation though did not indicate that they did know everything. It was obvious they had no qualms about eliminating people so if one of us had been a real danger to them we would be dead by now. This frame up smacked of something else. Like removing a minor nuisance from the scene. If I was a small nuisance only, then they could not know my connection with Hobson and the case, or maybe they did. Say they knew I was on the case but were not worried that I would find anything out. Yet they may be concerned that with my inexpert bumbling I may just get in their way. Not reason enough to kill me. That would result in a police investigation which would lead to them through my files; correction, file singular. It would be better for them to remove me from the picture some other way. Some way totally unconnected with Fairfax Inc.

That sat better. But why Chalky? Had we been under surveillance that morning? And if we had which party did the ungodly think they were keeping their eye on? The daughter of their pawn and her boyfriend, in other words, keeping a casual eye on Hobson's family to ensure nothing went awry, or the guy whose investigating could prove to be a nuisance and had to be dealt with one way or another? It had to be the former. Whilst I had been seen by Montford when I had collected Vicky from the office the previous day, as far as I was aware that was the first time he'd seen me and my surname had not been spoken.

Yet if they believed that I was merely the subject of Miss Hobson's affections why all this? They had to know who I was or killing Chalky and laying the blame on me made no sense at all. The only reason I could see that Chalky was in that winged circus in the sky was because he had spoken to me that morning. He was only dead because one of the parties he had spoken to was a danger to them. Other than Vicky he was probably the only other person they had seen me with. Also he was ideal for their purposes as he had no connection to Fairfax UK at all. The perfect person to keep me occupied.

All this meant that they knew me by sight and would also know I was in league with Vicky. What they may not know at this stage was whether she knew who I was. They may have believed I was undercover, trying to get closer to my subject. That must be the reason they had left Vicky alone so far.

There was only one other alternative, daft though it sounded, and that was Chalky had found his own way to my flat somehow and surprised the forces of the ungodly at the scene. Now I was going around in circles. How had Chalky found me? Nothing but unanswered questions and dangerous assumptions. Just like a join the dots puzzle only without the dots. I had to get from A to B with nothing in between. No known facts anyway. I was working with one assumption on top of another. Going in circles was right. Ever increasing circles.

A sound even rarer than a ringing phone interrupted my thoughts. The buzzer heralded a visitor wanting admittance to the building. Not necessarily anyone to see me, probably a neighbour who had locked himself out. I lifted the intercom handset to see who had buzzed the wrong flat when to my surprise the caller announced himself as Cox. I pressed the door release button a much relieved person.

"What have you been up to now?" was his greeting as I opened the door a minute later.

"Not a lot," I replied. "However, it might take a long time to prove it. You'd better sit down."

"OK. Shoot." A rather unfortunate choice of word in the circumstances or it would have been if Chalky had been shot and not knifed.

"Well," I began, sitting also, "a funny thing happened to me on the way to the circus." And I related the events that had brought me to that current state of affairs, on a need to know basis of course. Those facts that he needed to know to be of assistance in my present predicament. I told him I was on a case but not in too much depth. I then told him about the body. Then came the tricky bit. How to own up to knowing the identity of the body when I had already informed his fellow officer that I didn't. Cox gave me no time to think on it.

"So do you know who the dead man is?"

"Well, at first it never clicked but maybe I do," I admitted. "Only this morning, when I was helping somebody out, I met a guy called Chalky. He was a clown at a circus but he wasn't made up when I met him. That's why I didn't make the connection right away. I couldn't say for definite but it's a bit of a coincidence."

"Too much of a coincidence it seems to me," observed Cox thoughtfully. "Exactly what time did you discover the body?"

"3.17."

"And you put in the call to me at 3.24. Why?"

I knew what he was getting at. If I'd only just realised the possible connection between the victim and myself why had I needed his help so drastically that I placed an immediate call to him?

"I preferred to deal with someone I knew."

"For a witness statement?" asked Cox, sceptically. "I don't think so. I think you knew it as soon as you saw him. After all it's not every day that one meets a clown. Knowing this you tried to make immediate contact with me. You'd better come clean. I cannot help you if you don't.

"Alright." I gave in. It was excrement or bust time. "Yes, I knew who it was. I mean I guessed. Until all that stuff is off his face I couldn't swear to it."

"So you knew if the connection between yourself and the victim came out you would be Number One suspect." It was a statement not a question.

"It's worse than that. A lot worse." I swallowed hard. My mouth and throat had suddenly turned as dry as a particularly arid desert. "I think the knife is mine. I didn't touch it but there is one missing from my kitchen." Cox was silent, staring directly at me. "It's a frame up," I protested, arms open wide in appeal.

Cox was silent for a few moments longer, during which time I wished I was somewhere less complicated, like one of the more surreal episodes of 'The Prisoner'.

Finally he spoke.

"Why? Is it connected to this case you're working on?"

"I don't know. It might be," I conceded. "This guy Chalky wasn't directly involved with the case. Hardly indirectly either. He was the solution to a parallel problem."

"What exactly is this case about?" Cox wanted to know.

"I can't really say at this moment in time," I informed him. "However, I can say that it is more in the manner of preventive action. No crime has been committed ... " The 'yet' died in my throat.

"Other than murder," Cox commented drily.

"If the murder turns out to be connected," I pointed out. "I've been getting a headache thinking about this current turn of events and I cannot tie it up with anything to do with the case. It makes no sense to me."

"How can I make any useful comments if you won't tell me everything?"

"I can't give you the details of the actual case. Client confidentiality and all that." Not that I felt my client merited any such trust but if I alerted the police their own enquiries would send the ungodly to ground. Or worse, make them even more ruthless. Despite not having much of a life I was still very much attached to it. Yet I knew I had to cough up something. "I will tell you everything except for the specifics of the case."

Satisfied with this, at least for the time being, Cox told me to proceed with the story. I'd already told him in my previous briefer explanation that I had been employed to watch someone. I now told him how I made a mess of it and was caught by the daughter of the person I was supposed to be watching. I didn't tell him about the gun in case someone in authority decided to revoke the licence. One never knew, I might be glad of Vicky's armament one day. One day soon the way things were going. I told him about the car accident and Hobson's loss of memory, not though giving him the name. It would achieve nothing implicating Chalky in the accident so I omitted that part. The visit to Chalky was easily explained. As no person from his recent past had jogged Hobson's memory his daughter had thought an old pal from the distant past might do the trick. I explained about Chalky being Hobson's ex-partner but not in what. I told Cox all this and hoped it would be enough.

"So in essence you were employed to keep an eye on someone on the assumption he might be up to no good. You were found out by his daughter, teamed up with her to prove his innocence and ended up trying to restore his memory after an accident?" Cox succinctly summed it up.

"That's about right," I agreed.

"Then this clown, Chalky, who you met for the first time today turns up dead in your building with your knife in his chest?"

"Unfortunately."

"How is it I feel you're holding something back?" Cox asked suspiciously.

"Only the specific details of the case," I stressed. "Actual names and such. Surely you can see it's not connected?"

"Maybe, maybe not."

Cox rose from his seat and wandered to the window. He gazed out over the car park busy with his thoughts. "What if," he continued, after a few seconds, "this guy you are watching is mixed up in what he's suspected of? Maybe someone doesn't want his memory restored."

"Enough to kill for it? And why involve me? It's his daughter who would be pushing more for that."

"I cannot say yet. I've not had time to digest this."

In a knowledge of just a few minutes he had probably come up with what it had taken my hours to deduce. A great big fat nothing. However, it turned out that I was doing Cox an injustice as his next comments displayed his quickness of thought.

"Number one," he began. "As you only met this fellow

Chalky for the first time today I would say that you were followed. Two. If someone was keeping tabs on you then in view of the outcome I would say it was some person or persons who do not have your welfare at heart. Three. From the little I know there are two parties who could wish you ill. Either the people involved with the person you have under surveillance are on to you and want you out of the way or perhaps there is a connection to the previous caper you were involved in."

This latter possibility was something I had not even contemplated at all. It proved one thing. Cox was certainly better able to think along criminal lines than I was. He was on their wavelength.

"I hadn't thought of that," I had to admit. "But if it is revenge why just frame me for someone else's murder? Why not kill me?"

"Maybe somebody wants you to suffer for a long time rather than experiencing a brief moment of pleasure themselves by snuffing you out." Cox was deadly serious. "Either way you're in a right mess."

He was telling me. Why did he think I'd rung him in the first place? When one is being welcomed into the arms of the mother of all quicksands you want someone to pull you out. "Heh, do you know you are sinking" is the last thing you want to hear.

"There is another possibility." It was one that had only just occurred to me. It was unlikely but I decided to air it anyway. "What if I'm not the victim here just the scapegoat. Maybe Chalky had enemies and one of them saw me as the perfect patsy to take the fall. Maybe they were keeping tabs on him and spotted me meeting with him today. What better way to confuse the police. Frame someone who the murder victim had met for the first time that day and had no connection with the murderer."

"Anything is possible," said Cox. "It gives us three lines of enquiry but doesn't help you right now."

"What do I do?" I wasn't actually on my knees wringing my hands together but he knew I was pleading for his help.

"To tell you the truth I haven't got the foggiest idea," Cox owned up. "It's more than my job is worth to conceal evidence. Not that I could anyway. We have the body and the knife. It will not take long to make the connection once enquiries are under way. The best way is to come clean and rely on the things in your favour."

"Such as?" I enquired, all ears, for there was scant little on my side as far as I could see.

"Motive and opportunity," he replied. "There is no motive. Further, if this witness corroborates your story that she followed you from the car park that will prove you didn't have the opportunity. That is provided the autopsy confirms the time of death as just before you found him. Otherwise you could have done the deed earlier and got an accomplice to dump the body at a time when you could build an alibi.

"I personally know you didn't do it. I can give you a character reference for what it's worth. Then things will depend on the knife. Either it will be completely clean or your prints alone will be on it. I would bet upon the latter. No point in using your knife and wiping the prints off."

"But wouldn't there be smudges over my prints if the killer wore gloves?"

"Could be. Depends how inventive he was?"

Things didn't look too good for me. This was the equivalent of throwing myself on the mercy of the court.

"What if I wrote out my statement here and gave it to you," I suggested. "Then I wouldn't need to visit the station."

"Yes you would," Cox disagreed. "You have to view the body and you have to admit that you knew the victim. Always presuming it does turn out to be this Chalky. In addition I would be obliged to disclose what you told me about the knife. The fact that you offered this information voluntarily will sit well on your side."

My face must have been a picture. It was with increasing alarm that I could see my cry for help would be in vain.

"Don't worry too much," said Cox. "Honesty is the best policy, as we policemen like to say. There is enough in your favour.

Especially the timing. The fact that you discovered the body in the lift has upset someone's plans I feel. If your witness is any good it will prove you cannot have been in two places at once."

There was silence for a few moments. I was too deep in dread thoughts and Cox was no doubt postponing the inevitable. Eventually he said it though.

"We'd better go to the station now and get this over with." He looked at me and shrugged resignedly. There was no doubting his expression. He wanted to help and would where he could but he couldn't grant me any special favours.

In his car we travelled to my date with destiny. On the way there was not much discussion. What Cox was thinking about I couldn't guess. Me? I was too busy with my despair. All thoughts of the case, Hobson, Vicky and the ungodly had been swept from my mind. I felt like the French aristocrat travelling to the final meeting with Madame La Guillotine, only I knew there was no Scarlet Pimpernel to save me.

Things could not have been any worse. A phrase that should be banned from the English language. As it turned out events thus far had been as jolly as a Famous Five outing: Stephen King was to follow.

# CHAPTER 11

"I'm late! I'm late!"

"For a very important date?" I suggested.

"Precisely," said the White Rabbit, consulting his pocket watch.

I laughed. "Even he can get a date," I thought to myself. He took no offence but sped off into the distance. I laughed again. "I'm in Wonderland. I wonder where Alice is?" This wasn't the Wonderland I'd read about though. There was deep snow on the ground. Soon I couldn't see the White Rabbit's tail bobbing up and down any more for it had merged into the landscape. I looked up. Fluffy white clouds floated in the sky. They seemed low. Looking ahead again a white dust cloud was visible and it was coming my way.

All of a sudden I was scared. The whiteness was closing in on me. The clouds were lower now, almost completely blocking out the blue of the sky. The dust cloud was getting closer. I wanted to run but my feet would not move. On looking down I saw they were buried in the snow. Also I was dressed all in white. In panic I pulled up my jeans and sighed with relief as I saw the tops of my red socks, but they changed before my eyes. Oh no! White socks!

The whiteness was closer, all enveloping. The sky had gone, snow was up to my knees and the dust cloud was almost upon me. Except it was no longer a cloud. It was a white knight charging on a white horse, or was that galloping on a white charger. Either way he was not alone. On his right was a white elephant with gleaming white tusks. On his left was my friend the White Rabbit but he'd changed though. He was now at least eight feet tall and hopping in great leaps. It's Harvey, I thought nervously, although he certainly wasn't invisible. And behind them there were hundreds of rabbits, elephants and horses, all white, all hopping, trumpeting and galloping in my direction until they all merged into one massive white blob bearing down on me. I tried to figure out why but my mind was like cotton wool, white and fluffy. I opened my mouth to cry out but nothing emerged and the whiteness swallowed me up. Damn Danny Baker and his Daz Doorstep Challenge. These whiter than white whites had a lot to answer for.

I opened my eyes. The whiteness was still there. I closed my eyes again to shut out the white. Why was everything so white? My mind was blank. After a while I opened them again, surely things would be OK now. Everything was far from all right for everything was still all white. I just lay and stared at the whiteness, willing it to go away but it didn't.

There can be few people who have not at one time or the other awoken from their slumber to realise that they don't know where they are. And I don't mean those waking up after an all-night session of booze or drugs. Or those waking up in a strange bed because they can't remember picking up the stranger beside them the night before. No, I mean those occasions when the eyes are open but the mind is floating somewhere in the oblivion between the conscious and subconscious parts of the brain. It only lasts a short time, mere seconds, and usually on awakening in unfamiliar surroundings for the first time, not necessarily after a passionate one night stand, certainly not in my case.

That was how it was with me on that particular morning. As I lay staring at the whiteness, waiting for my mind to catch up with my body, it seemed that the whiteness wasn't as white as white but more a dirty cream colour. Suddenly, my mind had travelled the void to full awareness bringing with it the harsh facts of reality. I now wished it had stayed where it was.

I was wide awake now but somehow it did not matter. There was no need for me to sit up and survey the scene for it was etched on my memory. A seven by four foot space. Yellowing white paint on the walls, ceiling, floor and door. One hard-backed chair, a tiny table, a bunk bed and a jerry can. I knew where I was. Even with full blown amnesia I would have known. The bars on the windows and the small opening in the door were a dead give-away. I was a guest of Her Majesty.

In prison! Me! Who had never so much as dropped a piece of litter in the street let alone had a parking ticket. For the thirteenth time I rued the day I made the decision to leave the safety of employment to embark on the downward spiral of self-employment. Unlike the other times there was no self-pity, there were others to worry about. Vicky, her father and maybe Jenny too. They were all connected to me and I was in the proverbial, not just up to me neck either, I needed a snorkel.

To say I was in such a predicament through no fault of my own would probably have been stretching the truth a little too far. I was, however, innocent of the charges laid against my door but the frame was neat and secure, like that around a Constable landscape. I was guilty though, of a lack of foresight and the exercising of care. I had walked right into the neatly spun web with about as much suspicion as a victim of 'This Is Your Life'. It had been quick, efficient and unfortunately as watertight as a duck's rear end after an application of Thompson's Waterseal. Drug trafficking and murder tend to be taken very seriously, hence my current abode.

I went over the events in my mind and even with hindsight, I could see no way that I could have acted any differently. I could hardly believe it was less than a week since Mrs F had tripped into my office. So much seemed to have happened in such a short period of time. My first and highly likely final case, Hobson, Vicky, the car accident, Hobson's amnesia and Chalky's murder. Funnily enough it was the latter I was worried about at the time in question. I had been worrying too early.

On that Saturday, the trip to the police station had seemed as far to the bottom as I could travel. Things were grimmer than a Grimm fairy tale without the happy ending. I should have been more optimistic for there was more to come. However, first came the calm in the storm before the hurricane, which lulled me into a false sense of security.

First, I was left for a while in a room with only a mute P.C. for company. I assumed Cox was explaining the situation. It didn't take that long before someone appeared. It wasn't Cox. "I understand that you have not been entirely honest with us, Sir," Pinky announced. "Would you come with me please?"

I remained as quiet as a monastery mouse. I didn't know how much Cox had disclosed and whether D.S. Pink was trying to trip me up. The person we went to see had also taken a vow of silence, involuntarily of course, it was Chalky. Cleaned up now he was how I remembered him from our brief meeting. Hard to believe but it was less than twelve hours ago. Time flies when you're being done.

Perkins was there. "Is this the man you knew as Chalky?"

"Yes!" Accompanying this acknowledgement with a nod of the head.

"Right! We're going to have a nice little chat and I would appreciate the full story this time."

"Where's D.I. Cox?" I needed to know how much he had said.

"This is not his case," Pinky pointed out abruptly. "Come on!"

I found myself back in the room I had recently vacated. The P.C. had gone but Pinky and Perky were both present, which left me piggy in the middle.

"From the beginning please," Perky requested as I resumed my seat.

So I started again from the discovery of the body and basically reiterated what I had stated before, but it wasn't going to be that easy. Whilst there were no actual discrepancies, there were areas of clarification that needed to be addressed.

"Mr Robel. In your initial statement you did not mention that you knew the identity of the victim. Why was that?"

"At the time I didn't," I replied, in what I hoped was a totally innocent tone.

"But you have just correctly identified him."

"Yes. Now he's had all that muck removed from his face."

"Then tell me, Mr Robel, how did you come to know the

victim?"

This was one of the crucial areas and I had to tread carefully. As careful as a clogged Amsterdamer picking his tulips.

"I met him for the one and only time this morning."

"Where was this?"

"At the circus where he works ... er ... worked."

"And how did you come to be there?"

"Oh, I was just there with a friend who went to see him." I tried to sound flippant. "I was there in a purely observational capacity only."

"This friend being?"

"Is that really necessary?" This was really a rhetorical question. I knew that he would need to check out any acquaintances of the dead man, even brand new ones, and I knew that he knew that I knew. But did he know that I knew that he knew that I knew?

Apparently so as he did not deign to answer.

"Miss Victoria Hobson," I owned up.

"Address?" So I gave it. "And why was Miss Hobson so keen to see the victim?"

"I never said she was keen," I pointed out.

"The question still stands," said Perky.

There was no choice but to tell the truth. If I lied and Cox had disclosed the reason for the visit I was going to be in even more trouble. "Well, it was a bit of a nutty idea if you ask me. Rather a long shot." Raised eyebrows only. "Her father has amnesia," I continued. "She thought that someone from his distant past might jog his memory."

"So Miss Hobson's father was a friend of the victim?"

"I wouldn't go as far as to say that. I believe they used to work together, some years ago."

"So it is your contention that when you saw the victim in the lift you did not recognise him. You did not know it was the man that you'd met only hours earlier?"

"No ... er ... I mean yes. I didn't know who it was at the time."

"Yet you saw him only that morning?" Perky was disbelieving. "You knew he was a clown I take it?"

I nodded glumly.

"So you encounter a dead clown and did not connect this to the other clown you had met that day."

Words were not going to help so I just nodded again.

"Just how many clowns do you know?" demanded Pinky. A bit late I thought to take the role of bad cop.

Depends on your definition of clown, I mused. A couple of new acquaintances in authority might qualify. "Only Chalky."

"Now, after finding the body, you are positive you did not touch either it or the murder weapon?" Perky changed tack trying no doubt to trip me up.

"Definitely not! I never even set foot in the lift."

"So you never touched the knife?"

"No!" I had to make a quick decision and hope I jumped the right way. "However...."

"Yes!" Perky had perked up.

I swallowed hard. "I didn't know at the time but there is a knife missing from my kitchen." I looked directly into his eyes but he just returned the stare. "It was of a similar type," I added.

"And just when did you happen to discover this?" Pink demanded, sarcasm paramount in his voice.

"Not until later. It's not something you think about, is it?" A little bit of sarcasm crept into my voice. "Oh, look, a dead person. And what a nice knife. You know, I've got one just like that. I wonder ... "

"There is no need for dramatics," said Perky. "This is a serious matter."

Pinky wasn't as sympathetic. "And you're in it up to your neck. If you didn't already know." Bad cop coming up on the rails.

I, of course, did know but I hadn't known how much they knew. Their act had been quite convincing but they had made a slip. Not enough surprise about the knife, ergo they already knew of it. Cox must have told them everything so it was important that I corroborated what he had told them by doing the same.

"I'm sorry." There was no point in antagonising them. That wouldn't have got me anywhere except maybe a night in a cell. "It's just that you're treating me like the prime suspect. I discovered the body. I couldn't have done the dirty deed and been in place to discover the body." My hands were wide in appeal. "There was a witness," I reminded them.

They chose to ignore this, which was worrying as I had no idea if my neighbour, such being a relative term as she lived on another floor, had backed up my story.

"Now!" Perky getting back on track. "This knife taken from your flat. Were there any signs of a break-in?"

"Not really," I had to admit. "I would have reported it if there had been. There are some scratches around the lock though, if you look closely."

"Very convenient," was Pinky's view.

Perky ignored him. "So apart from the missing knife you would not have known that there had been an intruder?"

"Correct," I affirmed. "And if I hadn't seen one like it earlier I would not have even thought of an intruder. I would have just assumed I had mislaid it."

Then I got a real surprise. Perky arose from his position opposite and declared, "That will be all for now. However, you will have to remain here for a while." He motioned to Pinky with his head who made as if to follow him out of the room.

"Oh! Just one more thing." Perky turned at the door. "Why did you ring D.I. Cox and not dial 999 like anyone else?"

Not a question I had been expecting but it should have occurred to me that it would be asked. The local boys would want to know why I had recruited my own help. I doubted whether the response would make much difference to the state of affairs. "Because I had dealt with him before. Better the devil you know."

"It was a good job someone else had the common sense to ring the emergency services." As a parting shot it left me no wiser as to how I stood in his eyes. With this he was gone, Pinky in his wake. Immediately P.C. Mute was back.

I sat there for a good while, and paced about for a good while more, until Pinky returned. "You can go now," he said. He didn't seem too happy about the prospect and tried to cheer himself up by adding, "I wouldn't go too far though. We'll be wanting to see you again."

Minutes later I was being driven back home by a strangely silent Cox. It seemed as though he was reluctant to divulge anything, at least voluntarily, so it was up to me to ask.

"What now?"

"Now you stay out of trouble," he answered. "You've been lucky so far. Don't push it."

"What do you mean lucky?" I snorted. "I'm prime suspect in a murder enquiry. How is that lucky?"

"You're not inside, are you? You could be. They had enough to hold you, certainly for forty-eight hours."

I was slightly taken aback. "They never even took my fingerprints."

"You think not," grinned Cox. "Did you get a cup of coffee?"

I thought of the small plastic cup and wondered why they would bother with such subterfuge when they could have taken my prints legitimately. This was more like TV than TV itself.

"What's going on," I demanded to know.

"They will be checking on your story," came the reply.

Which meant questioning Vicky, and I wanted to keep her out of it. I hoped this wasn't going to alert the ungodly that their frame was not yet secure, they might then try something more permanent. "How much did you tell them?" I asked.

"All of it."

"Every last thing?"

"Everything," Cox confirmed. "Or at least as much as you told me."

I should have felt relief at not being locked in a cell but I didn't. The police – I never referred to them as pigs although with names like Pinky and Perky it was hard not to - would be questioning the Hobsons and the ungodly would soon hear of it. If it were the latter who had set me up I could be lucky because to have been able to do so they would have had to have seen Vicky and me together at the circus. Therefore, they would not be unduly suspicious if Vicky were questioned by the police; in fact it would be expected. However, it would upset the finely balanced apple cart as her parents would probably also find out, depending on the tact shown by the police, although obviously Hobson himself would not be able to react to it. I wondered whether Mrs Hobson would buy the story. Maybe. She would be as eager as anyone to see him recover. I hoped Pinky and Perky were going to be discreet in their enquiries. If the ungodly did not already know I was an investigator I didn't want them to find out third hand. Of course, if they didn't know then in all probability they had not set me up, which left Chalky's enemies or my old one.

In the final analysis all this conjecture was useless until I heard what actually had taken place. It was as pointless as one of King Henry's VIII's wives worrying about dandruff. All I could do was warn Vicky and see what developed, always supposing that the ungodly had not taken action against her too.

Cox dropped me outside my building and drove off, saying he would be in touch if he heard anything and warning me to keep my head down. The first thing I did in spite of the early hour on Sunday morning was ring Vicky's number, hoping that the phone would not be answered by her mother. It wasn't. After the opening pleasantries such as "What the hell do you mean by ringing me at this ungodly hour?" I ploughed on with my information, noting silently her appropriate use of the adjective to describe the hour.

"So expect a call or visit from Perkins and or Pink any time tomorrow," I eventually finished.

"I think I had better stay here until they arrive," suggested Vicky. "There are too many people at the hospital who do not need to know about this."

"My sentiments precisely," I agreed, glad that she saw

things from my point of view.

"Yes! I don't want to cause Mother any more grief and we don't want to alert the watcher."

OK, she didn't see it from exactly my view. Still my prime concern was to extract myself from the extremely tangled web I had woven, her goals were different.

There was not much else to say and we soon broke the connection.

As it turned out I never found out what happened until much later and by that time it mattered as little as not having a washing up liquid bottle when watching Blue Peter on the day they were using sticky back plastic. Things were beginning to career out of control faster than a novice skier on the piste. In other words it was downhill all the way.

# CHAPTER 12

That all seemed such a long time ago, in another time, so far detached from it did I feel in that depressing cell. They had taken my watch away so I had no idea what the time was. A calculated action to keep me off balance. The passing of time is strangely comforting, particularly if it is approaching clocking off time, and to be deprived of this can be disorientating. This was probably something someone was hoping for.

Everything was as quiet as the grave, my grave. There was nothing to hear and nothing to see. It was inevitable therefore that my mind drifted back to earlier events, those events which were, to use an insurance expression, the proximate cause of my incarceration.

The start of the slippery slope was a phone call that woke me on that same Sunday morning before I had even taken one wink far less forty. I figured it had to be urgent, either that or it was Vicky getting her own back, so I jumped out of bed to answer it. I'd always wondered what an anonymous caller sounded like. "If you want to know who set you up be outside the Town Hall at 6.00am," announced a deep, gruff voice. "Come alone."

"Who is that," was the classic response but Billygoat Gruff had hung up.

I was on the horns of a dilemma and it was jolly painful. Did I go, possibly walking into another carefully laid trap for the completely obtuse? Did I call Cox for reinforcements? Did I call Vicky and take another earful? In the end I decided to bite the bullet. I doubted whether at that time on a Sunday morning I would be able to reach Cox in time and, of course, as a veteran of numerous cop shows I knew instinctively what to do, turn up early and keep watch on the spot I was supposed to wait to see if I could see who would be waiting for me to get there. This meant leaving straight away. Two freezing hours later, one surveying where I was due to be, one waiting on the spot, and I had had enough. Returning home I knew I had been taken in again. The reason took no great feat of cranial power. Someone wanted me out of my flat for a while. I soon found out why.

They were waiting for me when I arrived. Not outside the flat but inside, sitting there as cool as you please. I might as well have had a revolving door for all the good locks did me.

"Who the hell are you and what the hell are you doing in my flat?" I demanded in outrage.

"Waiting for you," replied the tall thin man with dark hair and moustache, dark piercing eyes and a cruel mouth. I would have placed him in his late forties. "Let me introduce ourselves," he continued. "This is Detective Sergeant Cummins and I am Detective Inspector Bristow."

"All very nice," I said, acidly, "but what right does it give you to break in to my flat?"

"Does it look like we broke in?" asked Cummins, as tall as Bristow but broader with blond hair, blue eyes and unbelievably an honest face. "We merely effected an entry." Not the strong silent type I had pegged him for.

"Which we have the power to do if we think a crime has been committed," Bristow embellished.

"And what crime would that be?" Surely not the murder rap already. There had not been sufficient time to corroborate my story.

"You've been a busy boy haven't you?" Cummins wagged his finger.

"We know about the murder yesterday," Bristow informed me.

It hardly seemed like yesterday to me. "I was framed."

"So you say, and for now you are being given the benefit of the doubt on that." Cummins was taking the harder line. For a double act this was better than Pinky and Perky. "Do you want to do the honours, Sir or shall I?"

"Be my guest, Sergeant."

"Do you know this man?" Cummins asked me, drawing a

photo from his inside pocket with all the dexterity of Wyatt Earp on speed. Said photo portraying a thin weasel of a man with dark greasy hair in a dirty raincoat.

"No idea! Is he a flasher?"

"Don't get funny," he warned me. "This is, or should I say was, Leslie Knox, a well-known junkie. A clever one though, for although we busted him for possession a few times we could never locate his supplier."

"Until now that is," Bristow added with menace.

I didn't like the way he looked at me as he said that. In fact I never liked the way people in authority looked at me but in this instance I didn't think I was being overly paranoid. I have never professed to be fey but I would have bet my non-existent pension that there was big trouble on the way and it was nearer than just around the corner. And trouble was the last thing I needed; I had more than enough already. I was attracting it better than Wyatt A. Lottatroubles, the Trouble Magnet Supreme of the Trouble Annual Fair, Troublesville, County Trouble. There was nothing like a Blackadderism to make one feel better. Not this time.

"We found Knox's body yesterday evening," Bristow informed me.

"Oh?"

"And we found your name and number on his person," Cummins embellished with relish. "On a well-used scrap of paper."

"I've told you, I've never met the guy!" What was supposed to be a calm denial came out as a high pitch wail.

"He died of a lethal dose of heroin." Cummins acted as though he had not heard me.

"Well, you won't find an aspirin here," stated I with the utmost confidence.

The trouble with confidence is that when it is at its utmost it turns out to be completely misplaced.

"We didn't," confirmed Bristow.

"We found this instead." Cummins was doing his gunslinger bit again, whipping a polythene bag of white powder out of his other inside pocket. It could have been sugar, salt or flour, but somehow I figured not. "And this," ambidextrously drawing another bag containing hypodermic needles.

"In the toilet cistern," added Bristow. "Not a very clever hiding place."

"It's been planted!" I croaked in shock. "On my life I've never seen that stuff before." If I had been angry I was now downright terrified.

"We also found this." Bristow stood up, handing me a ledger book that he had been sat on. "Perhaps you would care to have a browse through it, although I'm sure you will be familiar with its contents. It seems Knox was behind in his payments."

The book was about half full, with names, dates and amounts in a neat hand. I just stared at the last used page because I was about as incapable of speech as a Trappist Monk with no vocal cords. I couldn't believe my eyes. The handwriting was mine. I sat there mesmerised, gazing at the entries I had never seen before yet in a hand indistinguishable from my own. I felt as though the walls were closing in on me as surely as the walls of a prison cell would surely do. I thought I had been framed before but the murder of Chalky had just been a mere teaser. Now I had fallen beautifully into a trap of flawless manufacture and as far as I could see there was no way out. The position was hopeless. The Spice Girls, as yet unknown until later that year, had more chance of overtaking Elvis in all-time record sales. Still I had to try.

"I don't believe it! I have never seen this book before in my life. And yet ... " I was at a loss for words.

"The writing is yours?" asked Bristow.

"Yes," I agreed before I could stop myself. "That is it bears a striking resemblance to mine but I can assure you that it isn't."

"I would say it bore more than a resemblance," Cummins observed. "We have checked samples of your own handwriting and the entries tally to the last dotted 'i'."

"I don't know what to say. I just don't understand it."

"Oh, come off it!" Cummins was getting annoyed. "You can't

get out of this and you know it."

"For Christ's sake," I bellowed. "Call yourselves policemen. You wouldn't suspect a set-up if you yourselves were the victims." I paused to take a deep breath. I'd never played poker but knew that I was trying a king-sized bluff although the outburst was only partly an act. I was tired of being done up like a kipper and I was fed up with their Punch and Judy act.

"Just think logically for a moment," I continued. "One. If I was going to run a drugs ring I wouldn't do it from my own living room. Two. Even if I did I definitely wouldn't be so stupid as to keep an incriminating record of illegal transactions. Three. If I was going to write off a bad debt I would check his pockets to make sure nothing could lead back to me. Three good reasons for looking past the obvious to try and find the truth. Given time I could probably think of more."

"Very succinctly put," admired Bristow. "But tell me, if this is all a put up job to incriminate an innocent person, as you claim yourself to be, what do you think, as such an innocent person, you have done to merit such unwanted attention as a set-up like this would require?"

"I haven't got a clue," I replied and in truth I hadn't. I was getting way out of my depth. This frame indicated an efficient, smooth running organisation of the first degree. "Whoever it is they don't like me and they're good."

"My thoughts exactly," agreed Bristow to my astonishment.

My face must have been a picture. My bluff had worked. Maybe I should start playing poker. Or was it a counter bluff.

Cummins was grinning.

"I don't think you've been entirely frank with us," Bristow carried on. "However, I think I know why. Let me tell you what we know so far. Please sit."

We all sat. Bristow and Cummins on the two seater sofa and me on the only other piece of sitting furniture, my piano stool.

"Firstly, you will be relieved to know that we do not believe you murdered Knox," began Bristow. "We thought it funny that he had that piece of paper on him. If he had been knocked off by his supplier, as you say, he would not have left this bit of paper pointing a finger at him. So we were left with two scenarios. Either it was a false trail or he had been killed for some other reason."

"That was before we found the stuff here," Cummins intervened.

"Yes. We had to check the lead out. It didn't take us long to find something. It was too easy especially having the record as well. We did check the handwriting from various bits lying around and as you saw it is identical. On face value we had you bang to rights."

"What changed your minds?" Now out of immediate danger of incarceration I was curious.

"A couple of things. We had already checked you out as soon as we found the name on the paper. We learnt of yesterday's happenings and spoke to your friend D.I. Cox. He was sure you were being set-up. In fact he felt this new twist could all be part of the same frame."

"Then there were a couple of other points that we discovered ourselves," Cummins supplemented. Now that he was not being accusing he was positively friendly.

"Such as?"

"Such as the footprint in the bathroom."

I must have looked puzzled. "Someone had split powder on the bathroom carpet," explained Bristow.

"Athlete's Foot Powder. I dropped the container this morning." I was losing track of time. "I mean yesterday, Saturday morning." An age ago when things were much simpler and there had been two more people in the world.

"No matter," smiled Bristow. "What is important is the print that was left. The tread didn't match any footwear we could find here but of course you could well have been wearing them. However, we did not need to wait until you got back to know something was afoot, if you will excuse the pun. All the footwear we could find were size 10."

"What big feet you have," joked Cummins.

"Goes with the big nose," I said.

"Lucky for you," pointed out Bristow. "The footprint in the bathroom is about an 8 or maybe 9. I'm not sure. What I am sure is that it is too small for a 10. We measured it to make sure. A person with a small foot can make a bigger print by wearing larger shoes but someone with big feet cannot leave a smaller print"

"Unless it was put there on purpose of course." Cummins liked to have his input.

My thoughts exactly. A size 8 would fit a hand.

"In this case there was no reason for a deliberately placed footprint," resumed Bristow. "If the person or persons planting evidence wanted to make it they would have used one of your own shoes. If you were really guilty then why would you create such evidence? To throw us? But you wouldn't know we were on our way and if you did you would have just removed the drugs. No! It has to have been left there by the person who planted the drugs."

"I've never been so glad to have large appendages," I announced almost happily, a great weight not exactly lifted but certainly supported by more than my own shoulders. "What was the other thing?"

"Another kind of print."

"A fingerprint?" That would be even more conclusive.

"Forefinger and thumb to be precise," Cummins informed me.

"This person obviously wore gloves except at one point," explained Bristow. "This being the time he placed his evidence in the toilet system. He obviously didn't want to get his gloves wet. We have the prints where he held the neck of the polythene bag when he placed it in the water."

"They were not great prints," said Cummins, " but good enough to eliminate yours which are all over this place."

"So you mean to tell me that you've been playing me along ever since I walked in the door." My voice was quiet and slow.

I was trying to keep a lid on my fast emerging anger which was replacing the relief that had taken place of the initial fear. I was totally fed up with being messed about and having my time wasted. "Was it you lot who took me off on a wild goose chase, standing around freezing for two hours."

"Regrettable but necessary I'm afraid," stated Bristow. It was about as near to an apology as I was going to get. "We got a tip but because of what Cox told us we wanted to check first. You gave us three hours but even so we had to do a rush job. We kept you on the spot to make you reveal everything you knew but as it happens you've not told us more than we knew already."

"OK! So you know I've been framed. What happens now?"

Cummins did not answer this time. It seemed now that we were on the same side the double act was suspended.

"That depends entirely on you," Bristow smiled. "You're obviously a threat to someone. This is the second incident in twenty-four hours."

"Less actually," I pointed out.

"Still, if you won't tell us what you're working on there is not a lot we can do."

"Well, Cox knows most of it. I'm sure he briefed you when you contacted him. I have no more to tell you. It's a starting point for probably Chalky's murder and this. I'll leave it up to you what to do about it." My cover must have been shattered to itsy bitsy teeny weeny yellow polka dot molecules by now.

"Right, we'll make a deal," offered Bristow. "As of yet we have no real evidence against anyone for either the murders or the drugs so we won't muddy the waters and queer your patch. However, if we get any real evidence we'll move in. That's our part of the deal. Now, if you turn up the identity of the killers you inform us immediately, regardless of the consequences to your case. Agreed?"

"It's a deal. If I turn up the murderer he's all yours." And they were welcome to him, or them, I was fast getting out of my depth.

Soon after, Bristow and Cummins left. I knew I had not heard the end of the matter and no doubt would see them again in the near future. As usual I was wrong. I never saw Cummins again as he was shot dead outside his home. An attempt was made on Bristow too but he apparently escaped and had disappeared, presumably to save his own skin. I was not aware of these incidents until later and not until much later did I realise that they were as a result of what I was involved in.

What I did realise was that I was still in trouble, real trouble. The kind that twists your guts with fear and leaves you wishing you were on your maiden flight down the Cresta Run instead. It dawned on me all too soon. I'd gone back to bed to try getting some sleep but I was obviously destined for sleep deprivation.

The trouble arrived in the form of two other policemen, D.I. Baxter and Sergeant Fox, only a couple hours after their colleagues had left. On the whole I preferred Bristow and Cummins. Basically because they hadn't kicked my door off its hinges and used me as a punch bag, far less take me into custody. I was informed that I was being arrested for murder and drug dealing. It was when I protested my innocence and explained that I had been cleared by Bristow that I learnt of his disappearance and Cummins' death.

I was told some new evidence had come to light and I had been arrested on the Chief Constable's orders. I had a nasty feeling that the things that could not be any worse had taken a turn for the even worse.

I soon found myself in a police cell but something was far from right. I was not asked to make a statement nor offered a lawyer. There was a definite conspiracy going on. My speed of transfer to prison was surprising. It was harder to escape from a prison cell than a police cell, not that the latter was a piece of Mr Kipling. I had one chance on the transfer to escape and it all hinged on who carried out the task. I lucked out. It wasn't Group 4 so I did in fact make it to prison. I didn't know which one because I was blindfolded. Events had taken a corkscrew twist and

I was literally in the dark.

Within the walls I was kept incommunicado. I was honoured that in these days of prison overcrowding I had a cell to myself. If indeed it was an honour, which I very much doubted.

And so it was after my first night in that cell that I had awoken, fleetingly blissfully unaware of reality but soon plummeting to the depths of despair. I climbed down from the top bunk and drifted over to the barred window. All I could see was a walled exercise yard, the extent of a prisoner's freedom. I had a funny feeling though that I wasn't going to be a prisoner very long. Soon I wouldn't be much of anything.

# CHAPTER 13

I remained in solicitous contemplation for some time. Rodin's Thinker would have seemed fidgety compared to me. Eventually a klaxon sounded which I presumed was equivalent to a bugler's reveille. At this my ears were assaulted with a cacophony of sounds. Moans, groans, curses, protesting bedsprings, scraping chairs and even someone singing. It was then I realised how deathly silent it had been before. In my case the emphasis was on deathly for I feared that I would not be among the living much longer. Unless, of course, I could escape. Easier said than done despite the numerous times it had been depicted on both the large and small screen as being more than possible. Still it is said that a drowning man clutches at straws and if I wasn't drowning then Robert Maxwell was alive and well and soundly managing a pension fund. I knew that even if the slightest chance at a bid for freedom presented itself, I had to snatch it with both hands, irrespective of the consequences.

How did I get myself into this mess? It all seemed so far removed from a little case of surveillance. Either I had blundered into something which was far more complicated than I had been led to believe or I had been played for a patsy from the beginning. Neither possibility left me feeling good about myself.

It had been a humdinger of a trap with a two tier construction. I had been too worried about Chalky's murder and my possible tie up with it to concern myself with what else had been done whilst the ungodly had been present in my flat. The first tier, the murder, I had survived as no doubt they had expected. They could not create events to be absolutely watertight not knowing my exact movements. It had though, thrown me off balance for the coup de grace. The drugs must have been planted when the knife was taken from the flat. It had worked a treat.

No, I had to revise my thinking there. It hadn't gone according to plan. Bristow and Cummins had not fallen for it and now one of them was dead? Cox had put them on the right trail. Where was Cox? And Bristow? That cannot have been the intention of the ungodly. When a member of law enforcement was killed no stone was left unturned in the ensuing investigation. They would have done better killing me off. This was the ultimate intention I had no doubt but they wanted me as far removed from their own area of play as possible so that any investigation did not inconvenience them. If I was found dead then my business, such as it was, would come under scrutiny which would lead to Hobson and the Fairfax Corporation. If a minor drug dealer was killed in a prison fight there would be no further questions. Similarly if I was killed trying to escape.

One thing was for certain though. This had taken time to prepare, more so than just the week I had been on the case. It probably took longer than that just to forge my handwriting in that ledger. How had that been done? It would seem that I had been set up even before I was working on the case. Only Mrs Fulwood could comment on that and I was positive now that she was not who she said she was. As the person who had appointed me to the case she was the only one I knew with prior knowledge of my possible involvement.

There was something else too. The question of my incarceration. It had been too speedily carried out. No chance of a phone-call, let alone a lawyer. My transfer from police cell to prison cell had been amazingly swift. I smelt police corruption. Where I had been led to believe I was dealing with a small criminal element from the States intending to make a raid on the assets of the Fairfax Corporation, what I had in reality was an organisation so powerful it had allies in the police force and probably the prison service too.

The only flaw in the plan had been Bristow and Cummins. They had been supposed to arrest me on the spot faced with overwhelming evidence of my guilt. The ungodly had known soon after that this had gone wrong and had taken steps to rectify it. These corrective measures had been swift and, as far as Cummins was concerned, deadly. That in itself smacked of them having eyes and ears inside the force. Bristow and Cox were probably both in hiding, not knowing who to trust. Would either be able to help me? There wasn't a lot of time left to find out.

The clanking of the cell door brought me out of my despondent reverie. There were two guards stood outside the cell. Big and mean looking with truncheons dangling at their sides but within easy reach. One entered with a plate and cup and placed it on the tiny table whilst the other remained wedged in the doorway. Neither spoke.

When they had left I got off the bed and went to see what was on the menu. The smell was enough to put me off and the grease in what the offerings were swimming in nearly made me retch. I wasn't hungry anyway. I drank the coffee. It was black, weak and without sugar but at least it was hot.

I could hear from the clatter of cutlery and buzz of conversation that other prisoners were eating together not so far away. They were certainly taking pains to ensure I didn't mix with the other inmates. No bonding in bondage. As far as I could remember from prison fare on TV, only high security prisoners ate alone. I was certainly high on someone's security but if they were to get rid of me, as I believed, then they would have to let me out of the cell sometime. I had to interact if I was to get in a fight with a fellow inmate. I had to be out of the cell to make a break for it.

After breakfast I heard other prisoners leaving to start whatever work they each did to buy basic necessities. Even in prison one had to work to live, or rather exist. Not me though, I was kept in my cell. Not that I was in the mood for working in the laundry or garden anyway but at least it would have improved my chances of escape. I would have to create a chance before the one they would present me with.

I tried to think of a way but anything I could think of was easily outweighed by the host of points against it.

My mind was taken off this dilemma by another clank of the door. It was one of the silent ones, who did not break his vow but gestured me out of the cell. So soon? These guys didn't hang around. I tried to stay alert whilst appearing deflated. I trudged along the way I was ushered more scared than I had ever been in my life. Finally, I was shown into a small room and to my complete surprise there was a man sat at a table, a closed briefcase lay before him.

"Good morning, Mr Robel," greeted the man, holding out his hand. He was tall and dark, with a comforting smile and twinkle in his eye. "My name is Fairweather, Justin Fairweather, and I have been appointed to your case. My client has asked me not to divulge his name but let me assure you I only defend those I believe to be innocent and I have never yet lost a case."

All the while he had been moving towards the door and as he uttered the last word he wrenched it open to reveal one of my guards who fell into the room so hard he'd obviously had his ear pressed to the door.

"My discussions with Mr Robel are strictly private and confidential, as I am sure you are aware," he said to the guard who was looking rather sheepish as he got up from the floor. "This direct conflagration will be reported to your superior. Now go!" After closing the door he came back to the table and opened his briefcase. "Now before we begin I'll just take a couple of minutes to read through these notes and refresh my memory on events."

"Be my guest," I offered. "I'm not going anywhere."

Instead of papers he took from his briefcase a little black box from which he extended a small aerial. He flicked a switch and played it around the room. Apparently satisfied he pushed the aerial home, turned the box off and replaced it in his briefcase. Next he went back over to the door, opened it just a crack and peered through. Again satisfied he returned to the table and sat down.

"Just checking for bugs," he explained, although I had already guessed. "I have already discovered that there are no hidden cameras."

By now I was very much confused. The man's actions were not those one would expect of a lawyer. I thought I detected Cox's hand in this. After all, who else would want to help me? The answer was not long in coming.

"Now that I know we will not be overheard I can begin," said my mysterious visitor. "My name you know and I am qualified as a lawyer. However, I am also a registered private investigator and a friend of Detective Inspector Peter Cox."

I had been right. "How is he? Where is he?"

"In answer to your first question he is fine. As to your second I am not at liberty to divulge that information. Suffice to say, you seem to have stirred up a hornet's nest and he has to lie low in order not to get stung."

"What about Bristow?"

"Ditto."

"I know they're in danger," I said. "There is something big going on. There's even police corruption involved if I'm not much mistaken." Too late I realised that this guy could be trying to find out how much I knew for the other side.

"I know. Apart from yourself, I am the only person Peter feels he can trust. There have already been three attempts on his life."

"Really! Someone is moving fast."

"Precisely," Fairweather agreed. "And that is why we have to move fast. As the Americans would say, your life won't be worth a plugged nickel if we don't get you out of here."

"While I'm sure you're a very able lawyer I don't think I'll live to see my trial."

"I fear you may be right. I had to raise quite a stink to get in to see you. However, you may be pleased to know you only have to survive until this afternoon."

"You've arranged a break?" I asked eagerly, prospects distinctly brightening.

"All fixed up," confirmed Fairweather. "There will be no slip ups, we have employed the best, although a prison break is a new line for them. The A.C.C.S. are doing it, I take it you have heard of them?"

"Who hasn't," I declared. "The Anti Crime and Corruption Squad were so much in the news last year that more people know what A.C.C.S. stands for than BBC."

"Right. You are going over the wall but not by conventional means. When you are out in the yard after lunch listen out for a chopper. It's going to drop some knock-out gas so wear this." He pushed over a small piece of plastic, large enough to cover nose and mouth, which would be held in place be a piece of elastic around the head. "You will have to hold your breath until you get into the chopper. I hope you are fast at climbing rope ladders."

"If it means getting out of this place I'll be up it in seconds flat," I assured him. "What worries me though is that I might not be in the exercise yard. They've kept me strictly incommunicado up to now."

"Leave that to me," he grinned. "I've got a little speech planned about prisoners' rights."

"What happens when I get out?"

"I was not told any more. Need to know basis. No doubt you will have to lay low for a while. Now I think our business is over and you can go back to your brief internment."

"OK. Just one question."

"Shoot."

"How did you get that gadget in here? I would have thought with the way they feel about me you would have been strip searched."

"I was practically but fortunately I have a Bond case."

He left it at that and I was soon back in my cell, plastic mask inside my shoe where I had put it in case I was searched on leaving the room.

I now had reason for a little optimism, although an optimeter reading at that time would have shown the needle in the pessimistic zone. It would certainly sway into the positive if two miracles could be achieved. Firstly, I needed luck with the weather. Not brilliant sunshine just Fairweather. He had to get me into the exercise yard and based on my total isolation so far, my captors had a fear of me mixing with the other prisoners. Secondly, and more importantly, I had to stay alive to reach the exercise yard. If I got there my troubles would be as over as the bluebirds to the rainbow.

With the A.C.C.S. on the case there was no doubt of the outcome from their end. This group had first entered the public eye about a year before and any of their exploits was guaranteed headline news, provided a well-known celebrity hadn't been seen shopping. No one knew who the members were or even how many there were but one fact was indisputable, the A.C.C.S. had prevented more criminal acts and recovered more criminal proceeds in the past year than any law enforcement agency, and at a tiny fraction of the A Team's armament expenditure. They always seemed to know when a raid or other nefarious activity was planned and managed to stop it before it happened or foil the escape attempt. All proceeds were returned minus a 10% operation fee which the insurance companies were quite willing to pay for in view of the larger claim they had been spared.

I was extremely surprised that they were going to spring me from prison for they had always operated within the strict confines of the law up until now. I could only assume that believing I was innocent they felt that helping me to escape injustice, at the worst, was no crime. After all they were, as their title suggested, anti-corruption as well as anti-crime.

Something else had occurred to me. I would have to lay low for a period of time and what better opportunity would present itself to get in well with the A.C.C.S., who with their skills and contacts would be a huge asset in my current fight against an unseen and for the moment unquantifiable enemy. They could probably hide Hobson and his family away somewhere until the nightmare was over. That would ease my burden. I would only have to worry about my safety then.

They say exercise is good for you and if I could get mine that day then things would certainly be looking up. I would need some luck though, more so because prison issue clothing did not run to red socks, mine were languishing wherever prisoners' property languished.

Still, it was about time that something went my way. I was beginning to feel like a puppet and I had to find out who was pulling the strings. I had the time to review events so far to see if anything hit me.

There had been the unannounced arrival of the American Mrs Fulwood to the office offering a job. The feeling I'd had that she'd known more about me than she should have done. Other than that things had gone as much as I would have expected based on what she told me. Hobson was certainly under pressure from some quarter and certainly the surveillance seemed justified. Despite doing a spectacularly poor job of it, I had lucked out in teaming up with Vicky. That had been my ace in the hole. The turning point had been when Hobson had taken a hand, playing his joker. Since then things had gone downhill faster than a mat on a greased helter-skelter.

Chalky's death was completely out of the blue. Vicky and I had thought we were being clever tracking him down but it had led to his death. His murder was on our hands, mine particularly because his life had been forfeited to try and implicate me. Even that had been a half-hearted attempt. Whoever was behind all this had thrown that in as a red herring and the irrelevance of human life to these people made me angry.

The drugs plant had been clever. It had been well planned and therein had to lay the answer. It had taken time to produce that ledger with a decent copy of my handwriting. The only person who in my opinion knew of my involvement in time to prepare such a planned attack was Mrs F. Back to the beginning. But I had checked. Fidelity Insurance Corporation did exist and it did have an employee of that name. So was I just a pawn in a large corporate game of cat and mouse or was Mrs F not the real Mrs F?

I was either the watcher being watched or there was a completely different agenda being adhered to. My previous thoughts had been along the lines of the former. Mrs F on behalf of F.I.C. had placed me in between the real surveillance team and Hobson, knowing if I was seen it wasn't the end of the world. Knowing I was green and unlikely to learn anything but hopeful I was useful for prompting a mistake which others could pick up on. Now I was off this idea. Even if this had been the case, surely the powers that be would not have let it go so far as murder and their innocent pawn in jail for life. Or would they? Did the ends justify the means?

I was now leaning heavily towards the other option. Yes, I had been set up but for another purpose. Mrs F was the key and I resolved to hunt her down as soon as I could. I had the distinct feeling she was still in the U.K. and not back in the States.

But that was the future and I had to deal with the present.

One thing I had noticed on my brief excursion that morning was that my two constant companions were not in the running for Prison Personality of the Month. I would have thought that in prison a certain relationship would build up between the prisoners and the guards, after all many were not hardened criminals but ordinary folk, first time offenders, who had strayed just the once from the straight and narrow. If there was mutual hate between the prisoners and guards life would be unbearable for both sides. On my constitutional I had seen on three separate occasions a camaraderie between the two factions but I had also noticed something else. Not one other person had let on to my two escorts and I had even spotted a covert thumbs down from another guard that we passed. I assumed the gesture meant me and I suddenly felt like the gladiator on the floor with a sword to his throat when the Roman emperor had exercised his prerogative. I had to assume from this that whoever had these two as companions was for the high jump. Obviously they were only assigned to special prisoners. I wondered how many were still alive.

The thing that disturbed me was that whilst they were obviously disliked and associated with matters distasteful, the practice was tolerated. The prison governor had to be involved and that didn't bode well for Fairweather's chances. If this was a usual routine, and the other guard's reaction had said as much, why had no one spoken out? It seemed that whilst not condoned, the practice was suffered by the others. What hold did the governor have over his honest employees? Whatever it was didn't really matter. I was under a close, restrictive guard with no possible contact with anyone else and it seemed no one was about to interfere.

If the recent past experience was anything to go by, I would be kept in splendid isolation until the time of execution arrived. That was what concerned me. I had to be with the other prisoners in the exercise yard after lunch. If not I was lost. Despite Fairweather's assurances I felt that some action from myself would be needed. I had to get rid of my personal guards, then assuming there were no other specialists to take their place I would be under normal supervision.

Time was of the essence so I decided to try something straight away. This would give me time for another attempt if this one failed and with my success rate on this case even Ladbrokes wouldn't have offered odds on me not achieving my goal.

My cell door was locked but I'd noticed it could be unlocked automatically or by a key and I was banking on the latter. Both guards were on the catwalk outside. What they were meant to be guarding with me locked in a cell I'd no idea but it suited my purpose just then. I lay on the bottom bunk and started moaning, lowly at first but then in increasing agony supplemented with angst writhing. It was the oldest trick on TV but it worked. I heard a key in the lock and I increased my writhing for visual effect. One of the guards approached the bunk with his companion staying in the doorway. I bunched my legs and shot them at the one peering over me. The effect was better than I could have hoped for. The guard I hit went careering backwards and crashed into his colleague, catapulting him backwards with such impetus that he went over the rail and fell screaming to crash below. That had halved the odds in one swoop. Moving swiftly, I grabbed the remaining guard's truncheon from the floor where it had dropped when I kicked him and applied it to its owner's skull. Already groggy he went down like a sack of potatoes. No sooner was he out cold than I started yelling the place down. Soon I had three guards of the conscious variety on hand.

"What happened here?" one growled as he approached.

"I might well ask the same question," I replied indignantly. "They were plotting to kill me. The only reason I'm still alive is because they couldn't agree on when to do it. That guy on the floor wanted to do it straight away so he unlocked the door and came straight at me with his truncheon. The other one told him not to be so rash and pulled him back. For his pains he got pushed over the rail. This one dropped his truncheon in the struggle so in self-defence I hit him over the head."

I was secretly surprised as to how plausible it sounded. Usually I found it very difficult to tell lies, everyone could just see it in my demeanour because I was too honest for my own good. Things had changed though. This was a life and death situation. Lie and live. There was no alternative. Anyway, I felt I was on safe ground.

My assumption of the reputation of my bodyguards seemed to be correct for these others merely nodded as though it came as no great shock. Still I was taken to see the Governor and he was less likely to be on my side.

I reiterated my version of the events that had resulted in one death and one unconscious guard with possible concussion to come. The Governor was a lean and greying man that seemed to be deep in thought when I'd finished. There was no way I could tell if he had swallowed my story but it had the desired effect, by lunch time I was eating with the other prisoners. He had looked distinctly worried as I and my entourage left his office, probably because he had no other dependants to nurse-maid me.

By taking action I'd now managed to manipulate circumstances in my favour. Now that I wasn't being given special treatment by my ex baby-sitters I was now on a par with the other prisoners. The luncheon fare was not great but I wasn't particularly hungry, I was too eager to be rid of the place. I vowed to myself there and then that whatever circumstances befell me in life, I would never even put one toe over the criminal line for I could never have tolerated any time in prison and even the greatest criminal gets caught in time.

In the yard during exercise period it was not the old English film act of plodding around the yard in line. This was free time and the inmates could do what they liked, although I don't think waiting to escape fell within the permitted pastimes. Around me prisoners talked in groups or carried out their own individual exercise programmes. There was even a game of football taking place. I just stood by a wall watching, playing the outsider I had been cast as and waiting for freedom to call.

My ears were strained to the limit to catch any sound of approaching rotor blades although I did refrain from searching the sky; that would have been a dead give-away to the watching guards. One would have thought that it would have been impossible for a helicopter to make a soundless approach but until it rose into view from behind the far wall I had not heard it.

Canisters were dropped into the yard billowing smoke. I had my little mask in place in seconds but because I'd had no warning I had still taken in a small amount of the gas. Not enough to be a problem, or so I thought. Not so the others who were falling like ninepins in front of Fred Flintstone's bowling ball, leaving me unopposed in my run to the rope ladder that was hanging from the chopper.

The pilot must have been very skilled and had nerves of steel. He was hovering with the blades inches away from the top of the prison wall so that I could reach the bottom of the ladder. No sooner had I grasped it than I was whisked upwards and it was then I knew I was in trouble. I felt increasingly giddy, no doubt due to the combined effects of the gas and the quick upsurge through the air. I had just about managed to haul myself up so my feet were on the bottom rung but I could not progress any further up the ladder. My circle of vision was getting smaller and I knew I was blacking out. I wrapped my legs and arms around the rope ladder, not even having time for a prayer as blackness engulfed me.

# CHAPTER 14

For the second time in twenty-four hours, I resurfaced from oblivion not knowing where I was. This time I was with sound mind, I just didn't know where I was. I didn't mind at all for compared to last time this was bliss. The bed was comfortable and there was no whiteness chasing me. My aching head offered only the merest fraction of discomfort.

I was free. Free! If I felt like that after only a day in prison god knows what people felt on being released after years inside. But I'd thought too soon. The door to the room was locked from the outside, I found. Still incarcerated. Out of the frying pan into the fire.

However, my fears proved to be groundless for after rattling the handle for a few seconds I heard a key being turned in the lock and the door opened. What met my eyes convinced me I had in fact gone mad after all and was really in a padded cell, for the person on the other side of the door was none other than Mickey Mouse. He beckoned me out of the room and I followed in rather a bemused state. Along a corridor and into a spacious lounge where I met Mickey's friends, Donald and Pluto. I was waved to a seat.

"Please forgive these melodramatics," Mickey apologised. "They're completely necessary I assure you. Our identities must remain a secret as I'm sure you'll understand." The voice was educated and confident.

"Don't mind me," I told him. "I've always wanted to visit Disneyland." My joke did not seem to go down very well for they sat in silence and gave each other covert looks, or so I presumed because it was difficult to tell what was going on behind those masks. They probably just thought me ungrateful. "I'm sorry. I didn't mean to be rude."

"It's OK," said Mickey. "We know you've been through a trying time recently."

"Not half. I have to thank you guys for getting me out. You are the A.C.C.S. aren't you?" With their obsessive compulsion to keep their identities secret they had to be.

"We are," confirmed Mickey. "Please take a seat."

I looked at the three of them. They were all roughly the same height and build. I couldn't see the hair as the masks were those rubber types that go right over the head instead of just the face. I noticed something else too but decided not to comment on it just then.

"How long do I have to stay here?" I asked. "Wherever here is."

"Impossible to say at the moment," Mickey replied. "Depends how much you are wanted?"

"I can't stay here too long, I've got work to do." Not that I knew what I'd be able to do. When the ungodly knew I'd escaped I'd be living on borrowed time. "I don't know how much you know but there are people in danger because of me."

"We know part of it. You've upset the wrong people and were framed to keep you out of the way." It was really noticeable that only Mickey could talk. "The only reason we broke you out was to keep you alive. If you leave here too soon you would be back in the same position or even worse. Don't forget that the police are after you as well now. You're a fugitive."

"But I have to get back to help the others," I protested. Not too strongly it seemed to me. Part of me wanted to just let it go but I couldn't. People were not exactly depending on me but to me it felt like I was responsible for them. Hobson, Vicky and Jenny too. If I could offer any help, I had to and the sooner the better.

"Stay here for a while. We'll check up on the situation. When you're not front page news any more you can venture out. You'll have to be ultra careful though and also change your appearance."

I couldn't argue. It made sense. My flat would be being watched as would the office, by both sides. Jenny would be questioned and probably kept under surveillance. I wouldn't stand a chance as me. Even as not me, a stranger, I would have to tread more carefully than an elephant in a minefield. I gave up, for now. "If I'm going to be here with you for some time are you going to keep those ridiculous masks on permanently?"

"We won't be here with you. Now you're conscious we'll be leaving. This is one of our safe houses. It's out in the country with no other residence for a few miles. You'll be absolutely safe here. You can even walk around the grounds but no further afield. One of us will check by from time to time but in the main you're on your own."

I was somewhat surprised. However, this was not their usual line of work and they seemed to be taking me on trust. "Can I use the phone to check some things out?"

"Not from here you can't. This doesn't have an outside line, it is only a means of communication between here and our base. Besides it wouldn't be too wise anyway. The persons you may wish to contact may be tapped." I didn't think he meant tapped in the head. "You can use it to get in touch with us though. Press 1. Our number's on speed dial." Mickey got up from his seat. "We'd better be off now in fact. Things to do, including checking on your priorities."

"I haven't told you what they are yet."

"We know enough." He was about to leave and the others got up to follow. This was bad. I needed to know more. I needed to know if they could help me, or if not, where Cox and Bristow were. If I had any choice at all I preferred not to continue with my one man show, so far the reviews left a lot to be desired. In the circumstances I said the only thing I could think of. "Are you identical triplets?"

That threw them. They all stopped in their tracks and looked in my direction. "How did you know?" asked Mickey.

It had been a shot in the dark but an educated one. Donald and Pluto were wearing watches on their right wrists as opposed to the popular left. Mickey wasn't wearing a watch and on the inside of his right wrist there was a purple mark, a birthmark I assumed. My guess was that his Disney chums had identical marks which they were covering with their watches. Same birthmark, same birth, or as same as made no difference.

They were waiting for me to reply. "Just an educated guess," I told them.

"Based on what," asked Mickey, a touch suspiciously I thought. Did they think they had been set up too?

"Your birthmark," I replied. "And the fact that your compadres have their watches on the wrong wrists. I assumed this was not just to shy away from convention."

"Very astute," growled Pluto, from which I discovered their voices were curiously alike too.

"Well, it's now pointless keeping this on," declared Mickey, pulling off his mask to reveal a young and pleasant countenance. Blue eyed, blond haired, as were his brothers when they de-masked. Like peas in a pod. If I'd known them for years I couldn't have told them apart. But what astonished me more was that I knew them or rather one of them, though which one I hadn't a clue.

"Which one of you is Howard Kelly?" I asked.

"None of us," replied Mickey, "but you have made the connection. Howard is our brother."

"Well, I never would have believed it!" I never would have either. Howard Kelly, who had erupted onto the Formula One racing scene less than twelve months earlier and had won every Grand Prix since, had three identical brothers. I was slightly confused and voiced my reservation. "In a recent interview I seem to recall that Howard stated he had no living relatives."

"Only three people in the world know there are four of us," Donald declared, which sounded a bit Irish to me.

"Harvey!" growled Pluto.

"Cool it you two," advised Mickey, but Donald was not finished.

"I said all along that this was a stupid idea," he went on, waving his mask. "Look, we checked him out and he's clean."

"He may as well know the whole story now," agreed

Mickey.

"But what if it gets out before we're ready," protested Pluto.

"Excuse me," I interrupted the family argument. I was torn. I wanted to get back on track, meaning my own problems, but also I would have liked to know more about the A.C.C.S. just in case they could assist me in any way. "I'd love to hear your story, after all I've nothing else to do at the moment, and I assure you I will not divulge one word of it. It would gain me nothing."

Pluto had no more objections it seemed so we all sat back down.

"First of all," began Mickey, "in answer to your first query, Howard Kelly has no living relatives because Howard Kelly does in fact not exist. Kelly is an alias we use because our true name must remain secret for the time being. Our first names are our own. I'm Herbert, that fine figure of a duck is Harvey and that is Henry."

"Pleased to meet you. And if you don't know already my name is Thomas Robel."

"We were told of a little of your plight," Mickey, that is Herbert, informed me. "That's why we agreed to help."

"So what's all the secrecy about?"

"Well, to begin at the beginning you have to go back to our great, great grandfather," said Harvey.

"I'll tell it Harvey," said Herbert. I would have bet on him being first out of the womb. He seemed to like to take charge of the situation.

"OK!"

"Our great, great grandfather was greatly passionate about medieval history and commissioned the building of a castle on part of the vast land our family used to own."

"Quite the real thing it was too," Harvey chipped in. "Courtyard, battlements and a moat. Straight out of the pages of King Arthur."

"It'll be quicker if just one of us tells it," pointed out Henry.

"Precisely," agreed Herbert.

"Sorry!"

"The castle, or Knightscourt as it's called, is now the family seat and is passed down to the eldest heir. Thus it passed to our father. Now father had a brother who is a lot younger and what you might call the black sheep of the family. As a youth he was always managing to get mixed up in one kind of trouble or another, although grandfather always managed to keep him out of the clutches of the authorities.

"Now the important point is that if our father had no heirs the title etc. would have gone to our uncle which is not what grandfather wanted at all for he feared that the family name would be disgraced. The problem was that our father's wife could not bear children and adopted children in this case would not be entitled to be heirs. This, of course, was all very pleasing for uncle for he was certain to get his hands on the estate in the end, but he was impatient. There were a series of accidents which nearly proved fatal for our father and he became suspicious of his brother. To safeguard his own life and the future of the estate a desperate plan was devised by our father and his wife." He had been talking with a faraway look in his eyes and he had been trying to exclude all emotion from the narration. Now he looked me squarely in the eyes. "Notice how I never call our father's wife 'Mother'."

I'd noticed immediately. It was something that most people would have. 'Our father's wife' is not a phrase commonly used.

"The reason will soon be clear." There was bitterness in that comment but it was soon gone for he was soon back in emotionless monotone. "Because our father's wife could not have children it was decided that he should conceive with someone else, a girl in the village was chosen. As my father feared for the life of any heir, the girl was to be paid to bring the child up as her own and only at the time of father's death would the heir become apparent. Yet all did not go according to plan for the girl gave birth to quads and while a single child could have been hidden from prying eyes, it would have been impossible with four. So our mother had to move away from the village and bring us up elsewhere. Father wrote a will and made a point of informing his brother that there was a condition that if he was killed in suspicious circumstances then the estate would go into trust. Our uncle knew he would have to wait then and he is still waiting, but it will be in vain because the solicitor who drew up the will knows that it will be us four who benefit."

"I can see that you've a nice little surprise in store for your uncle but you might have to wait years to claim your inheritance. Maybe twenty years. Twenty years of hiding, not being able to reveal your true identities."

"We have considered that possibility," admitted Herbert. "In fact we created the A.C.C.S. to try to speed things up."

"How does being Britain's answer to the A Team help?" I was curious. "Apart from finding lodgers for Her Majesty's institutions, making the various law enforcement bodies look like rank amateurs in the apprehension of villains and generally keeping Britain tidy?"

"It may seem to you and the rest of the country that we are just waging a private war against crime and corruption, as our name suggests, but we do have our own agenda. Our uncle, as I've already said, is the black sheep but we discovered that he's so much more. He is head of a vast crime syndicate which operates all over the UK and sometimes abroad too."

"When Herbert says discovered," interrupted Henry, "what he really means is that we've turned up some very disturbing facts but have absolutely no proof whatsoever."

Henry, I'd noticed, was the cautious one. So far he had only spoken to advocate prudence.

"We have our connections in the underworld," put in Harvey, "yet even though we're sure that all the crimes we've foiled have been initiated by our uncle, the lines of command are such that his hands are never dirtied."

"The syndicate is into everything." Herbert took control again. "Robbery, drugs, kidnapping, hijack, hit squads, you name it; they do it. Each activity seems to be undertaken by separate units with no connection to each other. We've not been able to tie any two together and so point a finger at a common source. All we need is one slip so we can put him away and lead our normal lives."

"This is very interesting." And it was to me because there was the faint possibility that there may be a connection to my own predicament. "Tell me. If someone from the States wanted to recruit some bodies to pull off a few jobs, would your uncle be the person to contact?"

"Could be," replied Herbert thoughtfully, "although they wouldn't deal with him personally. Like I said he keeps himself at arm's length. He may agree to hire out one of his units, for a cut."

"Maybe we could work together," I suggested. "It's possible the people I'm up against are tied in with your uncle and sure as beans mean Heinz I need help."

"We'll certainly help if we can," said Herbert, "but we may have another job on. Howard is out working on it now."

"Isn't it dangerous for him being so well known?"

"No! He is, to coin a phrase, a master of disguise. That's what allows him to lead a double life. It's also how we operate, so if we get seen he's not in trouble."

"So why no disguise now? Why just the Disney party?"

"Once a job's finished we scrap any disguises. If we're seen at the scene, as we often are, any description is useless. More protection against the criminal fraternity tracking us down than anyone else. After each job we lie low at one of our safe locations, except Howard who has his racing lifestyle to uphold."

It was a complex scenario to me. They couldn't use their true name and they couldn't even look their true selves. What type of father would put them through that? Though the latter burden they seemed to have taken on themselves. What father would not want to see his kids grow up? Just to keep the family name going. As a foursome would they not have been safe living with their father? Their uncle surely wouldn't have thought he could get away with five murders?

Still it wasn't for me to get involved in family feuds. It was their help as the A.C.C.S. I needed. However, if they had something else to do then fair enough. They had helped me out more than I could have expected anyway. I couldn't get any more information from them. Protecting their sources was paramount to their success. How they operated and obtained their information was going to remain a mystery.

Not long after they left to check in with Howard about their possible forthcoming operation. I was left to my open prison. Free to do as I liked as long as I didn't leave the grounds. It was getting on for about six o'clock by this time. I must have been unconscious for over three hours. Realisation of how time had flown brought awareness to two basic needs, three if you count a visit to the bathroom. I was hungry, nearly six hours had passed since my last repast and even then prison fare couldn't be called a meal. I also felt dirty, real dirt and sweat but also that of the death and corruption I was mixed up with. I was on a see-saw of indecision; food or a bath. I compromised by eating a packet of chocolate biscuits in the bath.

An hour and a half later, feeling fresher and more like my old self, not that being my old self gave me any great pleasure, I was in front of the TV with a microwave meal. Unusually, I couldn't concentrate on what was on screen. My mind was too preoccupied with matters I was trying hard to forget for the present. The phone was a great temptation to do an E.T. to see how the land lay, but this was lessened by the fact that I could only get through to the number that the brothers H could be contacted on, in other words no outside line. My only link to the outside was the TV or radio news broadcasts and I wasn't on any of them. Somebody was going out of their way to keep this quiet and I didn't know if that boded well or ill as far as I was concerned. I could only hope that the Kelly clan came up with some news.

As I couldn't concentrate on my usual Monday night fare I turned off the TV and went to bed. I wasn't tired though. Three hours uninterrupted slumber was a full night's sleep for me. In the end I got up again. Trying to keep my mind off unprofitable and bladder weakening scary thoughts, I found some paper and a pen and turned my mind to the further adventures of Sindy Cobweb. It took me a minute or two to recall where I'd got up too but then, unlike the horses in the 1993 Grand National, I was off.

That did the trick. By the time I had finished another chapter I was tired and no sooner had I put my pen down I headed for my bedroom. Not that I had a bedroom. I'd a choice of four but I automatically entered the one I'd awoken in earlier that day. Sleep didn't come easy but I eventually drifted off, my last thought being I hoped I wasn't in for another white nightmare.

# CHAPTER 15

It was a sort of a depression I suppose. I had been awake for ages it seemed but was unable to muster any energy or enthusiasm to face the day. I should have been over the moon at my new found freedom but I wasn't. I was still in prison in a way. An open prison. Nice and comfortable, with the freedom to move around but with no place to go, or no place I was allowed to go, so therefore no purpose. All I could do was think and my thoughts tended to be of the darker "what if" variety. What if Hobson had been found out? What if Vicky had been captured? What if I had to be a fugitive from justice for the end of my days? What if there was ever a last series of Friends?

I could have lain there all day, just staring up at the ceiling, with worrying but non-productive thoughts steaming through my head like a Casey Jones-less Cannonball Express. I needed a spur, some catalyst to get me going. Then suddenly a stray thought popped into my head and I was out of bed quicker than Speedy Gonzales with his tail on fire. I had just remembered something extremely important. Channel 4 were rerunning 'Bewitched' at 8.30 each morning.

I needed a laugh and for twenty-five minutes I forgot about the mess I was in, losing myself in the antics of Samantha, Darren, Tabitha and the various relatives of witchiness. Nearly thirty years old and it was still funny. Who would laugh at 'Holding The Baby' in thirty years from now? Who would laugh at it today?

When it was over I felt slightly better. I was up and about but still lacked purpose. I couldn't just watch telly all day. Most of it was rubbish. The first thing to do was get breakfast. The most important meal of the day to many people. So important that I hardly ever partook. Perhaps that was my big mistake in life.

Over cereal and toast my mind meandered over the week's events trying to bring a semblance of order to the proceedings. A task more difficult than persuading Prince John to place a coin in a blind man's begging bowl. Fortunately, I was saved from this cerebral countdown conundrum by a visitor. One of the Brothers Kelly, my saviours and absentee captors, arrived bearing gifts of the hair colouring variety.

"You'll have to change your appearance before you leave here," Herbert pointed out. "You can experiment with these."

"What? No false beard?"

"Not very practical and you know it."

"True. One thing though. Can you get me a pair of glasses, with clear lenses?" I could take a leaf out of Mrs F's book.

"OK. It will take a couple of days."

"Well, I don't seem to be going anywhere soon," I said. "Unless I've been miraculously cleared of all trumped up charges. Tell me the news, if there is any?"

"Not much," admitted Herbert, "but I'll tell you what we've learned so far."

"Shoot!" I must stop saying that, I thought to myself, one day someone might take me seriously.

"Well, the first thing is that both your office and flat are under surveillance."

"That was to be expected."

"Not just by the authorities. Someone else is anxious to locate you too."

Again this was no surprise to me. "The people who set me up I imagine."

"Our thoughts too," agreed Herbert, "but at this present moment in time we have not been able to learn who he, she or they are."

This was a little disappointing but I was also gratified that they had been trying. "What else?"

"Your secretary, Jenny, is followed wherever she goes. They obviously think she can lead them to you."

"Is she in any danger?"

"We don't think so. Both sides are watching her and should the bad guys try anything then the authorities would no doubt pounce."

"But the authorities, or at least someone with authority, is mixed up in all this!" I protested. "How do you think they got me into jail in the first place?"

"There was always that possibility," Herbert concurred. "Indeed, we all felt it was highly likely. However, with the number of men on surveillance they can't all be crooked so I think we can assume they would take action if necessary."

"I hope so for Jenny's sake," I said. "Anything else?"

"Naturally your phones are tapped."

"Naturally."

"Peter Hobson is still in hospital suffering from amnesia, his wife and daughter constantly in attendance." After a pause he added, "Well, that's not quite right. Mrs Hobson is in constant attendance but Miss Hobson has spent some time trying to find out what happened to you."

"Really?"

"When she heard you had been arrested, she tried to visit you in prison but did not get very far. Since you escaped she has been everywhere trying to find you."

"Everywhere being my flat and the office?"

"And some circus."

"Which means that all the people that have been keeping an eye out for me have seen her looking for me too?"

"I'm afraid so."

"And that's it?"

"Yes. We were lucky to find out as much as we did in so short a time," Herbert pointed out.

"I know. Don't think I'm not grateful," I placated. "It's just that nothing seems to have changed, apart from me being missing that is."

"Don't worry about it. It means you've missed nothing." He stood up. "I've got to be going now. One of us will check in again tomorrow."

"OK. Just one thing. How did you come by your information?"

"We have our sources," he grinned. Then he was gone.

It was about 10.30 by this time and the day stretched out endlessly before me like a stretchy endless thing. How was I to keep myself occupied cooped up in that house? As any housewife, or house-husband for that matter, will tell you daytime TV is lousy in the main. There was no one to talk to because the phone wasn't connected to the outside world. I could have experimented with my hair colours but it just wasn't a good dying day. In the end I decided to explore the far reaches of my open prison, the limits of my current existence, by walking the grounds.

Outside the front door there was a gravel forecourt from which a driveway led away through a band of trees and out of sight. There were green lawns up to the tree line but that was as far as I could see. That was all I could see from my bedroom too, trees. It said much for my state of mind that I had not tried to observe the surroundings from the other upstairs rooms in the house. I could still do that but felt I needed some exercise.

I figured the best way to explore the layout of the grounds was to start at its nethermost region. I followed the driveway, which seemed to go on forever through sparse woodland, not dense enough to be called a forest. Eventually I came upon a pair of wrought iron gates. There was no lock, padlock or otherwise. They were obviously electrically controlled and the push button intercom on a metal post on the outside confirmed this. There should be a gate release inside the house, I said to myself, making a mental note to check it out later.

There was a road outside the gate but it seemed a quiet country lane, certainly no traffic passed whilst I stood there. Each side of the gate was bounded by a high wall, at least ten feet in height. Curiously the wall whilst sturdy was of an age considerably greater than the construction of the house which was a fairly modern affair. I could only assume that the wall had once surrounded a contemporary building which through fire or demolition contractors was no more.

I turned left and walked along a narrow avenue with the trees on one side and the wall on the other. No trees grew beside the wall, nor did any branches overhang it. The place was certainly as impregnable as possible without dogs and electric fences.

I walked the length of the front wall but instead of a right angled corner it bent around to the left so I followed the contour. After about half an hour it started to rain. I could have sheltered beneath the trees but the rain felt refreshing and it was good to be out in the fresh air. It was only a light rain anyway.

So suddenly it came as a surprise, I stepped out into the open. I could see the back of the house and a panoramic view of a huge garden, with flower beds and pathways. My bedroom being on the front of the house I had missed this. I could also see where the wall circled about a quarter of a mile away. This being the case I left the pacing of the perimeter in favour of treading the path through the gardens. Not that there was much to see it being too early in the year but I could tell it was well kept and either the K Team – as I had decided to call them - were green fingered or they had employed a gardener. There was even a rock pool full of Koi carp and a bench to sit on. The rain had ceased so I sat to watch the fish for a bit.

It was peaceful out there and for a fleeting moment I could relax, forgetting the plethora of problems facing me. It was hypnotic seeing the golden fish glide and dart through the water, or it was until I detected a pattern there. There was one fish smaller than the rest and a different colour. Whether it was a different species or just an oddity I didn't know but he was an outsider and I could relate to that. The other fish were, for want of a better word, bullying it, bumping and prodding it. It was him against all the other residents of the pool. I could relate to that too. At seeing that fish in a similar plight to my own all my troubles came flooding back faster than the two halves of the Red Sea after Moses' centre parting. I was back in the real world, or what constituted my real world these days, a world of dead bodies, prison and a puppet on a string, namely me.

The mood was broken, the moment gone. I got up and made my way back to the house. I was filled with a new resolve. I was fed up with doing nothing. I was convinced action was required on my part to see things through to a satisfactory conclusion. It was time to start being proactive instead of reactive. Unlike the fish I had the chance to fight back. The only question being how? The most obvious thing was that before I could do anything, I would have to change my appearance, so after a quick bite of lunch it was a question of never say 'dye'.

I probably spent a little too long over a light lunch of cheese on toast, unconsciously delaying one of my pet hates, doing anything with my hair. It was and always had been problem hair. A bad hair day wasn't in it, more a bad hair life. It was fine so always fell forward and couldn't be brushed back. Though fine it grew thickly, so reminded one of a bush and had the tendency to stick out at the sides or on top. It was very dry after having just been washed but got greasy quickly. I had a double crown too which didn't help. All in all I had no style just an unruly mop. I liked it cut short but the shorter it was cut the more it stuck up. I never put gel or mousse on it although there had been one failed attempt at the former, when instead of enabling me to brush it back it had stood on end, making me look like Lofty from Eastenders. Needless to say that didn't last long.

I had never contemplated dying my hair before but had seen enough adverts on the TV on the subject. I thought it was as simple as shampooing in but not according to the boxes Herbert had brought. There was a bit of mixing of liquids and application via a squeeze bottle reminiscent of Grecian 2000 and once again I wondered if that particular product would be changing its name after the Millennium.

I had three colours to choose from; blond, black and ginger. I chose the latter first because it seemed the least likely and also I was getting the beginnings of an idea on how to proceed. It was a time consuming and messy process but that was probably because I was unskilled in the make-up and personal appearance department.

When I had finished to the best of my ability, which was hardly Vidal standard, I chanced a look in the mirror. My first impression was one of shock. Who was that guy that looked like an uglier version of Chris Evans? My second impression was one of horror. It's just me with ginger hair. It was too. Same non-style just a different colour. I wondered if anyone would be able to see my brown roots.

It certainly wasn't going to stay but for the time being it could have a purpose so I cleaned up the bathroom and started work on the idea that had been establishing a foothold in my brain.

I couldn't yet go back to Manchester. I knew I wasn't in the North West anymore because we were not in the Granada region. According to the ITV channel on the TV we were in the Central area which presumably meant the Midlands. I was thinking though, that I could visit somewhere else where I wasn't known but could still obtain some answers pertaining to the case. London and the offices of the Fidelity Insurance Corporation. There was only one person who could possibly be there that knew me and I had a nagging feeling that even she wouldn't be there. All I had to do was plan out the route, which meant knowing from where I was starting. As well as the minor issue of appropriating some money from somewhere.

I thought that the former issue would have been achievable but as usual I was wrong. There was no phone book to even pinpoint the local area and even though I carried out an exhaustive search not one envelope from which I could have gleaned the address did I find. In hindsight it was not surprising. This was a safe house after all and the A.C.C.S. were as professional as one could get.

I decided that I would have to let the K Team in on my plan. Logic dictated this, as Spock would have said. They were my saviours and I did not want to go against their wishes. I needed them to tell me where I was, unless I broke out, so to speak, and maybe put their whole operation at risk. Also who else could I ask to lend me money at this time? It was time to use the Bat Phone.

Picking up the receiver seemed to automatically set the phone ringing at the other end. It was answered at the second ring.

"Herbert," announced the voice at the other end. "What do you want Tommy?"

Of course he knew it was me. Who else would be calling on the direct line from the safe house? I quickly explained my idea and I could tell from his reaction he was not very keen. He said he would have to discuss it with the others and get back to me. I agreed but asked him not to take too long about it. I also stressed that this would not be a dangerous assignment for myself or the A.C.C.S. as a group. It was not like I was going back to where there were people on watch for me. It could also provide useful information on the case. He promised to get back as soon as possible.

Now I had to kick my heels waiting for a response but this was hardly crucial as it would have been too late to start now anyway. Still I was anxious to learn if my plan met with approval, at least then I would have some purpose. Until I heard from the K Team I just had to keep busy and that meant some more time creating the exploits of Sindy Cobweb.

Some time later I put me pen down with disgust, not too happy with what I had written. As a parody of James Bond the first chapter had been OK I felt but each chapter since seemed to be shorter and definitely less funny. I was running out of ideas faster than a bionic Linford Christie. The bit I had just written about Watt and Over was just a space filler. Although circumstances were not in my favour, only the first instalment having been written in the comfort of home with no outside pressures for my mind to deal with, I decided there and then that the next chapter would be the last. I would just hope that it would satisfy the customer. Mel Brooks would have to look elsewhere for his next spoof.

It was gone five by this time and I was getting impatient for the decision from the K Team. If they said no there was not a lot I could do. I would have to wait it out until they deemed it safe for me to return north. Not that it would ever be really safe, not if I wanted to finish what I'd started. If it was just me then maybe I would have chickened out but there were others to think about.

Eventually the call came and to my surprise they agreed to my request. This is it, I thought to myself. You're on your own on this one and I would have said if I hadn't been an atheist, God help me.

# CHAPTER 16

And so it came to pass that the next day I was collected by Herbert and Henry, duly blindfolded and driven to Birmingham New Street station. Rather like Spaghetti Junction I guessed we had arrived there by a roundabout route. Even though I'd had to keep the blindfold on nearly the whole way I knew the K Team would take no chances in me locating where their safe-house was.

I felt like a little boy being dropped off at the station before his first unaccompanied train ride. I was even given some spending money. I also had a briefcase with me, containing nothing but a writing pad and pen. I was dressed in a dark business suit, white shirt, sported a bright red tie and wore black shiny shoes. My idea on what to do in London had been developing since the time I had received permission from my temporary guardians. It was time to hone my acting skills or, if it turned out I hadn't any, then to bluff outrageously.

During the journey I had time to think. Unfortunately, train travel makes me sleepy and so I ended up dozing, arriving in Euston no wiser. Stepping off the train I was a bit nervous. I'd only been to the capital once before and that was a kid on a primary school trip. I hardly remembered anything about it except a trip to a museum where I had bought a plastic model of a T-Rex. Certainly I had no idea of the layout of the city and I had to consult the street guide the K Team had thoughtfully provided.

At least I knew the best way around London was via the Underground or Tube. The offices of F.I.C. were situated on Fenchurch Street and according to the street guide there were four stations I could alight at, depending at which end of Fenchurch Street I wanted to be at. The trouble was I didn't know, so unlike the man hanging on the edge of a cliff with an itch I would have to chance my arm. Or I thought I would but the street guide had other ideas. It had an Underground map on the back. It took me a while to understand the multi-coloured plan. There were more lines than at the employment exchange on signing on day. I had thought the Tube was just an interconnection of stations in the city on one track so to speak. I hadn't realised it was so extensive and diverse. There were eleven different lines and whilst many interconnected at some stations it seemed impossible at first glance to be able to get from one place to another without having to change trains at least once. There was the Northern Line, black, which ran north to south and vice versa, although it must have just run one way initially from the south otherwise it would have been called the Northern Southern Line. There was the Central Line, red, which funnily enough ran through the centre of the city although it ended up going north at both ends. The Circle Line, yellow, surprisingly was more of a bottle shape and the other names made no sense at all. The District Line, green, was not located in one district but ran through at least twenty. The Piccadilly Line, dark blue, actually ended up at Heathrow. The Bakerloo Line, brown, didn't go through any station by that name and whilst the Victoria Line, light blue, went through Victoria station it was actually between Walthamstow and Brixton. The Hammersmith and City Line, pink, should have been the Hammersmith and Barking Line, and as for the Jubilee Line, grey, and the Metropolitan Line, mauve, I could not read anything into their names at all. Which left just the East London Line, orange, the shortest. It started in the East and ended shortly after. Oh for another short Eastender.

Things improved, however, once I found that Euston was only on the Northern Line and then my answer was clear. Of the four stations suitable only Bank was on that line. I headed for the Underground sign but unfortunately ten thousand other people had the same idea. It was like playing sardines whilst on the move, especially on the escalators, and it was so hot I was sure steam was coming from my armpits. And that was before I was flush with embarrassment.

Firstly, I had to purchase a ticket. Simple enough one would have thought. But not for me, cosmopolitan traveller that I was. There was the ticket office, with a queue representative of the one that would wind around Old Trafford when tickets went on sale for the Champions League Final, if we ever made it. Alternatively, there were ticket machines, where the waiting time would be a lot less. Not being a patient person, I tried the latter but I made the people behind me even less patient whilst I tried to work out the operating procedure. Then I realised it was requesting the correct change only, of course I only had notes so I then had to join the queue for the ticket office which seemed to have lengthened to England World Cup Final proportions. Now that was real fantasy. Once I had my ticket, or rather tickets as a return meant two tickets and not one that could be used on both journeys, I had the red face trying to get through the ticket barrier, or gates as it seemed more appropriate to call them. I had seen them open for people when I'd been in the queue but only with a passing eye. I hadn't seen them insert their ticket; I thought they were just operated by magic eyes. My interrupted walk through brought a guffaw from the surrounding crowd and I had to be shown where to insert the ticket by a little old lady.

Embarrassment seems to produce heat and I was nearly passing out now. The platform was even worse with people standing ten deep. I should have expected this with it being connected to a main London railway station. I had to let the first train go as I couldn't force my way inside but on the second was fortunate to hold onto a nose pressed against the door position. I know that I'd, in times of loneliness, wanted to be close to people but this was ridiculous. What was more at the next station even more people tried to push on and miraculously half of them even made it but not the woman screaming "Move down inside!". She had a point as most everyone was squashed around the doors when there was standing space in between the rows of occupied seats. Unfortunately for her those barring her way were either deaf or indifferent.

Eventually, after having elbowed a fat guy in the belly and getting my briefcase caught between a lady's legs, it was time to alight. It was a fight I nearly lost as those wanting to get on were not about to wait for those wanting to get off. I launched my way through and earned some angry exclamations. I didn't look back but made for the exit. It seemed a long walk to obtain freedom and I was bathed in sweat.

According to the guide I had to walk down Lombard Street to get to Fenchurch Street. It took me a while to find the right way as Bank station lay on a junction with numerous options. After two false starts I at last got my bearings and strode towards my destination. I'd made at least two strides in the right direction before I stopped in my tracks. What was I to do now? I needed a plan. How to gain entry and learn something to my advantage. It was easy on screen. Courier. Pizza delivery. CID. Health and Safety. I'd seen it done many times. Simon Templar could do it. Axel Foley could do it. Even Frank Drebin could do it. All it needed was a prop or two, usually bought over the odds from a passing courier or pizza delivery guy.

Fortunately, I didn't need that amount of fabrication. I needed to make a phone call and for once my luck was in as a phone box was visible a few yards down the street. It was in two ways incredible. The phone wasn't vandalised, in Manchester it would have been inoperative again before the BT van had left the street after repairing it for the umpteenth time, and it was vacant, disproving the theory that you only see an empty telephone box when you don't need to call someone.

I dialled the number from Mrs F's card and was promptly answered. On asking for her I was told that she was not available. Would I like to speak to somebody else? No thank you, I would ring back later. Leaving it a few minutes I then located the building that housed the Fidelity Insurance Corporation and entered, hoping that the receptionist was not the person that I had spoken to on the phone. A forlorn hope really as most receptionists double as telephone operators.

Luck was with me so far. It was one of those buildings with

a watchman in the lobby to whom one had to report before proceeding further. He certainly wasn't the person I'd spoken to.

"Hello," I greeted. "I've come to see Mrs Fulwood at Fidelity Insurance."

"I'm sorry," he said, "but I don't recognise that name; I'll have to check."

"She's American, from the Chicago office," I volunteered.

"Even so I'll have to check. Who should I say wants to see her?"

"Pratt! Henry Pratt! Of Pratt, Pratt, Wally and Pratt."

I could hear from his side of the conversation that he was being told what I already knew. The person on the other end was obviously consulting someone for he held on silently for a couple of minutes. Then he acknowledged instructions and replaced his receiver.

"Mrs Fulwood is not available but if you'll go up someone else may be able to see you. It's the third floor. Take the lift, the stairways are being painted." I wondered what would happen in the event of a fire.

On the third floor I was confronted with double glass doors emblazoned Fidelity Insurance Corporation - Reception. On entering I was greeted by a middle-aged, bespectacled woman guardian. I could see the modern switchboard and knew she was the one I had spoken too. I had to hope she didn't recognise me as the caller of a few minutes ago. Fortunately I had disguised my voice.

"Can I help you?" she asked as if she had no idea who I was instead of me having been announced by the watchman who had been instructed to send me up anyway.

"My name is Henry Pratt. I was hoping to have a word with your Mrs Fulwood but I understand she is not in today."

"I'm afraid not." Information point number one, she wasn't in the building. On the phone I was told she was not available which didn't necessarily mean the same thing.

"Would it be possible to see your Claims Manager then? It is rather important?"

She didn't have to check and I guessed she had been briefed already. She pointed the way down the corridor and gave me directions to his office. When I got there Mr Erdlington proved to be short and fat with sweaty palms. After we had slipped hands and sat down he asked me what he could do for me.

"I assume that you are fully in the picture regarding the reasons why Mrs Fulwood has been sent over here from the States?"

"I have been briefed on the matter," he confirmed.

"I was hoping to be able to speak to her directly," I sounded disappointed. "There is a small problem that needs addressing."

"It is unfortunate that she's not here but then she's hardly ever here anyway." Did I detect a note of criticism in his voice? "Out following up her own line of investigation," he quickly added. One had to promote a united front to the general public.

"Well, in that case I suppose that I will have to discuss the matter with you," I said in such a way that he was left in no doubt I was granting him a great honour. "You will know, I take it, that Mrs Fulwood hired my company to carry out some surveillance work."

"I do. It was I who authorised the cheque she paid you with."

"Not me but one of my employees," I pointed out. "And therein lies the problem. He has got himself mixed up in some ruckus or another and has been arrested."

"Nothing to do with us I hope?" said Erdlington.

"Certainly not," I assured him. "Nothing to do with the case in hand, although it does present me with certain problems. I'll have to brief another operative now and I cannot find the file built up by this other fellow Robel. Would it be possible to have copies of anything that was given to him?"

"I think that might be arranged," agreed Erdlington, "Although I must confess I seriously believe this is a huge waste of time and money."

I didn't want to get into an argument on the merits of the case. He obviously thought the States were suffering from paranoia and whilst I could have assured him that they were not, it was not in my favour to do so. "Not my place to say. We just perform the duty asked of us."

"Quite." He nodded his agreement. "Where do we send the documents? To the same address as before?"

"I was hoping I could take them with me now. If that is not too much trouble."

I could see it was but he was gracious about it. "Not at all. I will just arrange it," he said and left the office to do so. Five minutes later he was back.

"It'll take a few minutes," he told me.

"That is perfectly alright." Time for a little fishing. "You said before that you felt this investigation is a waste of time. Why is that?"

"I would have thought that was obvious."

"Not to me. Robel was the one briefed by Mrs Fulwood. He tends to operate with a lot of autonomy. It's only now that he is indisposed that I need to get involved."

"Well, the whole thing is based on supposition. Sure, there has been an alarming downturn in the profitability of the Fairfax account but so far there is no concrete evidence of foul play. Then to say there will be a repeat of it over here is complete paranoia. But if they want to send over one of their own to check who am I to argue."

"It must be quite unusual investigating claims before they have happened."

"It's not what I'm used to," he admitted, "but then it's not me that's involved in it. It's not my case, I've only been notified as a matter of courtesy, although the underwriters will be more concerned. Mrs Fulwood is running the show. In fact she is the show. Apart from asking me to draw a UK cheque she has not involved anyone here. No one knows where she goes and we have instructions not to concern ourselves."

"It doesn't seem an efficient state of affairs to me."

"Me neither but my hands are tied."

"Tell me. Is this Mrs Fulwood good? She must be for them to

have sent her over rather than let you use your own manpower."

"She has a certain reputation in the States," he confirmed, grudgingly.

"But this is the first time she has been sent to investigate in England?"

"As far as I'm aware. Why?"

"Well, I know Robel wondered why she chose our firm which is after all a new organisation with no track record."

"Beats me. Like I said, she's her own boss."

"I take it then that you had never met her before she arrived."

"No. Wouldn't have known her from Adam."

"Surely you mean Eve?" I quipped, relaxing into my role.

He wasn't in the mood for smiling. "I'll go and see if the copies are ready yet." He didn't have to. He could easily have used the phone but I think he had realised he had said too much and didn't want to be drawn further. Precisely four and a half minutes later I was back in the street with copies of the information previously provided in my briefcase.

I was about to head back to the Tube to head home, or what was home for the time being, when I suddenly had the urge to check the hotel at which Mrs Fulwood was staying. She said she was staying at the London Hilton, only the best for our Mrs F.

There is an art to obtaining the room number of someone staying at a hotel. Despite the ease with which such an endeavour is tackled on TV, I imagined that most hotels would not divulge the number of someone's room if asked, especially one as high class as the Hilton. A good ploy I had seen used a good number of times was the message left at the desk which the receptionist helpfully places in a box showing clearly the room number. I doubted whether it could be so easy. Hotel managers and security chiefs watch television and surely had taken action to avoid such an easy dupe. I had my own idea which may or may not have worked. Either way it was back to the telephone box for me.

Firstly, I obtained the Hilton's number from directory enquiries. Easier said than done. On asking for the number of the Hilton in London I was asked which one, there were six. Was it the London Hilton, London Olympia Hilton, London Regents Park Hilton, London Kensington Hilton, the London Hilton at Gatwick or the Langham Hilton. I pondered for a moment. I either had to take down all six or make a guess. I opted for the latter but made an educated one. She had said the London Hilton so I opted for that one. I was right first time but even after steeling myself for action I was nearly caught by surprise by the speedy answer on the first ring.

"Hello! Can you connect me to room 1169 please?"

"I'm sorry sir, our room numbers do not go that high. To whom do you wish to speak?"

"A Mrs Fulwood."

"Fulwood ... Fulwood. Ah, you need Room 230. I'll connect you."

I was banking on her being out. If she was in I would speak to her as Pratt, putting the phone down would just have been suspicious.

The phone rang out for some while before the voice at the other end said, "I'm afraid there is no answer sir. Can I take a message?"

"No thanks, I'll ring later."

Part one of the plan complete. Now I had to find out where the hotel was actually situated. I asked a passing likely affluent person and was informed it was on Park Lane. That sounded familiar but only because I was rather good at paying at hotels that other people had on Park Lane in Monopoly.

According to my street guide Park Lane ran alongside Hyde Park and there were two tube stations I could use depending on which end of Park Lane I wanted. The problem was that I didn't know and as eeny, meeny, miny, mo seemed inappropriate I chose Marble Arch as this meant I could take the red route, the Central Line, straight from Bank to Marble Arch.

On my luck to date I was bound to be at the wrong end of Park Lane and I was. I found The Dorchester about halfway down but The Hilton was right at the other end, a stone's throw from Hyde Park Corner. Once I found it I stood some way off looking and thinking, trying to plan a strategy on the hoof. I tried to remember every little ploy I'd seen in films and on TV for this sort of situation. A message that had to be given person to person, a delivery, flowers were the best bet as I doubted the guests rang out for pizza, or just the unannounced sneak through. I had the inkling of an idea but I had to be careful as a doorman dominated the entrance.

I sauntered over and stood just away from the steps, looking anxiously at my watch and then the surrounding area. Eventually I asked the doorman for the correct time and fiddled with my watch to make him think I was adjusting it. Having now established that I was waiting for someone I had a bit of time to catch the right opportunity.

Every few seconds it seemed a cab stopped in front unloading its occupants and in most cases replacing them with new customers. Many of those vacating the cabs were loaded down with purchases. The doorman opened the cab doors for the passengers to alight and the cab drivers helped load up the passengers. In the case of those with compulsory purchases disorder, additional help was summoned in the form of bellboys. Eventually I saw my chance. Two cabs arrived together and the doorman approached the first and as the couple inside seemed loaded down with bags and packages he summoned a bellboy. In the other cab there was an elderly lady with a few bags and quick as a flash I had grabbed them off the driver and smiled at the lady who preceded me into the hotel. Once inside I suggested I would wait at the lift with the bags whilst she got her key. I was trying to be my most honest, helpful and charming self and it worked. I ended up carrying those bags to her door. I was in and even got a five pound tip for my trouble.

As luck would have it her room was on the floor two above the one I needed. I took the stairs believing there was less chance of me being seen that way. Except for two couples, a businessman, an air stewardess and a vicar, no one saw me at all.

Either healthy living had even taken a hold in hotels and guests preferred the stairs to the lifts or the lifts were out of order.

Arriving at Room 230 I found the corridor empty. The next problem was how to get into the room, assuming it was still vacant that is. My unanswered phone call had been over an hour previously and the elusive Mrs F could be once again resident. I had to knock to check, knowing I would have to bluff it out if by misfortune she was there to answer. Would she recognise me with red hair? Would a dog smell a rabbit even though it had just had a bath?

I knocked and waited with bated breath, whatever that means. Fortunately, there was no response so I found myself in the position of numerous investigators of the TV variety. There were various methods available to me; pick the lock, force the lock, try to persuade a chambermaid that I was locked out of my own room so she could let me in with her pass key or pay for the adjoining room and use the connecting balcony. Although I had seen it done with everything from a hairpin to a paper clip, I had about as much chance of picking the lock as Lovejoy passing over to the police an antiquity which had fortuitously fallen at his feet from the back of a lorry. However, the lock was only a latch lock and as everyone who watches the box knows it only takes a piece of plastic to circumvent such things. I had a variety of them to choose in my wallet; Royal Bank of Scotland cash card, Tesco Clubcard, Burton Gold Account card, library card and local video shop card. Choices, choices.

Five broken cards later it was time to look for a chambermaid. There was obviously a knack to this method of entry which everyone from school kids to grannies demonstrated admirably in the world of televised fiction. Even an American Express card wouldn't have done nicely at that moment.

Far from having to turn the next corner to find a member of the hotel staff willing and able to use her pass key, I had to wander about for ten minutes before I spotted a likely linen trolley. I was at a momentary loss. You see the thing was, it was such an obvious ploy to say that your wife had the key that surely by now hotels had rules against it. Still I had nothing to lose. It was either that or hope that she still had to do 230 and enter as though belonging there when she was working in there with the door open. To my mind this latter option was too much of a risk. She may have already done that room and, even if not, I was sure to be spotted lurking suspiciously if I waited around. I had to go for the tried and telly trusted method but with a variation on the theme.

I burst through the open door of the room she was working in only to find out it was a he, fortunately my plan did not base itself on gender. "Come quick!" I yelled at him.

"Why? What is wrong, sir?"

I was dancing around holding my bottom. "My wife's got our key and I need to get into the room fast." I prayed he wasn't going to offer me the bathroom facilities in the room we were in but that must have been bad form for he followed my awkward run, one hand on my behind, to 230 and unlocked it. I doubted he heard my thank you as I bolted through the door slamming it behind me. Hopefully, he would just stroll back to his work a bemused smile on his face.

Now what to do? Search the room obviously. I'd never done this type of thing before but had seen it done numerous times. It was a large room with en suite bathroom. I checked the bedside table first but this was empty except for a Jackie Collins paperback and that other not to be missed bedtime reading, a Gideon bible. Next the set of drawers. Inevitably I started with the top drawer. "Oh, knickers," I said to myself, enjoying a good rummage through them. I found nothing except that Mrs F was into sexy silky lingerie. The other two drawers revealed nothing either. The wardrobe was next and this was full of clothes. I looked at some of the labels out of curiosity. Most of the designers meant nothing to me but something else did. I knew absolutely nothing about women's dress sizes but I was intrigued that all the outfits but two were size 10. The two exceptions were size 8. I at first wondered whether like footwear it depended on the outfit, myself I sometimes could do with a size nine whilst at other times I had to have a size 10. However, it seemed odd. The majority of the outfits were really I suppose business wear, dark jackets, trousers and suits. To my untrained eye one of the size 10 outfits and one of the size 8 looked identical. And if I didn't have to swear to it I would have said it was the suit that Mrs F had been wearing on her visit to my office.

It was a mystery but at the time I didn't rate it as very important although it took on a new slant minutes later.

There was only one other place to check as far as I could see and that was the three suitcases perched on top of the wardrobe. Two large ones and a much smaller one. The two large ones were empty but in the inside pocket of the smaller one I found something of interest, a passport, or two to be precise. One was in the name of Jane Fulwood and showed a woman not unlike the one who had presented herself at my office. It wasn't though. This one was slightly fatter in the face and although only a head shot I reckoned she would have been a slightly bigger build than the alleged Mrs F. The second passport was in the name of Rosalind Pincher and the picture was of a quite stunning woman. Hair flowing to the shoulders and unlike a passport photo a happy smiling face. It was difficult to compare with the serious and prim picture in the first photo but I knew the woman who had visited me was not Jane Fulwood but Rosalind Pincher. The two sizes of dresses made sense. Mrs Fulwood's clothes were here but where was she. No doubt the impostor knew but I was not waiting to find out.

I felt even more out of my league now. I had gambled to try and discover some more information on my employer. I had succeeded beyond my wildest dreams but realised I was caught up in something even more complicated than I thought. I was still pondering on the implications on the train journey back to Birmingham.

# CHAPTER 17

It is amazing how clear thinking one can be at times. Less than twenty four hours ago my mind had been so bogged down and slow that compared to me a Valium addict would have seemed on Viagra cloud nine. It was like my mind had been in a darkened room with many doors all of which had been locked. Finding the key to one had unlocked all the others, a master key if you will. Each locked door had been a puzzle and whilst I still didn't have all the answers at least I was making my way to the heart of each maze.

It was the morning after the day of discovery before. It was early. I couldn't sleep because my mind would not allow me to turn it off. I knew I wouldn't be able to just sit and kick my heels any more. I had to get back into the game, no matter that it would be as a soccer player entering an American football game without the padding.

The woman that had got me into this mess was not who she said she was and that complicated things but conversely made things a lot clearer. It complicated things because I was totally confused about my fellow contestants in the game. How many were there? Who was who? The things that were clearer were the things that had happened to me since I had taken on the case.

Behind each door lay the answer to a question that had been bugging me and now that the doors were unlocked the answers presented themselves. The question on Door Number One had been who was Mrs F? I'd had my doubts about her from the start. Mrs Fulwood, the one I had met, was not the real Mrs Fulwood but an impostor, one that went by the name of Rosalind Pincher. Pincher by name and pincher by nature, having misappropriated an identity, passport and two suitcases of clothes. She had needed to take the real Jane Fulwood's place and that had been done somewhere on the journey from the States otherwise why the need for the oversized clothes in the hotel room. It must have been a fast switch and Pincher had been left with the luggage and just added a small bag of her own with her size clothes in it.

Jane Fulwood did exist and did work for Fidelity Insurance in the States. She had flown to the UK for a reason. The Claims Manager of F.I.C. in London had been aware of it. This told me that the actual case I was working on was real, only the angle I was working from was off. If I hadn't been employed by the good guys that meant I was being manipulated by the ungodly. But why?

I had a theory. It was based on certain assumptions but they fitted the facts and frankly I could see no other reason behind it.

The losses of the Fairfax Corporation were fact and I figured the concern of the F.I.C. management was real. They obviously felt some fraud or grudge was involved and had feared it might spread to the UK. So far so good. This much I had been told and this much I had a gut feeling was true. The best deceptions are those that don't stray from the truth too far. The real Jane Fulwood had been despatched to the UK to prevent trouble starting here. Her intention probably to employ an investigator or team of investigators to keep an eye on the UK operations of Fairfax UK. Somehow the ungodly had found out about this and had decided to take their own counter measures; whether because the UK involvement was crucial to their plans or because any cock up here would lead to them over there, I couldn't say but the reason hardly mattered.

In a nutshell then. Jane Fulwood was to employ investigators in the UK. Both F.I.C. HQ and London knew of this. London knew she was coming but no one had met her before. The ungodly put their own woman in, so far so good. However, an investigation had to be started and a firm employed to do it. She had autonomy but HQ would be expecting to pay out fees and receive reports. The latter she could make up herself but she needed someone on the payroll as a front. So what had she done? She had employed the newest firm in the right area. The one with no experience and the least likely to achieve any results. Enter yours truly.

That was the answer to the question painted on Door Number Two in red ten feet high letters. WHY ME?

Door Number Three was easy. It was a question I had asked myself quite early on in the case and one that Vicky had also posed at our first meeting. Was I being played as a patsy? The answer to that was obviously a resounding three letter word in the affirmative. I'd thought that just maybe I was being used in the front line so others more professional could observe from a safer distance. Now I knew this was not the case. There was no doubt that I had also been under surveillance but not for that reason. I had been fed Hobson, true, but they hadn't expected me to learn anything and afterwards, I had the feeling, he would have been silenced. He had been an expendable pawn in the game, as was I.

Door Number Four was a double D. Drugs and death. Chalky had been a half-hearted attempt to frame me. I guessed we had been seen with him and probably not knowing why the ungodly had realised we had been asking him for help. They had been trying to kill two birds with one stone. They had obviously known he had not given us what we wanted and had silenced him before he could change his mind. Equally obviously they didn't know about Hobson's amnesia ploy or they would have dragged him from the hospital or eliminated him. They had used Chalky's body to frame me but it had been hasty and they had a backup plan if it failed. That's why they had planted the drugs at the same time as taking the knife. If I had gone down for Chalky's murder the drugs would still be in my flat.

I had wondered all along about that. How had they got onto me? Where had I made a mistake? From the beginning in fact. They had known all about me. I was there as window dressing for the opposition but if in the unlikely event I learnt too much I had to be taken out of the picture. In the final analysis it was all because of Vicky. If I hadn't come across her I would have still be as ignorant as I had been at the start.

Certain of the doors whilst unlocked still had rusty hinges and were still hiding their answers from me. How big was this thing I was caught in the middle of? I didn't know how big but I knew it was big. How else could you explain how the ungodly could tap into the police corruption in this country, have me jailed on a bum rap and take out those law enforcement personnel who believed me and were on my side. Also, the American end? Everything in America's big and so was this question. So big it was painted over double doors. If I could fathom that out, I instinctively knew, I would be a lot further along. And more importantly, where did I go from here?

I was on my third cup of coffee but I was as far as I could go cerebrally. What I needed was some sustenance so I went through the kitchen to use my finely honed culinary skills to prepare some cereal and toast.

Chewing on the latter covered in marmalade, I decided I had to get back to Manchester. Everyone I had been in contact with on the case was in extreme danger, especially Vicky and Jenny. Jenny more so, I thought, because as my secretary she would be expected to know most of what I knew. It was still a slight possibility that the ungodly didn't know how much in cahoots Vicky and I were. If they hadn't seen the initial contact and didn't have the Hobson house bugged then maybe they were under the impression I was using Vicky to get to her father.

Who was I kidding? I hadn't been able to fool anyone so far except myself. They were both in danger. I knew they were under surveillance because the K Team had told me so. They were therefore still in circulation but for how long? Maybe, just maybe, if I contacted the bogus Mrs F as one of the PPWP partners, I could quit the case due to lack of progress. Then Jenny would be in no more danger and Vicky would be alright as long as her father could keep up his pretence. Of course, I would still be a fugitive but one couldn't have everything.

No sooner had this thought entered my mind than I discounted it. I couldn't rely on the ungodly to leave anyone alone. They would want to tie up any loose ends no matter how remote from their plans. Also, I hated to turn tail and run. I had been pushed too far and I wanted someone to pay. And anyway, if I didn't try to resolve matters I couldn't clear myself.

As I cleared the breakfast things away I resolved to leave that day, subject to the approval of mine hosts. Fortunately, they were in when I called. They were not too happy about the situation but were unable to dissuade me, so in the end reluctantly agreed. Warning me at the same time that they would not be around to assist as they had another job to do. I hadn't expected anything else although it would have increased my chances a thousand fold to have them on my team.

It was the same procedure as before. Blindfolded and transported to Birmingham station. I was given some money and the clear framed spectacles I had requested. My hair was now black. The ginger had looked ghastly and I had been seen in that disguise. I would never have got away with blond so black it was and I'd used the more permanent dye. I was as far removed from the appearance of Thomas Robel as I was going to get.

After wishing me luck Harvey drove off. I was on my own again. If no man is an island why did I feel like a small atoll?

The train was delayed by fifteen minutes but I was too caught up in thought to notice. One half of me was cursing the other half of me for being the worst kind of fool. One who knows he's being foolish but still goes ahead as planned anyway. A fool who doesn't know he's a fool can be forgiven for his ignorance. A fool who knows he's a fool but foolishly persists in acting foolishly has only himself to blame. I was a bigger fool than the lawyer acting on his own behalf.

The reason half of me felt this way was obvious. I was a fugitive from both sides. Justice on one hand and the ungodly on the other, although to all intents and purposes they were the same. Those who professed to be on the side of justice were heavily influenced by the wishes of my enemies. The true forces of justice had been brought to death or condemned to hiding for their lives. Not only this, I was walking back into the lion's den with a disguise which would fool Mr Bean for about ten seconds.

If one was being charitable one could have said that the half of me that was being criticised for being foolish was in fact brave. Rushing out gallantly to face the enemy head on. Don't you believe it. If it wasn't for Vicky and Jenny, and to a lesser extent Hobson and his wife, I would have been halfway to Lapland by now.

What did I think I was playing at? I didn't even have anywhere to stay. I couldn't use the flat because it was being watched. I'd have to be most careful even about contacting the office. There was in fact no one I could rely on who wasn't already in the frame.

As I realised what I was heading into the panic started to rise in me like lava simmering in a pre-eruption volcano. To try to take my mind off it I started going over the case in my mind again to see if I had missed anything and Eureka, suddenly another of those doors swung open.

I had been thinking about how things had started, all those incidents in the States. Co-ordinated they had been. There were too many coincidences for them not to have been. Therefore there had to be an overall aim. One party that would benefit, be it a group or an individual. Whoever it was had either an enormous grudge or expected financial benefits. Perhaps both. The acquisition of money was certainly involved. Take the two cases of paralysis. Induced paralysis, I felt it was safe to say. With both victims dead and the damages disappearing along with paramours who did not exist. That was a cool $8,000,000 to start with. Michael Caine's Italian Job persona would have been over the moon with such a sum, especially as it wasn't contained in a coach precariously balanced over a cliff. However, we were dealing with big league here. $8,000,000 was small potatoes.

Looking at the fires and thefts. These seemed to be aimed at valuable areas of the Corporation. Maximum loss and disruption. In the case of the thefts there was also the fact that most of the items taken were individually high value, low bulk. The fact that none of these had yet turned up on the black market did not disprove my theory. Someone was playing a waiting game. A cat playing with the mouse. In the end when the furore died down I guessed those items would be sold but the ill-gotten gains would be peanuts compared to the rest. Even the paintings.

If there was one person controlling things it had to be someone in the know. The intelligence of the A.F.G. was too good. It was either someone with excellent connections or it was an inside job and if the latter it was someone in authority. I had been over this ground before when I had been trying to make sense of it at the beginning. That conjecture had been useless but now I had another piece of the puzzle. It was just a case of where it fitted.

The last thing one needs when one is trying to concentrate on a cerebral problem is a kid running around tooting a toy trumpet. To say that he broke into my train of thoughts was a bit of an understatement. It must have been right against my ear and I must have jumped about ten feet in the air. He was off before I could catch him, blowing a victory fanfare. I hadn't taken much notice of my fellow passengers so didn't know who was in charge of the little bugler. Fortunately another guy had not been so preoccupied and after getting a blast himself he turned around to a woman who was dozing in her seat. She must have been used to the noise. "Unless you want me to make him eat that thing you'd better take it off him," growled the man. The woman shrugged, called the kid over and took the offending instrument. The crying that ensued was only slightly lower in the decibel level. The glare of the man was enough to lower this to a mere whimper.

I turned my mind back to the problem in hand and found that the near shattering of my eardrums had cleared away some of the cobwebs. Previously I had discounted the possibility of profit for two reasons. Firstly, the stolen items had not been off loaded but I'd changed my thinking on that now. Secondly, it was impossible that one person could profit from the insurance money as it was paid to different divisions with independent financial controllers.

I had been wrong. I didn't have one extra piece of the puzzle I had two. Mrs Fulwood, nee Pincher, was one and the modus operandi regarding Hobson was the other. OK it was all guesswork on the part of Vicky and myself but it was educated guesswork. Hobson was being coerced by a threat to his family. The same thing could have happened in the States but on a larger scale. The UK operation was really just one division with Hobson as controller and to get him to do what was required his family were being used. I wondered if all the controllers of the Stateside divisions were under similar duress. Not only would this mean that they would do whatever was required to assist the A.F.G. but also would be in a position to pass over the insurance money. Of course it wasn't just as simple as that because the disappearance of the money would have to be explained. Nevertheless the planning had been perfect so far and I was sure that whoever was behind it had fathomed out that problem also.

So we had a person in a position of high authority in the Fairfax Corporation but what about the other piece of the puzzle? Where did that fit? The fact that the ungodly had known about the real Jane Fulwood's visit and had felt the need to intervene suggested that someone at F.I.C. was also involved. Again someone at a very senior level Stateside. Two people working together maybe. No. Mr Big was probably using his contact at the insurance end too. Perhaps that was his first conquest and the reason for it all. Once he had an ally in the insurance company's camp, whether assisting willingly or not, it would have been so much easier.

For a brief second I felt like a great burden had been lifted from my shoulders. I was as light as a Special K flake. Then the whole thing came crashing back down weighing heavier than before. Big Daddy had just removed himself off me after his famous Splash only for an elephant to sit on me before I could get up off the canvas. Who was I kidding? I had a wild theory and nothing more. Sure it fitted the facts but I had no tangible proof. If I could have got someone to check up the angles in the States maybe I could get things moving but my contact was as much use as a  padlock on the stable door after the horse has bolted and been killed in a motor accident. I couldn't even report to anyone in the UK. Those I could trust were either dead or missing.

The train was just pulling in to Manchester. The time for action was at hand but I felt oppressed with the enormity of the task. The kid had got his trumpet back and was blaring away. It sounded like the Last Post to me.

The obvious place to start was the office. It was only about fifteen minutes' walk from the station. I knew it was staked out but what choice did I have. The phone was bound to be bugged. Even a cryptic conversation on the phone would alert them to my presence. By innocently walking into the building with my new look I may just get away with it. If the office itself was not bugged at least I could have a few words with Jenny.

As I came to the corner before the street where the office building was situated I consciously altered my stance. People had told me I tended to slouch a lot with shoulders drooping so I therefore stood up straight and sauntered jauntily along swinging my arms. The only reason I wasn't whistling was because I couldn't. Pucker up your lips and blow. Trouble was when I did that all I achieved was a raspberry.

I figured that the outside would definitely be under a watchful eye, either from a parked car or someone loitering in a doorway. Without appearing to notice I saw five possibilities. Three cars on the street had occupants. Two were on a meter but one was on a double yellow. I discounted him as he would surely be moved on. There was also a young guy stood drinking out of a soft drinks can, idly as if waiting for someone. Finally, there was a bag lady, sat with all here paraphernalia around her. It was impossible to know who it was. Maybe there was more than one. Indeed it was likely, as the K Team had said, that there were watchers from both sides, even though both sides were the same side.

Not giving any of them a second glance, I stopped and studied the nameplate by the door of the building two up from my objective. Not seeing what I sought I continued sauntering to the next doorway. Take two. Finally with a pointed finger jabbing at a nameplate on my own building, not my own, which was merely a scrap of cardboard, I entered and began to climb the stairs. No one seemed to be following but I passed the second floor and continued to the third and top floor. I walked all the way round the maze of corridors until I was at the stairwell again. Still no sound except the quiet murmur from nearby offices and no one in sight. Satisfied, I made my way back down to the second floor, meeting no one on their way up. Outside the office I glanced up and down the corridor. Still unobserved, I swiftly opened the door and went in.

"Oh! Can I help you?" Jenny was clearly startled and became more so when I just stood there and grinned at her. It might have been the day she had started and me just returning from hiring a car. So much had happened in between it seemed impossible that life could have been so easy and yes, boring. What I wouldn't give for that boredom now.

Incidentally, my hire car should have been returned ages ago. I wondered if the company had recovered it from my flat. Was there such a thing as a black list in respect of car rental?

Crazy thought. Back to reality. "Jenny, it's me."

"Tommy!" she cried.

"Shhhhhh! Not too loud," I begged her. There well may have been bugs in the office and even that one word would have given me away. I had to pray that no one was listening in.

"Where have you been?" she whispered. "I've been worried sick?"

"It's a long story and I haven't got time to tell you now," I told her. "Please just fill me in on what's happened whilst I've been away."

"Nothing much."

I couldn't believe it. "Nothing much?" I'd been running for my life and here things had been meandering along at a snail's pace. Although there were things happening that she wasn't aware of.

"Not really," she affirmed. "Peter Hobson is still in the hospital with amnesia, although I think they are about to let him go home, hoping the familiar environment will jog his memory. Vicky's been on a number of times to ask if I'd heard from you, other than that it's been very quiet and boring.

I'd been out of circulation for a week and whilst it seemed a lot longer to me because of what I'd been through, when you really come down to it a week is only seven days.

"Where have you been?" asked Jenny.

"Out of my depth." I was surprised she had not heard via news reports. Perhaps the authorities were trying to keep it quiet, or rather those shady members of authority were, to keep themselves out of it. But then I remembered that the K Team had told me that Vicky had tried to see me in prison when the news broke. Jenny was obviously aware of that then, she must have meant since I'd broken out.

"Can I help in any way?" she offered.

"Unfortunately, I've got a feeling that nobody will be able to help me out of this mess," I said. "Things have taken a distinct turn for the worse. The best thing you can do is to close up the office and stay at home for a few days."

"Why?"

"Please don't argue," I beseeched her. "I haven't got time."

"OK. You're the boss." And she started packing up her desk, though what she had to pack up was anybody's guess. There can't have been any work to do.

"Wait a minute." I was having second thoughts. "Best leave it until the end of the day when you would normally leave. Just don't come back in tomorrow. Act as if you are ill until you hear from me." I didn't want to start getting the watchers suspicious. "And before I go I'd like you to do something for me."

"Anything I can do to help," she offered.

The whole conversation so far, except for Jenny's initial surprised exclamation, had been done in whispers. If there was a listening device in the office I didn't know whether the level was low enough to be indecipherable. I had the vague feeling I had read somewhere that even turning on a shower was not sufficient these days. If we had been overheard it was too bad. If they hadn't stormed the building by now, then they were playing a waiting game, which suited me. They might even leave Jenny alone now I'd in effect taken her out of the picture.

I put my fingers to my lips, picked up her pen and wrote on her message pad. I asked her to arrange a meeting with Vicky. Just two girls meeting up to catch up on things. When they met up she was to let Vicky know where and when I would contact her.

Not wanting to hang around longer than was necessary I told her I would be in touch and left, after having warned her to be extremely careful.

I didn't want to leave by the front of the building. If anyone had overheard our conversation they would be more vigilant now and I might not get past them. I wandered around the ground floor looking for a back door. There was only a fire door. I pushed the bar and an alarm started screeching. I ran for it and didn't stop until I was halfway to the station.

I had a lot of time to kill until I could meet Vicky. I wanted to go back to the flat but that would have been ludicrously dangerous. That place would be under close surveillance for sure. I had to get lost somewhere I wasn't expected to visit. This excluded therefore the office, my flat, Vicky's house, the hospital and the Fairfax offices. I decided to jump on the first train and get off at anywhere that took my fancy.

Not as easy as it sounded. I would have to buy a ticket to somewhere. According to the departure board there was a train to Crewe leaving in ten minutes. This was ideal as it was on the same line as Alderley Edge, the nearest station to Vicky's house. I bought a ticket, got on the train, sat back and contemplated my next move.

From those we were about to deceive may the Lord make us truly sneaky.

# CHAPTER 18

I wet my trousers. Not because I was scared, although given recent events I had as much right to be as Gazza has to cry over a packet of crisps, but because I tripped over a branch and put my knee in a puddle. I was already scratched and bruised but then walking through a strange dense wood at nearly midnight tends to do that to you.

Hopefully, Jenny had been able to tell Vicky that I would meet her at her home at midnight. As they intended to meet in the open and Jenny intended to get this piece of information across within a lot of girlie chat, the forces of the ungodly should be more in the dark than I was. Even so I was taking no chances and was approaching the house through the wood at the back. I had taken a cab from the station and got the driver to drop me off a couple of miles away, making my way across fields and below hedges. If the house was under surveillance I had done as much as I could to arrive undetected.

Vicky had left the back door open as per instructions. I had been well trained as a kid and took off my trainers so I wouldn't leave any wet marks on the kitchen floor. Most of my best intentions go awry and as my socks were also saturated so did this one. I also thought I'd been as silent as a church mouse on Valium but I totally spoiled this when I opened the door out of the kitchen and jumped back, arms flailing and knocking a set of pans to the floor. It was rather startling to open a door to find a gun pointing at your head.

Vigilant Vicky. She switched on the light and stood there smiling as I lay on the floor, down with the pans. She was that amused that she didn't seem to see the trail of dirty footprints leading across the tiled floor, no linoleum here. As there was a distinct lack of danger she put her gun in the classic position, in the waistband of her jeans in the small of her back.

Probably needlessly, I placed my finger to my lips as I got to my feet and dragged my dignity from the floor. I'd made enough noise to alert every eavesdropper in the county. Well, they would be straining their ears for nothing. I motioned her outside.

After replacing my trainers we wandered down the garden, not hand in hand but then one can't have everything.

"Well!" she demanded. "Where the hell have you been?"

"It's a long story," I said and related events since that phone call just after Chalky had been killed. When I was finished she was lost for words for once. Perhaps it was the realisation of what we had got ourselves involved in and the ruthless people we were up against. Maybe she was having second thoughts about helping me.

"You were mad to come back," was her eventual comment.

"I've started so I'll finish." It didn't take a mastermind to see that I was very mad indeed. "What's been happening here?"

"Not a lot," she responded, confirming Jenny's assessment. "After your call I rushed to the hospital and stayed there two days but nothing out of the ordinary happened. Mother is there all the time, she is staying in a hotel near the hospital."

"Is your father still playing his charade?"

"No change there. If it is phoney, as we're as positive as we can be without any actual corroboration, he's a much better actor than I thought he would be. No one has any suspicions as far as I'm aware."

"I'm surprised he's still in the hospital."

"Not for much longer. He's coming out at the weekend. The doctor says there is nothing that can be done except wait. At least in familiar home surroundings his memory is more likely to return. "

"It'll be easier to keep tabs on him then."

"True, she admitted." As long as he keeps it up he will have no reason to go anywhere in connection with this business."

That was one problem solved then I thought. As long as the ungodly didn't wise up. That left us free to concentrate on tackling the real issue, stopping the bad guys in their tracks, although what to do next was the question.

"What do we do next?"

"Hand it over to the proper authorities," suggested Vicky. "We have some proof now with what you have found out about the woman purporting to be Jane Fulwood."

"It's not conclusive," I told her. "Besides who do we tell? There is obviously corruption at a high level involved here. I was placed in prison on a trumped up charge and the only guys I can trust on the Force are dead or in hiding."

"What about the American end? Why don't you report it to the insurance company, either the London office or the office in the States where Jane Fulwood is based?"

"Because again there is corruption in that organisation. How else would the ungodly have known about her visit and be able to abduct her, substituting their own person? I would think the London office is clean, otherwise they wouldn't have had to use an American, but I can't believe that there isn't some way for them to discover anything of interest that turns up there."

"What about the A.C.C.S.?"

"I asked them but they are on another job."

"Do you mean to say that you didn't arrange a way to keep in touch?"

"Well, they did give me a mobile number but stressed that I only use it in a dire emergency."

"Don't you think that the position we are in merits the term 'dire emergency'?"

"Not exactly," I had to tell her. "Matters are no worse than when I left them."

"What other choices do we have left?"

"Only one," I said.

"And that is?"

"Justin Fairweather."

"Who?"

"The lawyer who sprung me from jail. It only just occurred to me but he said he was in contact with Cox. If I could get in touch with him then maybe we could make a plan."

"So how do we contact this guy Fairweather then?"

"Well, that could be the tricky bit. Understandably he couldn't leave me a card at the time and I haven't seen him since. I suppose it's possible that he may make contact with me eventually but we can't afford to wait. He said he was also a licensed private investigator. We'll have to hit the Yellow Pages."

"Let our fingers do the walking," said Vicky.

"Probably not," I disagreed. "The one you will have in the house will only cover South Manchester. I don't even know if he came from this area."

"What about his accent?"

"I'm not too good on accents," I admitted. "Mind you I can tell you he wasn't Scottish, Irish, Brummie, Geordie or Scouse."

"Well, that certainly narrows it down." Vicky's natural sarcasm was coming to the fore.

"Nobody said it was going to be easy," I pointed out. "Nothing in this whole business has been easy. If he's not in Manchester South we will have to hit the library tomorrow. They will have all areas."

That was a plan.

We both turned and started back for the house.

"No talking inside," I warned her. "We'll just look through your Yellow Pages, which won't take us long and then I'll be on my way."

"No sitting down on the furniture with those wet and muddy clothes on," said Vicky. "You can stand up in the kitchen."

Her words made me remember how cold and wet I felt. "Perhaps a coffee whilst we work," I hinted.

"Perhaps," she replied.

Once inside we were as silent as two Trappist monks who have fallen out and were not speaking to each other. Vicky stationed me on the tiled floor in the kitchen and went to fetch the Yellow Pages which she plonked on the counter. Whilst she made the coffee I browsed through law firms and private investigators with not high hopes and in that I was not disappointed.

I conveyed this lack of success with a shake of my head and then we just sat at the kitchen table sipping our coffee.

It could have been one of those moments when a man and woman gaze longingly into each other's eyes but it wasn't. Partly because Vicky was miles away, her eyes glassy and a vacant expression on her face, but mainly because of the large man who smashed through the kitchen door.

Actually, Vicky couldn't have been as far gone as I thought because she grabbed my hand and pulled me from my seat before the door took the brunt of a broad shoulder. She had seen a shadow across the window which I had missed as I had my back to the window. Even before I could utter my disclaimer against damage to carpets from muddy footwear, she had dragged me out of the kitchen. She made off down the hall to the front door but unfortunately someone was engaged in knocking that one down as well. She had to make a quick decision, into the lounge or up the stairs. She chose the latter and, let me tell you, I wasn't being dragged at this stage I was pushing her ahead of me.

She dashed into a room and slammed the door behind me. We stood still and over our rasping breath heard a thud as one of the doors caved in. I hoped it was the back one. At least I could get some malicious satisfaction from the fact that some energy and muscle had been wasted there. The door had been unlocked all the time.

We heard a lot of crashing and banging from downstairs. Presumably they were searching for something. Then after a few minutes it all went deathly quiet. Even after waiting another fifteen minutes not another sound was heard. It was weird. They knew we were there. They had to know we were upstairs. Why had they not been up to get us?

We waited another ten minutes but still all was quiet as the grave.

"Do you think they've gone?" whispered Vicky.

"I don't know but if they are still down there they must be asleep," I replied, in similar low tones. It was doubtful that they were listening outside but conversing quietly just seemed the right thing to do.

"What do you think they wanted?"

"Me, you, both of us, but from all appearances it seems they were looking for something that they thought was here."

"That doesn't quite ring true," Vicky stated. "They wouldn't have left the upstairs, particularly as we are here."

She had a point. If they had gone, and there was no reason to think otherwise, either they had found what they were looking for or they had not been after us or anything else, in which case it had just been a warning. The trouble was that matters had progressed well beyond the warning stage.

We had delayed going downstairs long enough. We both knew it but neither of us seemed to want to be the one to broach the subject of leaving our sanctuary. In the end I turned the key unlocking the door. Vicky nodded.

Ladies first. I was a gentleman and let Vicky precede me although it was less an act of chivalry than of self-preservation. She had the gun and knew how to use it.

We crept down the stairs and surveyed the wanton destruction. It was probably enough to have made some weep. Her mother may well have done so on seeing the desolation but Vicky just got mad. She started to rant and rave, waving the gun in the air. I was distinctly worried because the safety catch was off and I began wishing she would engage it again before she actually shot something or more importantly someone.

A wish too soon. The lounge, kitchen and the other rooms on the ground floor were clear of intruders but not wreckage. Unfortunately, there was one place we forgot to check and just when our guard was down our friends erupted from the cupboard under the stairs guns in hands. Vicky was quick. She had been standing in the lounge doorway and got off a couple of shots before diving through. As she was the danger they concentrated on her. I was already in the lounge and had ducked quickly behind the sofa. Vicky flung herself behind a tall bookcase and from around the side kept her gun pointed at the door. One of the guys dived through and behind an armchair just inside the room. Vicky's shot took a chunk out of the wall and his shot from cover just nicked the edge of the bookcase. Vicky was stuck now. The guy behind the armchair could pick her off if she even peeped around the side of the bookcase. She knew it and so did the other guy who took this opportunity to enter the room also.

It was up to me. I considered jumping the guy behind the armchair but his buddy would just pick me off from where he had flattened himself on the opposite end of the bookshelf to Vicky. I peered around the end of the sofa furthest from the gunmen so Vicky could see me. She was motioning with her fingers. One, two, three. She must have thought I had a clear view of both men for the gun flew through the air in my direction, in slow motion it seemed to me. I had seen this done before and knew what to do. Catch the gun, insert the finger through the trigger guard, aim and fire all in one smooth motion. How come no one I had seen do this on TV or on film had actually caught the barrel.

"Yow! That's hot," I yelled, dropping our only protection to the floor.

It was all over. With hands up, Vicky came out from her hiding place glaring at me. If her eyes had been lasers I would have been an instant piece of fried chicken. I also emerged looking decidedly sheepish.

"What is the meaning of this?" Vicky demanded.

"You know very well," came the reply from one of the men.

"No! I'm sure I have no idea."

"We want him."

"Take him then," she said. "He's of no importance to me."

"It's not that easy lady," grinned the other one. "All for one and one for all. Where he goes you go."

"How did you know I was here?" I asked for something to say.

"The house is bugged," I was told.

"But we never spoke in the house."

"No, but no one person pours two cups of coffee for themselves."

So that was it. The coffee. It must have been an extremely sophisticated listening device to have picked that up I thought to myself, but then I was hardly the master of undercover surveillance techniques as had been proved not so long ago.

"Time for forty winks," declared the first one, removing a hypodermic from one pocket and a phial of some clear liquid from the other.

This was an increasingly alarming trend that had cropped up in my TV viewing. No longer was a quick cosh on the head good enough these days. No chloroformed cloth would do. Anyone apparently could give an injection. One didn't need a medical degree. I knew I couldn't do it. I wouldn't even have been able to find a vein. At least he squirted a bit out first to remove the air bubbles. As I drifted into blackness I reflected on the injustice of it all.

I don't know how long it was before I regained consciousness but when I did I had a head like a savagely squeezed sponge. There were also a few moments of disorientation. It was dark but there was noise and movement. I was in a van. My hands and feet were tied tightly and I couldn't help remembering that time not so long ago when in a similar predicament I had managed to escape, right back into the hands of my captors. This time was different for I wasn't chained to a ring and so was mobile after a fashion.

I rolled around trying to locate anything to assist in a bit of rope cutting but I found nothing except someone's lap with my head. It had to be Vicky and I guessed she wouldn't have been too pleased at that moment. Tied up in the back of a van going who knew where, she was a strong girl and could cope with that; but my head in her lap, that was beyond the pale.

I managed to get myself back up into a sitting position next to her. Despite me calling her name and nudging her with my head she remained out cold for some time. It was difficult to judge sat there in the dark, unable to look at a watch, but I would have guessed thirty three minutes and six seconds elapsed before she started to come round.

Unfortunately, I had no time to brief her because all of a sudden the van stopped and seconds later someone was unlocking the rear doors. Light poured in, showing us the two intruders of what must have been the night before. One of them got into the van and untied my feet then shoved me roughly to the doors where his colleague waited with a pointed gun. "Get down," he drawled. Vicky was dealt with in a similar way although she was more bewildered having only just regained consciousness.

I looked around. The van was parked just off a dirt track in some trees. There were open fields over the other side of the track and dense forest before us. We were shepherded the hard way through the forest. The further we went the denser it became until it was difficult to tell if it was day or night. We were just pushed through getting scraped and scratched, the two behind us having an easier time with us having trampled everything for them. With our hands still tied behind our backs we had more than our fair share of stumbles too but they didn't care, they just kept pushing.

Trudging through that seemingly impenetrable vegetation I was deep in thought. What strange twist had events taken now? Abduction in the middle of the night. Drugged and transported to an unknown destination. And now jungle training. We were being taken somewhere specific that was obvious but for what purpose. I had a nasty feeling that we were just being taken to a place deep in the forest where our bodies would never be found. There was no other obvious explanation why we were being shoved along on foot. But then this was too much trouble. We were obviously miles away from where we had been taken, at least eight hours journey time. There was full daylight and we had succumbed not far after midnight. Maybe we were going somewhere else.

Even so, I was on the lookout for a chance to turn the tables but none presented itself. In one way our two captors reminded me of my old friends, Tweedledum and Tweedledee. They were the strong and silent type. However, these two did at least have a brain cell between them. They always kept themselves at arm's length except for the occasional shove in the back. They both had guns trained on us and there wasn't a chance in a million of jumping them and getting away with it unencumbered, that is without carrying a bullet, even if Vicky and I could co-ordinate our efforts which we couldn't because we were not allowed to converse.

A cry of pain broke into my thoughts. Vicky went sprawling full length and sat there nursing her ankle. It was badly twisted as could be seen from how swollen it was when she took her boot off. We could all see that she wouldn't be able to walk but that was no problem for our captors. Whilst I would gladly have carried Vicky over a threshold, I sincerely hoped that we did not have that far to go now. One of them could have carried her much more easily than me, they had muscles. That would have left only one of them with a gun and they were too wary for that. So I was the beast of burden. At least crashing through the undergrowth was a thing of the past. Now one of them was in front clearing a path. Also my hands were no longer tied and the shoving from behind was over too.

If Vicky had just kept her feet for five minutes longer. That was all it took to emerge from the trees. I was damn glad about it too because that tramp from the van had taken its toll. Not that we had travelled that far, I estimated we had only done a mile or so, but it had been a fight all the way. The thick foliage was more reminiscent of the Amazon jungle than an English forest and machetes would not have been out of order. When we had clambered through the last bush I was battered, bruised, tired and had soaking feet from the damp grass and puddles we had encountered. Yet my misery was soon forgotten when I spied our destination, or what I assumed was our destination, which was clearly visible about a quarter of a mile away. Not that it wouldn't have been visible over a greater distance

We had emerged from the forest at the edge of a large lake and across from the water rose this resplendent castle straight out of the stories of King Arthur. It was square in shape with a tower at each corner and was surround by a moat which seemed to be fed by the lake via a small stream. I could see a road leading to the castle which ran to the left of the lake and this was where we now headed for. The distance to the castle may have been a quarter of a mile in a straight line but skirting the lake made it more like a mile.

I could have thought of less obtrusive ways of making an entrance than three men and one woman strolling up to the gates, well two strolling and one staggering under a labour of if not exactly love then companionship in time of trouble. Still we made it without any further mishap.

The moat was indeed fed by the lake and was about twelve feet wide. Entry to the castle was inevitably by drawbridge, which had been in a vertical position at first but someone was expecting us or was keeping a good lookout for as we neared it lowered and the portcullis was raised. We made our way to the gatehouse and entrance passage which were flanked with octagonal towers three storeys in height. There was no one there to meet us.

Outside the gatehouse the passage we had been following emerged into the courtyard and I got a real glimpse of the grandeur of the place. The passageway led onto a gravel drive which was just wide enough for a vehicle. At first, bordered by green lawns, then widening out into a forecourt in front of what must have been the main hall. It covered nearly all the back wall and half of the right hand side wall of the castle in an 'L' shape but with a little protrusion at the top so it really looked like a 'J' with half its top cut off. The hall was three stories in height but even so the battlements were five feet or so above its roof. The lawn to the right of the gravel drive was a square bordered by the forecourt, end of the hall and right hand corner of the castle walls next to the gatehouse. Whereas the gravel drive spread out into the forecourt on the right, on the left it bent around giving half the shape of an M with the central drive and ending in some other buildings along the right hand wall which appeared to be stables. The remaining space between the top end of the stable block and the hall was also lawn.

There were two vehicles parked on the forecourt, a green Range Rover and a metallic blue Mini. Not many vehicles for the occupants of a building that size but then unless I missed my guess most of those inside wouldn't be needing a vehicle, or it was probably more correct to say that they desperately needed one but would not be allowed near one. Perhaps that was a reason for only the two, less temptation. There were some people standing at the main door to the hall awaiting us. Now that breaking down bushes and low hanging branches was not required I was in the lead, still carrying Vicky and trying my best not to stumble with the exertion. Both of our minders were now behind, guns prominent.

There were only three people there to greet us when we made the steps leading to the hall. I had spied another two before but they had now disappeared. One of the three remaining came forward.

"Good, you have them," he greeted our captors. "You can leave them to us now. Here's your money." He passed them a briefcase which had been handed to him by one of his colleagues.

Our companions for the last few hours just shrugged and started back the way they had come taking the briefcase with them. Even in the dream state I seemed to be in that surprised me in two ways. Firstly, they never counted the money nor even checked to see if, in fact, there was money in the case. Secondly, I would have thought they might have requested a lift back to the van. They must have known beforehand that this was out of the question and resolutely set out for the return trek through the forest. Mind you, it would be less strenuous for them this time, especially if they backtracked our original approach.

"Welcome to your new home," announced the man who had handed out the money. He seemed to be the one in charge. "Shall we go inside?"

# CHAPTER 19

We entered a flagstone entrance hall with the obligatory standing suits of armour and shields bearing various coats of arms adorning the walls. Ahead lay a wide grand staircase and there were three doors leading from the hall, two on the right and one on the left. There was also a long corridor off to the right with more doors off it. We were ushered through the left-hand door into a luxurious sitting room. No flagstones here but a thick pile, gold coloured carpet. Heavy velvet curtains hung at the windows. There were modern and comfortable leather arm-chairs and sofas, glass topped coffee tables and even a TV and Hi-Fi. Even the stone walls had been plastered and painted. Walking from the hall into this room was like walking through a time barrier. From medieval times to present day. It was weird and incongruous.

Our host took a seat and waved us to do the same. I still had Vicky in my arms and carefully laid her down on a sofa. I sat on the arm.

"Did you have an accident?" he asked. "Not the fault of my men I hope."

"It's just a twisted ankle," came Vicky's terse reply. "But it is almost certainly the fault of you and your men. If we hadn't been abducted in the middle of the night it wouldn't have happened would it."

"Listen to the innocent," he purred looking at the other two men who were standing guarding the door. "Consorting with a known criminal who is wanted by the police for drug pushing, murder and jail break."

"All put up jobs as I'm sure you're fully aware," I retorted angrily.

"As a matter of fact no. But then that doesn't concern me. My job is here, and now that you are here that means you two too." He smiled as a shark might smile on meeting a school of tuna, all that protein and no tin to open. "As you will see," he continued, "we have a large accommodation here and we need to have because we have a fair few guests. Most of them I'm afraid, like you, are reluctant guests but that doesn't mean their stay is any less enjoyable. There are rules here of course, and if you obey them you will come to no harm. Just a peaceful rest away from the rigours of home life. If not, your time here can be made very uncomfortable. I'm sure your fellow guests will inform you of the rules when you have a chance to meet them. For now you will be shown to your rooms, and, my dear, I will have some ice sent up for your ankle." He stood up to leave. "Roger and Dirk will show you the way. I have things to do before dinner. Enjoy your stay."

He left and the lasting impression he'd had on me was that I didn't like him. He was in charge of course and had a veneer of urbane civility but it was the thinnest layer, I felt, and he was hard pushed to keep it. He was tall, muscled and in his late thirties, I would have guessed. For all the world he reminded me of an East End hood put in charge of a game of country house charades.

His two cronies escorted us up the stairs. Nothing was said, they let their gestures do the talking. I couldn't put my finger on it but one of them seemed vaguely familiar. I knew it wouldn't come to me if I was trying to drag it from my subconscious, so instead, I concentrated on looking at the portraits of someone's dead ancestors which hung on the walls all the way up the stairs and beyond into a corridor. A family history in a series of paintings. I couldn't catch any of the names without moving for a closer look and as I was still carrying Vicky it was not the best time. It was something I could investigate later. If I knew the family name I maybe could find out where we were. The place must surely have a library.

The corridor we found ourselves in had five doors. Two on the left and three on the right. We were shown to the end door on the right which we entered. It was a bedroom, obviously occupied because there were some clothes strewn around the place and an open suitcase on the four poster bed. There were two doors off this room. One of them was open and I could see it was an en suite bathroom. The other was closed and one of our escorts opened it for us. It was another smaller bedroom although there was still a four poster bed in it.

"You stay here," announced the one who looked like Lurch out of the Addams Family. He then left leaving us with the other guy, the one who gave me this feeling of familiarity.

I was just about to lay Vicky on the bed when he spoke. "You don't half get around don't you?" I was so surprised that I nearly dropped her.

"Hey! Watch it!"

"Sorry. It's just that I know that voice." I turned and the guy was grinning at me. I didn't recognise him by physical appearance but the voice was a dead give-away, although whether it was Henry, Herbert, Harvey or Howard I could not be sure. One thing I was now sure of was the feeling of familiarity which had been bugging me, the watch on the right wrist.

"Will someone mind telling me what is going on," demanded Vicky.

"You better tell her," I said. "I'm nearly as much in the dark as she is."

"Later," was H's reply. "I have things to do."

He turned to leave but Vicky gave a snort of disgust which made him turn around. "Do you mean to say that I have to share this room with him?" She knew how to hurt a person. "Share the same bed with him?" Things were definitely looking up.

"I'm afraid so for now," he replied. "For the time being that is. When you meet the other guests there may be some bed-hopping."

"And what is that supposed to mean?"

"Wait and see."

This time he did go and we were left in our room. We could clearly hear a key being turned in the lock. We were prisoners although things were not as bad as they could have been. The

A.C.C.S. were obviously on the case, although how they had got involved was beyond me. When I had asked them for assistance they had intimated that they had a prior engagement. Of course, Vicky wasn't aware of their presence and I didn't know how much to tell her.

"How is your ankle?" I asked her, for want of something better to say.

"Sore. What's going on?" Her eyes were trying to read my face and I had to make an instant decision. One on which lay not just our lives but those of everyone else in the castle who were on the side of the angels.

One of the Kelly brothers was on hand, that much I knew for sure. Maybe they all were. The fact that he had said as much as he did seemed to indicate there were no listening devices in the room. The A.C.C.S. wouldn't have overlooked such a necessary precaution. His comments, guarded though they were, would have been enough to make any listeners suspicious. I had to believe therefore that it was safe to speak.

"I don't know for sure but things are not as black as they seem," I assured her. "By some strange coincidence the A.C.C.S. are here or at least one of their number is."

"That guy that just left?"

"Right. Though don't ask me which one he is because I don't have a clue."

"Where do you think we are? Things seem to be totally out of control now."

"They're certainly out of our control at the moment," I agreed. "As to where we are I have no idea of the location but I have a feeling I know what this place is used for."

"What?"

"A holding cell." She gave me a questioning frown so I tried to explain my thinking further. "You remember when we talked about the possibility of your sister being in danger? The fact that she might be held to force your father into co-operating?"

"God. I'd forgotten all about Sam." She sounded ashamed of the fact.

"Don't beat yourself up. A lot has happened recently. And if I'm right your sister could be here."

"How do you come to that conclusion?"

"Well, I've had longer to think about this than you have, particularly as you must have been worrying about your father most of the time. It all starts with what happened in the States and that is what I tried to concentrate on." She remained silent so I carried on. "The problem about this case has always been that if there was a conspiracy going on over there it seemed impossible that one person could benefit with each division of the Corporation being financially autonomous. Each one has their financial controller or equivalent and each of these individuals would receive any insurance money for losses concerning their own divisions. Taking this into account unless all the finance people were involved jointly how could it work?"

"I would have to agree," admitted Vicky. "There doesn't seem any way one person could manipulate this to profit from it."

"I have been worrying at this problem on and off since I was given the case. Without realising I think we hit on the answer when we were trying to work out the change in your father's behaviour. We agreed that the only way he would cooperate with the forces of the ungodly was if the family were being threatened, particularly if your sister was being held hostage."

"You mean she is being held here?"

"I'm almost certain of it. That is how it's been worked, even in the States. If family members of each person they wanted to control were abducted and held as hostages then everyone would do as they were instructed. I'm sure that if it could be checked it would be found that all the money from the claims already paid will by various means have been transferred to one central fund accessible by one or maybe two people.

"If we take this scenario a bit further we can assume that all the hostages are being held together. A smaller force can hold them together than each one individually. Therefore if we assume that any person that they need to use in the UK has close

PRATT, PRATT, WALLY & PRATT INVESTIGATE

relatives in the hands of the bad guys then they would all be held together and I suspect that we are at that place. That guy in charge said that there were other guests, remember. Reluctant guests."

"So what do we do now?" Vicky was still dispirited. "We are caught in the trap we were trying to prevent."

"All we can do for now is wait. I don't know any more, and what I do know is mere conjecture, but we do have at least one person here who's on our side."

She pressed me for more information but I felt it was not fair to build up her hopes when I was so unsure myself of what was going on. In the end she gave up and settled back on the bed to rest her foot.

After about twenty minutes we heard the key turning in the lock again and H was back carrying a bucketful of ice. "Here, put your foot in this," he said to Vicky. "Sorry, we have nothing to use as an ice pack. You will have to sit on the edge of the bed."

Vicky shuffled to the edge of the bed and tentatively put her foot into the bucket, big toe first as if testing the temperature of bath water. Personally, I always thought it was better to take the full shock effect by thrusting the foot in rather than inching along. It was certainly quicker.

"What's going on H?" I asked our friendly captor.

He look bemused but only for a split second after which he gave a broad grin. "I'm Harvey."

"OK Harvey, nice to see you again but my initial question still stands."

"I don't quite know the full story yet and I haven't got a lot of time to explain." He went and closed the door and dragged a chair over to the bed so he would be facing us. "We are OK to speak here. All the other rooms have microphones and cameras but this room wasn't earmarked to be used I gather. You two are a bit of a priority surprise and this freedom will not last I'm sure."

"What freedom is that exactly," snorted Vicky sarcastically.

"Freedom of speech." Harvey remained unruffled by her caustic comment. "Believe me there are not many places where you can do that here. Your best bet is not to say anything that you don't want anyone else to hear."

"It's going to be damn difficult planning an escape then." I tried to inject a little levity to lighten Vicky's mood.

"There will be no escape," Harvey warned. "Not yet. There is much more to this than you can possibly imagine."

"Not at all," I intervened. "This is where the ungodly are keeping the unfortunate relatives of those they need to manipulate."

"I didn't mean that," said Harvey, a little too fiercely. "This is personal!" Then a little less aggressively, "Do you know where you are?"

"Haven't got a clue."

"This is Knightscourt."

I hadn't expected that. The Kelly family seat. It was personal then, no doubt about it. The fact that they were here in the middle of my case when I was in my direst need of assistance must have been a total coincidence. Still, I always stood by the maxim 'Never look a gift coincidence in the mouth'.

"What's the agenda then?" I was keen to know their plan of action so I could plan my own.

"To play it by ear," was his reply. "Herbert is here with me but the others won't be joining until later. They are trying to tie up loose ends, or they are as far as Springer is concerned. That's the guy who is calling the shots around here. Really they are digging up what information they can on what exactly has been going on around here."

A beeping noise sounded from inside his jacket. "Got to go. Be back later."

"That complicates things," I sort of murmured to myself but Vicky must have thought I was talking to her. "What do you mean?" she asked. Then in a Tina Turnerish sort of way, "What has Knightscourt got to do with it?"

"It's a long story but I suppose we have the time for it, especially if I give you the short version."

"Look, you playing the fool is not going to cheer me up," Vicky declared. "So you may as well stop your funny one liners, especially as they are not funny."

Seeing as I hadn't been trying to make a joke that time I agreed, although silently to myself. It was time to be what I had often been criticised for, being serious. Too serious, many people had said, but in our situation there was no such thing as too serious. So I related the events the K Team had told me and swore her to the strictest secrecy. She wasn't even allowed to let the K Team know that she knew.

"So you can see," I summarised, "whilst I originally thought the A.C.C.S. were here to help me they are really here to sort out long overdue family business. It's just one hell of a coincidence that we are here too."

"It still helps us though," pointed out Vicky.

"Without doubt," I agreed. "We would have had no chance of escape on our own. The trouble is we will now have to work to their agenda. You heard Harvey, they don't want any escape attempts yet. Presumably they don't want to upset the apple-cart until they have all the answers."

"You mean like why is their family home being used for criminal purposes? And where their parents are?"

"Among other things. I think it is safe to assume that their uncle is heavily involved with this. Whether just by letting this place to the ungodly or maybe by being part of the plans. He is some sort of kingpin in the UK crime scene and we know that local talent is being used."

"And we just have to hang around until your friends are ready?"

"Well, we can't do much without their co-operation, although I'm very well aware, as no doubt they are, that speed is essential." For Vicky it was, because who knew what was happening to her father. Had they cottoned on to his wheeze? Or was he still trying to beat 'The Mousetrap' for acting longevity? However, for me we were in a crucial area right where we were.

If we could not just escape but basically free all the hostages then Fairfax and his cronies lost their bargaining chips.

"We are close to breaking this thing now," I told her. "Just be a bit patient."

I was about to advise her not to tell too much to her sister when they met but at that moment we heard the key in the lock. It wasn't Harvey this time but the other guy who had escorted us. "Come on," he growled.

We were shown downstairs again and into a different room than before, with me acting as beast of burden again. It seemed full of people. Mainly women but a couple of men also. No sooner had we entered than there was a shriek and someone rushed over. "Vicky!" The girl threw her arms around Vicky and I, by virtue of the fact that I was still carrying her, was included in the embrace. I naturally assumed that this screaming banshee was sister Sam. My attention, as was everyone else's in the room, being on those two I didn't see the person who appeared at a more leisurely pace in Sam's wake.

"Hello Tommy"

You could have knocked me down with a Milky Way. It was Jenny and the shock must have shown on my face. My speech capabilities were certainly affected and I stood as if auditioning for the stupid part in a movie about goldfish.

"I'm surprised to see you here," said Jenny.

"Not as surprised as I am to see you," I told her, as on being released from Sam's death grip I lowered Vicky onto an empty armchair.

"Well, this is all very nice," a voice announced from behind us. "Now if you've finished playing happy families." I turned and saw Springer. "Everyone, we have a couple of new guests," he continued. "As you can see they are not quite strangers to all of you. I am sure you will make them welcome and ensure that they are aware of the establishment rules. Eh, Mr Thomas?"

I followed the direction of his eyes and noticed that one of the two men in the room who were not on Springer's team had his arm in a sling. There was blood showing through it too.

When I turned back Springer had gone and so was the goon who had escorted us down. We four were still the centre of attention and I still felt like a goldfish, in a very small glass bowl. I felt it was up to me to say something as everyone in the room other than us four seemed to be silently waiting. But what could I say? Not to worry, that I was the great white hope, newly arrived to save the day. Even a cock-eyed dyed in the wool optimist wouldn't swallow that one.

"Hi everybody. I'm Tommy and this is Vicky," perhaps a mere introduction was what was needed. "I hope you don't mind us dropping in."

"We don't mind but you will," said the guy in the sling. "It's as good a place as any for the last supper."

"Oh, do be quiet Jerry!" Pure exasperation exuded from the elderly lady who had uttered these words. As if she had been having a running battle with Jerry for some time and was getting quite fed up with it.

"Why don't you lot believe me?" demanded Jerry. "None of us are leaving here. Don't you realise that yet?"

"We do not want to listen to your pessimistic paranoia," the lady stated. This was her final word on the subject it seemed, for she chose to ignore his indignant snort and turned back to me. "Nice to meet you Tommy, Vicky. I see you know Sam and Jenny. Perhaps they can do the introductions."

Sam had obviously been there the longer. After all, I had seen Jenny in the office only twenty four hours ago. Had that only been yesterday? So it seemed inevitable that Sam would do the honours. "Everyone, this is my sister Vicky," to which there were a chorus of greetings. "And this is er ... Tommy."

"He's my boss," Jenny added by way of explanation.

Again there were a chorus of greetings before it was back to Sam to introduce the others to us. There were seven ladies plus the two men. The lady who had slapped down the man with his arm in a sling was Mrs Mary Watson. She was the oldest there and she appeared to be a bit on the frail side physically but she had true grit. The man she had been verbally sparring with was

Jerry Thomas, he looked to be in his late thirties or early forties, solidly built with dark hair, he had a lot to say and mainly it led from pent up anger and frustration. The less forthcoming members of the group consisted of; three thirty-something ladies - all attractive in their own way, two blondes and a redhead, all married or so said their fingers and answering to the names of Jennifer (Gascoigne), Alison (Fairchild) and Fiona (Robinson), a young woman in her early twenties - slim with long dark hair, called Nina Roberts, two middle-aged ladies - well groomed and well jewelled, Roberta Simons and Elizabeth (Liz) Gray, and finally the other guy, younger than Jerry, in his mid-twenties, blond and muscular, known as Tony Watts. A mixed bag you might say.

I wondered if they had any idea of what was going on. A pound coin to a penny they were all connected to someone working for the Fairfax Corporation, and by now they probably all knew that about each other so they would know that was the common link. I also wondered what Jenny had told them, for she had a more overall picture and I wasn't sure that it was in our best interests that they could all see it. I needed a quiet word with Jenny but that seemed out of the question at the moment.

The questions came flying at us. Did we know why we were here? Who was behind it all? How long was it going to last? And so on. I couldn't blame them. Any new person that arrived was probably a very welcome distraction from the frightening but ultimately mundane existence of the kidnap victim. Most of the questions came my way as Vicky was closeted in the corner with her sister.

"Listen everybody," I announced to the room as a whole. "I, or rather we, have no idea why we are here either. All we can do is wait and see what happens." I hoped that Springer was picking this up. He probably knew I knew more than I was letting on, but by not doing so I wasn't letting him know that I in fact knew more than he thought I knew. Also, I wanted it to seem as though we were just going to remain reactive to what might happen, rather than proactive which would make him put us under closer supervision.

"That is what I have been telling him," declared Mary Watson, nodding in the direction of Jerry. "If he had listened to me he would not have his arm in a sling."

"Why, what happened?" I asked, glad to move the centre of attention from me.

"He tried to jump one of them," explained Tony in a tone that said it had been a stupid thing to do. With his physique I would have bet on him having a go at them but then maybe he didn't have the heart to go with the body. Or maybe he was just smart.

"Why don't you people listen to me?" Jerry was a mere lava flow from a full eruption. "If we don't do something we're all going to die."

"We don't know that," said one of the other ladies, Roberta if I had put the face to the name correctly.

"Oh come off it! What's this in my shoulder? They're deadly serious this mob, with the emphasis on dead."

"Then why did they just shoot you in the shoulder?" asked Mary.

"They're just playing for time that's all. You mark my words."

"Look, there is no point getting all heated," I told them. "We have to stay calm and we have to stick together. If we do this there is a chance that we will all walk out the other side. Now who can tell me what these so called rules are?"

"Simple really," said Mary. "Behave and no harm will come to you."

"And they all believe that!" Jerry snorted.

Mary chose to ignore him. "We were told that as long as we comply with their wishes we would be released when this is all over?"

"Whatever this is," put in Roberta.

"It's really not too bad," Mary stated. "We have the run of this side of the main buildings. The other wing is out of bounds due to building works. Of course, there are guards all over the place watching us but they don't interfere. Unless of course one tries to jump them and take their gun," this with a withering look towards Jerry who elected not to respond. "There are three basic rules. Firstly, there is a ten o'clock curfew. Everyone has to be in their room by that time. By the way we all double up, which was easy with eight women and two men. Then Jenny arrived so she is on her own at the moment. Now you two are here. I don't think you will be sharing, no fraternisation allowed.

"Secondly, if you want to eat, you eat at the allotted meal times. Miss out and you go hungry until the next one. We all eat together in the dining room. Thirdly, if you are asked to do something you have to comply. That's it. Otherwise everyone just muddles along as best they can."

"Sort of like an open prison only less open," I mused.

"Oh, open too. We are allowed out into the courtyard at any time except after curfew. With the drawbridge up there is nowhere to go. It's the only way to exercise."

"I don't think I will be doing much exercise for a while," said Vicky, sat with her foot upon a hard backed chair.

Just then there was a loud clanging sound. "Lunch is served, announced Mary."

I couldn't believe I still didn't know the time. I still hadn't looked at my watch but I did now, it was one o'clock and this tied in with my suddenly materialising hunger.

Everyone started to file out but as I was about to lift Vicky again Mary said, "You would be better staying here dear. The dining room won't be able to accommodate your foot."

"I'll bring some food in and eat with you," offered Sam.

I offered too but was told that whilst Sam would probably be allowed no one else would. Everyone had to eat together. Vicky's ankle was a mitigating circumstance but only one person needed to attend to her.

We all trooped along to the dining room which conveniently was just opposite. I don't recall what I ate because I was too busy pumping for information. By the end of the meal I

thought I had as much as there was to know without having given myself away. Anyone listening would have just heard
people telling me how long they had been there and how they
got there. Nothing abnormal about that. Of course, even before our arrival all the prisoners had been speculating on what
they were caught up in. They had obviously compared notes
and had realised the Fairfax connection. Each one of them was
connected to someone who worked for the Corporation. Wives,
girlfriends, one husband and a toy-boy. I already knew this but
anyone listening also presumably knew that the others had
worked it out for themselves and were not worried about it.

I also learnt how Jenny had been taken. It had been right
after she had met with Vicky. So someone had overheard us
when I had been in the office, or the girls when they had met.
No wonder they had been ready for us when I had turned up at
Vicky's.

Jenny was the new kid on the block. The others had been
there three weeks at least, some of them nearer a whole month.
Many of them were dispirited but Mary had inner strength that
was inversely proportional to her frailness of body and she tried
to keep them going. I couldn't tell them that it was nearly over
one way or another. It was hard not to give them some hope
and encouragement. It was going to be harder still to just kick
my heels and do nothing. I hoped the K Team were in a position
to act soon. With the right luck we could tie the matter neatly
with a red bow and present it to the authorities.

"We're not badly treated," Roberta was saying as I resurfaced to the present conversations. "The real problem is boredom."

"Sure. We've got TV, video, music and even a games room,"
said Jerry, "but it's still like a stinking prison. Nowhere to go except a walk in the car park". By which I assumed he meant the
courtyard.

"It can be a problem," agreed Mary. "Let's face it, daytime
TV is not great unless you are a Richard and Judy fan or get a kick
out of Jerry Springer. It becomes a question of filling in time be-

tween meals."

"All I want is to kick out at another Springer," growled Jerry.

"I know, why don't you finish recounting your earlier adventures?" suggested Jenny, in an effort to diffuse the situation I assumed. "He has been telling me how he ended up becoming an insurance investigator. It will take our minds off things for a while."

"No Jenny, I don't think now is the time for stories." I wasn't in a Jackanory mood but the others must have been really suffering from ennui.

"We could do with something different," said Roberta.

"Why not," muttered Jerry. "Bugger all else to do."

"Manners, Jerry!" Mary rebuked him.

I was still reluctant but when we returned to the other room, Vicky put in her tuppence worth, if two pence was worth anything these days. "Come on. Entertain us." I didn't know whether she was mocking me or wanted something to take her mind off her sore ankle. In the end I relented because I needed something to take my mind off current events too. Even those present who had so far kept their own council were nodding in approval.

"OK, OK. Is everybody sitting comfortably, then I'll begin. Not that long ago, in a galaxy not so very far away ..." And I began to bring them up to date on the story that I had narrated to Jenny in instalments. Jenny should have been disinterested during the recap but didn't appear to be and I noticed a sort of aura of increased alertness as I reached the part I had left off last time.

There wasn't that much let of the story untold from that point. The two cronies of the main bad guy were dead at my flat but he was still at large. I told how I was put in a safe flat which had proved anything else but and how I had been visited by Mr Big. He intended to put my lights out but after a struggle over a knife I managed to put his lights out instead, with a chair over the head.

It seemed to go down well. Maybe too well if truth be told.

# CHAPTER 20

The room was deathly silent. I was the centre of attention and now that my tale had ended I was painfully aware of it. All eyes were on me and I felt not just in that room. As Yogi said when he carved a replica of his little mate out of a log, I thought to myself, I've made a boo-boo.

"My god!" ejaculated Tony. "We've got the right guy here. I vote that we put him in charge."

That was the last thing I needed. "In charge of what?" I asked innocently.

"Why the Escape Committee, of course," he replied.

"You have an Escape Committee?" I was as incredulous as an atheist who has just been addressed by a burning bush.

"Not really," Mary told me, the voice of common sense. "Obviously we have talked about the possibility, even thrown a few plans around, but none of them were really practical."

"You see we don't have any experience of this sort of thing," spoke up one of the other ladies, although I had forgotten which was which.

"But he has," insisted Tony. "Now we can make some real plans."

It was time to nip this in the bud.

"Look, I'm no James Bond," I told them. "I sort of exaggerated a little with that story. I'm no fighter and I got lucky on more than one occasion. Believe me, if there is one person you don't want in charge it's me."

I looked across at Vicky for some affirmation and incredibly she seemed to cotton on to the fact that I wanted to remain as inconspicuous as possible. "Let me tell you," she said, "I've known this guy for only two weeks but I am in no doubt that to put your faith in him is like trusting Mr Magoo to pick the right path through a minefield. I mean, would you trust somebody who went out on surveillance at night dressed in white." She laughed and a couple of the others did too. Was she backing me with telepathic unerringness or was that her true perception?

"Anyway, even Bond would have trouble getting out of here," I pointed out. "Guards with guns, locked in a castle surrounded by a moat and none of Q's gadgets to hand."

"Looks like you're just as lame as the rest of us," said Jerry.

Maybe I was but my main concern was lulling Springer in to a false sense of security. We were being watched or listened to or both. It was as sure as the fact that any unfamiliar face within a landing party on a strange planet in Star Trek belonged to a dead man. Undoubtedly, Springer knew who his two newest guests were and he would be aware that of all his wards we would be the ones to cause trouble. I had to make him believe that I was just a chicken livered coward trying to live the fallacy of being a private investigator, hoping that he would not twig that metaphorically speaking I was very much watching him watching them watching me watching them.

It was only mid-afternoon and the rest of it was spent in desultory conversation for the main part, although after a while I wasn't part of it because Tony suggested a game of snooker in the games room and that whiled away a couple of hours. We didn't speak much. There wasn't much to say. He was the archetypal strong, silent type but could we rely on him at the moment of crisis? It was the other guy, Jerry, who had had a go, but then again from what the others had said it had been hot headed and reckless. Apart from the K Team and my crack team of a virgin investigator, disabled partner and newly employed secretary, these were the only other two we could rely on to help and what a pair, a possible coward and an impulsive pessimist. I had to find out if they were going to be assets or not. I had them both together, Jerry had followed us to watch, and there would be no better time.

"So what do you make of it all?" I asked Tony.

"Blowed if I know," he replied. "Has to be for some sort of ransom, although multiple victims is unusual. However, we are all tied in with this Fairfax Corporation in some way and that must have something to do with it."

"Of course it has," snapped Jerry, "but we will never know what. We are all dead meat."

"He's right," agreed Tony, somewhat surprisingly. "I wouldn't admit so much to the ladies but it is rather obvious when you take into account that none of our captors bother to hide their faces nor have any objection to using names in front of us."

So Tony might be worth having on our side after all. He was gallant and thoughtful. He was the toy-boy and I had errone-ously had him pegged for an easy ride gigolo. If he knew he was going to die but was deliberately keeping this from the women and trying to keep their hopes up it pointed to him being very brave too.

"That's why I say let's have a go. If we are going to check out let's go down fighting." Jerry was brave too but gave no thought to his actions. If we went his way we would have a blood bath in very short order.

"If they were going to kill us why haven't they done so," said I, not wanting to let on that I agreed with them, less for their sake than for listening ears.

"So they can prove we are still alive when it is time for ask-ing for the ransom," suggested Tony.

"I suppose."

Silence once more ensued other than the clacking of the balls. I thought it might be an idea to let Tony in on the full facts so he could be ready for action. About Jerry I wasn't too sure. If he knew of the lic of the land it might make him more patient but a change in his restless nature might show Springer that there was something afoot. It was the K Team's call.

Not at that time though because it was the gong's call. Time for dinner and the three of us trooped into the dining room. All the ladies were there, even Vicky, who was braving her foot in favour of a communal meal, not that there was much conversation. Now that the initial excitement of two newcomers had waned the strain of three weeks captivity was taking its toll again.

The evening was spent in watching TV or for some, reading. Nothing exciting happened, until that is the BBC 9 O'clock News aired. The main story was about an explosion at a bottling plant. The bottling plant of Fairfax Bottling.

"Oh, my god!" cried Roberta. "That's where my husband works!"

I was surprised but then again I wasn't. I was surprised because in the circumstances we now found ourselves in the Fairfax case, or at least that side of it, was the last thing on my mind, and I hadn't anticipated or been expecting the next move. I wasn't surprised at the action nor that one of my fellow hostages was related to the head of the bottling plant. No doubt the nine hostages prior to the addition of Jenny, Vicky and myself were related to the heads of each UK division of the Fairfax Corporation. As had been previously mentioned they had all discovered the Fairfax link, but I had not discussed my thoughts on the subject because I didn't want Springer to catch on to how much I knew.

Roberta was sobbing and repeatedly saying 'No! No! No!" The other women were trying to comfort her but she was inconsolable. It was obvious she thought her husband might have been caught in the blast.

"Look, Roberta," I said, "this happened in the middle of the night. Your husband wouldn't have been there then would he?"

She looked up at me through tear filled eyes and grabbed on to the hope of a lifeline I had thrown her. "Not usually," she replied in a low voice. "The plant is run twenty four hours a day on three shifts but John is only there at nights if there is a problem."

There had certainly been a problem but if things ran to form her husband would not have been there. His wife had been taken so he would not interfere and the best way for him to do that was stay away from the place. Of course, that still left the rest of the workforce on the night shift.

But in this thinking I was wrong. Due to Roberta's outburst

we had missed the rest of the news story but it was later confirmed on News at Ten that there had been a warning and the plant had been cleared. There had only been enough of a warning to clear the plant but not for the bomb squad to find the explosives.

This news came later though and prior to this Roberta was still extremely worried. Not wanting to be seen to be taking charge I had a quiet word with Jerry who was already noted as the mouthy one. He opened the door to the lounge and called to the guard, one of which was always outside any room occupied by any of the hostages. "Get Springer in here," he demanded.

At first I thought the guard was going to refuse but then he just nodded and mumbled into a walkie-talkie. Three minutes later Springer entered the room. "You asked for me," he said to Jerry.

"This woman has had a severe shock." Jerry indicated Roberta. "As you probably know of the explosion at her husband's workplace can't you let her know whether her husband is OK?"

"Why would you think that I knew about this?" Springer was giving nothing away.

"We're not stupid, man! As soon as we all started talking to each other we knew the connection was the Fairfax Corporation."

"Well, you know more than I," Springer told him. "My orders are just to hold you all here. I don't know who you are or why you are here. However, I will make some phone calls to see what I can find out."

With this he left on his errand and I was left with conflicting thoughts. Did he or did he not know what was going on? Sure, local talent had been employed for the UK work but there was still American control. It was possible that there were two separate units. One to hold the hostages and one to lift the hostages and carry out the attacks. Or maybe there were three units with the hostage snatchers separate from the attack unit. If so then Springer would appear to be just in charge of watching the hostages and may really not know the true connection.

There would obviously be someone in control of all units and my guess was the American, Montford. I had already suspected him of being in the country at the time of Hobson's accident because he had arrived too quickly after. He was probably always in the background pulling the strings but had to come out into the open when Hobson could no longer assist in their plans.

For the time being then I had to assume that Springer was on the level, or about on the level as a multi-kidnapper could be. Even so he was back within ten minutes to assure Roberta that according to his sources, which were impeccable, her husband was alive and well. She cheered up appreciably at the news and seemed ashamed of her initial reactions. She was the first one to retire to bed but soon most of the others followed until only my own little team was left. It was well past the ten o'clock curfew by this time and I could only assume that Roberta's plight was the reason for this. I gathered that the nightly ritual was to watch the news at nine then retire for the night. However, that night what with waiting for Springer to check out the situation and then wanting to see News at Ten for corroboration things were a little lax.

We still couldn't converse without being overheard and we couldn't huddle together and whisper in case there was video as well as audio surveillance. We just talked generally about the situation. I aimed to talk to Vicky later in our bug free room and then Vicky could pass this on to Jenny. Two girlfriends conversing in low voices was less likely to attract attention. In this too though I was baulked and Harvey's comments on bed-hopping were correct.

Prior to Vicky's and my arrival there had been eleven hostages, two men and nine women, including Jenny. The two men would obviously be sharing a room and the ladies would be paired off. Jenny as the newcomer was in a room by herself. Springer wanted to separate Vicky and me to stop us plotting and there was also his no fraternisation rule, although Vicky's previous comments blew that possibility out of the water. Vicky would no doubt want to room with her sister, so I guessed that Nina who had been in the same room with Sam was now Jenny's room-mate. This meant that I, of course, as usual, would be by myself.

The guard who had been outside the door came in. "Curfew's gone," he growled, which we all took as a sign to make a move. What was astonishing to me was his voice. He was dark, lean and swarthy. The gruff voice matched perfectly. The only trouble was that this was the guard who had brought Vicky the ice. This was Harvey, but not only did he not look like Harvey he now didn't sound like Harvey either. Then again in their line of work being masters of disguise and mimicry was no doubt essential.

He ushered us up to the rooms on the first floor where another guard sat with a view of the whole corridor. Jenny said goodnight and entered the room she was using.

"That's your sister's room," growled the guard otherwise known as Harvey, with a wink, pointing two doors down. "And you are in that one," gesturing at another door.

So the team was split and I entered my room. Being by myself might have its advantages, I thought, but Springer had other ideas. The light was on and my bed partner was sat up reading a book. They were taking this no fraternisation rule a bit too far, it was Mary.

"So they put you with me," she observed.

"Hi," I said, lost for words.

"Don't look so put out. It was fairly obvious what they were going to do. They were not going to let Vicky and yourself remain together. You are not part of the original plan, hence all the shake-up, and therefore you two must have been of some trouble to the organisers of this kidnap plot. As partners in anti-crime they were not going to let you remain together to plot against them." She was a wily old bird that was for sure and she wasn't finished. "Looking at our party you can see their thinking on the subject. There were originally nine of us. Jerry and Tony are obviously already sharing as the only two men. Jerry is outspoken but is not a leader, Tony is rather quiet and thoughtful, although his stature would seem to make him leader material. Not so. Certainly all the ladies look to me for guidance. Perhaps because I am the oldest and more experienced in life or perhaps because I was the first to arrive here. So I was kept apart. Jennifer and Alison, Fiona and Nina, Roberta and Liz were all paired off. I was on my own until Sam came. Then Jenny arrived so she was on her own. She had also obviously been of some trouble to them and they didn't want her conversing too much. Finally Vicky and you arrive. They had to split you and Vicky up but also keep Vicky and Jenny apart, although I guess Springer knew Sam was her sister so that was not going to be a problem. Jenny could stay where she was and I swapped with Vicky.

It was very succinctly summed up. I could see why everyone looked to Mary Watson as the leader. She was smart, observant and calm in extremely trying circumstances. Maybe she could provide some answers.

Mary had kept to the right side of the bed so I sat on the left. I had to be careful because of those listening but then again they would expect me to ask some questions and would be suspicious if I didn't.

"So you were here first?"

"That is right. I have been here over a month now?"

"How many of them are there?" A reasonable question to ask and one they would have expected. It was also one I needed the answer to.

"I cannot be certain of that but apart from Mr Springer I have noticed eight different guards. They tend to work in shifts so there may be some who have been permanently on night shift who I have not seen."

So there were a definite nine and hopefully four of those were the K Team, although if Henry and Howard had not been here at all that meant eleven in total, seven in the ranks of the ungodly.

"Have they given you any idea of how long you are to be kept here?"

"No. We've asked of course, many times. I think only

Springer knows what is going on and we don't see him a great deal."

"You mean he is away from the castle a lot of the time?"

"Oh no. He is in here right enough but he keeps himself to himself and only appears when there is a problem to sort out."

I had hoped for a precious moment that Springer was absent at times and one of these could be used to overcome his subordinates, with a little help from my friends, of course. I didn't know Springer at all but it was obvious he was in control of that part of the operation and the rest were probably in the dark, unless he had a trusty lieutenant. If he had the K Team would know who that was. Anyway this was all idle conjecture as it appeared that Springer was going to be there at the time of the attempted take-over, whenever that turned out to be.

"Tell me, Mary," I said, my mind turning to another track, "have any of you been in communication with your families since you got here?"

"Yes, we all have. Every week we are all videoed with that day's paper to prove the date. We are only allowed to say that we are all right."

That was interesting. That was what you would expect according to TV fiction, confirmation of life whilst a ransom was being organised. But there was no ransom involved here as such. I was as concerned as the rest that the people holding us hostage had not bothered to hide their appearance. My gut reaction was that if things ran their intended course then no one was going to leave that place alive.

After a few more desultory questions I apologised to Mary for keeping her up.

"That is quite alright," she said. "At my age you do not need that much sleep. I usually read until midnight."

"Please do. I wouldn't be able to sleep anyway. I'll just lie here and try to sort out my thoughts."

I mulled over the facts. A lot had happened in a short space of time. Was it only eleven days ago that that woman had tripped into the office and started a train of events that had led

PRATT, PRATT, WALLY & PRATT INVESTIGATE

me to this? A tall tale had been fed me that day, all the taller because it was nearly the truth but from the wrong perspective. I had really known all along that something was not on the level and now after being charged with drug running and murder, imprisoned, breaking out and now kidnapped, the events which I had allegedly been hired to prevent had started. However, the reason behind them was still not so clear. OK, so the modus operandi was now understood. The person in charge, the fat spider controlling all from the centre of this web of death and deceit, had a plan. Each move had been meticulously thought out like a chess game. He, she or even they, knew which persons had to be coerced into helping the plan along and to ensure they did so their closest relatives were held hostage. These coerced people were those in a position to either turn a blind eye or otherwise assist the felonious attempt, be it theft, fire or something else. Either that or they were money men. The latter were the important ones. They had access to the insurance monies and by controlling them the ungodly could get their hands on this money. So reason number one was obvious enough. However, the acts continued even when the insurance company became suspicious and held back claim payments which begged another reason. Such wanton destruction had to mean revenge. Someone was out to destroy the Fairfax Corporation. That was also obvious now. To blow up one of the UK plants, knowing that because of the problems in the States no money would be paid out without a thorough investigation, left only that reason. To begin with it was a way to make money but now all that mattered was destruction. Who had such a motive?

The things the woman, formerly known as Mrs F, had told me had to be taken with an extremely large pinch of salt but no doubt the American police authorities had been and were looking at the revenge angle. They would be looking at all the parties that had ever sued the Corporation or sent crackpot letters. Something told me it was much closer to home. The fat spider controller had far too much information on all aspects of the Corporation and that said to me someone at the top. Mrs F had told me that one of the top two men, Simon Fairfax, was suspected. Was this a bluff and James Fairfax was involved? Was it a double bluff and neither were involved? Or was it a holographic bluff i.e. it didn't really exist and therefore Simon Fairfax was the man? How I wished I had a reliable American contact to check things out. Not that I was in a position to contact anyone at the moment but I needed to be. Things were coming to a head and if I and my compatriots were not going to finish up at a dead end, with the operative word being 'dead', some action had to be taken. I had to be able to speak to the K Team, or at least one of them in private. I had to persuade them to act now even if they had not yet fully discovered what had become of their father and his wife.

I thought I had as much chance of forcing their hand as there was of 'We Wish You a Wombling Merry Christmas' being re-released and becoming an Easter number one. But unbeknown to me events were working in my favour.

At that very time in a galaxy in the nearby vicinity a meeting was taking place.

*********

I knew nothing of the meeting that was going on at The Galaxy, a pub within convenient travelling distance of our place of captivity. It took place in one of the rooms let out to overnight guests and the guest who had let this particular room was a Roger Smith, a very original alias for none other than Howard Kelly. I only heard about the meeting later but it was crucial to the outcome of events.

The K Team were all there except Herbert who was still on duty. As far as Springer was aware, out of the gang of four he had hired two were yet to arrive, Howard and Henry, and Harvey had requested leave of absence after receiving a call on his mobile that his mother was seriously ill. Springer had consented but had requested the name of the hospital. Fortunately, that possibility had been foreseen and should he have contacted the hospital to check he would have been given full details of how at death's door Dirk Dangerfield's mother was. Or he would have done if he had not already been made aware that Dirk Dangerfield was a pseudonym, for Harvey had made it plain that his team of four did not want to be identified and were using false names. Indeed, Springer might have expected this. Having asked for and been told the symptoms he could ring the hospital, describe these and probably be able to get the real name of his underling. If he did another false name was awaiting him.

When Harvey arrived, after having thoroughly checked he had not been followed, he could see that his brothers were consumed with anger. They must have found out something and it didn't look like good news.

"What did you find out?"

"That utter bastard," spat out Henry. "I'll kill him." Which in itself wasn't an answer but spoke volumes.

"Come on," urged Harvey. "Spill the beans."

After his outburst Henry let Howard who was just as angry but a lot more controlled do the telling.

"We've been asking around discreetly, trying to establish when the last time that either Lord or Lady Knightscourt have been seen by the locals," he explained. "We found out that it was not for some weeks. In fact," and here his voice took on a hard note, "the local doctor was the last person to see them and that was on a visit to the castle just over a month ago. He was summoned to fix a broken arm."

"Whose?" asked Harvey.

"Father's. The doctor was told he had fallen down the stairs. He set it but told Father to go to the nearest hospital to have a plaster put on. While we were with him this doctor, at our request, rang the Outpatients Department of the hospital. There is no record of Father having been there."

"This looks bad," Harvey observed. "Was Uncle Nathan involved?"

"The doctor knows him by sight. He was present when the doctor made his visit but according to his account the atmosphere was very strained."

"There was something else too," put in Henry, who had regained a smidgen of control. "Margaret also needed the doctor's attention. She had a cut on her forehead where she had allegedly been caught by a door."

"There is something very wrong with this picture." Harvey was trying to process all this information quickly. The others had had time to contemplate what it may mean. "We all know what Uncle Nathan wants but he is not likely to arrange events so openly. They must have been real accidents."

"Then why did Father not go to have his arm set. He would be agony if this was not done properly." Howard had the truth of the matter. There was no point just having your arm in a sling if it was broken. It had to be immobilised. "Yet the doctor was called."

"It is confusing," agreed Harvey.

"But it is explainable," said Henry. "We know that Knightscourt is being used for nefarious purposes. Father would not have allowed that to happen but it is right up Uncle Nathan's street. Therefore, we can assume he is in control and Father is out of the picture, either dead or held somewhere against his will. Margaret also. The fact that the doctor was called out to relieve some of the pain would suggest that they were not intended to die, not yet anyway. Uncle Nathan must have a use for them. So let us assume they are still alive. We have to locate where they are before we can act."

"Whatever Nathan's plan is it has to be desperate because if he is openly involved, and circumstances seem to suggest this, then after all this has blown over things can never go back to the way they were. No more pretence of happy families. Nathan must be going for broke and with Father alive I don't know how he can succeed." Harvey was voicing all their thoughts.

"We checked with Bob," Howard informed him. "Father has not submitted any changes to his will."

That was important to them. The only way that their Uncle Nathan could succeed in his quest to obtain the land and title was to get rid of his brother but not before forcing him to change his will.

"What about the old place?" said Henry. "What is the situation?"

"It's a babysitting job as we were told." Harvey went on to put them in the picture including the surprising news that I was back in their lives. "I also think I know where Father and Margaret are being held."

"Where?" the other two chorused together. "Have you seen them?" Henry added.

"No but I have my suspicions. One wing of the house is out of bounds. Springer says it is being refurbished. All the interconnecting doors are locked. Yet on the first night I could swear I saw a brief flicker of light when I looked out of my window. It makes sense. Keep them under wraps but where an eye can be kept on them. I've not seen Uncle Nathan around, neither has Herbert. He may be the one watching over them to see they do not spoil his plans."

"Well, if you are sure," said Howard, "it would seem that the time to act is now."

"Agreed."

And so the plan of action was discussed and when sufficient time had elapsed for Harvey to have made his trip to the hospital and back he made his way back to Knightscourt, but not before running forward the mileage on the clock the necessary number of miles for such a journey. Howard and Henry were to put in an appearance early the next day.

A bloodless coup had been meticulously planned. The trouble with meticulous planning however, is that most of the time one little miscalculation throws it all out of the window.

# CHAPTER 21

I had spent a sleepless night, tossing and turning. Metaphorically speaking that is. In reality I hardly moved my position at all for fear of waking Mary. I had had plenty of time to think. Far too much in fact. I had been over everything that had happened a million times or so it seemed until my head was spinning faster than a Battling Top.

Just as light was breaking and the dawn chorus could be heard I drifted off. Ten seconds later, or so it seemed, a gong sounded. "Breakfast in ten minutes," explained Mary, who was already dressed for another day of inactivity. Obviously no lie-ins allowed as it was only 7.00am. I would have thought that sleeping longer would have been better for all concerned. Less guarding needed as far as Springer was concerned. And for the prisoners every hour asleep was one hour blissfully unaware of their current plight, unless of course they were having nightmares about it, and also one hour less of enforced captivity to endure consciously and totally bored out of one's skull.

On the other hand, of course, Springer wanted all his eggs in one basket or at least in the same hen house. If all his prisoners were allowed to rise at their own convenience that could mean twelve people all wandering around to bathrooms etc. at different times. Difficult to keep track of and increasing the possibility of attempted escape as the captors were spread thin in covering such a wide area. Not to mention having to cook twelve breakfasts at varying times.

In any event there was no point arguing. I followed Mary down. Joining the others as they left their rooms. The occupation forces stood at regular intervals to check we didn't deviate from our course down the stairs to the dining room. This was the first time I had seen more than two in one go. I scrutinised the faces without seeming too but couldn't tell whether any of the K Team were present. Not until I saw a dark bearded guy with a bandaged right wrist. His watch was on his left as normal but that bandage could hide a birthmark. He saw me watching him and looked directly at me but there was no recognition there just cold haughtiness.

We were all sat down for breakfast by 7.15 and this time there was a choice. Everything was laid out on a side table like a running breakfast buffet. There were various cereals, bacon, sausage, egg, mushrooms, toast, jam, marmalade and coffee or tea. I tend to stay away from fried food and opted for cereal and toast with lots of coffee to wake me up. Everyone else seemed refreshed as they could be in the circumstances but my eyelids felt as though each had a sumo wrestler sat on it. Also I was the only one who had on the same clothes as the day before. Even Vicky had managed to borrow something from her sister I observed. I had even slept in mine but no one mentioned it.

There was no conversation at all. I supposed first thing in the morning was the worst time. Waking up from the ignorance of sleep to the harsh realities of being a hostage must be like the Monday morning blues one hundred times over. But suddenly something happened which made good digestion an impossibility. I was steadily munching my way through a piece of marmalade laden toast when I heard it. We all heard it. Everyone paused without exception. Forks and spoons halfway to mouths and masticating terminated. Gunfire! It had sounded some way off but had been clearly audible. Not individual shots but a stutter of a machine gun.

"Hell!" muttered the guard who was watching over us and ran to fling open the door. It was the one with the bandaged wrist. And if it was one of the K Team then obviously things were not going to plan. Forgetting us, his charges, he rushed off presumably towards the sound although I couldn't have guessed where it came from.

It was going down now whether planned or not so I followed in Bandaged Wrist's wake. He ran along the corridor towards what was the out of bounds wing. Just before he got there another burst of gunfire was heard and simultaneously the door for which he was heading was strafed with holes. He was already diving to the ground. I stopped dead but another guard ran past me a machine gun in hand. By this time Bandaged Wrist was now stood with his back to the side wall and had drawn his handgun from a shoulder holster. "You go first," he yelled to the onrushing guard who without stopping applied a kick to the considerably weakened door. As it collapsed inwards and he with it, Bandaged Wrist caught him a mean chop behind the ear with his handgun.

"Heh!" yelled a voice in my ear and I turned to see another guard lining up on Bandaged Wrist. I reacted instinctively. I hate rugby but it was a good tackle and it threw us both against the wall. He must have had his finger on the trigger because his gun went off but fortunately the deadly hail went up the wall and then the ceiling as we fell to the ground. I was on top and I couldn't let go of his arm with the gun. He was strong and I was the weak silent type but desperation must have given me some Hulk-like qualities, if only for the few seconds it took for Bandaged Wrist to backtrack to our position.

"Drop it!" he said with deadly menace in his voice and the guy let go of his weapon and went limp.

I clambered to my feet.

"Can you use this?" said Herbert, ex Bandaged Wrist, handing me his handgun and taking up the machine gun.

"On past record no," I admitted, "but I know a girl who can."

"Good, you look after the prisoners. I'm needed elsewhere. Come on you!" This to the guy on the floor who Herbert walked like a shield through the doorway into the next wing which was now strangely quiet.

I turned to go back the way I'd come but the pounding of feet told me I would meet some other guards head on. My first instinct was to play possum but that would leave Herbert's rear unprotected. I hid by a corner and stuck out a strategic leg as someone came hurtling round. It had the desired effect and he went stumbling. I was over him with the gun in a split second.

"Tommy! No!" came a yell from behind me. I looked and Howard was rushing up, ginger wig in hand. "God! I thought you were going to shoot. That's Henry."

"Sorry," I apologised to Henry. "I wasn't going to shoot anyway."

"It's OK. You were not to know we were not the enemy and no harm done," said Henry as he picked himself off the floor then removed his long blond wig.

"Where are you off to?" asked Howard.

"To watch the prisoners. Herbert told me to. He's gone into the other wing."

"Right. That means two of us over there already. I'll go and back them up. Henry, you see if you can mop up the others."

Howard went off after his other brothers and Henry and I quickly made our way back to the dining room. On the way he told me they had taken out three of the ungodly and the communications room where all the cameras and listening equipment were monitored. That was five of the other team's players out of action. The odds were looking better.

We met no one in the corridor until we got to the dining room where all my fellow captives were milling around the doorway. Vicky and Jenny were trying to get them all back inside where it was safer but after being restrained for so long and now feeling their leashes being slipped off they were full of curiosity even if not eager to join in the action. Leaving me to assist, Henry left to try and round up the rest of Springer's men.

Eventually, we got them all inside again. Surprisingly, so little time had passed that the dishes were still steaming but no one could rediscover their appetite. Under protest from Vicky I gave her the gun and left her in charge. Distracting as this whole kidnap episode had been, I still had my own job to do and whilst, however unlikely, Springer may have some of the answers to questions that were nagging me. I set off to the room we had met him in on our arrival. The room was empty but just as I entered I could have sworn I heard a click as if a door had been closed to quietly. The trouble was there were no other doors in that room. However, if that was Springer's own private sanctuary he would not have picked it unless there was a back door escape route. This was a castle wasn't it and according to the best Scooby Doo traditions all castles and mansions had secret passageways. Normally behind a bookcase.

There were three bookcases in that room but I discounted two straight away as they were on the outside wall on either side of a window. That left just one and I knew I had guessed right when with my Sherlock head on I noticed the groove in the thick pile carpet showing where the bookcase had repeatedly swung open. I had two options. Waste time trying to fathom out how to open it or try and guess where Springer would make for. Obviously he would be making a break for it so he needed to reach the outside but the drawbridge would be up so he needed to get to the controls wherever they were located. As in most things I was totally wrong in this assumption as was proved a short time later.

I had no idea where the drawbridge was raised. In the olden days it would have been raised by winding a wheel or lever or some such in the gatehouse but in these times it could probably be done automatically from somewhere inside the castle. As I knew not where, I thought I might as well waste my time trying to find the entrance to the bookcase. In many cases I had seen that a book was the key. I glanced at the titles. They were all hardback and classics, maybe first editions for all I knew. I saw 'The Arabian Nights'. It couldn't be surely. I tried to pull it out but instead of coming out it came down like a lever. There was a click and the bookcase was no longer fully flush into the wall.

"Open says me," I murmured to myself, paraphrasing from Ali Baba and the Forty Thieves.

I pulled the bookcase fully out and entered the dusty passageway behind. I had no means of illumination with me, so it was fortunate that someone had thought to put a line of light bulbs along the passage. Like a long trail of fairy lights but with no varying colours. To my left was a blank wall which was no doubt the outer wall so I could only go right. I walked at a fast pace not wishing to advertise my pursuit by pounding along and sending echoes through to my quarry. After a couple of minutes the passage split into two and I was in a quandary. It was about then I noticed that the passageway was not as dusty as it should be. There were no hundreds of cobwebs and not enough dust on the floor to trace footsteps. Mind you the mark on the carpet in the room I had just left spoke of fairly frequent use which meant that Lord Knightscourt had presumably used it for some purpose. If it had been totally unused the way to go would have been clear but as it was I mentally had to toss a coin. I was just going for two out of three when a brief exclamation came from the right-hand passage so I travelled along at greater speed.

"Where are you taking me?" "Shut up and move!" I heard voices ahead. I recognised them both. Springer had Vicky and was forcing her somewhere. I couldn't see them though for there was a corner ahead. I reached it at a sprint but could not see them ahead. I did see some natural light though and stormed through the aperture I found. I was in the dining room and there were dazed looks all around me.

"What happened?" I demanded to know.

"Springer took your friend Vicky," replied Mary, who seemed less traumatised than the rest.

I turned to head back into the tunnel. "Here, you might need this," called Tony. It must have been Vicky's discarded gun. He tossed it over to me and this time I didn't drop it.

I sped along the passageway until it split again. One headed up via a flight of stairs and one remained on the level. I stopped to listen but they must have been too far ahead to hear anything or else Springer had gagged his captive. I was just about to follow the passageway ahead on the assumption that to make his escape Springer would need to remain on the ground level when a gunshot rang out. They couldn't have been that far ahead because a bullet ricocheted off a wall and whined past my head. It came from an upper level. I heard a slap and a snarled "If you do that again it will be the last thing you do." They were close now so I edged up the stairs slowly and peeked around the corner at the top. The passageway led to the right only but it was empty. There was another set of stairs further on though and I could hear scuffling steps going up. I crept up these as silently as I could. I didn't think Springer knew he was being followed yet but I was sure surprised that he was heading upwards.

The steps seemed to go on forever but eventually they gave out to another passageway. Again it was empty but this time I was pretty close because I could hear Springer. "Move it! Up those stairs!" There was more light streaming through another gap in the wall and as I peeped outside I glimpsed them just disappearing up another set of stone steps ahead.

I stepped out of the passageway into the main castle again. The corridor into which I had entered was carpeted. There were doors off it but directly opposite the secret entrance I had just exited were these stone steps. No carpet and fairly narrow. They also spiralled which told me we were heading up one of the towers. Why was he cutting off his avenue of escape by aiming for the topmost part of the castle the only way he could escape from there is if he could fly. Then it hit me, a helicopter. He had to have access to one, there was no other explanation.

I leapt up the stairs now desperate to catch them before they reached the top but I didn't achieve this objective. I heard the helicopter before I even reached the door at the top. There was not that much room on top of the tower but it had managed to land and Springer was pushing Vicky in and she was doing her best to kick him off. It was a losing battle for he got her pushed across and jumped in himself. Before he had even got the door closed it started to lift off. Just then I saw Vicky connect with a violent punch to Springer's jaw. She was out of the door and onto one of the helicopter's runners before he could recover. I was directly under them now. "Jump!" I yelled and without a second thought she did. I caught her but couldn't keep my balance and fell with her on top of me. My head took a crack on stone and it suddenly became night again.

I had a propensity for passing out at the wrong moment.

The next thing I remember was coming to in a four-poster bed. Vicky and Jenny were there sat by the bed and so was Howard, devoid of disguise now. They all seemed surreal though as in an indistinct dream. I tried to lift myself up but didn't manage an inch.

"Easy there, Tommy. It's all over now," said Howard.

I tried to tell him it wasn't. It may be for them but there was something important I still had to do. I knew it was important and I tried to tell him but for the life of me I couldn't remember what it was. As I struggled to get my message across they were fading away until they disappeared and it was night again. "It's not over!" I said or maybe I just thought it before I was gone.

# CHAPTER 22

It wasn't like I thought it was going to be. One of the three things I had always wanted to learn to do and it was a great disappointment. What were those three things? Play the piano. Ski. Ride a horse. It was the latter that left a lot to be desired. Brought up on 'The Adventures of Black Beauty' and 'Follyfoot' plodding along in single file at walking pace was as much out of sync with my aspirations as the dubbing of that other great classic 'White Horses'. Still I was a novice and it was a case of not being allowed to gallop, or even canter, before one could walk.

One thing watching all those horsey programmes didn't prepare you for was the saddle, which really was a pain in the rear. Ignoring this, the pace was so sedentary that I had time to mull over events. It was hard to believe that I was out in the open air on a brisk but clear day with a lot of other first timers on horseback. It was all over or should have been but there was still a shadow hanging over me. One that was threatening to engulf me even if it wasn't actually going to.

When I had surfaced into the realms of consciousness again after breaking Vicky's jump from the helicopter, I knew that there was something I had forgotten but I didn't know what. The K Team's fight was over, or so it seemed to me, but I was still fighting the opening skirmishes. In the final analysis though I was never that greatly involved again. It may have been because they thought I was out of my depth or perhaps because it was loosely tied up with their own troubles but the four brothers took the whole mess off my hands and sorted it in quadruple quick time. It was like they were literally Qualcast Concordes, a sort of faster than the speed of sound lawn mower, and the butts of the ungodly were grass oh so ripe for cutting.

It started with a meeting. We were all there. The ex-captives including Jenny, Vicky and myself, the four strong K Team and Lord Knightscourt, arm in a sling, with his wife. Having been unconscious it seemed ages since the coup but in fact it had only been an hour. I had resurfaced briefly after only a few minutes then had blacked out for a further half an hour. Then stressing an urgency that I felt but couldn't put a finger on I got Howard to convene the meeting. I divulged all that I knew. At all exclamations of disbelief corroboration was provided by variously Vicky, Jenny and perm one from four of the Kelly brothers.

I felt greatly relieved when I had finished. Now that it was all out in the open it was as if Giant Haystacks had been lifted from my shoulders. I suppose in a way too it was a relief to our fellow captives to learn why they had been taken, but in another way it was distressing because other than Roberta the others all had loved ones still under coercion. Not for long though because it was immediately suggested that each one contact their partners to let them know of their safety so removing the lever against them. This, of course, still left them prone to actual physical violence but not when the K Team swooped into action.

Now that they had achieved their objective in locating and freeing their father there was in its place a total obsession to raze to the ground the whole conspiracy. Springer had escaped but not so their Uncle Nathan. He had been holding Lord and Lady Knightscourt captive when Harvey burst into the room in the out of bounds wing of the castle. Only seeing an unknown armed protagonist he turned to fire and it was that first burst of gunfire that had alerted us all at breakfast. Harvey was already diving and took out his uncle with two shots to the heart from a silenced automatic. They could pick loose his criminal webwork at their leisure but as he had been involved in the whole caper, although not directly with the still unidentified kingpin, they felt a duty to clean up the mess. And like when they had broken me out of prison, to decide to do a thing was to act. They knew a lot of people in the forces and within hours all the locations of Fairfax operations were covered. The roving hit squad were caught with their hands on the paraffin tin prior to another torching. They were all British recruits, the American Montford, if that was his real name, had done a bunk, probably tipped off by Springer, but had been apprehended in the States.

All this was achieved within twenty-four hours by which time all the detainees at castle Knightscourt had been returned to their homes. And this was when the real clean up started. Cox and Bristow were able to come out of hiding and were instrumental in bringing to book the corrupt officials who had made the case so much more difficult. Baxter and Fox were minor fish. There had been people much higher up pulling strings to have me incarcerated. They were going to get a taste of their own medicine and I doubted very much if the A.C.C.S. would be breaking them out.

That just left the American end. With the guidance of Justin Fairweather I drafted a report of all I had learned and that which I had surmised. This was for the British case but a copy was given to the American authorities and also one to both the London and Chicago offices of Fidelity Insurance. There was a massive operation in the States with hundreds of undercover operatives who managed to confirm that all the financial heads of each Fairfax division had close family members missing. They were eventually tracked down to where they were being all held together. Cleverly, this turned out to be an enormous luxury yacht that kept changing its position to be near to wherever a pick-up was to be made. This yacht was owned by a holding company but on backtracking it was discovered that this lead to James Fairfax III. A red herring, as it turned out. The suspicion had been on Simon Fairfax from the start and he had set up this dummy company in his brother's name in case of investigation. It took a while to sort out but the fact that Simon Fairfax had disappeared told its own story. The same dummy company had three bank accounts loaded with money from the insurance swindles. It also owned numerous warehouses which when raided were found to be full of the property stolen via the various raids carried out on Fairfax locations.

That was it then. It was all over. And for me it was an anticlimax. I had carried the baton from day one when the impostor Mrs F had first laid it all at my door, but my last action had been to get myself laid out by a falling aerial person, in other words I had fumbled feet from the finishing line. Someone else had picked up the baton and won the race.

At least there was the reward to look forward to. That must come to a hefty figure. Ten per cent of millions. Don't count your wonga until the bank cashier has stamped your paying-in slip. Fidelity Insurance UK were of the opinion that as any losses they would have been expected to cover would not have been paid due to connivance by the policyholder there was no money saved so no reward. As far as the head office in Chicago were concerned I was too far removed from their end to justify a reward. Discussions were ongoing but I had referred them to that distinguished insurance tenet Proximate Cause, 'the active, efficient cause that sets in motion a chain of events which brings about a result without the intervention of any force starting and working actively from a new and independent source'. I even gave them the case law, Pawsey v. Scottish Union and National 1907. I was the active, efficient cause. Ever since I had been appointed to the case there had been one long unbroken chain of events leading to their recovery of most of their outlay. Discussions were still ongoing.

At least there was the girl. The hero always gets the girl. What girl?

The Hobsons were now one happy family again. Miraculously Hobson's memory had returned. Everyone was grateful, of course, and I had the key to their front door so to speak but Vicky had never seen me in that way. A friend OK but anything else no way. Anyway, the boyfriend she had never mentioned was due to leave the Marines any time.

So all in all a very atypical ending. I wasn't too upset about the money. I still had most of the £20,000 left, at least F.I.C. hadn't asked for that back, and I would get something for my efforts. The voices of the K Team, Cox and Bristow had been raised loud in my defence. Something would eventually come of it. Vicky was a different story though. Considering what we had been through the time had never been right for romantic overtures but I had felt that we sparked well off each other and made a good team. As someone who would have been turned down by Baldrick's ex dates, I had been placing too much emphasis on our close, what had to be termed, working relationship. Still not every story can have a happy ending.

Did I say ending? The fat lady had not even squeezed herself into her posh opera frock yet.

It was the Monday a week after the weekend of adventure at Knightscourt that I reopened the office. I had given Jenny a week's holiday with pay. Not that we needed to be in that day or any other subsequent day. The one case we had was resolved and I was back at square one. Older and very much wiser. I had a decision to make on whether to keep the firm going. The only job we had done was one specifically targeted at us because we had no experience to do it properly. That the result of choosing PPWP had had the opposite effect was no real reflection on me. I felt I had made all the mistakes in the book and even invented a few new ones. A person had been killed because of me and several more could have been. The only reason I considered staying open was so that Jenny would have a job. But what job? There was nothing to do.

In the end the decision was made for me by the arrival of an air mail letter that very morning. The note inside was short and to the point. YOU ARE DEAD spelled out in newspaper headline cuttings. There were only three people in the affair that were not accounted for; Mrs F, Springer and Simon Fairfax. The fact that the letter originated from outside the country leaned towards the latter.

I had two choices. I could trust in my friends on the force or I could get myself lost. Thinking back to my last bout of protective custody I would have been safer in a Group 4 van, even though now the corruption had been eradicated. No, I had to rely on myself. Where could I get myself lost without having to look over my shoulder all the time?

When the answer came it was like a bolt from the blue. It was so corny it could work. I made my arrangements that day. I had no time to waste. The death threat sent by air mail could mean Fairfax was still outside the country on the other hand it could be to lull me into a false sense of security. He may have been outside at that very moment. Once my booking was made on the phone I wrote Jenny a cheque for £6,000, six months' pay, and I also wrote a short note to D.I. Cox enclosing the death threat and its envelope. This I asked Jenny to post as her last duty until I contacted her again.

That was four days ago. Now here I was with a sore bottom but no fear of being spotted by my erstwhile executioner. No one knew where I was so no one could give me away, even inadvertently. Center Parcs had been surprised when I had asked for a six month booking but they had acquiesced and here I was. I hadn't even gone for Nottingham which was the nearest but had travelled further afield to Elveden Forest. I felt as safe here as anywhere I could think of. Unbeknown to me that Group 4 van was looking decidedly as good as Fort Knox.

After the, what felt like, bare bum riding I eased myself onto as many cushions as I could find back at the villa. This one could berth four but it was the only one available at short notice and then only due to a cancellation that had occurred minutes before I had rang to book. I sat there eating one of those meals for one that look like a plateful on the box but it is only after you have cooked it you realise that they used a saucer for the picture. At first I had taken to eating out at the various eating establishments. I had tried them all. My favourites were the Dutch Pancake House and the Italian restaurant. My least favourite, once tried never again, was the American Diner. It wasn't that the food they served was not to my liking, they just used too much fat. My stomach couldn't cope with it for some time afterwards. After a few days eating out proved too repetitive and also heavy on the pocket and I had therefore stocked up the villa with supplies bought from the on-site supermarket with the intention of only eating out twice a week.

At Center Parcs you can do as much or as little as you liked. If you were sporty you could play anything from five-a-side football to mini golf. If you just wanted to unwind there was the swimming complex and places to pamper yourself with massages, saunas and the like. You could do either, both or none at all. As a UK holiday resort it had everything except a beach but for me it was slightly different. I wasn't vacationing, I was, in effect, living there, for the time being. Initially the spectre of death overshadowed me but soon I forgot this in my efforts to try as much as possible, before I realised that in that way lay future boredom and with it a relaxing of the vigilance I still needed to maintain, just in case. Try everything in the first week and then what did I do to keep myself occupied for the balance of six months? If six months proved long enough for Fairfax to be apprehended, that is. I intended to contact Cox from time to time to obtain an update. I was hoping staying out of the way long enough for Fairfax to be taken was the answer. If he hadn't been captured by the end of six months I would have to rethink my strategy.

One problem with Center Parcs is that even with so much to do it is no place to go by yourself unless you were just going for the pampering. Me? I wanted to partake of the various sporting activities but of course had no opponents to play so I only had a chance when the tournaments were on. Unfortunately, at that time of year they were being cancelled due to lack of entrants. That is the midweek ones were, I was told it was different at weekends i.e. Friday to Monday which out of season were the most popular of the three types of available breaks; Weekend (Friday to Monday), Midweek (Monday to Friday) or Full Week (Friday to Friday). This being Friday there was a Badminton Tournament that afternoon for which I was entered. Prior to this I had a couple of hours. I had brought my typewriter with me and so far had typed up all the various miscellaneous scraps of hand-written chapters of 'Doctor! Oh No!' I was not that impressed. After the first chapter which I had thought rather good, things had fallen away into corniness far worse than old JB's one liners. I had decided to tie things up with the final chapter.

When I had finished, I had to face it - it was rubbish. The first chapter was fine. As a parody of James Bond it had run along the established lines of one of those stories, the initial assignment meeting with M (P) and the gadget training from Q (I). From Chapter 2 onwards I had seriously lost the plot and the final chapter had just been a rushed finish to get it over with. Although I was quite pleased with some of the other titles I had created, especially 'Loos Never Flush Twice'.

I would just give it to the woman who had asked me to do it so she could pass it to her Bond obsessed boyfriend. If he didn't find it funny, too bad. Writing funnily was a lot harder than it looked. Especially if you use up all the best gags in the first chapter.

That last chapter, if one and a half pages can be called a chapter, had taken ninety minutes. Just time to get changed and make my way to the Jardin De Sports for the badminton tournament.

The competition was a lot harder than I expected. I was only an average player, once a week if that. I was definitely not to league standard which some of my fellow competitors seemed to be. It ended up being a doubles tournament as most had come in pairs. I was the odd one out as usual so the tournament organiser had to partner me. We were split into two leagues with each team in the league playing each other. The winner of one league would play the runner up in the other in the semi-final and vice versa. My partner, Chris was good, definitely far better than me, and so although there were a few tight games we won our league. The runners up in the other league were two young lads. They were fit and could play but Chris had just too much savvy and we were in the final. At that point I expected that we would win. Of course with such confidence coursing through my veins we could do nothing but get tonked. It was a husband and wife team and they were good. Well, she was good but he was unstoppable. Definitely league standard. They ran us ragged and were hardly out of breath at the end.

Prizes for these tournaments were medals, gold, silver and bronze, and by that I mean gold, silver and bronze coloured metal. I swung my silver one around by its tape on the way back to the villa, too self-conscious to hang it around my neck like Medallion Man. A few minutes later I discovered that what I needed to be swinging around in front of me wasn't a cheap medal but a mace. The latter would have been of much greater assistance in the circumstances.

On entering the villa I immediately noticed it was a lot colder than before, like someone had left too many windows open. I knew I hadn't left any open and the new found sense of ease and security I had found in my sanctuary quickly disappeared. I hovered, my hand over the light switch and ready to run for the hills but the starter never even got his pistol out of his holster. I suddenly saw a red spot on my chest and I had seen enough TV to know that it wasn't a sudden zit or the forerunner of measles. It was an infra-red sight.

"That red dot is an infra-red sight," announced a voice out of the darkness. "You'll be dead before you even turn to run. Stand completely still and turn on the light." Not wanting to point out the contradiction in his instructions just in case he couldn't stand criticism I complied.

Pickfords had obviously paid a visit. The furniture had moved around. The dining table had been pushed over to the far wall covering one of the bedroom doors and the bathroom and an armchair had been dragged over from the living room area having been positioned so any occupant was directly facing anyone entering the villa. This particular occupant was tall, as far as one could tell of someone in a sitting position, certainly he had long legs which were crossed, pointing to the windows as he sat at an angle. He had black hair, gelled and brushed back and a moustache that was either naturally oily or had been gelled also. His eyes were dark and hooded with pronounced eyebrows. His smile was wolfish. He was nattily dressed in pinstripe suit including waistcoat, brilliant white shirt and red tie. His shoes were so highly polished they would have made a sergeant major positively green with envy. If my attention had not been held by other things I may have wondered how he had walked through a holiday village dressed like that, but as it was I couldn't take my eyes off the firearm pointed in my direction. Not only did it have an infrared sight but it had been fitted with a silencer and not a Kwikfit fitter in sight.

"Mr Fairfax I presume." It was hardly a shot in the dark. His speech told me he was American and he was the only person connected with recent events unaccounted for.

"So you are the busybody who ruined all my plans?"

"I suppose I am," I admitted. "But you needn't have come all this way just to meet me."

"I came all this way to kill you," he snarled. "Without you I would have got away with the whole thing."

"You mean lining your pockets with insurance fraud money whilst bringing the corporation your grandfather founded to its knees?"

"No. So Mister Smart Alec you don't know everything."

"Well tell me what it was all in aid of then."

"Why? What do you think this is? A James Bond film? Where the egotistical villain has to fully explain his actions before setting an elaborate method of killing a person who could just as easily be shot in the head?"

"Works for me."

"I'll not explain myself to a mere bug that I would not even scrape from the bottom of my shoe."

"Hit you hard didn't it?"

"What did?" He was a bit taken aback now. I was trying to give the impression that I knew something he didn't think I knew. I did know something. Something that had been mentioned to me in the days following the events at Knightscourt when all the cleaning up operations both here and overseas had been going on.

"When your father made your younger brother president of the company and you only senior vice president."

"You better believe it! The company was mine! I was the

eldest. It was my right!"

"So you wanted to make your brother look bad. See Father, how poorly my brother presides over the company. Fires, thefts, insurance frauds. You were painting your brother black with one hand and pocketing the ill-gotten gains with the other."

"Money was never the issue. I have more than a little worm like you could even dream of spending in a lifetime. I wanted what I was due. I kept the money and most of the other stuff to put back into the business once I was in power."

"You really think this charade was going to work?"

"It was working. That irritating do-gooder brother of mine was just about to be stripped of his position. You spoiled that. Now I'll never be in charge. I am a fugitive: never able to set foot in my own country again. The Corporation was my life and now there is no reason to go on. My life is forfeit and so is yours."

There was to be no tying me up beneath a gradually lowering blade. No time for the hero to extricate himself from a sticky end. It was going to be one shot, from less than ten feet and even I couldn't have missed. It was goodnight Vienna, or even Elveden.

"Out!" He rose from his seat still covering me with the gun. He motioned with his head to the patio doors which opened onto the rear of the villa. I say patio doors but one of them was just a frame because a patio chair was lying inside it surrounded by glass fragments. No wonder it had felt chilly.

He was going to dump me in the lake. I knew the lake could be reached from the rear. The ducks that foraged for food outside the patio doors had told me that much. It could only be a few hundred yards away. Not enough time for me to think myself clear, not with a brain that was processing information slower than a snail on a go slow.

I climbed through the glassless door and he followed. He pointed me through the trees and I paced as slowly as I could. Strangely enough he didn't try to rush me along. Maybe he was a sadist and wanted me to suffer imagining what death would be like for as long as possible. He acted cool but I reckoned there was less than a hairline breadth between sanity and a chocolate bar short of a selection box. His speech in the villa had been half the ranting of a madman at times and I had noticed his hand was not entirely steady. This made it trickier. His finger was probably already applying half pressure to the trigger. In the end it was not me that initiated the bid for freedom. I had heard of being saved by the bell but never by a duck. Fairfax was behind me but not following exactly in my footsteps and he must have disturbed a roosting duck for suddenly there was an angry quacking and I heard an almost instantaneous silent spat of his gun. It had been a mere reaction and his aim was off me for a second. As I flew through the air in a headlong dive to grapple him I noted it would not be Duck a l'Orange for supper as he had missed.

I made contact before he could shift his aim and we both went down, the gun flying from his grasp. He may have still be this side of sanity but he fought like a madman. I was on top but he got his legs underneath me and propelled me off. I fell on my back but quickly rolled to gain my feet. Fairfax couldn't find his gun in the dark so he just rushed me. He came charging at me head down like a mad bull but just before he would have butted the wind out of me I brought my knee up into his face then let out a cry of pain. I hoped his face felt worse than my leg. He got up from where he had fallen and came again but slowly this time, swaying from side to side like a boxer.

On TV there are two types of fight. The one quick punch that knocks an opponent unconscious, a Simon Templar special, or one of those fights where punch after punch fall still leave both fighters standing and even after crashing through furniture, doors and walls they still carry on fighting. A slightly more serious form of a Clouseau Cato contest. This was one such. We stood there and slugged it out. I had never been in a proper fist fight before. Not that it was just fists. Feet, elbows and head all played a part. He lost it and was just pummelling me anywhere whereas I tried to defend and place my efforts in strategic places. Eyes, stomach and the area of the crown jewels.

He was hurting me. Sometime his wild punches caught a more vital area than the arms or chest. One sock to the jaw made me slightly light headed for a few seconds and one to the stomach half winded me. The punches I landed seemed to be having no effect at all. His madness made him oblivious to pain. It looked like he was going to wear me down. We spent less time on our feet and more time on the ground either rolling around, each other trying to get on top, or throwing punches at any exposed area. I was near the limits of my strength when we both crashed through some undergrowth onto the bank of the lake. Some more ducks went quacking wildly out of our way. We rolled apart again and both staggered to our feet. I had my back to the lake and he rushed me. It was now or never. I took a step back and aimed a kick straight between his legs. I pretended I was volleying the winning goal at Wembley following through on the ball. That got through to him. He stopped in his tracks clutching at the stricken area. Quick as a sloth I grabbed his collar and propelled him into the lake. Knowing I had to finish it now I waded after him and held his head underwater. He struggled but not as hard as I thought he should have done. Maybe he was half unconscious from the pain. As soon as he stopped struggling I dragged him to the bank and left him lying with his legs still in the water. I didn't know if he was alive or dead and I didn't care. I just sank down on the ground to recover.

After five minutes he still hadn't moved but he had been moaning so I knew he was alive. I took off his tie and bound his wrists behind his back. Then I pulled his legs out of the water. Luckily he had laces in his shoes. I removed them and tied them both together before securing his ankles. Then I headed off back to the villa to get help.

Only after I arrived back through the broken patio window did I remember that there were no phones in the villas. Calls had to be made from phone-boxes placed at various intervals on the service roads that ran outside. They were the old red telephone boxes that have long since disappeared from the streets. Fortunately there was one only a few hundred yards from my villa.

As I opened the door to call the police or site security or whoever I let out a huge sigh of relief. Now it was all over.

# CHAPTER 23

Back where it all started. A rainy Monday morning, sat in the office waiting for a client. Well, not just waiting because I was for all intents and purposes finishing off my one case file. I scrawled the words 'Case Closed' across the front and filed it away again. The only extra item that hopefully would need to be added to that file was a grateful thank you letter from Fidelity Insurance attaching a big fat cheque but I guessed I would be brushing away cobwebs from the file before I added such a letter.

It didn't matter that I had no other clients because I had decided to close the business down. I had to face the fact that I was not much of a success as an investigator. If it had not been for Vicky and the A.C.C.S., I would have failed dismally. I would be six feet under now with not even a gravestone in memorial. Anyway, one such adventure was enough in a lifetime and I had had two in mine. I wondered how Jessica Fletcher coped with such cases every week, even though you would expect a writer, who by definition must spend many hours alone er … writing, would have little time for such encounters. Not for me thank you very much. Death is so permanent.

I had advised Jenny of the situation and told her she need not come in even though her week's holiday had finished. I told her she could keep the six months money I had given her. That meant both Vicky and Jenny were now out of my life and I was back to just worrying about myself. That was enough. After my life and death struggle with Fairfax, which of all the episodes in the case was the one where I had been so near to death, life could never be too mundane again. Thank God it was all over.

Deja vu. I was sat in my office thinking of how to tie up loose ends, such as could I get someone to sublease for the remaining period of my lease. Suddenly, as in a time long ago, I heard the outer office door and footsteps coming towards me. I wasn't expecting anybody but then again I wasn't anticipating danger.

For a few seconds I didn't recognise the woman before me. She was in a black leather catsuit, had shoulder length blonde hair and a wild look in her eyes. She was breathing heavy and must have run up the stairs. It was a few seconds before she got any words out but even before the strong American accent I had realised who it was. The severe bun, owlish glasses and business suit were gone but the real reason I had not recognised her was because this time she had not tripped over the carpet.

"You Limey bastard! I'm going to get you!" She pulled a small gun out her pocket. It was one of those small peashooters that can fit into a woman's purse. I didn't know if it carried just one bullet, but it didn't seem large enough to hold more. If I could just dodge it then it would just be a friendly bout of mixed wrestling, no holds barred.

"There's no need for this," I said as soothingly as one can when one's tongue has swelled to the size of a melon and is restricting airflow. "You would do better to just make a clean getaway. I promise I won't call the police."

"You don't get it do you?" she said waving the gun about. Her voice was low, more of a fierce whisper really. "He was mine and you killed him."

"Fairfax?" That was a turn up for the book but it all fitted. "He's not dead. He's in custody."

"And what do you think will happen when he is extradited? At least two deaths will be on the list of offences. The death penalty for sure. You did this and now you are going to pay."

Where had I heard that before? She was not going to march me to some secluded spot though. She was beyond reason. If I was going to rush her it had to be soon.

"Don't you see? My life means nothing without him." She had suddenly gone all melancholy and I tensed myself to jump. "We've been together for ten years." I was in the middle of my pre take-off checks when I heard something. A stealthily opening door.

"But it's not really my fault," I said loudly so her attention would be on me. "It was you who put me up to the job. Bad judgement on your part, I would say."

"True," she agreed snapping out of her dream state. "And now it is time to rectify my mistake." She was taking no chances, she wanted to be as close as possible so as not to miss. She came towards me, gun outstretched and I could see her knuckle whiten as she started to apply pressure to the trigger.

Three things happened simultaneously: she pulled the trigger, I dived behind the desk and someone unseen by me smashed a chair over her head whilst the bullet embedded itself in the wall directly where my head had been.

"Tommy! Are you alright?"

It was Jenny. "I came round to say goodbye in person."

I gingerly picked myself off the floor. "I'm so glad you did. If you still worked for me I'd give you a raise."

"Is there anything I can do?" she asked.

"No Jenny, I don't think so. It is all over now."

And now it was.

THE END

# BOOKS BY THIS AUTHOR

## Trouble Cross

This is the full novel which is the Pratt, Pratt, Wally & Pratt Investigate storyline plus the back story (T is for ...) and the James Bond spoof (Doctor, Oh No!).

## T Is For ...

The back story to Pratt, Pratt, Wally & Pratt Investigate as included in Trouble Cross.

Thomas Robel is working as an insurance broker and visits a new client. Not long after, he believes the client is acting suspiciously so tries to carry out his own investigation which leads to his own kidnapping and further attempts on his life. As just a pen pushing office worker, can he survive?

## Doctor, Oh No!

The James Bond Spoof from Trouble Cross.

S.P.I.D.E.R. Sindy Cobweb (W7) has her most ludicrous assignment to date. She must rescue the kidnapped scientist, Profession I.C. Nutting, and his new eyesight formula from the clutches of the combined enemy forces of S.M.A.S.H. and S.E.P.T.I.C. in their Eygptian lair. Can she succeed?

## Rewind

Jason West, forty years old, wakes up in his eight year old body back in 1971. Every one at one time or another has wished to go back and have a do over. It turns out not to be so easy.

## Once Upon A Week

A collection of seven brand new fairy stories, each based on a proverb. A week's bedtime stories for children with a life lesson thrown in.

Printed in Great Britain
by Amazon

36284980R00165